UNTAMED HUNGER

THE INFINITE CITY #4

TIFFANY ROBERTS

UNTAMED HUNGER

She's a lone human on the run—but he has her scent, and he will not stop until he possesses her.

It should have been an easy job. Deliver the ID chip, get paid, and get out. But when Drakkal sees a beautiful human in his client's private zoo and instantly recognizes her as his mate, the situation gets complicated. The motto Drak's long lived by —don't be stupid—is cast aside as the beast within demands he take this female and make her his no matter what he must do. And when she runs from him, the hunt is on.

After being impregnated by her dirtbag ex-boyfriend, abducted, and sold to be a breeder in a rich alien's basement menagerie, Shay has to admit things aren't looking great. But she's determined to give her unborn child a decent life. Her first opportunity appears in the form of a gruff but insanely attractive azhera who forces Shay's owner to sell her to him. Refusing to trade one alien master for another, she escapes him at her first chance. Yet Shay can't forget the intense azhera and his heated stare—and soon realizes that he's not going to forget her either.

But Shay's former owner also remembers, and he's determined to retrieve his prized possession and have his revenge on the one who took her.

Check the author's website for detailed content warnings.

Copyright © 2019 by Tiffany Freund and Robert Freund Jr.

All Rights Reserved. No part of this publication may be used or reproduced, distributed, or transmitted in any form by any means, including scanning, photocopying, uploading, and distribution of this book via any other electronic means without the permission of the author and is illegal, except in the case of brief quotations embodied in critical reviews and certain other noncommercial uses permitted by copyright law. For permission requests, contact the publishers at the address below.

This book was not created with AI, and we do not give permission for our work to be trained for AI.

Tiffany Roberts

authortiffanyroberts@gmail.com

This book is a work of fiction. Names, characters, places, and incidents are products of the author's imagination or are used fictitiously and are not to be construed as real. Any resemblance to actual events, locales, organizations, or people, living or dead, is entirely coincidental.

Cover Illustration by Donovan Boom

Character Art by Sam Griffin

❦ Created with Vellum

To my one true love, for all your dedication and devotion.

DRAKKAL
UNTAMED HUNGER

ONE

Arthos, the Infinite City
　Terran Year 2106

DRAKKAL WASN'T SURE HOW, but he'd get back at Arcanthus for sending him on this delivery.

He'd arrived at the client's manor—one of the largest residences in the Gilded Sector—ten minutes before the appointed meeting time, eager to conclude this business and be on his way. Per the instructions he'd been provided, he'd used the tunnels below street level to access a hidden entrance, where he'd endured suspicious glares and firm questions from the security guards. They'd finally allowed him inside, and he'd had the privilege of weathering a forty-minute wait in the kitchen as over a dozen servants prepared an immense meal.

Even after the volturian guard who'd stared at Drakkal with cold, blue eyes during his entire stay in the kitchen had finally led him to the client's study, Murgen Foltham—the immensely wealthy durgan businessman Drakkal had come to see—still hadn't shown his face.

Drakkal folded his arms across his chest. His tail flicked restlessly, and his ears drew back.

And here I'd thought Arcanthus was a pain in my ass...

Releasing a heavy breath that ended in a low growl, Drakkal scanned the room. Everything here was ornate nearly to the point of sacrificing functionality, right down to the oversized desk and the chairs positioned around it.

Like most other manors in this part of the city, this place was more a status symbol than a home. It was an elaborate, excessive, unnecessary display of wealth, and just being inside it irritated Drakkal. Such residences presented an illusion of freedom and beauty at odds with the subterranean, gritty nature of the Undercity. It was all fake, it all stank, and the expensive, exotic scents these people used to cover the stench only made it worse.

Drakkal strode forward and sat in one of the chairs in front of the desk, resting his tail on the cushion between his thigh and the armrest. Just as he'd guessed it would, the chair forced him into a rigid posture that provided no comfort.

The volturian guard stepped closer. "I didn't say you could sit."

Drakkal glanced back at the scowling volturian. The discomfort caused by the chair seemed a fair price for the guard's perturbation. "And I didn't ask. Where's Foltham?"

"Master Foltham will be here when he's available. He doesn't plan his schedule around the likes of you."

Lifting his cybernetic left arm, Drakkal activated the holocom built into its wrist. His wait was approaching the fifty-minute mark.

Drakkal settled his hands on the armrests and pushed himself to his feet. "Tell your boss that he can contact us when he's serious about concluding our business. Any future meeting will be conducted at a neutral location at a time of our choosing."

He walked toward the door. The volturian stepped into Drakkal's path, tilting his head back to meet Drakkal's gaze.

"You don't belong here, you overgrown sewer skrudge," the volturian spat, "but Master Foltham has chosen to do business with you. So you'll stay here and wait like a good little animal until whenever he declares the transaction completed to his satisfaction."

"I don't care who he is," Drakkal growled, baring his fangs. "I'm not going to have more of my time wasted. Stand aside or draw your blaster to save me the dishonor of an unfair fight."

"You skeks-sucking—"

The door to the study swung open, and the volturian snapped his mouth shut, keeping his intense glare fixed on Drakkal.

A large alien walked through the open door—Murgen Foltham. He was perhaps two or three centimeters taller than Drakkal, but his body was huge, with thick, trunk like limbs and a round belly that dominated his overall shape. He had no neck to speak of, and his fleshy jowls hung low enough to rest upon his chest. The most solid part of Murgen Foltham seemed to be the pair of four-centimeter-long tusks jutting up from his lower jaw. He wore a loose black tunic with silver trim that was secured around his waist by a wide, violet sash from which dangled countless gold and platinum trinkets, many of which were embedded with gems and crystals.

"Ah! You're finally here," Murgen said in a rumbling bass voice. "Our appointment was forty minutes ago. I was beginning to wonder if—"

"I've been here for nearly an hour," Drakkal said, gaze locked with the volturian's, "and I'm on my way out now."

Murgen made a sound that was half-grunt, half-groan, and shuffled closer. The metal adornments on his sash clinked together as he moved. "Come now, I've set aside time from my day for this meeting, and I'm quite busy. Money doesn't earn itself—at least not quickly enough for my liking."

Gritting his teeth, Drakkal suppressed the growl threatening to rise from his chest.

Doesn't matter if I'd like nothing more than to gut these pompous gresh navari. *This is just business. Besides, don't want to give Arcanthus any ammunition to use against me by botching a simple deal.*

Drakkal doubted that any of the Infinite City's billions of residents could manage to say the words *I told you so* with as much smugness as Arcanthus could.

The volturian stepped aside as Murgen neared.

"Come, then," Murgen said, settling a hand with three short, thick fingers on Drakkal's shoulder. "All's forgiven. No one's perfect, after all, and it's unfair of me to expect too much of folk from lesser social strata."

Just business, Drakkal repeated in his mind. The thought didn't cool the angry fires that had been lit in his chest.

"So generous of you," was the best he could manage to say.

"It's a small thing." Murgen lifted his hand only to drop it on Drakkal's shoulder in a heavy slap.

Drakkal clenched his fists, pressing the claws of his right hand into the heel of his palm. He always told Arcanthus to remain calm. How hypocritical would it be for Drakkal to lose control of his temper now? It didn't matter if part of Drakkal's mind insisted he was shaming himself by letting Murgen's comments slide; he'd moved on from the azheran concepts of pride and honor long ago, hadn't he?

"So is the ID chip you ordered," Drakkal replied. "If you have the credits, I have your chip. Let's be done with it."

Murgen chuckled, producing a booming sound that made the flesh of his throat expand as though it were filling with air. "No, no. Let me show you something special, something people like you rarely have an opportunity to see."

Keeping his tone as neutral as possible, Drakkal said, "Maybe another time."

"Come now"—Murgen squeezed Drakkal's shoulder—"I insist. Your forger, he does good work. Let's solidify our relationship with this little treat."

Drakkal found himself glad that he'd put on a thick jacket to cover up his sleek prosthesis despite the way such clothing sometimes irritated his fur; he had a sense that Murgen's direct touch would've been far more uncomfortable. Murgen was the sort of person Drakkal had dealt with often during his years as a gladiator on Caldorius—friendly only so long as one served a purpose.

After drawing in a steadying breath, Drakkal nodded.

"Good! Come along, azhera." Murgen turned away, glancing at the volturian as he moved. "Nostrus, accompany us. We're off to the menagerie."

Nostrus glared at Drakkal again. Were his eyes any colder, there'd be ice crusting his eyelashes. "Yes, sir."

Drakkal said nothing. It seemed holding his tongue was the best course of action here if he meant to be done as quickly as possible, even if it meant suffering Murgen's condescension and Nostrus's ire. His only consolation was that Arcanthus was charging Murgen well above the standard rates.

He followed Murgen into the hall. Nostrus fell into place behind Drakkal, and the azhera could feel the guard's gaze, chilled and heavy, on his back. A hint of unease colored Drakkal's irritation; he was in an unfamiliar place with people he didn't know. Dangerous people. Murgen had already made it clear that he viewed Drakkal as a lesser being, and Nostrus seemed hungry for conflict.

Drakkal forced his tail to still. He'd learned long ago that it served as a tell that could cause trouble in situations like this. Besides, he'd been in worse places. He'd dealt with people like Murgen and Nostrus countless times.

Just have to get through this. Then I never have to see either of these two again.

What was a few more minutes at this point?

He would soon discover that, if nothing else, *a few more minutes* was a gross underestimation.

Murgen stopped at a blank section of the wall. "I trust that, given the nature of your...profession, you understand that you must divulge no details regarding what you're about to see?"

Drakkal grunted his understanding.

Murgen's big, dark eyes widened along with his grin, and for the first time, his mask slipped, revealing a hint of the real person beneath—a person who would devote countless credits to destroy the life of anyone he deemed an enemy.

Drakkal held the durgan's gaze until Murgen looked away.

Murgen extended an arm and pressed one of his thick fingers to the wall. A large section of the wall slid upward, disappearing into the ceiling and exposing a set of sturdy metal doors. A moment later, the doors slid apart, opening on an elevator car.

Drakkal's fur bristled. His current relationship with Murgen and Nostrus wasn't exactly built on trust, and elevators weren't the most comforting spaces. The relatively tight confines were extremely restrictive when it came to combat; things tended to get brutal and desperate in such conditions quickly.

Murgen stepped into the elevator first, turning to face the hall. Drakkal didn't allow himself any hesitation; he stepped in after Murgen and positioned himself with his back against the far wall. Nostrus entered last, leveling his cold, hard gaze on Drakkal even as he turned his body toward Murgen.

"What a happy bunch we are," Murgen said as he pressed a button on the controls. The doors closed. "You'll have to forgive Nostrus, azhera. He's worked for me for many years and takes his job quite seriously. The finest security professional in the business, this one."

Drakkal offered no response. He kept his gaze on the doors, watching in his peripheral vision as Nostrus watched him.

Without a sound, the elevator began its descent; Drakkal felt it in his gut, and some primal part of him railed against moving even farther from natural light. It didn't help his unease. In his experience, it was the wealthiest clients who most often decided the terms of an agreement no longer suited them at the last moment, who were the most likely to *negotiate* a change of said terms. Of course, those last-minute changes usually occurred at blaster point.

But there was more here, something Drakkal couldn't place. It was almost...a sense of inevitability that eluded definition, somehow related to a scent on the air that was too faint to isolate and identify.

Drakkal's tail twitched. He leaned back against the wall to prevent it from swinging restlessly.

The elevator drew to a smooth halt.

Murgen twisted his torso to glance back at Drakkal. "This must be terribly exciting for you. I imagine it's not every day you're offered such privilege as this."

Not for the first time, Drakkal was stricken by a powerful urge toward violence. It certainly wasn't the sensible solution, wasn't the moral solution, wasn't the *right* solution, but sometimes it was the only way to force people like Murgen—people who thought themselves the most important thing in the universe whether they were talking business or taking a shit—to alter their perspectives a little. Drakkal hadn't survived his one hundred and fifty bouts in the fighting pits of Caldorius only to feign interest in the garbage a person like Murgen had to say.

The best way to show someone they weren't untouchable usually involved a few well-placed punches.

The elevator doors slid open silently.

Drakkal's nostrils flared. Both that sense of inevitability and the accompanying scent were immediately stronger, though he still couldn't identify either.

Murgen stepped off the elevator and into a sleek corridor with dark floor panels and walls that curved at both their bases and peaks. The air—which was recycled and pump-circulated throughout most of the Undercity—had an enhanced crispness here. Murgen's waddling gait carried him toward an open-topped hovercart.

Drakkal looked at Nostrus. Brows low, the volturian gestured for Drakkal to exit the elevator. Clenching his jaw against an instinctual growl, the azhera shoved away from the wall and strode forward.

Should've just made Foltham deal with me in his office. Who the hell would've cared if he took offense to it?

Murgen climbed a set of low steps to enter the hovercart's rear compartment, which was oval shaped with a wide seat on each side. The craft bounced and swayed as Murgen sat down on the left seat. "Join me, azhera. Nostrus will drive."

"Master Foltham," Nostrus said, "this is ill-advised. We can't trust this—"

Murgen raised a hand and waved it, silencing Nostrus. "All business, yes? I'm sure our friend here is a consummate professional. At any rate, I imagine he will soon be too captivated to even contemplate anything untoward."

Once again, Drakkal kept silent; Murgen was confident in

his control of the situation, and there was no reason to shatter his illusion. Ultimately, Murgen's mistaken belief that Drakkal could so easily be intimidated by flagrant displays of wealth would work in Drakkal's favor if the situation took a turn.

And there was plenty of time for this to go bad, especially given Nostrus's demeanor.

As aware of Nostrus's presence behind him as ever, Drakkal climbed into the cart, seated himself opposite Murgen, and wedged his tail beneath his thigh to keep it still.

The volturian's boots clacked across the floor as he walked to the front of the vehicle and climbed into the operator's seat. A moment later, the vehicle's engine hummed to life. The back steps rose and folded up, sealing the rear wall of the cab, and Murgen grinned around his blunt tusks.

The hovercart moved forward. Drakkal felt the gentle hum of its antigrav engines beneath him.

"This is a real treat," Murgen said, settling a hand atop one of his thick thighs. "My collection is the best in Arthos. You've never seen its like."

Drakkal would've asked what Murgen was talking about if only to garner a better understanding of what was happening—which he *should* have done before coming this far—but the answer became apparent before he could open his mouth.

The hovercraft passed a shallow recess in the wall—a large observation window at least two meters tall by four across. Beyond the window was a lush, dense section of jungle, within which stood several big, squat, golden-scaled creatures. They were khochi, native to the swamps of Zanjin—popular quarry for intergalactic trophy hunters.

"All genuine," Murgen said. "Holographic displays don't do the animals any justice. It's always best to see directly with one's own eyes, I say."

They drove past a few more displays, each containing

unique environments and creatures, some familiar to Drakkal, many not. Drakkal glanced toward the front of the vehicle. The corridor stretched on and on ahead, bisected by intermittent perpendicular corridors.

This place was a zoo. A damned *zoo*, right beneath the Gilded Sector.

Drakkal's unease intensified. All these cages, all these cells...

Murgen's eyes gleamed with pride. "I've rare species from across the known universe here. Some of the most beautiful, most dangerous animals in existence. It's taken decades to build this collection."

All Drakkal could do was nod and force his expression to remain neutral. His eyes flicked from cell to cell; the hovercart must've passed a dozen such displays on either side before Nostrus guided it around a corner into a wider corridor. The mysterious scent strengthened further; it was reminiscent of sundrinker flowers, a fragrance Drakkal hadn't smelled since before he was enslaved nearly twenty years ago. But this scent was spiced with something exotic, something foreign, something...alluring.

Murgen chuckled, making his body shake. The hovercart trembled. "We're almost to the best part, my friend. The heart of my collection. The specimens that make it truly unique. You know, I..."

Though Murgen continued speaking, Drakkal didn't hear the words. The azhera's chest was tight, his blood hot, his stomach knotted. He'd spent several years of his life hunting and fishing, but seeing these creatures caged in a place like this, held by a person like this...it woke something within Drakkal, a primal rage that railed against *all* cages.

Drakkal clenched his fists at his sides, barely resisting the urge to bury his claws in the seat cushion beneath him. And

Murgen kept talking, jowls jiggling, his voice reduced to a meaningless, self-absorbed drone in Drakkal's perception.

But Drakkal's rage only intensified when the vehicle came to a stop in a large, circular chamber with viewing windows all around. The fires burning in Drakkal were momentarily overpowered by a chill so strong that it threatened to freeze his blood.

"These are the real prizes." Murgen grasped the edges of the cab and pushed himself onto his feet; the cart wobbled with his efforts. The rear steps unfolded. "Animals that think themselves more than what they are. Smart enough to learn some language, perhaps even to reason on a rudimentary level"—he grunted as he stepped down—"but little removed from beasts, regardless."

Nostrus turned his head to glare over his shoulder at Drakkal, but the azhera barely noticed.

There were people in these cells. *People.*

Powerful memories clawed their way to the forefront of Drakkal's mind. It didn't matter how long ago he'd earned his freedom—freedom that had been his all along—it felt like only yesterday that he'd been kept in a cage, that he'd been treated like an animal himself.

Only that smell, that sweet sundrinker fragrance, stronger here than before, kept him grounded and afforded him a modicum of self-control. He stood up and exited the vehicle, his movements slow and stiff.

"Of course, my interest in these creatures is largely based in scientific curiosity." Murgen walked toward the nearest window without a backward glance at Drakkal. "I've always said I'd have become a scientist, were it a career that actually earned any money, and I've gone so far as to hire on a few researchers to help guide my pursuit of knowledge."

This is just business. Endure it for the sake of business...

That thought only soured Drakkal's stomach. Pressing his lips together, he forced himself forward, joining Murgen in front of the window. Nostrus's footfalls were light as he moved to stand behind Drakkal.

The interior of this cell was plain compared to the others Drakkal had seen thus far, much closer to the quarters of a slave —or a prison cell. The walls were decorated with simple paintings depicting animals and people in basic shapes and lines. Two people were huddled together on the cot attached to the far wall, both with pale gray skin, long white hair, and dark claws. Drakkal knew their species only because of one of Arcanthus's more memorable clients.

They looked lost. Afraid. And so young.

"Zenturi," Murgen said. "Fascinating creatures. They've a venom they can deliver in their bite that is deadly to most other creatures. The few tests I've performed thus far have supported that. Quite strong and agile, as well—don't let their appearances fool you. With proper training, I think they may prove exceptional guards and soldiers. Of course, my true ambition is to use these as a breeding pair once they've matured."

Murgen turned and walked toward the next window. Drakkal's gaze lingered on the zenturi for a few seconds before he numbly followed his host.

"I find the science around breeding and genetics to be engrossing subject matter. It's been proven that the mutative compound administered by the Consortium has side effects on certain species that allow them to interbreed with unrelated species. Imagine the potential combinations!"

Drakkal grunted; he wasn't sure if the sound came off as agreeable or not.

The next cell contained a lone alien. Drakkal wasn't familiar with its species. It looked bigger than him—standing well over two meters tall—and had thick, powerful limbs, shaggy brown fur, and a bony crest sweeping up from its forehead that split into two large, curling black horns. The creature was pacing restlessly along the far wall of its cell.

"Another rare one, and just as primitive as the zenturi. It's called a halthid, though no official name has yet been entered into the Consortium's database. I'd imagine this species barely knows how to harness fire. Still, it's been implanted with translators like all the rest, and they all seem capable of following simple instructions."

Don't be stupid, Drak. That's a simple instruction.

Drakkal had the sense he'd not leave this place without violating that directive.

Murgen finally turned to look at Drakkal again. "Even if the scientific aspects of all this are beyond your comprehension, I'm sure the spectacle is well worth the extra time. You may be one of the lowly, but you have far more in common with me than you do these creatures."

Drakkal drew in a deep breath. *Don't be stupid. Don't respond. Just keep your mouth shut.* But the words came anyway. "Only science I've studied is anatomy. Seem to have a mind for those facts."

"Oh? I personally find alien anatomy fascinating. Do you have a particular species you've focused on?"

Drakkal kept his face toward the viewing window, but he wasn't focused on the halthid inside. His attention was on a faint reflection in the glass—the ghostly blue face visible behind his own dark reflection. "I'm a generalist. Benefits me more. So I know things like how tralix have two hearts, and that one of them isn't protected by their ribs. Or that the average volturian has six liters of blood—and can lose two-point-nine liters before succumbing to blood loss."

There was a faint rustling of cloth behind Drakkal.

Nostrus's indistinct reflection shifted slightly but didn't move any closer.

Murgen laughed that deep, booming laugh that inflated his jowls. "A practical individual, I see."

"Yeah. You ready to finish this deal?"

Waving a hand dismissively, Murgen walked on. "One more to show you, azhera. Can't let you go without gazing upon my most valuable prize. After you see this, you'll be the most popular person in your, uh"—Murgen glanced back at Drakkal, features tightening—"in your...social circles."

"And here I thought people liked me for my natural charm," Drakkal muttered. He glanced at Nostrus; the volturian's brows were low, and his eyes, for once, were no longer cold—they burned with anger.

Drakkal bared his fangs in an expression that would have been considered a smile only by someone with poor eyesight before following his host.

Murgen bypassed the next three cells, each of which contained one or two aliens of species with which Drakkal was unfamiliar. All of them had that gleam of intelligence in their eyes.

As he finally drew to a stop in front of the fourth cell, Murgen said, "An ertraxxan who used to live in the neighborhood had one of these creatures for several years. He used to parade it around the city. But I've done better. I've obtained two for the price of one."

The unease within Drakkal built to a sense of dread. He'd known this delivery would be an unpleasant experience the moment Arcanthus had given him the details, but he'd not realized just how unpleasant it would be. He didn't care how much Murgen Foltham was willing to pay, Arc would no longer be conducting business with this durgan.

Drawing in a deep breath, Drakkal moved to stand beside Murgen and turned toward the cell.

His eyes fell upon the female inside—the female *terran*—and widened. He'd never seen her before, he was certain of it, but she seemed familiar all the same—and she was the most beautiful thing he'd ever seen.

She was sitting in the corner, legs bent with her arms draped around them. Long golden hair hung over her pale, bare shoulders concealing her breasts. Shapely brows arched over bright, piercing blue eyes, angled toward a small, narrow nose, and her full, pink lips were downturned. She looked so small, so delicate. She was...stunning.

She was also clearly with cub.

TWO

Murgen interlaced his fingers and settled his hands on his prodigious gut. "A female terran, currently pregnant. She has a few months to go, by my estimates, and I'm terribly eager to observe the process firsthand. I understand it's rather painful for their kind."

Drakkal's gaze roamed over the female, lingering on the blotchy bruises scattered around her body, the thick collar around her neck, and the matching cuffs at her wrists and ankles. The cuffs weren't attached to any visible tethers, and the skin around each was red and irritated. Drakkal tightened his fists; a powerful instinct had sparked within him, as though his very essence rejected the sight of this female in her current condition. She should've been free, should've been unharmed, should've been...*his*.

"The expected offspring is fully terran, of course, but these terrans have proven remarkably adaptable." Murgen moved closer to the glass. "Though there's not enough research by which to draw concrete conclusions, it seems her species—after the Consortium's mutative treatment—can reproduce with almost anything. The compatibility is astounding."

Separating his hands, Murgen brushed his fingers lightly over the glass. "I'm not normally inclined to partake directly in my research, but I find myself tempted by this one. What would we produce?" He cleared his throat and stepped back suddenly, jowls jiggling as he spun to face Drakkal. "For science, of course. You'd be a fine male specimen to breed with some of my collection, now that I've mentioned it. I've seen many azhera, but none built quite like you. Normally I would charge for the privilege, but in your case, I might pay to have you breed with some of my subjects. I trust your...*equipment* is in working order?"

Drakkal dipped his chin slightly, willing away some of his shock and confusion. He needed to conclude this business and leave, but that sundrinker scent perfumed his every inhalation, and he couldn't take his eyes off the terran.

"Why is she chained and bruised?" Drakkal asked.

"Because she is amongst the most dangerous creatures in my collection. Nostrus can personally attest to that fact."

Nostrus, still behind Drakkal, released a bitter, affirmative grunt. In Drakkal's imagination, a brief scene played out of the volturian striking the terran and leaving one of those bruises. Drakkal barely resisted the urge to turn and hammer a fist into Nostrus's face.

"We mustn't allow her demure appearance to deceive us," Murgen said. "She's sent several members of my security staff to the infirmary with varying injuries. Nothing life threatening, of course. But when she's ready to breed again... Well, I've access to potent sedatives and exceptional restraints. Unless, of course, she's awoken something more primal inside of you. I understand that even those of more evolved species sometimes wish to simply rut like animals. I'll pass no judgment regarding that; it's not as though you've a reputation to protect."

Clenching his jaw, Drakkal pried his gaze from the terran and settled it on Murgen. He reminded himself again that all he had to do was exercise a bit of self-control, make the deal, and go. It didn't matter how this place made him feel, didn't matter if seeing all these people caged stirred old, bitter memories, didn't matter what connection he thought he might've had to the terran.

Conclude the deal and walk away.

Drakkal's ears slapped down flat against his head, and he asked through his teeth, "You have the credits for this chip or not?"

Murgen frowned, brows falling low. "Not the reaction I'd hoped for. I suppose I understand if you're too uncultured or uneducated to appreciate—"

"Then give me a closer look," Drakkal snapped. "Open the cell and let me see her face-to-face."

The durgan recoiled as though he'd been physically struck, and Nostrus's boot came down heavily as though he were advancing to attack.

"All that I've shared with you, and you take this tone with me?" Murgen said; Drakkal couldn't tell how much of his host's offense was genuine, but he didn't care.

Drakkal growled. "You want me to come back later to fuck her, I need to see her up close. I need to smell her, to touch her. I need to see if she sparks those *animal* urges in me."

Just the thought of being close to her, of touching her, heated Drakkal's blood. His cock stirred, threatening to emerge from its sheath.

Kraasz ka'val, I already feel those urges. What's wrong with me?

"Time to go, azhera," said Nostrus.

Murgen shook his head sharply. "No, Nostrus. Not yet. Azhera... Why should I let you close to my prized possession? You've just demonstrated that you're barely in control of yourself. I won't tolerate disrespect in my own home."

Drakkal took a slow step forward, releasing a huff through his nostrils; he was surprised that smoke didn't flow out given the heat of the fires raging inside him. "Then stop disrespecting my time. Let me see her face-to-face or pay me for this ID so I can leave. A simple choice."

"Perhaps this attitude works with the other sorts you do business with, but I will not be swayed by intimidation, azhera."

"You're the sort I usually do business with. A criminal," Drakkal replied. "You have the best security in the business glaring at my back. You afraid I'll hurt your pet? Maybe you weren't serious about breeding her."

Murgen narrowed his eyes and stared at Drakkal for several seconds, stroking his fingers along his dangling jowls. Drakkal kept his focus on the durgan; there'd be a signal, perhaps a subtle one, that would precede Nostrus's inevitable attack, but so long as Drakkal was ready for it...

"I was right about you, azhera," Murgen finally said. "When I looked at you in the study, I thought you were a prime candidate for breeding with my pets. You're big, strong, and bold. Direct. A male who knows what he wants and isn't afraid to reach out and take it. You remind me a little of myself. I'll put your rudeness behind us this time." He lifted his hands and activated the holocom on his right wrist. "You're the perfect male to breed with my terran. An exceptional specimen. Of course, we'll have to finalize the details later, but for now, yes. You may see her up close. I *know* you'll enjoy what you find."

Nostrus stepped forward, his brows angled down over the bridge of his nose. "Master Foltham, I think it best to finish your transaction and have this azhera escorted off the premises."

"Haven't you paid any attention, Nostrus? This azhera is a prime specimen. Exactly what I'm going to need access to in the future. Why, he seems the sort who might even pull himself up out of poverty and become something respectable someday." Murgen twisted to glance over his shoulder at Drakkal. "He may even be the sort whose services I employ for other sensitive endeavors. The two of you may one day be colleagues."

Nostrus didn't try to mask his disgusted sneer.

Drakkal clenched his fists tighter still, and the claws of his right hand dug into the rough flesh of his palm. He flicked his gaze to the terran. She remained hunched in the same spot, her position seemingly unchanged, her beauty somehow greater than it had been a few moments before.

That only further sparked Drakkal's desire and rage. His want for her had already grown into something undeniable and overwhelming. His fury was like a maddened beast, a snarling thing antagonized by Nostrus, fed to immense size by Murgen, and now threatening to break out of its cage at the sight of this trapped, suffering terran.

Murgen's fingers moved with surprising dexterity, manipulating the controls on his holocom. A soft *whoosh* called Drakkal's attention to the left. A section of the wall—likely one of countless concealed doors in this place—had opened between this observation window and its neighbor. Drakkal stepped backward to grant himself a better angle; the opening revealed a long corridor with dull gray walls and floors. Two doors stood across from one another a few meters beyond the entryway, lining up with the cells on either side.

Murgen cleared his throat and walked through the opening. "This way, azhera. A rare treat, indeed, especially for such as you. Why, this terran…"

With the concealed door open, that sundrinker fragrance was even stronger.

Drakkal tuned out Murgen's words, shifting his attention back to the terran. She looked so small and fragile, so...*broken*, and he wanted to draw her into his arms and make her feel safe and sheltered. But there *was* something more to her. Drakkal sensed it in the same way he sensed the gentle air current created by the ventilation system brushing over his fur, or the scents riding that air, even if he couldn't define it.

What are you thinking, Drakkal? Don't be stupid. Take your look and get out of here.

He followed Murgen into the corridor. Nostrus fell into place behind Drakkal, bristling with palpable agitation. Murgen stopped in front of the right door.

Turning his head toward Drakkal, Murgen smiled. The expression created lines of strain around his jutting tusks and pulled his jowls taut. Drakkal did his best not to reflect upon the arrogance, condescension, and eagerness conveyed in the durgan's features.

Murgen's was the epitome of what Drakkal and Arcanthus considered *an extremely punchable face.*

The interior door slid up when Murgen touched his holocom control screen again. Murgen's smile widened, and he stepped into the open cell.

About to walk into a cage with a man who says he wants me to breed with his pet. Guess I'm making nothing but great decisions today.

Heat pulsed up Drakkal's spine. His fur bristled, his ears flattened, and his tail whipped from side to side. His every instinct warned against this, told him it was foolish, that it was a trick, a trap. Every instinct but one—the one that demanded he go to the terran *now*. He didn't understand that drive or its origin, but it was more insistent than all the rest.

Don't be stupid, he reminded himself.

He followed Murgen into the cell.

Before Drakkal registered anything else, the sundrinker-laced fragrance—which permeated the air within the cell—dominated his senses, so potent that he felt it spread through his body, trailing delightful tingles in its wake. The exotic aspect of that perfume remained unidentifiable, but it was undoubtedly warm, sweet, feminine, and alluring.

It was undoubtedly *her*.

Drakkal swung his gaze to the terran, who remained huddled in the corner, her stunning, blue-eyed gaze locked on the males who'd entered her cell. The defiance and intensity in her eyes belied her meek, vulnerable posture.

Her eyes met Drakkal's, and the tingling sensation within him intensified. Hers were the eyes of a fighter, of a fierce, unbroken spirit.

Hers were the eyes...of Drakkal's *mate*.

It seemed impossible that he could know it with such certainty, but now that the thought had blossomed, it was indisputable. This terran was meant to be Drakkal's.

Murgen stopped a couple meters away from the terran. "She's docile now, but I assure you she's quite...energetic when it matters."

Nostrus shoved past Drakkal to stand beside Murgen.

"Come now, Nostrus," Murgen grumbled, "she's restrained. She cannot do me any harm."

"It's my duty to anticipate potential risks, Master. And nothing about this"—he glared at Drakkal—"is safe."

To his annoyance, Drakkal couldn't help feeling a kinship with Nostrus. He understood the headaches of running security for someone who didn't seem interested in following simple rules to maximize safety.

That didn't ease his desire to knock the volturian's head into the wall.

"Stand up, terran, so my guest may have a better look at you," Murgen said.

The female's eyes shifted to Murgen and narrowed; it was the only movement she made.

Murgen huffed, his smile falling. "As I may have mentioned, this one hasn't quite learned her place." He activated his holocom, flicked through the options, and brought up a new menu. "We've had to implement certain gentler means of control thanks to her spirit."

As Murgen manipulated the controls, small green circles lit up on the terran's bindings. Her features hardened, and her muscles tensed, making the cords on her neck more pronounced. She bared her teeth as she stood up with jerky motions—though it seemed more to Drakkal like she was *pulled* up.

"I've considered investing in these for my other pets, though our more typical means of discipline have worked well in keeping their behavior acceptable. The collar and cuffs are bound to each other as a unit but are also tethered to an energy field within the walls. They can be manipulated through my holocom or synchronized to handheld remote controls," Murgen said. "To put it in terms you might better understand, think of it like...magnetism that is entirely at my control. I can adjust the length and strength of all the tethers with a few finger gestures. It's proven quite effective with this one."

Murgen adjusted the controls again. The terran female growled as her head was pulled backward toward the wall, nearly dragging her on her heels. She straightened stiffly. Her arms swung down to her sides, hands about half a meter from her hips, and her legs spread apart to widen her stance, baring her naked form fully.

"Our traditional means of discipline are currently off limits with her, and she's clever enough to understand that I don't want much harm done to her for the sake of her expected offspring. We've been forced to get...creative."

Drakkal studied her body—he was helpless but to do so. Standing upright, she was around one hundred and seventy centimeters, about the same height as the other two female terrans he'd encountered. Her stomach was rounded, and she had generous curves, including flaring hips, delectable thighs, and large breasts tipped with dark pink nipples, but the strain in her stance revealed tone muscle beneath that surface softness. His gaze fell to her hairless mound, which was open to reveal the delicate petals of her sex.

Unbidden, his cock hardened, pushing out from its sheath to press painfully against his pants. His ears rose, his nostrils flared with a fresh inhalation of her heady scent, and his tail sped its restless lashing. Without thinking to, he stepped closer to her.

He needed to have her, to take her, now. It didn't matter if she was carrying another male's cub, this terran was his. His mate. Her scent alone was enough to drive him wild, and it was only Murgen's voice—pompous and condescending—that halted him.

"Yes...I see this will work out well," Murgen said. "Cleary she's awoken something bestial your kind hasn't quite evolved beyond."

Don't be stupid, Drakkal. Remember where you are, who you're with.

Drakkal shook himself and pressed his claws into his right palm, producing pricks of pain. That pain was just enough to draw him back to his senses and force him to look at the larger picture.

The terran's eyes were upon him again, glaring beneath

eyebrows that were slanted in fury. Despite her strained stance, she held her chin up, creating the odd impression that, though Drakkal towered over her, she was looking down at him. Somehow, that only rekindled his desire; he forced it aside with all his willpower.

Her earlier position—sitting on the floor with her arms wrapped around her legs—had only displayed a few of her bruises. More were visible now, some dark blue or purple, others faded green or yellow. There were some on her arms and legs, one on her cheek, but the ones that told the clearest story were those on her knuckles, elbows, and knees.

She was tiny, yes, but Drakkal didn't doubt that she'd injured a few of Murgen's guards. She was a fighter. What he'd initially mistaken for meekness or defeat had only been patience—she'd been biding her time, awaiting an opportunity.

"Those bruises don't suggest gentle treatment." Drakkal pried his gaze from her to look at Murgen.

Nostrus turned his head to stare heatedly at Drakkal.

Pursing his lips, Murgen grunted. "Most of them are self-inflicted, the results of her struggles. As I said, quite spirited, this one. Of course, none of that is your concern. Should we come to some agreement, your only obligation is to fornicate with her. I'd prefer the natural methods over any sort of artificial insemination, just from a scientific standpoint. Any such contact would be observed and recorded, mind you, for the same, uh...scientific reasons.

"At any rate"—Murgen turned to face Drakkal fully, settling his hands over his gut and locking his fingers together—"you've had your closer look, and your interest, however crude or primal, is quite apparent. We can discuss the details at a later time, when I have the appropriate liaison available to explain the terms to you in a manner you'll fully comprehend. Shall we return to my office to conclude our business regarding the identification chip?"

Drakkal flicked his gaze from Murgen to the terran.

Don't be stupid, Drakkal.

Don't. Be. Stupid.

She's my mate.

"How much for her?" Drakkal asked.

Kraasz ka'val, you idiot. What are you doing?

"I thought I'd explained already that she won't be available for such interactions until after she's delivered her current offspring," Murgen replied.

Already been stupid. Might as well go a little further.

"No, not how much to rut with her. How much *for* her."

Murgen reeled backward. For a moment, it seemed as though he'd topple onto his backside. "Excuse me? I would think it clear to anyone with more than half a brain that she is not for sale. Even if she were, someone like you wouldn't be able to meet my asking price."

"What did you pay, Foltham?" Drakkal took a step toward Murgen.

Nostrus inserted himself between the durgan and the azhera, drawing back the side of his suit jacket with one hand and reaching for the holstered blaster beneath his arm with the other. He met Drakkal's gaze with his cold eyes and held it. A mere meter of space separated them.

"It's quite rude to discuss financial matters of this sort openly," Murgen said, shaking his head behind the volturian. "Just as I had begun to consider you a respectable professional, you've gone and shown your true nature, that you're no better than any typical piece of scum from the streets, that—"

Whatever frayed string that had been tenuously holding back the fullness of Drakkal's rage snapped in that moment. He was tired of inaction, tired of having his patience abused, tired of being insulted. He was tired of being treated like something less than a person by people like Murgen Foltham.

Drakkal lunged forward. Nostrus was fast; the volturian managed to pull his blaster completely free of its holster before Drakkal covered the volturian's hand with his armored prosthetic hand, halting Nostrus's arm. Drakkal squeezed. Bones crunched.

Screaming in pain, Nostrus swung his left fist. Drakkal blocked the blow with his right forearm.

Need to get the terran out of here.

Pushing himself forward, Drakkal slammed his knee into the volturian's midsection. Nostrus doubled over with a wheezing grunt.

Drakkal hammered his right fist into the side of Nostrus's head. The volturian swayed. A second blow had the volturian's knees buckling. After the third blow, only Drakkal's hold on the volturian's shattered hand kept Nostrus up. Drakkal struck his opponent one more time—mostly because it felt satisfying—before prying the blaster from the volturian's limp hold and letting him collapse.

Murgen, with eyes so wide they seemed about to burst from their sockets, backed away from Drakkal. He lifted his arms and reached for his holocom, which still displayed the controls for the terran's restraints.

Leaping over the unconscious Nostrus, Drakkal lashed out, caught hold of Murgen's holocom, and tore the device off the durgan's wrist. Murgen staggered backward with a quivering cry and slammed into the wall hard enough to send a jolt through his entire body.

Drakkal tossed the holocom aside, switched Nostrus's blaster into his right hand, and continued his advance on Murgen. He thrust his cybernetic arm forward, grabbing the durgan by his fleshy throat and pinning him against the wall.

Drakkal jammed the barrel of the blaster against Murgen's cheek.

"Rude?" Drakkal growled. "I'm not going to let a *gresh navari* like you call me rude after the way you've behaved."

Murgen's lips quavered, releasing a series of stammering, unintelligible sounds.

"Suddenly don't have much to say? I should've done this thirty-five minutes ago." Drakkal leaned his face closer to Murgen's. "You ready to listen for once in your life?"

Swallowing thickly, Murgen nodded as much as Drakkal's hold allowed.

"You're selling me the terran. One hundred thousand. Since you're no longer receiving the ID chip, I'll add the advance you paid on top of the price."

Murgen's eyes somehow rounded further. "That's...that's... a-an insult, an outrage, a-a—"

Drakkal tightened his left hand, silencing Murgen. "Big picture, Foltham. One hundred thousand, your advance, and your *life*. She's leaving with me whether you agree or not."

Murgen gasped and sputtered, struggling to respond. Drakkal allowed it to continue for several seconds before easing his grip.

"All right," Murgen croaked. "I accept. I-I agree. Sh-she's yours!"

Those words triggered another wave of rage in Drakkal. The terran was already his; Murgen had no say in that, no right to declare it. This was just another example of the merchant's inherent arrogance.

Drakkal wanted to pull the trigger. He'd taken many lives in his time; what was one more? Murgen Foltham had very likely harmed a lot of people apart from the ones in these cells.

But the uproar it would cause... Foltham's death would get the Eternal Guard involved, and Drakkal had undoubtedly been captured on the manor's surveillance system. Murgen Foltham's wrongdoings would not shield Drakkal from repercussions—not after the merchant was dead.

But they could while Murgen was alive. The revelation of a private, illegal zoo—including sapient captives—would prove costly in a multitude of ways, and people like Murgen cared about their wealth above all else. It was the only sort of loss they understood.

Still, it took a considerable amount of Drakkal's willpower to loosen his hold on Murgen's throat. That willpower was dragged through the crimson haze of Drakkal's rage in the process, and he nearly succumbed to his instinctual drive to protect his terran by eliminating this threat.

"This is all between you and me, Murgen. Understand? That's the only way I keep quiet about your *collection*. You give her up and you get to keep everything else." Growling, Drakkal stepped back, pulling Murgen by his neck before heaving him aside.

With a choked cry, Murgen stumbled forward and fell heavily onto hands and knees.

Drakkal turned toward Murgen, aiming the blaster at him. "Lie face down."

The sputtering durgan seemed about to protest. He twisted to look up at Drakkal, and his eyes widened when they stopped on the blaster. Breathing heavily and grunting with the effort, Murgen lowered himself onto his belly.

"Don't move," Drakkal ordered. Keeping the blaster directed at Murgen—and the still unmoving Nostrus—Drakkal eased back to the discarded holocom. He flicked his gaze toward the terran as he crouched.

Though she couldn't change her position, she had changed her expression. Wariness remained in the hard set of her mouth and eyebrows, but the new gleam in her eyes suggested hopefulness—or perhaps, more accurately, the recognition of an opportunity.

Drakkal held her gaze as he picked up the holocom from the floor. Fortunately, the screen hadn't locked. Adjusting his hold on the blaster, he studied the restraint controls for a few moments.

A simple flick of his finger across the appropriate option was all it took to deactivate the invisible tethers. She stumbled forward as the tension on her restraints vanished. Remaining upon her feet, she turned toward Drakkal, one arm raised to shield her breasts while she cradled her belly with her opposite hand.

Drakkal returned his attention to the controls; unlocking the restraints wasn't quite as straight forward as releasing their tethers.

There was a dull *thwump* from near the terran.

When Drakkal looked back at her, she was standing a little straighter, and the light in her gaze had shifted to say *What?*. He flicked his eyes down; though she hadn't moved from her spot, Nostrus was now laid on his side rather than his front, still unconscious.

One corner of Drakkal's mouth twitched up.

"You're making a mistake," Murgen said, voice strained. "Letting her loose is stupid, and crossing me is even more foolhardy!"

"Still trying to talk big?" Drakkal asked as he looked back at the holocom controls. "Guess you have more balls than I thought. Let me tell you what else is stupid—threatening the person who's holding the blaster. You agreed to our deal."

"Under duress! That...that's illegal!"

Drakkal selected the option to unlock the restraints. With several simultaneous clicks, the cuffs around the terran's neck, wrists, and ankles unfastened and clattered to the floor when she shook them off.

"Is that really your argument?" Drakkal asked. He stalked forward and settled a foot on Murgen's back, extending his toe claws as he leaned his weight on that leg. Shuffling the holocom and blaster between his hands, he quickly shrugged off his jacket and tossed it to the terran.

She caught it and stared at Drakkal with narrowed eyes for a second before pulling the jacket on and zipping the front. The garment dwarfed her, making her appear even smaller. The hem, which came to Drakkal's waist, hung to her knees, and the sleeves dangled well past her hands until she rolled them up.

Something about the sight rekindled Drakkal's earlier desire. This terran in his clothing—and knowing she wore *nothing* beneath it—was the most erotic, arousing image he'd ever seen.

But the insistent protective instinct she'd awoken in him was more powerful than his lust. Keeping his left hand free, he removed his foot from Murgen's neck and grasped the back of the durgan's shirt. He hauled Murgen up and tossed him backward. The durgan landed in a sitting position against the wall with a startled grunt.

Drakkal crouched near Murgen, keeping the blaster aimed at him. "If I don't let my friends try to argue ethics during illicit activities, I'm definitely not going to listen to you blather about the rules. Owning people is illegal, *zhe'gaash*. Lift your arm."

Lips quivering, Murgen hesitantly lifted his right arm.

Drakkal glanced at the terran over his shoulder. "Clamp that collar around his arm."

The female bent and picked up the collar. When she straightened, she approached Murgen without a hint of fear in her expression. If Drakkal was correctly reading the fire in her eyes and the slight upward slant of her lips, she was taking satisfaction in this.

She clamped the collar around Murgen's raised arm.

Drakkal shifted over to Nostrus and quickly removed the volturian's holocom. He crushed it in his cybernetic hand and tossed it aside. "Now get the others on our favorite volturian."

Hand on her belly, the terran squatted and gathered the cuffs. She secured a pair around the volturian's wrists and paused to tug off the volturian's boots before closing the remaining manacles around his ankles. That done, she stepped into Nostrus's boots, covering her little feet.

Drakkal's smirk grew more despite the seriousness of the situation.

Once the terran had stepped away from Nostrus, Drakkal accessed Murgen's holocom again.

"What are you doing?" Murgen demanded.

"Ordering lunch," Drakkal answered.

The lights on the restraints came on when Drakkal activated them. Murgen grunted as his arm was forced back against the wall. Nostrus stirred as he slid across the floor, dragged by the cuffs on his limbs. Both the volturian and the durgan were forced into upright positions, their restraints locking into place against the wall—close enough to each other that their bodies were pressed together.

Nostrus groaned as his eyelids fluttered open, head lolling.

Drakkal fished a credit chip out of his pocket—unmarked and untraceable, the only sort he used—and briefly linked it to his own holocom to load it with credits.

The read out ticked up to one hundred and eighty-thousand credits.

He flicked the credit chip onto the floor in front of Murgen. "Your payment. She's mine now. Forget that, and there will be consequences. Let this be proof—you're not untouchable."

THREE

The female terran's scent would've been all Drakkal could focus on were it not for the feel of her supple little body tucked against his side. When he'd first put his arm around her shoulders and pulled her close, her tension had been unmistakable, but she'd offered no protest—unlike Murgen Foltham, who'd blathered on and on as Drakkal had walked the female out of the cell. Only the closing door had silenced the durgan.

In fact, the terran hadn't said a word as, following the map on Murgen's holocom, they'd driven the hovercart to a rear exit that led from the zoo into the Undercity's maintenance tunnels. They'd been unable to take the cart beyond that point, and Drakkal had left Murgen's destroyed holocom on the driver's seat.

Drakkal glanced over his shoulder. The dimly lit tunnel stretched on behind him, as empty as it had been since they'd entered it. These tunnels crisscrossed Arthos, providing discreet pathways to the savvy.

Though being forced to travel on foot had slowed them down, Murgen's predicament likely hadn't been discovered yet.

There was still time. And if things came down to a fight before they made it back to the hovercar, Drakkal had Nostrus's blaster strapped to his belt.

The terran was as much a distraction as she was a motivation. Drakkal had to remain mindful of potential pursuit, had to ensure they were following the correct path through these confusing tunnels, had to keep the terran safe—all while his groin ached and his cock struggled against the restraint of his pants.

Apart from his ceaseless battle against lust, this all seemed too easy. They'd walked out the back door of Foltham's zoo unchallenged—no guards, no alarms, just a blast door that had opened after a prompt from the stolen holocom. Was Foltham's security truly so lax, or was there more to it?

Arrogance. That gresh navari likely never imagined anyone would have the balls to pull something like this.

The female, too, didn't seem quite right. She'd been quiet and cooperative thus far. Where was the fierce little creature Murgen had described? Where was the warrior who'd injured several security guards? She was Drakkal's mate—there was no denying that—but she was more than she appeared. She was cunning, and Drakkal knew nothing about her. He needed to remain wary.

Don't be stupid.

Or stupider, anyway.

And yet his attention continually returned to her lovely scent, to her delectable little body—how he craved to peel off the jacket and bare her skin to him again, to feel that skin against him—and the fleeting, random brushes of her soft, warm breath over his fur.

Focus. Time to start thinking this out.

They'd escaped Murgen's manor, but the danger hadn't passed. Drakkal had crushed Murgen's holocom and left it with the hovercart to avoid having it traced, but there was at least one other means by which Drakkal and the terran could be tracked.

He halted, placed his hands on the female's shoulders, and guided her to stand in front of him, facing ahead. She attempted to pull away, but Drakkal held her firmly in place. He took extra care with his prosthesis; though he'd had the cybernetic limb for a year, he still sometimes underestimated its strength, and he had no desire to harm this female.

"Be still," he said. He slid his right hand up her neck, sweeping aside her long, golden hair to press his fingertips over her spine.

She stiffened. "What are you doing?"

Drakkal paused, ears perking. Though her voice was hard, demanding, and guarded, it was also amongst the sweetest sounds he'd ever heard. His hunger for her intensified.

Clenching his jaw, he forced his fingers up slowly, moving them toward her skull. "Murgen likely implanted a tracker in you. Most of his type do that with their slaves."

"I'm not a slave."

Drakkal halted his fingers when he felt a tiny nub beneath her skin; it moved when he shifted his finger from side to side. "Something tells me he sees it differently. Hands on the wall."

She turned, raised her hands, and flattened them against the wall. "The last guard who told me to put my hands on the wall wound up with a broken arm."

Drakkal guided her head forward until her forehead also rested against the wall. The threat she'd made was as comical as it was endearing, given their size difference. Her bravado was almost enough to heighten his desire, but he'd been a fighter for long enough to know not to underestimate anyone based on size alone.

"You'll want to try breaking my arm in a second," he said, "but you'd just hurt yourself more."

She widened her stance and took a deep breath. "Whatever it is you're going to do, do it."

He gathered her hair together, twisted it into a loose bundle, and moved it aside, clearing the patch of skin where he'd felt the tracker. Placing his right hand on the side of her neck with his fingers beneath her jaw and his thumb pressed against the back of her skull, he forced her head forward to a sharper angle; her resistance was brief but surprisingly strong.

Raising his prosthetic hand, he formed the hardlight claw at the tip of his forefinger—a hooked blade that looked like translucent red crystal—and lowered it to the skin over the tracker. He slid one foot forward, bracing a leg between hers and pinning her against the wall with his hip.

She tensed. "What the fu—*ah!*"

Drakkal slid the claw over her skin.

The terran's hiss became a low, pained hum as she slapped her hand against the wall. Blood welled along the incision and trickled down the back of her neck. Drakkal's stomach churned; for a moment, he felt as though he were about to retch.

Blood had never bothered him before, not once in his entire life. Why now? Why did the sight of her blood—and the knowledge that he'd spilled it—make him sick to his stomach?

Swallowing thickly, he forced himself to work. He dismissed the hardlight claw and pinched the incision from its ends, opening it like a tiny, bloody mouth—a resemblance that caused a resurgence of his nausea, but he wouldn't let himself vomit.

Stop acting like a fucking zhe'gaash *and do what needs to be done!*

The tiny, crimson-coated tristeel orb was barely visible

amidst the glistening blood. He shifted his right hand, curled his fingers to extend his natural claws, and pinched the orb between them. He drew it out slowly, revealing the hair-thin wires attached to it a millimeter at a time.

"Hurry the fuck up," she snapped. Her hands were curled into fists against the wall, and her entire body was rigid and trembling.

Drakkal clenched his jaw. He'd hurt her already, but he knew this was the worst part, and despite everything he'd seen and done in his life, he didn't want to do this. He didn't want to cause her more pain.

But this was the path he'd decided to walk. The time to choose had passed.

He pulled on the orb. The wires went taut, clinging to their anchor points somewhere deep in the terran's flesh. Drakkal gave the orb another sharp tug, and the wires broke free.

A high-pitched cry burst from the terran's throat, and she went slack. Drakkal hurriedly tossed aside the tracker, looped his prosthetic arm around her middle, and lifted his knee to take her weight onto his leg and keep her upright.

SHE INHALED DEEPLY and flattened her palms against the wall, running them up and down slowly. Her exhalation was soft and slow as she released the breath, only to suck in another, as though breathing through her pain.

Drakkal's insides twisted and flipped. He'd spent years physically harming people in arena bouts and had never felt remorse over it. But hurting her, hurting his *mate*...it was too much. He dropped his right hand to his belt and felt along it until his bloody fingers touched his small first-aid pouch. After a few moments of fumbling, he tugged a bandage out of its little dispenser and raised it to her neck.

"We're done." He pressed the bandage over the wound. The bandage activated immediately and faded into her skin, sealing the cut as it vanished.

Slowly, he removed his leg from between hers, allowing her to support her own weight a little at a time.

She was still for a little while before she hesitantly eased away from the wall and turned to face him. She swayed unsteadily, and her body sagged toward him. Drakkal's heart leapt. He caught her upper arms, stopping her before she fell. Had he done too much damage, pushed her too hard, inflicted too much pain? His familiarity with terran anatomy was relatively shallow; he wasn't sure how much punishment they could endure.

He needed to bring her home to the compound. Urgand had been studying terran medicine for the last year—ever since Arcanthus took Samantha as his mate—and would be far better equipped than Drakkal to examine and treat this terran.

Her palm settled on his thigh. For an instant, Drakkal's blood reheated with desire, and conscious thought ceased. She slid her hand slowly up toward his waist. Her touch, even through his pants, sparked an electric current across his skin that made his tail twitch and his fur stand on end. He craved more of it—*now*—despite their situation.

"No," she said, stepping back to press herself against the wall, "we're not done."

Drakkal's brows and ears fell; her tone, now firm and confident, snapped him back to reality. He glanced down to see the blaster he'd taken from Nostrus—the blaster he'd dropped into the empty holster on his belt—in the terran's hand, its barrel pointed at his chest.

Whatever he might've expected from a female in her condition, especially given what she'd been through, it wasn't this.

And her hand was absolutely steady—not even the faintest tremor moved the blaster.

Well, Drakkal, you did it. You were stupid. Again.

"Step back," she commanded.

Drakkal took a large step back and lifted his eyes to her face. The rage and hatred he'd seen in her eyes when she'd looked at Murgen and Nostrus was back, but it was controlled, it was *cold*.

He slowly raised his hands, displaying his empty palms. "I'm not going to hurt you, terran."

"You already did."

"That was necessary."

"I know. That's the only reason I let you do it. Now shut the fuck up and take off your belt."

His tail flicked from side to side. This was his mate. Surely she felt something of that, too. She wouldn't harm him, not now. Not ever.

"Strange way to show thanks after I took you out of that place," he said.

"For your own sick-minded fetishes. I'm not trading one owner for another."

"That's not—"

She lowered the barrel of the blaster and fired a single plasma bolt almost faster than Drakkal could register, producing a high, echoing sound that ran along the tunnel in both directions. The bolt struck the floor between Drakkal's feet; the metal flooring hissed in the aftermath.

Though Drakkal didn't move, heat and pressure built in his chest. He was angry, both at her and at himself, but he was also oddly thrilled by her actions—by her boldness, by her confidence, by her spirit.

"Take off your belt," the terran said. "I'm not going to say it again."

Drakkal's mouth twitched; he wasn't sure whether he was about to snarl or smirk, so he pressed his lips together instead. He lowered his hands and unbuckled his belt, removing it from around his waist. He tossed it to the floor between himself and the terran.

"Now your clothes," she said, gaze holding his.

"I guess that's fair," he replied, grasping the hem of his shirt.

"Why's that?"

"I've seen you already."

Her dark brows slanted farther. "Do you *want* me to shoot you?"

He pulled the shirt off over his head, wadded it up, and tossed it atop his belt. "Hasn't felt good the other times it's happened, so I'm going to pass on that."

For a moment, her eyes dipped to his chest and down his abdomen. She swallowed, then flicked the blaster's barrel toward his groin. "Let's go. Get 'em off."

Drakkal released a sharp breath through his nostrils and unclasped his pants. "You have a name?"

"Not that I'll be telling you. Pants off. *Now*."

He grasped the waistband of his pants and shoved them down; his half-sheathed, semi-hard cock sprang free. If nothing else, the relief was welcome.

"You serious right now?" she asked, aghast. "You're fucking hard over this?"

"Yeah. Nothing turns me on like getting robbed," he replied flatly.

She shifted her stance and tilted her head. "Well, it's impressive. I'll give you that much. And if you don't want me to shoot it off, you'll hurry up."

Drakkal couldn't prevent his lips from turning up in a smirk now as he lifted his legs one at a time to tug off his pants. He stared at the terran as he moved. Her gaze remained fixed on his cock, and a new, intrigued light had entered her eyes.

His heart thundered in his ears, and his shaft twitched, swelling further and sliding out of its sheath that much more. "You're pretty impressive yourself, terran."

He threw the pants into the pile and stood up straight, drawing in a deep breath to expand his chest. His ears perked, his fur bristled, and his tail lashed behind him. It took him a moment to realize that he was presenting himself for his mate—instinctually displaying his prowess.

Her breath hitched and her eyes flared as she took him in. Though she tried to hide it, Drakkal could see the interest, the heat, the confusion, the *hesitation* in those bright blue eyes.

"It's not too late," he said.

She seemed to shake herself and dragged her eyes away from his now fully erect, throbbing cock to meet his. "Not too late for what?"

"I was going to say it's not too late to let me put my clothes back on and bring you somewhere safe, but with that look in your eyes"—he trailed his gaze down her body, his imagination filling in what he knew was hidden beneath the jacket—"I'll go with it's not too late to take that jacket off and help me relieve some of this...tension between us."

A faint blush tinged her cheeks, but all traces of her desire vanished. Her eyes hardened again, becoming even colder than before. She raised the blaster until it was level with his chest. "Back up."

Drakkal walked backward until his back hit the wall. "You know I'm going to come for my belongings."

And for you.

She moved to the pile of clothing, keeping her eyes and the blaster trained on him. "You won't find me." She crouched and gathered the items into her arm.

"You don't sound quite so confident suddenly," Drakkal said. "But I am. I'll find you, female, wherever you go."

"Oh, I'm confident. I know how to hide. But if you *do* happen to find me, I'll shoot you." She backed away from him and continued down the tunnel, her bundle of stolen possessions clutched to her chest.

He didn't move but to turn his head and follow her progress. "It'd be rude to shoot someone with his own gun."

She smirked, her features easing in her amusement. "It's my gun now." With the hand holding the blaster, she reached back to quickly raise the jacket's oversized hood. Shadows obscured her face.

Drakkal's instincts were at war; it was only that inner conflict that held him in place. He wanted to give chase, wanted to rut with her, to claim her, but at the same time he knew she wasn't bluffing. It didn't matter if she was his mate, didn't matter if he believed she didn't *want* to shoot him—she would if he pressed her.

She wagged the barrel of the blaster at him as she reached the end of the tunnel. "Don't follow me, azhera."

And then she stepped into a side corridor, vanishing from Drakkal's view.

For several moments, Drakkal was frozen, his breath heavy and ragged, his cock aching and throbbing, as that internal war raged. He hadn't gone to Murgen's in search of a mate—he hadn't even thought about seeking a mate for many, many years. What was the point of it?

But now that he'd found her, now that he'd scented her, he knew he wouldn't be able to stop himself. Her threats didn't make a difference. Drakkal would hunt for her, and he would find her. Because she was *his*.

All she'd accomplished here was to gain a small head start.

Drakkal shoved himself away from the wall and stalked

after the terran, following her scent. Though her fragrance was so distinct, so intimately familiar to him already, the task was complicated by the simple fact that her smell had seeped into his fur through their clothing while they'd walked. He could scent it on the air, but it also wafted from *him*.

He turned into the doorway through which she'd vanished and hurried down a long, narrow corridor. It ended at a single sliding door—an elevator entrance.

"Vrek'osh," he growled as he pressed the call button. This was more than a *small* head start.

Seconds ticked by. Drakkal clenched his fists and paced along the corridor, his tail swinging with increasing speed and erraticism.

"Come on," he said through his fangs, mane bristling. Tension rippled through his muscles, filling them with anticipatory energy; he needed to run, to chase, to claim what was his.

The door began opening. Drakkal darted forward, forcing his way through the widening entryway and into the elevator car. Gritting his teeth, he forced himself to carefully press the inside control to direct the elevator to the surface. The last thing he needed was to break the control panel and make the elevator inoperable. He'd already lost enough time.

The door closed, and the elevator began its rapid, softly humming ascent. The air was redolent with her fragrance, and his cock stirred again, twitching and pulsing with a resurgence of desire. He lowered his right hand to it and grasped his shaft, squeezing even though he knew it would only momentarily ease the pressure.

When the elevator stopped and the door opened again, Drakkal charged out like a ravenous beast released from its tether. He emerged in a dark, dank alleyway that let out on a brightly lit street ahead. His nostrils flared as he scented the air, drawing in the stench of metal, concrete, and garbage that suffused the city, the smells of the sweat and skin of countless alien species, the aromas of exotic perfumes and spices. He was interested only in one scent—the sundrinker fragrance—and it was so faint, so diluted, so overpowered by everything else, though the terran couldn't have passed through here more than a few minutes ago.

He raced forward, ignoring the puddles underfoot, pausing only when he was out of the alley. He found himself on one of the many bustling retail streets of the Gilded Sector. People of various races, many of them well-dressed, walked along the edges of the wide street, which was lined with businesses presenting polished display windows and high-priced items. Across the street and about twenty meters to his left was a restaurant with an outdoor seating area that was cordoned off by forcefield walls. Sleek hover cars touched down and lifted off all along the street, dropping off and picking up well-to-do passengers.

Drakkal scented the air again but he could only detect the merest hint of the terran's scent here. He turned his head from side to side, scanning the street for any sign of her. The jacket she'd taken from him wasn't the pinnacle of fashion, but it was nice, and blended in well with the more casual of the pedestrians here—especially the ones who wanted to look *tough*. Paired with her smaller stature, which would allow her to fade into the crowd with ease, and the fact that she'd covered her golden hair with a hood, he had little chance of finding her.

A couple of grimacing ertraxxans made disgusted sounds as they walked past Drakkal, giving him a wide berth. Drakkal met their gazes and growled, baring his teeth and flexing his claws. The ertraxxans increased their pace.

Drakkal's growl dragged out, rumbling his chest, as he resumed his search. His body seemed to be torn in both directions. She could've gone anywhere; there were dozens of pedestrian pathways here, most of them at least as busy as this one.

"*Vrek'osh.*"

More of the people walking nearby were staring at him now, many of them putting on airs of offense—as though they'd never seen a naked body before. His pulsing cock softened, but it only brought minor relief from its ache. He turned his head to the left; a pair of gold-and-teal armored peacekeepers were posted on the corner less than fifty meters away.

Public nudity wasn't a crime in Arthos, but everything operated differently in sectors like this one. The city's wealthy residents—like most of the people here—typically got their way when it came to things they deemed *distasteful*. Drakkal wasn't foolish enough to think those peacekeepers would hesitate to drag him off whether he'd committed a crime or not.

He snarled and shook his head, ruffling his mane. He wanted nothing more than continue the chase, but the trail had already gone cold, and he wasn't in the mood for a trip to the nearest Eternal Guard outpost.

You win this round, little terran.

He lifted his left arm, meaning to activate the holocom embedded in his prosthesis, but stopped himself. What good would it do to call for help now? He couldn't very well stand here and wait for someone to pick him up, and he wasn't eager for the conversation that would arise when one of his friends arrived.

So, Drakkal...you released a terran slave and let her steal everything—including the clothes on your back? And how much smaller than you was she, exactly?

Releasing a frustrated huff, Drakkal turned and walked toward his hovercar, ignoring the put-upon pedestrians in his way.

At least the car was less than two kilometers away; it

would've been a long, long walk home otherwise.

DRAKKAL WASN'T SURPRISED to see Arcanthus waiting near the interior door when he drove the hovercar into the garage. The sedhi was leaning against the wall, one leg bent, with his dark cybernetic arms folded across his chest. His smirk was reflected in all three of his black and yellow eyes.

Drakkal parked the vehicle and climbed out.

Arc's eyes widened—and his smirk stretched into a grin. "Well, look what the cat dragged in," he said as Drakkal—still naked—approached.

"I told you to stop asking Sam for cat-related sayings," Drakkal replied, stopping a couple paces away from Arcanthus.

"Sorry. That one just seemed *purr*fect."

"Fuck you, sedhi."

Arcanthus chuckled. "Taking out the claws early, I see."

Drakkal ground his teeth together and spread his arms to either side. "Do I look like I'm in the mood?"

"You look like you're in *a* mood, at least. I suppose things got feisty at old Murgen's?"

That restless, fury-laced energy thrummed through Drakkal's body. His arousal had cooled—albeit slowly—during the journey home, but his drive to hunt and claim his terran had intensified. His patience for everything, including his usual banter with Arcanthus, was frayed.

"Yeah." Drakkal walked to the door, opened it, and strode into the corridor beyond.

Arcanthus fell into step behind him. "Naked *and* agitated, azhera? You have a story to tell."

"Maybe when you're ready to stop screwing around, Arcanthus."

"Now I'm even more intrigued."

Drakkal shook his head and increased his pace. "Fine. Let's talk in your workshop."

"Hold on," Arcanthus snapped. One of his cybernetic hands came down on Drakkal's shoulder.

A low, involuntary growl vibrated from Drakkal's chest as he halted. He shrugged off Arcanthus's hand and turned to face the sedhi. "What?"

"Samantha's in there. You can't go in like this."

Drakkal's brow furrowed. "You're telling *me* to get dressed?"

"Well, you're not going to parade around naked in front of my mate."

Any other day, Drakkal would've seized this opportunity to tease Arcanthus, to get under his skin—*it's only because you know she'll realize I'm more attractive than you* or something like that. But today, having encountered the woman he was certain was his mate, he couldn't bring himself to joke like that.

I want my terran.

Drakkal held out his right hand. "Give me your robe."

Arcanthus's eyes widened. "What? No. You have plenty of your own clothes in your room."

"My room is on the other side of the building." Drakkal began turning away. "Would rather just stop in your workshop on the way."

"All right, all right!"

Normally, the corner of Drakkal's mouth would've turned up in amusement at this petty victory, but he didn't feel any amusement now. He turned back toward Arcanthus, who was scowling as he removed his silky crimson robe. The sedhi's brows were angled down toward the bridge of his nose as he handed the garment to Drakkal—or rather shoved it hard against the azhera's chest.

Drakkal took the robe by the sleeves and let it unfurl. He held Arcanthus's gaze as he tied the robe around his waist, covering his groin with the main portion of the fabric.

Arcanthus's expression darkened. "I expect that washed and de-furred before you return it."

Drakkal gestured to Arcanthus's long crimson loincloth. "Now we're in matching outfits."

The exaggerated look of disdain on Arc's face should've been immensely satisfying, but it did nothing for Drakkal now. Part of Drakkal's mind remained outside, scenting the air and searching for even the briefest glimpse of golden hair.

"Let's get this over with," Drakkal muttered. He turned and continued along the corridor. Arcanthus followed.

These halls were familiar by now, but Drakkal still hadn't shaken the feeling that they were *different*. He and Arcanthus had moved their operation into this facility a little over a year ago, in the wake of their fallout with Vaund and the Syndicate, and though it was furnished similarly to their old home he couldn't help noting all the things that weren't the same.

He still wasn't sure if that bothered him or not. This place was home, but he'd always felt it was lacking something.

My mate.

The deeper Drakkal went into the compound, the stronger his agitation grew. He should've been thinking about a hundred other things—like the botched deal, or the potential of Foltham seeking vengeance despite Drakkal's threat to expose his illegal activities—but his mind repeatedly returned to his terran.

Drakkal entered the workshop just ahead of Arcanthus.

Samantha, dressed in leggings and an oversized hooded sweater, was seated on one of the couches. She looked up from the tablet she was drawing on and smiled at him. "Hi, Drak."

This workshop was small compared to the one Arcanthus had kept in their previous base of operations, but Drakkal preferred it. This space was warmer, cozier. Arc's desk—with its multitude of displays and controls—sat straight ahead, beyond the pair of dark red couches that were positioned to face each other. A counter with fabrication equipment, which Arcanthus used to create the physical ID chips, ran along the wall to the left. Sam's desk was beside Arc's; it was smaller and a bit cluttered, with several blotches of dried paint and a few bits of flattened, hardened clay marring its surface. The large cabinet behind it contained a variety of artistic tools. While she usually used her tablet, she'd also taken well to painting and, occasionally, sculpting.

Though Arcanthus had carried over the moody adjustable lighting and dark carpeting from his old workshop, this room seemed brighter and more welcoming. Samantha was largely to thank for that. She was also responsible for Drakkal's favorite part of the room—the large, stone fire bowl hovering in the space between the two couches, crackling with holographic flames. It reminded him of older, simpler times.

Samantha's gaze shifted past Drakkal to Arcanthus, and her smile took on a slight, mischievous tilt. "You two are wearing matching outfits."

The smile that crept onto Drakkal's lips was genuine, even if he didn't feel the humor as fully as he should have. "That's what I said. He's upset because I wear it better."

"*Now* you're in the joking mood?" Arcanthus dropped onto the couch beside Samantha, wrapping an arm around her shoulders and draping his tail over her lap. She set her tablet on the cushion beside her and leaned against him.

Drakkal sat on the opposite couch, stretching his tail out beside him. Its tip lashed back and forth rapidly. The warmth emitted by the fire bowl, usually soothing and comfortable, made his skin prickle with heat. "No. I'm not."

Samantha frowned, and Arcanthus's expression softened.

"Well? What happened, Drak? Why'd you come home naked?" Arcanthus asked.

Samantha's cheeks reddened. She cleared her throat and tilted her chin down, her hair falling over her face as though to hide. She'd been around the crew for a long time, was part of the family as much as anyone else, but she was still easily embarrassed—more often by what she said than what anyone else did. Drakkal understood well enough; Samantha was just a private person. She preferred to keep intimate matters between herself and Arcanthus.

"I was robbed," Drakkal replied.

Simultaneously, both Arc's and Sam's eyebrows rose high.

"By *who*?" Arcanthus asked.

Gritting his teeth, Drakkal shoved himself off the couch. His ears flattened and his fur bristled as another wave of restlessness rippled through him. "A terran."

"A terran robbed *you*?"

"It's not like we're completely harmless, Arc," Samantha said gently.

Arcanthus turned his face toward Sam and brushed a finger along her jaw. "I know, little flower. You're proof of that yourself."

Drakkal paced from one end of the couch to the other and back again; it wasn't enough to vent even a fraction of the energy building within him, but it was better than staying still.

"I sent you to the durgan's for a simple delivery," Arcanthus said.

Drakkal growled. "Murgen wasn't interested in simple."

Samantha snickered. "I know this isn't the time, but...his name is Murgen the durgan? Does that sound ridiculous to anyone else here?"

"Murgen the durgan," Arc echoed, grinning. "You're right. It has a certain comedic ring to it, doesn't it?"

Drakkal couldn't argue that, but it wasn't enough to ease his agitation. He needed to leave, to hunt, but how could he? The terran was one person in a sprawling city of billions. His first encounter with her had been so improbable as to have been nearly impossible, and the chances of another meeting were infinitesimal.

"Sorry, Drak." Sam's voice broke his thoughts. Her face was troubled, her concern genuine. "What happened?"

"I rescued a female terran from a fucking zoo," Drakkal replied, struggling to keep his tone as even as possible, "and she took my gun and used it to rob me."

Arcanthus lifted a hand to his face and covered his mouth. Mirth gleamed in all three of his eyes.

Drakkal jabbed a finger at Arc. "Don't."

Arcanthus shifted his hand, revealing one corner of his upturned lips. "But it's so hard not to."

"*Kraasz ka'val*, at least make an effort!"

Arc's tongue slipped out to run over his upper lip. "Was this one of those mythical three-meter-tall terrans? Did she overpower little Drakkal?"

Drakkal halted his pacing, spun toward Arcanthus, and roared, "*She's my mate!*"

Samantha and Arcanthus stared at him with wide eyes and slack jaws. Drakkal's thundering heartbeat and ragged breaths rose in volume to fill the ensuing silence. Slowly, his frustration shifted, altering into a combination of despair and a crushing sense of helplessness. He clenched his fists, resisting those emotions. He wouldn't allow himself to fall into that state of mind.

"That's...an unexpected twist," Arcanthus finally said. "Was this some sort of strange azheran foreplay? She steals from you, you track her down, then make love?"

"Yeah. Nothing turns me on like walking naked through

the fucking Gilded Sector. She has no ID chip, and she's not going to appear in any registries or databases. I don't even have a name for her."

"Oh. Well, we all face challenges."

Samantha smacked Arc's chest and glared at him.

Arcanthus winced and rubbed the spot she'd hit. "All right, sorry. I'm only teasing in what I can assure you is good nature."

"Good," Drakkal said, resuming his pacing. "Then it shouldn't upset you to know that Murgen isn't a customer anymore and the deal was cancelled."

Arcanthus's expression sobered. "What?"

Drakkal drew in a deep breath through his nostrils and told Arcanthus and Samantha everything—from his arrival at Murgen's manor to his bare-assed walk to his hovercar.

When the story was done, Arcanthus sat with the bridge of his nose pinched between a forefinger and thumb. "That's..."

"A blow to your precious reputation?" Drakkal suggested drily.

"Well, yes, but I was going to say *unfortunate*. Had I known about the whole slaves being kept in a zoo thing, I'd never have agreed to do business with him."

"And Drakkal would never have known his mate existed," Samantha said.

Arcanthus sighed. "What happened to *don't be stupid?*"

"Did you ever once listen to that when you were after Samantha?" Drakkal asked.

"I thought about it, even if I didn't always obey."

Drakkal grunted and dropped back onto the couch. He lifted his right hand and dragged his fingers through his mane. "You never obeyed. But it was me who messed up this time."

"Are you sure she's your mate?" Arcanthus asked.

Drakkal tipped his head back and turned his unfocused eyes toward the ceiling. He'd felt lust before, had felt attraction, had once even mistakenly thought himself in love...but all of that was nothing compared to what he felt now. This desire, this consuming need, this instant obsession, it was unlike anything he'd ever experienced.

And that scared him.

"Yes," he said.

"Then you didn't mess up. You did what you had to."

Those words were both comforting and unsettling. As head of security for this little operation, Drakkal had been cautious and disciplined for years. This lapse of self-control was uncharacteristic. It was *dangerous*—not just to him, but to Arcanthus, Samantha, and all the people they worked with and cared about.

"What now, Drak?" Sam asked after several seconds of silence. "You're going to look for her, right?"

Drakkal's brow furrowed. Finding his terran in this city would be like searching for a particular speck of dust amidst the vastness of space.

But he had resources—money, a network of informants and contacts, and access to Arcanthus, who was one of the best hackers in Arthos—and *tenacity*. There'd been a period in his life, before he'd met Arcanthus, when Drakkal had been on the verge of surrender, had been about to give up. That wasn't him anymore. He'd meant what he'd told his terran.

He lifted his head and stood up as bolstering fire swept through his veins. Whether it had been fate or just blind chance, the universe had put the terran in his path. It was up to him to do the rest, and he wouldn't let the odds deter him. "Not just going to look. I'm going to find her, no matter where she went."

FOUR

Three Weeks Later

THE SUDDEN, insistent blare of Shay's alarm startled her awake. Her fist reflexively flew up and smacked her nose, sending sharp pain across her face. With a curse, she lifted her head and fumbled with the holocom on her wrist, trying to remember through her grogginess how to turn the damned thing off. Once there was silence, her head fell back on the pillow.

Just another day in paradise.

She opened her eyes and squinted at the holocom's display, which was blaringly bright in the otherwise dark room. 05:01. Not that it meant much in the Undercity, which was locked in an eternal night broken only by the vibrant, obnoxious neons and holograms on almost every street.

With a groan, Shay rolled onto her back, rubbing the throbbing bridge of her nose as all her other twinges and aches made themselves known—stiff back, sore hips, immense pressure on her bladder. Despite all that, she enjoyed this rare moment of peace.

Slipping her hands beneath the blanket, Shay settled them on her rounded stomach and closed her eyes. Little feet kicked against her palm from within.

Shay smiled. "Good morning, Baby."

Baby. That was all she could call it. Shay didn't know whether it was a boy or girl, wasn't sure of the due date, didn't even know what she was going to do when the time finally came. But she did know this baby was the only good thing in her life regardless of its conception and despite the piece of shit sperm donor, and she'd do her best not to fuck this up like she had everything else. Shay might have made a mess of her own life, but she wasn't going to ruin her baby's. She'd do better for her child.

Just how she was going to accomplish that remained a mystery, but she *would*.

It didn't help that she'd been taken from everything she'd ever known, sold and thrust into this dangerous new world where some viewed her as weak and small, as a curiosity, a possession to be claimed. As a fucking *animal*.

Never again.

It'd been three weeks since her escape from that damned prison cell and every day had been a struggle. She was paranoid, always on guard, always looking over her shoulder, always anticipating the moment when they'd find her. And she was stuck here in Arthos. She had no ID chip and couldn't get one through the United Terran Federation because of her criminal record—she had at least one warrant out for her arrest back on Earth. If she went to the embassy, they were guaranteed to see that warrant, and she'd be taken into custody. She was royally fucked.

Well, you wanted a fresh start. Doesn't get much fresher than this. You're nobody here.

"So, we make do with what we got, right Baby?" she asked softly, running her hand over her stomach as the baby restlessly shifted.

Pregnancy was a state she hadn't wanted, one she couldn't afford, but she didn't resent it.

Fortunately, she'd been granted a better start than she might otherwise have had thanks to the azhera who'd *purchased* her from Murgen. He'd had chips with several thousand credits on them stashed in his pants pocket. But credits only went so far when you didn't have an ID chip.

"And money isn't going to make itself." Despite those words, Shay lay on her pathetic excuse for a bed—an old, thin, lumpy gel mattress on the floor—and cherished the quiet moment with her baby a little longer.

She didn't bother suppressing her groan when she finally rolled out of bed. "Lights on."

The overhead lights along the upper walls hummed and flickered on, low and dim at first before strengthening to an uneven glow. Several were burned out.

On her hands and knees, Shay slipped her hand beneath her pillow, curled her fingers around the handle of her blaster, and pushed herself to her feet. Her bladder chose that moment to remind her of how long she'd ignored it.

She hurriedly snatched clean clothes from the dresser and crossed the small studio apartment to enter the bathroom. She set the blaster on the counter, shoved her underwear down, and relieved herself. The moan that escaped from her was embarrassing, but who the hell cared? No one was around to hear.

She took a moment just to glare at the auto-washer embedded on the wall—it was a sliding door about a meter wide and tall, and like everything else in the apartment, it was unreliable at best. The wash function worked well, but it was crapshoot as to whether her clothes would actually be dry when the *done* light came on. More than once, she'd been forced to drape damp clothing over the shower rod and let it air dry.

Once she'd finished on the toilet, she took a quick shower and got dressed.

The bathroom contained a tiny shower stall, a sink, and a bowl protruding from the wall that was her toilet, and it felt about the size of a coat closet. Despite being crowded and leaving her with bruised elbows a few times, it was enough for her. Better her arms than her belly, anyway, which seemed prone to bump into everything. She wasn't used to being so...ungainly.

She was brushing her teeth when the door buzzer went sounded.

Shay paused, her mouth fully of toothpaste, and looked at the front door—which was behind her in the main room—in the mirror. She settled her free hand atop her blaster.

The buzz came again.

Trying to ignore how nauseous the toothpaste made her, she spat into the sink, set the toothbrush down, and quickly rinsed and wiped her mouth before stalking into the main room.

Pressing a shoulder against the wall beside the door, she raised the blaster and checked the charge. The view screen mounted near the doorframe hadn't worked since she'd moved in. Any time she opened the door, she was doing so blind, and that was especially concerning in a place like this.

Her visitor pounded on the door. Shay felt the vibrations through the wall.

"Who is it?" she called.

"Open up, terran," demanded Vrisk, her so-called landlord, his voice muffled through the closed door.

"What do you want? I'm busy."

"Your payment is due."

Shay pushed away from the wall to glare at the door as though she could see Vrisk through it. "The fuck you say? I paid for a month!"

"It's been a month. Hand over the credits or get out."

Righteous fury burned in her belly. Shay gritted her teeth, switched the blaster into her left hand, tucked it behind her back, and disengaged the locks on the door.

"I so don't have time for this shit," she muttered, slapping the *open* button.

The door—the only thing in the apartment in decent working order—whipped open to reveal her two-hundred-ten-centimeter tall landlord, an ilthurii with dark brown bark scales and crimson eyes. He was one scary motherfucker, but that hadn't stopped Shay from approaching him when she needed a place to stay, even if this was a dump.

Desperate times...

His hairless brow ridges were drawn down—whether in annoyance or in constipation, Shay neither knew nor cared. It was the look he always seemed to wear.

"It's only been three weeks," Shay said, glaring up at the overgrown lizard. "The deal was a month."

Vrisk leaned down, the spines around his face and head flattening as he grunted. "If I say it's been a month, it's been a month. I want my credits, terran."

"You'll get your damned credits in a week."

"I am not running a fucking charity." He held his hand out. "I want what is due."

Shay smacked his hand away. "You'll get what's due *when* it's due."

Vrisk snarled and stepped closer, shoving a clawed finger in her face. She barely managed to keep herself from shoving her gun into his.

"You will pay now, terran, or I will sell your room and everything inside it to another by the day's end," he said.

Shay's jaw hurt from how hard she clenched it to keep her words from spewing out. Oh, the things she wanted to say to this asshole.

Think of the baby...

Shay tucked her blaster into the waistband of her pants and hid it under her shirt. "Stay there."

She turned around and walked across the living space, listening closely for any indication that he might've followed her inside, to snatch up the belt draped over one of the chairs at the table. She fished the credit chip she'd been saving for next month's rent out of one of the pouches. When she turned back toward the ilthurii, he was still standing in the hallway—and still looking like someone took a shit in his breakfast.

Striding to the door, Shay drew her arm back and snapped it forward, releasing the chip. It flew through the air and struck Vrisk right between his eyes. He flinched and shuffled backward, scrambling to catch it.

"There's next month's payment. You try and cheat me again, and I'll blow your goddamned head off." She hit the control button. The door shut immediately, cutting off Vrisk's glare and any words he might have said.

A kick in her stomach startled Shay out of her anger. Shay settled her hand over the spot and closed her eyes, releasing a long, slow exhalation. "You're right. Mommy's gotta calm down."

Once her heart slowed, she opened her eyes and glanced down at her holocom.

Shit!

Racing to the bathroom, she snatched a hairband from the

counter, gathered her hair, and tied it back. She returned to the living room and shoved her feet into her boots, nearly falling over in her haste. The near fall was enough to give her pause.

Bracing a hand on the wall, she took in another calming breath and muttered, "Slow down, Shay."

After moving to the table, she placed the blaster atop it and picked up her tactical utility belt. Its weight was a comfort. Shay secured the belt around her waist and holstered the blaster. It wasn't the only weapon she possessed. The belt—the same one she'd stolen from the azhera—held a wealth of surprises, including an extendable stun baton, a knife hilt that formed a hardlight blade when activated, a small but well stocked first-aid kit, and two sets of deceptively thin but strong automatically activated restraints.

She never left the apartment without it.

She grabbed her oversized hooded jacket and swung it on before opening the door and making her way out into the Undercity.

THE UNDERCITY WAS a place of stark contrasts—deep, inky darkness clashing with bright neon lights and pulsing holograms; the silent, still alleys that flowed off every street like roots from a tree juxtaposed against the bustling cacophony of the crowded walkways; cool air flowing from ventilation systems fighting against the heat of the crowds, locked in perpetual stalemate.

There were more alien species, languages, and scents than Shay could count, more than she could've imagined possible— and many of those scents made her wish pregnancy hadn't sharpened her sense of smell.

But she'd dealt with nonhuman species on Earth, and even

though she hadn't seen a single human face since she'd been kidnapped and sold, this city seemed to share the same attitude prevalent in most large cities she'd visited. Most of these people were indifferent as they hurried past, acting as though the relatively small terran offering them floppy holographic flyers didn't exist.

Assholes, the whole bunch of them.

Shay dropped her arm to her side and clutched the stack of flyers to her chest. Her shoulders sagged. Loose strands of hair that had escaped her ponytail and fallen from beneath her hood tickled her nose, and she blew them aside with a huff. After hours of walking up and down this block, her ankles were swollen, her feet were killing her, and her voice was hoarse, but her attempts to be seen and heard had failed miserably.

Why was it harder to get someone to look at a damn flyer than it was to bypass the security system of a high-end store and rob it blind?

Don't these people understand that I'm trying to do things the legitimate way this time? Give me a break!

If she returned to her boss, Yorgaz, with all these flyers still in her possession at the end of her shift, he'd accuse her of laziness *again*. Then he'd launch into a rant about how her only job was to get asses into seats for the show, and if terrans were too stupid to do that, maybe he'd just ban them from his theater.

And Shay would bite her tongue and refrain from telling him that no one, no matter how alien, wanted to go watch trained skrudges—which were scary-looking, rat like animals—do tricks. Because she *needed* this job, she *needed* this fresh, legitimate start. She needed routine and stability. This was all she had for now. Once the baby came... Well, she'd figure out which branch to take when she reached that fork in the road.

Squaring her shoulders and setting her features in determination, Shay held a flyer out to the passing aliens. "Come see the Spectacular Skrudge Show!"

A tall, lean, four-armed dacrethian with pale pink skin glanced at her, snatched the flyer from her hand, and tossed it aside, walking on without even looking at it.

"Dick," Shay said as she retrieved the flyer from the street. She backed away from the thicker foot traffic. "Come see the best trained skrudges in this galactic sector perform the most awe-inspiring tricks!"

The cycle continued on and on. Shay's feet hurt more with each passing minute, her voice grew hoarser, her stomach was soon growling in hunger, and her frustration climbed to new heights. When another tall, powerfully built being passed her, Shay decided she'd had enough. Clearly her tactics weren't working. She'd have to *make* them look at her.

Without thinking, Shay reached out, caught the being by his arm—an arm encased in some sort of segmented armor—and gave him a tug. "Hey, check out—"

Her eyes widened as the male turned to face her and she looked up into his intense green eyes. He was an azhera, his dun fur run through with darker patches of brown, and his broad shoulders were at least twice as wide as hers. He was huge—and he was terrifyingly familiar.

His nostrils flared, and his dark lips peeled back to reveal his fangs. His brows fell low. "*You.*"

This was the azhera who'd taken her from Murgen. Who'd *purchased* her.

Who she'd robbed.

"Fuck," Shay breathed.

For what couldn't have been more than a second or two—but in her mind felt like forever—they stared at each other. Violent criminals had been a part of her life for longer than she cared to admit, but she couldn't recall having ever seen anyone look as angry and dangerous as this azhera right now.

Angry, dangerous, and kinda hot.

Where the hell had *that* thought come from?

The azhera eased closer to her. "I've been looking for—"

Shay released his arm and threw the stack of flyers in his face. The wobbly plastic pieces broke apart from each other the instant they were free, turning into a cloud of shimmering holographic advertisements that sent the azhera reeling.

Wheeling around, Shay ran. She had no destination, no plan, she just needed to escape. Even though this was one of the city sectors that seemed to have a very limited presence of peacekeepers, there were too many bystanders here, too many witnesses, for her to draw her blaster and start shooting. And even though Shay had done some shady stuff in her life, had broken a lot of laws, she'd never killed anyone—and she'd never hurt anyone that didn't have it coming.

A bestial roar boomed behind her; it was the sort of sound that would've made a lion bow its head and scurry for a hiding place. Shay glanced over her shoulder to see the azhera swipe away the last few fluttering flyers. His fur was bristling, and the look of rage on his face had only intensified.

He charged toward her, plowing through the pedestrians in his path like a wrecking ball crashing through a wall.

Her eyes rounded, and her eyebrows rose. "*Thaaaaat's* not good."

Despite her soreness, her weariness, her awkwardness, Shay pushed herself forward with everything she had. The surprise advantage she'd gained with the flyers wouldn't be enough to save her—she'd have to utilize anything she could to escape him.

And all she really had going for her right now was being a *little* terran.

Cradling her belly with one hand, she turned toward the center of the street, where the crowd was at its thickest, and plunged directly into the press of bodies. For once, her size was a boon—being smaller than many of the aliens allowed her to slip through the crowd with relative ease, using them to shield her from the azhera's view.

She could only hope it'd be enough.

Shay forced her way deeper into the ever-flowing river of alien pedestrians, twisting and turning as best she could to squeeze through the gaps. Her heart pounded, and her breath was ragged, but she didn't let herself slow. If she stopped, that'd be it. Exhaustion would take hold and ensure she didn't run anymore.

She *couldn't* let that happen. Saving her own skin was a great motivation, but it wasn't her primary drive—not like it had been several months ago. She needed to keep her baby safe. She refused to birth her child into slavery.

The awkwardness of running through a thick crowd resulted in more bumps and touches than she cared for, but she shielded her belly, sparing it from the impacts. The exasperated words spoken by the aliens she hurried past—sometimes uttered in languages her implanted translator had trouble deciphering—flowed over her like a hot breeze, uncomfortable but ultimately harmless. She didn't have the breath to spare for snarky retorts.

A series of near-simultaneous cries and shouts rose from the crowd behind her.

Shay's heart skipped a beat when those cries were answered by a guttural snarl—a snarl that was much too close. How long would this crowd hold back a very large, very determined, very *angry* azhera?

Not long enough.

More cries erupted from the pedestrians, drawing steadily

closer to Shay. For an instant, she pictured a slow-burning trail of gunpowder behind her, just like from an old cartoon, the little spark drawing nearer and nearer. Bad things happened when those sparks reached the character at the end of the line.

Her mind raced as she squeezed between a pair of tall, lanky aliens who were walking side-by-side; the aliens lifted their intertwined hands to glance down at her, opening a path for her to stumble forward.

If only her legs could move as fast as her thoughts.

"Out of the way," the azhera yelled. He was perhaps as close as ten or fifteen meters, by the sound of it.

There was no question in Shay's mind—even were she in peak physical condition, she couldn't outrun him, especially not in the mazelike tunnels and alleyways of the Undercity. Her only hope was to outmaneuver him.

The trams!

She'd used Arthos's public transportation—which the city provided as a free service—almost every day over the last few weeks. Without a private vehicle at her disposal, the trams were likely her only chance of escaping her pursuer.

Shay turned sharply toward the edge of the street; there was usually more room to maneuver near the shops and vendor stalls along the sides of the road. When she emerged from the thickest part of the crowd, she paused for only an instant—just long enough to lift her gaze and spot a glowing sign ahead. The largest letters on it were written in Universal Speech.

Public Transport.

She sprinted toward it, weaving around meandering shoppers and bystanders.

Shouts and curses from behind her called her attention back. She glanced over her shoulder to see the azhera burst out of the crowd, knocking over at least three pedestrians in the process. He came to an abrupt halt, snapping his head from side to side with his nostrils flaring as though he were scenting the air.

His gaze swung toward Shay and locked with hers. Reflected light from the myriad of signs and holos all around set his eyes aglow. He broke into a run, gaining more speed in his first few strides than any being his size should've been able to.

Releasing a sharp breath, Shay turned her face forward, let go of her belly, and pumped her arms, pushing her body as hard as possible. The impact rattled up her legs and through her body each time one of her feet came down. She felt it in every joint, in every bone, right up to her damned teeth.

When she reached the sign, she turned into the wide corridor it pointed toward. Her feet skidded, threatening to slip out from beneath her. Underestimating just how much her belly had disrupted her balance, she overcorrected, only to nearly fall in the opposite direction.

She could see the azhera barreling toward her from the corner of her eye.

Shay stumbled forward, grabbed onto someone's coat to steady herself, and hurried down the corridor. Alien faces, bodies, and colors zipped by on all sides, their details swallowed in a blur of motion. She could only focus on the place up ahead where the ceiling hit an angle and sloped down—the stairs to the tram station. It was the quickest route, but it was also the place where the foot traffic looked the most congested.

It's still better than stopping and waiting for an elevator, isn't it?

Prickles of heat spread across her back and crackled up and down her spine. Even were the grunts and cries from the crowd not giving away the azhera's approach, Shay could *feel* him drawing nearer. In a few more seconds, she'd feel his breath on the back of her neck. Then his claws would tear into her skin.

The stairs were only a few meters away now, close enough

for her to see how crammed full of people they were on both sides of the center divider.

"Stop, female!" commanded the azhera from directly behind her.

Sure thing, azhera.

Shay didn't allow herself a moment's hesitation. When she reached the steps, she slapped her hands atop that sloping central divider—which was perhaps two-thirds of a meter wide at best—and used her momentum to vault onto it. Every muscle in her legs screamed in protest as she swung them up and to her front. She landed atop the divider on her hip.

All the grace of a watermelon, Shay.

The azhera growled. Shay glanced back as he lunged, reaching toward her with his large, unarmored right hand. His fingertips brushed the fabric of her hood. Before he could take hold of the garment, Shay's momentum—and the power of gravity—carried her out of his reach.

"Oh shit, oh shit, oh shit shit *shiiiit!*" she whisper-shouted as she sped down the divider. She wrapped her arms around her belly to shield her unborn child and, somehow, twisted so she was sliding on her ass.

The people on the either side of the stairs, several of whom had limbs hanging over the divider or were leaning on the attached railings, recoiled as she passed. She reached the bottom within a few seconds. For an instant, she was airborne, and it felt like she nearly broke her back getting her legs beneath her and her torso upright.

Shay landed on her feet with a jolt that clacked her teeth together. Her momentum forced her forward, and her torso pitched forward. The only thing that stopped her from falling face first on the floor was the massive body of a tralix—he had to be nearly three meters tall and built of solid muscle. Fortunately, she managed to throw her arms up and let them take the brunt of the impact as she struck the tralix's backside.

She eased back from him, clutching her belly and groaning at the sharp pain in her pelvis. She sucked in a shaky breath and let it out thickly, willing the discomfort away.

A low, rumbling growl in front of her called her eyes up. She tilted her head back to meet the gaze of the irritated tralix, who had turned to face her.

The tralix leaned toward her. "I should crush you, you—"

"Nice ass," she said, offering the tralix a wink.

His brow furrowed, and his skin—a mottled blend of purples and blues—darkened as though in a blush. His lips curled in a surprisingly soft smile.

Shay made herself smile back despite her lingering pain and turned to seek her pursuer.

The azhera glared at her from the top of the stairs with eyes narrowed and ears flattened. Fortunately, the space between the crowds on either side of the staircase divider was too narrow for his broad-shouldered frame to fit through, and—

The azhera leapt onto the divider and began a rapid descent.

"*Fuuuuuuck*," Shay whined.

She spun away and hurried past the tralix, giving him a slap on the ass as she did so, and worked her way toward the platform, where a multi-car tram was loading and unloading passengers. The azhera roared again, and some of the heat drained from Shay's face. She didn't let herself stop; she could do this. This was her element. It was no different than any major city she'd been to on Earth, despite the alien population.

She fell into the flow of boarding traffic, hurrying past the slower passengers.

"Terran!" The azhera's voice carried to her over the din of the crowd, once again right behind her.

She chanced another backward glance to see him pushing through the crowd. He was rapidly gaining on her despite the thick press of bodies.

Shay stumbled through the open doors at the front of a tram car and—ignoring the protests of her aching legs and back—ducked to conceal herself amidst the bigger passengers as she hurried toward the opposite end of the car.

People frowned, glared, and swore as she slipped by, but she didn't slow. She found herself both thankful for having never been claustrophobic and cursing her overly sensitive nose. The stench of sweating bodies and exotic perfumes and spices was amplified in this tight space.

"I can smell you, terran," said the azhera from somewhere behind her. "No more running."

He could *smell* her? Even amidst all this? How bad did she stink despite her shower this morning?

And does nobody in this city see a problem with a big ass azhera chasing me down right out in public? What a bunch of assholes.

A chiming series of notes sounded overhead—the tram was about to depart. Shay turned her head; she was near one of the tram car's central doors. Beneath her feet, the tram's antigrav engines began to hum, creating barely perceptible vibrations.

This was her last chance. If this didn't work, she was done—she'd be caught.

The double doors began to slide shut.

Shay charged toward them, grabbing onto the people in her path to haul herself forward. The passengers' protests undoubtedly caught the azhera's attention. Heart racing, she flattened her arms against her sides and darted through the narrowing doorway.

The doors whispered shut mere centimeters behind her.

Shay's skin felt like it was ablaze, and she was itchy from

head to toe on top of her other discomforts. Breathing heavily, she slowly turned as the tram's hum intensified.

The azhera forced his way to the doors and met her gaze through the view windows; this time, he was the one caged, not her. Oddly, she felt no satisfaction at that. The tram began its smooth forward motion. The azhera pressed his hands against the doors as though to pry them open, his green eyes, hungry and burning, fixated on her.

Shay's heart leapt into her throat, and she stepped back. He was powerful and driven; she'd put her money on the azhera over the doors any time. It was frightening, but she still couldn't deny that thrill, that flare of eagerness. She knew the hunger in his eyes—it said he wanted to devour her in all the right ways.

Right ways? Wrong, wrong, wrong, Shay!

He wanted revenge. He wanted blood. What the hell was wrong with her?

The tram continued forward. Baring his teeth, the azhera slammed a fist against the doors. They shook, briefly warping the reflections on the glass. The vehicle's motion carried him out of Shay's view. A few moments later, the last tram car vanished into the tunnel.

Everything inside Shay felt heavy as she stood there with her chest heaving. She wanted nothing more than to allow her body to pool on the ground and give her screaming, trembling muscles a break, but she couldn't. Not here. The tram station was no safer for her here than it would've been on Earth were she to let her guard down.

Though the tram was the quickest route back to her apartment, Shay didn't wait for the next one, opting to take the long way back. She couldn't chance running into the azhera again. She didn't have it in her to make another run for it.

She slowly climbed the stairs out of the tram station, following the crowd of disembarked riders, and pretended her body wasn't in agony. Keeping to the busier streets and well away from all the dark alleys, Shay wound through the Undercity. Every step shot needling pain through her legs. She'd overdone it today at work, and that chase had pushed Shay beyond her limits.

Neon lights and flashing holograms blared down at her, advertising products, drugs, sex, and food. Her stomach growled for the latter. When was the last time she'd eaten? With no small amount of guilt, she realized it had been on her way to work hours ago. She'd been so focused on handing out those stupid flyers so she wouldn't get reamed by Yorgaz that she'd skipped her lunch break.

She rubbed her belly in apology. "Sorry, Baby."

And now she had a murderous azhera to worry about. She'd honestly thought she'd never see him again. What were the odds of it in a city of billions?

"Apparently pretty fucking good," she grumbled.

Though it was late, and her body was screaming for rest, the savory smell of food lured her toward a food stall. She ordered a noodle-like entrée filled with unknown vegetables. She knew for sure the 'noodles' were totally unrelated to human pasta, but she hadn't allowed herself to ask what any of the food in Arthos actually was. She had a sense that knowing the answer to that question would make her never want to eat again. Best to remain oblivious when it came to alien food.

Besides, she thought as she slurped a 'noodle' into her mouth and found a place to sit, *it tastes good*.

After she'd finished eating and had won the arduous battle of standing back up, she resumed her slow trek back to her apartment. Her feet objected to every step, and she was occasionally struck by sharp pains in her groin. She couldn't lie to herself—those pains scared the hell out of her.

Her life on Earth had always been almost nomadic, moving

from one score to the next, sprinkled with quickies here and there with her then-boyfriend, not realizing the jerk had been two-timing her—or more like *five*-timing her—for their entire relationship. She'd been so busy during all that, her thoughts so occupied, that she'd forgotten that she'd been overdue for another contraceptive implant.

By the time she'd realized her mistake, it had been too late. She'd already been nearly three months pregnant—which she'd learned from the one doctor she'd been able to see, a shady bastard who didn't ask questions about why his patients didn't want to use IDs and paid only in cold, hard cash. A month later, she was kidnapped by alien pirates and promptly sold to Murgen. She hadn't received any prenatal care after that diagnosis... Not that she would've gone back to that doctor, anyway.

Now, Shay was alone on an alien world with no one to turn to. She couldn't *afford* any help because she knew the credits she'd taken from the azhera wouldn't last long—not at the rate the scumbags in this city were sucking her dry. But she was doing the best she could.

"But I got you," she whispered, settling a hand on her stomach, and was flooded with relief when she felt an answering kick against her palm.

It took Shay an hour and a half after her meal to reach her apartment building. An hour and a half of pain, discouragement, and constantly looking over her shoulder and expecting the azhera to be breathing down the back her neck at any moment. She was exhausted to the very marrow of her bones when she reached the entry doors. She opened her jacket and swept back one side, exposing the blaster at her hip to settle her hand on it.

I didn't let Murgen beat me, didn't let the azhera beat me, and I'm sure as hell not letting this city beat me.

Walking with a prominent limp, she entered the rundown

building and headed toward the elevator. She pressed the call button and waited. The doors opened a few minutes later and Shay stood back as a group of aliens stepped out, crowding the hallway, their voices raised in conversation. There was a burly, pointed-eared borian and an ethereal, elf-like volturian, but most of them were cren, tall and leanly muscled with long pointed ears, brightly colored skin and hair, and tusks protruding up from their bottom lips. They ignored her—or outright didn't see her—as they pushed and shoved one another, two of them arguing over what Shay gleaned was a drug one had claimed the rights to.

Without waiting, she entered the elevator. The doors closed with a grinding, metal on metal sound, and the lift creaked and screeched during its ascent to her floor, its lights flickering gloomily like she was in a horror movie. Every time she rode this elevator, she was half-convinced it would be the last thing she did. Thankfully, her floor was only the second one up, so she didn't have far to drop if the lift failed.

Exiting the elevator, she moved down the hall toward her room. The odor hanging in the air was an alien mix of bodily fluids, mildew, and unidentifiable smells that triggered her nausea. There were holes and cracks in the walls and stains on the garbage-strewn floor. Sounds carried easily through the thin walls—voices raised in anger or passion, thumping music, people banging on doors, and alien TV shows with the volume turned up way too damned loud. It was a dump. But it was also the only place she'd been able to find that didn't require an ID chip and wouldn't break her budget.

When she reached her apartment, she shoved her hand into her pocket, pulled out her dinged-up keycard, and waved it in front of the reader on the doorframe. The door whooshed open.

Once she was inside and the door was closed and locked behind her, Shay stumbled toward her pallet and all but fell upon it, unsure of whether she'd be able to get back up. She certainly had no plans to get up any time soon. Her every muscle burned with exertion, and for the first time in a long time, Shay felt incredibly weak, both mentally and physically drained.

Peeling off her jacket, she laid it beside her. Her shirt was damp with sweat. Next came her boots and socks, which she struggled with. She hissed through her teeth once her feet were freed.

"Fuck," she said, tugging up the hems of her pants. Her feet and ankles had swelled so much that there was no longer any distinction between them—she'd gone full cankle. Harsh red lines marred her flesh, indentations from her socks and boots, and she had a few spots where it looked like blisters were forming.

For a moment, Shay could do nothing but stare at her feet. Pain pulsed through them like they had their own heartbeat.

"What am I doing, Baby? How are we going to survive?" The words slipped out without thought, but they were true.

How could I think I could do this on my own?

Anger, frustration, and helplessness swelled within her and tightened her throat, making her fight for every breath.

What would Dad think if he saw me now?

Something tickled her cheek, and Shay brushed it away with her fingers. She was startled when she realized what it was —tears. She was *crying*. When was the last time she'd cried?

Six years ago, when my mother—

Another tear fell, followed by another, and another; once they'd begun, they wouldn't stop. Shay bowed her head in defeat as she cried, taking in shuddering breaths between her sobs.

"What I am going to do?" she asked, voice thick with emotion. "I can barely take care of myself. How I am going to take care of you, too? How am I g-going to give you everything you deserve? Because you sure as hell don't deserve *this*."

Tears dripped from her chin, but she ignored them as she cradled her belly.

After her father's death, Shay had decided that she could take care of herself, that she didn't need anyone. Not even her mother. It had been a lie, and it was a lie she carried with her for years. She had done all right for a long while—not that most of what she'd done to get by had been particularly good. But right now... Right now, she felt like she really needed *someone*. She felt...so alone. She was scared—scared for herself and for her baby, and she knew she couldn't keep living like this. She had more than herself to worry about now. There was a life growing inside her.

What if something happens to me?

The thought wrenched a fresh sob from her and made her cry harder.

If something happens to me...what would become of my baby?

"I'll figure something out," she said, stroking the side of her stomach as she sniffled. "I swear, I *promise* you, I'll make things better for you."

If only she knew how.

FIVE

Drakkal kept his fists clenched at his sides as he stalked toward Arcanthus's workshop. Frustration, disappointment, worry, lust, and a small but resilient glimmer of hope were locked in a massive struggle, clouding his mind and making rational thought almost impossible. Currently, frustration was the frontrunner.

Somehow, he retained enough willpower to resist the most destructive of his urges—like raking the hardlight claws of his prosthesis along the wall to tear deep gouges in the material, or slamming his armored shoulder into a door to dent the metal and break the door off its sliding track, or punching a wall until his hand was numb and bleeding. None of that would provide any relief beyond a temporary, ultimately insignificant catharsis, an expelling of a modicum of the blazing, hungry energy thrumming through his body.

He growled. He'd been so close. *So* fucking close.

His body had reacted to the terran; his instincts had surged the instant he'd turned to discover that the sundrinker scent on the air hadn't been a figment of his imagination, that she was there, that she was *touching* him. He might've maintained control had things gone differently. He might've maintained control if she hadn't run.

Her flight had triggered instincts Drakkal could not ignore, had roused his desires to a feverish heat. His muscles had swelled—along with his cock—and his senses had sharpened. There'd been no choice but to give in, no choice but to give chase.

This was the aftermath—all this strength, all this energy, all this heat, and all for nothing. The prize he'd been meant to claim was lost. The relief he'd been meant to receive had been snatched out of his grasp. And his body refused to relax, his blood refused to cool.

She's not going to disappear again. I won't accept it.

Drakkal snarled as he reached the workshop door. His instincts demanded he go back out there to continue the search for his terran, for his mate, but he knew that wasn't the way to find her now. Any trail he could follow had again gone cold. But there *was* hope—he just couldn't take advantage of it on his own.

That realization was a bitter one, further confusing the maelstrom of emotions whirling through him.

Tensing the muscles of his right arm, he pressed the access button on the wall.

The door slid open freely. He couldn't deny his pang of disappointment for not having an excuse to break it down.

As Drakkal strode into the workshop, his nostrils flared with a heavy exhalation that did nothing to vent his frustration or ease the tightness in his chest.

Arcanthus was sitting at his desk, leaning back in his chair with his cybernetic legs propped on the desktop and his matching prosthetic hands folded over his abdomen. He turned his attention away from the holographic displays in front of him and met Drakkal's gaze.

"Oh, no. You have that look again," Arcanthus said with a sigh.

Drakkal strode across the room, ignoring his rogue urges to tear into the couches with his claws.

"So what is it this time, Drakkal?"

Drakkal walked past the desks and paced in the space behind them. His ears, already low, flattened against his head, and the claws of his right hand were dangerously close to piercing his palm. His lips peeled back, baring his teeth, but only a growl emerged.

"Cat's got your tongue?" Arcanthus asked.

Limbs nearly trembling with a fresh swell of rage, Drakkal spun toward Arcanthus. "*Kraasz ka'val*, you don't know when to quit, do you?"

For a few seconds, all he could think about was knocking that smirk off the sedhi's face.

That smirk only grew as Arcanthus lowered his legs and turned his chair to face Drakkal. "I certainly don't. And neither do you. You went looking for her again, didn't you?"

"Found her this time." The heat and pressure in Drakkal's chest intensified as he recalled the feel of his fingertips brushing over the hood of the terran's coat. He raised his right hand, holding his palm toward the ceiling with fingers partly curled. "Had her right here."

Arcanthus hummed thoughtfully. "But you botched it, didn't you?"

Drakkal growled and lunged forward, slamming his hand down onto Arc's desk. His claws clacked against the desk's metal surface. "I didn't botch anything!"

Arcanthus didn't so much as flinch. His smirk faded, but a

tiny, mischievous glint lingered in his eyes. "And yet here you are, upset and alone."

"I'm *not* upset."

"You don't have to admit it. It's clear in your every action, right down to your posture."

"We're not doing this right now, Arcanthus."

Arcanthus tipped his head back and studied Drakkal from head to toe—and simultaneously from toe to head, as the third eye at the center of his forehead moved in the opposite direction of the other two. He reached up and delicately tucked a loose strand of hair behind one of his horns. "It's all right to ask, Drakkal."

Drakkal's brow furrowed, and the fires of his frustration cooled ever so slightly beneath a mist of confusion. "Ask what?"

"For help."

"I was already going to do that."

"*Of course* you were," Arcanthus replied, rolling his lower eyes. "You've never once asked for even the tiniest bit of help, Drakkal."

With a grunt, Drakkal dragged his hand off the desk, claws scraping the polished metal with a brief, high-pitched whine. "I *was* going to ask you, you horned asshole. That's why I'm here!"

Smirking again, Arcanthus shook his head. "I know you're just trying to spare yourself the shame of not having the courage to ask before I prompted you. You azhera and your pride."

Drakkal lifted his hands and curled them into impotent firsts as he gritted his teeth.

The terran has had me out of sorts for weeks. Normally I wouldn't let Arc get to me so easily... Normally, I'm the one getting under his skin.

Though that thought didn't eliminate the emotional torrent

within Drakkal—it didn't even slightly diminish the storm—it restored a bit of his self-control.

"Let me correct myself, sedhi—I'm not asking you, I'm telling you. You're helping me."

"Why should I, if that's the attitude you're going to take?" Arcanthus asked with a shrug. He turned his chair back toward his desk. His lingering smirk suggested he was taking far too much pleasure in this.

"Samantha," Drakkal replied through his teeth.

Arcanthus snapped his head to the side to glare at Drakkal, his expression instantly darker. "Even in jest, I won't tolerate any threats to her, azhera."

"*Vrek'osh*, I'm not threatening her. I'd never harm Samantha. Do you remember how you acted when you first found her? When you realized what she was to you?"

Arcanthus frowned. "I acted like a damned fool."

Drakkal nodded. "More so than usual. But once you told me what she was to you, what did I do?"

"You called me stupid."

"After that, damn it."

"You helped. Which, for the record, is what I was about to do for you. I just can't resist a chance to get your fur in a tangle."

"Only thing that's going to get tangled here is my hands around your neck, sedhi."

Waving a hand dismissively, Arcanthus turned his chair forward again. "You're sure about this terran, Drak?"

"Yes."

"What are the odds? First that zenturi, then me, and now you. Terrans are one of the smallest alien populations in this city, and yet all of us are finding them as mates. Who do you suppose will be next? *Thargen?*"

Drakkal grunted; the thought of Thargen with a terran

mate almost made the corner of his mouth twitch upward, but it wasn't quite enough to break through his current mood.

"It's just that you've been down this road before," Arcanthus continued. "I only saw the aftermath of that a few years after it happened, but you were in a bad place because of it for a long, long time."

Drakkal caught his lower lip between his teeth and bit down, breathing out slowly to keep himself from making an angry retort. "This is different."

"How do you know? Clearly, this female isn't interested."

"Because it *is*, Arc. It just is. It smells different, feels different... *I* feel different. She's roused instincts in me that I've never experienced before. There's no comparison between what I had back then and what I feel now. You ready to shut up and help yet?"

"Fine, fine." Arcanthus shifted his attention to the many displays on his desk. "What do you want me to do?"

Drakkal moved to stand behind Arc and watch over the sedhi's shoulder. "Hack the city surveillance system again."

Arcanthus snickered. "We tried that the night you came home bare-assed. Lost her less than a minute after she left that alleyway."

"This time will be different."

"How can you know that?"

Drakkal clamped his jaw shut for a second. "I don't. But it *has* to be. I ran into her on Orcus Street in the Viraxis sector about four hours ago."

"That can be a rough part of town."

"They can all be rough. You going to do it or not?"

"Of course, azhera. You know it always excites me when you ask me to break the law," Arcanthus said with amplified huskiness in his voice.

"You break the law on your own every day."

Arc's fingers flew through the control screens on the displays, navigating options and commands faster than Drakkal could follow. "Yes, but that's for money, not for you. This is completely different."

Drakkal folded his arms across his chest and forced himself to remain in place despite his restlessness and agitation. "Just get to it."

"I am." Arcanthus continued inputting commands, pausing only to bring up another display. "But it'll take a few minutes. Might as well tell me what happened while you're waiting."

Drakkal grasped the armored plate that encased the bicep of his prosthetic arm with his right hand and squeezed; his brain registered the pressure and warmth through his neural connections with the limb, and he could even make out a hint of his palm's texture, but it wasn't the same as feeling it with his own flesh. It would never be the same.

He'd had a year to adjust to the cybernetic arm thus far, and over that time he'd developed a new admiration and respect for Arcanthus—who'd had to wear similar prosthetics on both arms and legs for better than a decade.

"Was out searching when I caught a hint of her scent," Drakkal said. "Tried following it, but the air was too saturated with other smells to get a clear trail. As I was walking, I passed a female handing out flyers for some show. She grabbed my arm to get me to stop...and it was her."

"You walked right past your mate?" Arc's tone was light with amusement.

"She had a hood on, and like I said, it was hard filtering her scent through everything else."

"Fortunately, she grabbed you."

One of Arcanthus's displays changed. Drakkal recognized the gold and teal seal of the Eternal Guard in the upper left corner. The Eternal Guard maintained a massive network of surveillance devices throughout Arthos, though many areas of the Undercity were only lightly covered—and there was almost no Eternal Guard surveillance in the Bowels, which lay below the Undercity.

"We didn't recognize each other until I turned around. Then she took off running. I chased her through the crowd but lost her in the tram station." Drakkal inhaled deeply. "At one point, I almost had her. Almost grabbed hold."

"Is this the street?" Arcanthus asked.

Drakkal leaned closer to study the still image Arcanthus had brought up on the main holo screen. "That's it. Think she was around Burik's Meat Emporium."

With a few flicks of his fingers, Arcanthus opened three more holographic displays, each showing Orcus Street from a different angle. He manipulated the feeds until all were focused on the street in front of Burik's Meat Emporium.

"There," Drakkal said, heart skipping a beat. He leaned closer still and extended an arm to point out the small, hooded figure with an armful of flyers.

Arcanthus adjusted the display to zoom in on the terran and scrubbed through the feeds simultaneously. The crowd around her moved at an accelerated speed; Arcanthus didn't slow the recording until a broad-shouldered figure with an armored cybernetic arm came into view.

"So, she doesn't even come up to your neck, but she outran you?" Arcanthus asked.

"Just keep going," Drakkal said distractedly. His attention was held by the image on screen—the terran's hand on his arm. He wished it had been for a good reason, wished it had been because she wanted to see him, touch him, and share his company.

Startlingly, Arcanthus complied without comment.

Drakkal's heartbeat quickened as he watched the chase. He

was so focused upon her and the way she moved that he barely noticed himself plowing through the crowd behind her. He'd not seen faces or people on that street—only obstacles between himself and his mate. But all his strength and speed hadn't been enough. He'd drawn close to her, but never close enough.

The angle shifted as Arcanthus jumped to different camera positions, following the terran's progress down the street. Drakkal curled his fingers into a fist as the recording showed the terran jump atop the staircase divider leading into the tram station, tightening his grip further as the display showed his fingertips brush across her hood.

Just a few more centimeters would've been enough.

The recording continued, following the terran down the sloped divider. Drakkal narrowed his eyes as the terran plunged into the crowd—leaving the tralix she'd bumped into with a parting slap on the backside. Drakkal clenched his teeth, and a deep, involuntary growl rose from his chest. Heat spread outward from his core, renewing his agitation. He could find that tralix, could find him and—

The terran slipped into the tram and vanished from the images. Arcanthus switched the main display to a feed from inside the tram car. Drakkal frantically searched the crowd on the screen, breath growing ragged, but he couldn't see her, just like when he'd been there in person, and he was going to lose her again.

Vrek'osh, what's wrong with me?

"The other side," he said, voice hoarse and tongue dry. "She went out the other side of the tram."

Arcanthus changed the main feed again to display the outside of the tram from the opposite side of the station. Just as the tram's doors began to close, the terran darted out of the car. She turned back as Drakkal appeared on the other side of the doors' view windows.

"Oh, Drakkal," Arcanthus sighed, shaking his head.

The tram pulled out of the station.

"Keep following her," Drakkal said, bracing one hand on Arc's chair and the other on the desk as he leaned his face closer to the screen, closer to the image of his mate.

"Drakkal, I don't think—"

"Keep following her!" Drakkal snarled. Arcanthus's chair creaked and groaned within Drakkal's tightening grasp. "I need to know where she went. Where she is *now*."

With a heavy exhalation, Arcanthus continued the recording. He switched camera feeds regularly to keep the terran in view as she exited the tram station and made her way through the crowded streets, subtly checking for pursuit as she moved. Though Arc played the recording at a faster-than-normal speed, the terran's pace clearly slowed as she traveled, and she soon developed a noticeable limp.

Drakkal's lips fell into a deep frown; the tightness in his throat and chest was no longer the result of rage but of sorrow and helplessness, of guilt. His mate was suffering, and he couldn't comfort her.

His mate was suffering, and he'd caused it.

Her route was meandering, including a stop for food, but she eventually reached what seemed to be her ultimate destination—a big, rundown apartment building two sectors away from Viraxis. She entered the building, and Arcanthus paused the playback a few seconds later.

Drakkal's heartbeat, slower now but even more insistent, filled the silence until he said, "Follow her into the building. Show me where she went in there."

"I can't, Drak."

"*Kraasz ka'val*, you really think I believe you can hack Consortium surveillance but not crack the security of a dump like that?"

Arcanthus changed the main display to a three-dimensional model of the apartment building and the surrounding structures. Numerous slowly flashing dots were scattered around the building, but none were on the building itself—or inside it.

"The place is dark," Arcanthus said. "If they have a system, it's a closed network, off grid. But places like that don't usually have surveillance at all. Less chance of liability for the owners when the peacekeepers come knocking."

"So what do we do?"

Reverting to the main recording feed—the one focused on the building's front door—Arcanthus scrubbed through the available footage. Aliens of dozens of species came and went through that entrance, but there was no sign of Drakkal's terran. There was no sign of any terrans at all. The feed slowed to normal speed when it reached current time.

"Either she's still inside or she left by another exit," Arcanthus said. "Either way, I think—"

Drakkal shoved away from the desk and turned toward the door.

"Where are you going, Drak?"

"To knock on doors until I find her."

"Stop, Drakkal. Please. You need—"

Nostrils flaring, Drakkal spun toward Arcanthus. "Did *you* ever stop? You know what she is to me, Arcanthus!"

Arcanthus pushed himself up out of his chair and stepped closer to Drakkal. Though the sedhi wasn't nearly as burly as the azhera, he was a couple centimeters taller—not counting his horns. The beast inside Drakkal, which hadn't stirred for over a year before encountering his elusive female terran, demanded he face this challenge directly.

"I know exactly what she is to you, azhera, which is why you need to stop and listen to me," Arcanthus said firmly, holding Drakkal's gaze.

Drakkal's fur bristled as a fresh wave of heat spread through him, concentrating in his face. "Stopping isn't going to help me find her."

"But it will help you keep her," Arc said. The weight of his expression, paired with the sincerity in his tone, broke through Drakkal's impatience and aggravation. It wasn't often that Arcanthus was so solemn.

"What do you mean?"

Arcanthus settled a hand on Drakkal's shoulder and gave it a squeeze. "Terrans are different from you and I, Drakkal, and I don't mean merely in appearance. Whatever you feel for her, whatever instinctual drive is pushing you toward her, she doesn't feel the same for you. They don't work that way."

"Sam loves you, Arcanthus."

"Well, who doesn't?" Arc replied with a smirk before lifting a finger and lowering his eyebrows. "Don't answer that. This terran may well come to recognize that she's your mate and reciprocate, but it's not going to be instantaneous. You need to win her, not conquer her. You know...*woo* her."

"I freed her from captivity and let her have the clothes off my back. Shouldn't that be proof enough of my intentions?"

"According to your story, you *bought* her and then she robbed you at gunpoint."

"All amounts to the same thing."

Arcanthus licked his lips, sighed, and closed his eyes, pinching the bridge of his nose. "You really need to try to consider this from her perspective."

Drakkal drew in a steadying breath, struggling to contain his once again growing anger. "I haven't exactly had the opportunity to ask her about her perspective, Arc."

"I have fantasized about having the chance to say this to you for a long time, Drakkal—*don't be stupid.*"

Having the words he'd so often said to Arcanthus thrown

back at him should've annoyed Drakkal. He was the careful one, the alert one, the half of their partnership who took the bigger picture and the long term into account. But he wasn't annoyed, or angry, or upset. Though he'd been unable to control it, Drakkal had recognized for weeks that his decision making was reckless while the terran was on his mind.

Don't even know her name, but she has all this power over me.

"The way she robbed you, the way she's evaded you, the way she took a deliberately convoluted path home, even the way she was checking for pursuit...to me, that speaks of experience." Arcanthus eased into his seat, slipping his long, powerful tail through the opening at the base of the backrest. "Criminal, law enforcement, or military. Maybe some combination of the three."

Drakkal almost disagreed, almost called it a stretch to draw such a conclusion, but his mind returned to the moment when she'd taken his blaster in the maintenance tunnel. Her hand had been steady—deadly steady—and she fired a shot that struck between his feet with speed and precision that few people could manage without experience.

Arcanthus leaned back and locked his hands together over his abdomen. "She's assessed you as a threat, Drakkal, and can you blame her?"

"I've only tried to help her."

One of Arc's eyebrows rose.

The next words that came out of Drakkal's mouth were a surprise even to him. "That's not fair, sedhi. Samantha says you look like a demon, an evil, corrupted spirit from old terran stories, but she still finds you attractive. I look like a cat—cute, warm, and cuddly. Familiar."

Arcanthus's eyes widened, and a slow grin spread across his lips. "Firstly, no. You don't look cute and cuddly. You put out the exact opposite of a welcoming air during your every waking moment."

"What's that supposed to mean?"

"Was that not clear enough? You look angry and unpleasant, Drak. It's your natural state."

"*Kraasz ka'val,* Arcanthus, I will—"

"Secondly, old friend, you can guarantee that you'll never live down having compared yourself to a cute, cuddly cat."

Drakkal clenched his jaw for several seconds, breathing heavily. "Don't see how this is meant to be helpful."

"Because you're still not listening. Let me *show* you." Arcanthus spun his chair toward his desk and manipulated the controls.

The recordings sped by in reverse, rapidly retracing the terran's path until she had just emerged from that first crowd on Orcus Street, no more than a minute or two after she'd thrown her flyers into Drakkal's face. The feed paused as the terran looked back over her shoulder. When Arcanthus spun the view angle around to face the same direction as her, a pang of loss and longing struck Drakkal.

Arc settled the viewpoint on the outside edge of the main cluster of pedestrians and advanced the recording at a greatly reduced speed.

Drakkal narrowed his eyes as a bulky figure burst from the crowd, knocking aside several startled bystanders—at least three of whom fell to the ground. Arcanthus paused the recording again and zoomed in on the figure's face.

Those features were at once alien and familiar; Drakkal was looking at his own face. But his eyes were ablaze with a predatory light, his fangs were bared in a snarl, and his mane was nearly standing on end. There was little evidence of conscious thought in his expression. That snarl, those flaring nostrils, and those hot, hungry eyes would've been perfectly suited to the face of a bloodthirsty wild animal.

"Fuck," Drakkal said with a huff.

"Mmhmm." Arcanthus pulled in tighter on Drakkal's face. "This is what she saw. Can you understand why she might've fled in fear for her life?"

Much of the directionless anger that had been brimming in Drakkal vanished. How had he not realized this before now? How had he managed to push his mate into thinking he was the biggest threat to her safety when he was supposed to be her fiercest protector?

"So...what should I do?" Drakkal asked.

Arcanthus lifted a hand, palm up, and shrugged. "Have you ever just tried to be...*cool*?"

"I'm usually the calm and collected one here, Arcanthus."

"You need to earn her trust. Show her you're not a threat, let her feel like she's in control."

"She's a fighter. If I show her weakness, she'll take initiative and attack."

"I'm going to guess she had the blaster she stole from you hidden on her person, but she didn't even reach for it."

Drakkal's tail flicked restlessly, and his ears twitched before flattening again. He tugged his fingers through his mane and shook his head. "Too many witnesses. She's not dumb."

"No, she's not. Use that. Make her understand what you can provide."

"She won't let me get close enough to do that."

"Come on, Drakkal. Are you a *kitten* or a *lion*?"

Drakkal glared at Arcanthus.

Arcanthus waved a hand. "If you need me to go with you and hold your hand..."

"No," Drakkal snapped. "I'll figure it out."

"Tomorrow. Give her—and yourself—some time to calm down."

Drakkal's instinctual reaction would've been to growl and refute that notion, but he resisted it. His current state of mind was not typical, and the more he relented to it, the more intense it would become.

"Good to see you finally embracing your motherly side, Arc."

Arcanthus grinned. "I guess you acting like an overly-sensitive cub brings it out in me."

Releasing a slow, measured breath, Drakkal nodded. That storm still raged inside him, but for the first time in a few weeks, he could hear his own thoughts over the rain, wind, and thunder. "For whatever it's worth, thanks, sedhi. You're a pain in my ass, but at least you're useful once in a while."

"I'm just grateful you didn't come home naked this time."

"Me, too. I wouldn't want to crush your self-esteem by making you feel totally inadequate."

Arcanthus chuckled. "I'm glad you're finally in better spirits. Now go take a tongue bath or something. I have work to do."

"Bite me, sedhi," Drakkal said as he turned and walked toward the door.

"Only after you've showered, little kitten."

Smiling, Drakkal entered the hallway. That smile faded as he walked to his room. Thoughts of the terran flooded his mind, stirring his longing, rekindling his lust. His groin ached with a need that had gone too long unfulfilled, creating a deep discomfort low in his belly. No matter how he controlled his breathing and adjusted his gait, that ache wouldn't subside.

By the time he reached his room, he was agitated again. He needed relief. He needed his terran.

He'd made mistakes in his dealings with her, but it wasn't over. He hadn't given up—he wouldn't. This time, he'd do everything right, he'd build something that would last, he'd build something real.

He entered the bathroom and undressed. With nothing to restrain it, his cock emerged partially from its sheath. His balls were heavy, sensitive, and felt overly full. Trying to ignore the discomfort, he moved to the control panel on the wall and started the water.

All he needed was a shower to clear his head, and then he could turn his attention to the important work—figuring out how to win the terran's trust.

Drakkal inhaled deeply, drawing in the steam that was already wafting from the shower stall. Its warmth made him think about the heat that had radiated from the terran's body as he'd escorted her out of Foltham's zoo. He could almost smell her now; they'd not had enough direct contact this time for her fragrance to have settled into his fur, but it was so clear in his memory that it was almost real.

He forced himself to step over the small ledge and cross the forcefield to enter the spacious shower stall. He'd never been so aware of the faint tingling the invisible barrier caused on his skin. He positioned himself in the center of the stall, directly beneath the stream of hot water, and let the world fade from his awareness as the water's gentle sound and caress enveloped him. Only his terran remained.

His eyelids fluttered shut.

Images of his terran—her naked body, which he'd seen with his own eyes, mixed with poses and movements from his imagination—flitted through his mind. His cock twitched, and his scrotum tightened. In his mind's eye, he reached for her, and she didn't move away.

Drakkal's right hand closed around the base of his now fully emerged shaft. A shaky breath flowed through his parted lips, spraying away droplets of water. His touch was as painful as it was pleasurable, but he couldn't relinquish it now; he *needed* release. In his mind, it was the terran's hand on his cock. After a deep inhalation, he shifted his hand up.

His fingers and palm were rough over the sensitive skin of his shaft. It was almost unbearable, but the flare of pleasure beneath that discomfort was undeniable, and it sent a shiver up his spine that shook water from his fur. He released a low growl.

In Drakkal's imagination, the terran smiled. She pumped her hand back down over the still-swelling knot near the base of his shaft, sending another jolt through him, this one more pleasant than painful. His hand mimicked her pace, sliding up and down his throbbing cock with increasing speed. The terran's full breasts swayed over her rounded belly as she moved.

Drakkal's knees threatened to buckle as the waves of pleasure grew in power and frequency, forcing the pressure inside him to build accordingly. Without breaking his pace, he staggered forward and thrust out his left arm, slapping his cybernetic hand against the wall to brace himself.

"Fuck," he rasped, tightening his grip on his shaft. He was on the verge of exploding, but he couldn't help wondering what her hand would really feel like—warm and soft, but also strong and confident?

What would her *sex* feel like, clamped around his cock, hot and slick with her desire?

The imagined terran's smile widened into a sultry, knowing grin.

Drakkal's hips bucked. For an instant, the pressure held at a level so great that he knew it would be his undoing; there could be nothing but oblivion after this. His muscles tensed, and— with a growled curse—Drakkal exploded.

His seed pumped out of him in a powerful spray, some of it

splattering his hand and coating his shaft as he pumped his fist with erratic movements. His hips gyrated with each stroke, but nothing more came out after the initial burst; it wouldn't unless he was fully seated in a female with his knot buried in her heat.

He leaned his forehead against the wall and drew in a shuddering breath. The imagined terran was gone, leaving only darkness behind his eyelids.

Drakkal released his shaft. His knotted cock pulsed and twitched, refusing to ease. It felt as though he'd been brought to the verge of orgasm and abandoned, as though he'd managed only to tease himself rather than relieve the pressure.

He still needed more, still needed her—and he had the sense that his body would accept nothing less.

"*Kraasz ka'val*," he grumbled, "this is going to be a long night."

SIX

Shay absently stirred the unappealing slop in the food tray. The brown, gravy-like substance contained chunks of unidentifiable gray meat. She shifted in her chair, which creaked and wobbled slightly beneath her weight; it was in only slightly worse shape than the dinged-up table she was sitting at. As hungry as she was, she didn't have much of an appetite—at least not for this crap. But it was all she had on hand.

Wrinkling her nose, she scooped up a spoonful of the food and shoved it in her mouth. She forced herself to chew and swallow the bitter, gelatinous substance, struggling to hold back the threatening rise of bile. She nearly lost the battle.

"Ugh!" She tossed the spoon down and shoved the tray forward as a shudder swept through her entire body. "Sorry, Baby, but even for you, I don't think I can tolerate that garbage."

Shay leaned back in the chair. There were places with decent food within walking distance, but she was trying to stretch her credits as far as possible, and her feet were still sore from working and running from the azhera the day before. At this point, she wasn't even sure if she had a job to go back to. She closed her eyes and let her head fall back, releasing a groan.

What the hell am I going to do?

The sudden, insistent sound of the door buzzer startled her from her thoughts.

"What now?" Shay muttered, pushing herself up to her feet. She grabbed the blaster from her belt, which was draped over the other chair, and made her way to the door. Once she was there, she raised her voice and said, "I already paid your goddamned rent, Vrisk. Go away!"

The buzzer sounded again.

Guess I'm shooting my landlord today.

Rolling her eyes, she slapped the control button. The door slid open with a whoosh. "I said go—oh fuck!"

Shay's eyes rounded, and she took a step backward, lifting the blaster to aim it at the big azhera standing in front of her. She'd known he was dangerous. He'd made short work of Nostrus back at Murgen's and hadn't seemed concerned by the possibility of running into more guards on their way out, and he'd looked terrifying while he'd chased her yesterday. But he was also the last person she'd expected to be standing there when she opened the door.

How the hell had he found her?

The azhera raised his hands, displaying his empty palms—one flesh and the other black metal. "Don't shoot, terran."

Shay's eyebrows dipped lower over her narrowed eyes as she took the blaster in a sturdy two-handed grip. "Why the hell not?"

"For starters, it's rude."

The azhera's dry tone and neutral expression left her unable to tell if he was joking or being serious.

Shay tipped her chin down to give him a droll look. "That's cute coming from you, kitty."

The azhera's lips turned down in an annoyed frown, but he quickly returned his expression to its neutral state. His nostrils flared with a slow exhalation. When he inhaled, his slitted pupils dilated, thinning the green irises around them. "Not here to argue. I want to start over."

"What do you mean *start over*? You fucking purchased me from that walrus to be your sex slave."

Something moved behind the azhera. It took her a moment to realize the movement was from his tail. His broad-shouldered frame filled most of the doorframe, leaving little of the corridor visible around him.

"I paid him so he would be forced to accept that you weren't his anymore. I wasn't going to keep you as a slave," he said.

"You expect me to believe that? You were there for a reason, with all that talk about deals and *rutting*."

The azhera bared his fangs to release a sigh that was punctuated by a low, brief growl. "He was a client. Didn't know about his zoo until he brought me down there to show it off. All I wanted was to conclude my business with him and get out, but the *zhe'gaash* wouldn't shut his mouth."

Shay's brow furrowed. She'd encountered words to which her translator could attribute no meaning, but never in direct conversation like this. "Zee gash?"

"*Zhe'gaash*," he corrected. "It's a word in an ancient Azheran dialect that fell out of common use a long time ago. It's someone who's...dishonorable, disgraceful. Cowardly. Those aren't exactly it, but it's along those lines."

She tilted her head, sweeping her gaze over his body. He was dressed in black pants with reinforced knees and cargo pockets that would've fit perfectly with the uniforms of most private security companies and law enforcement divisions back on Earth, and a gray shirt beneath a form-fitting jacket. Though she couldn't be sure what anything was made of here, the material of that jacket looked to be leather; it was a dark, rich brown with the slightest hint of red, and it brought out the subtle copper highlights in the fur on his face and mane.

He wore a belt similar to the one she'd stolen from him, its hip holster empty. Though his lower legs from mid-shin down were clad in black leather wraps not unlike the upper portions of combat boots, his feet were bare, and his toes were tipped with wicked looking black claws.

"Deciding whether you want to rob me again or not?" he asked, just as drily as before.

She met his gaze. "Maybe. Some of your other stuff sold for more than I expected."

He narrowed those intense green eyes and asked in a slightly strained voice, "Did you sell my belt?"

"I think you mean *my* belt."

His ears flattened against his head, and he muttered, "*Vrek'osh*, that was my favorite belt." Moving slowly, he lifted his right hand and combed his fingers through his dark mane, tugging the fur back. "Look, terran, when I said I wanted to start over, I—"

Shouting from down the hall called the azhera's attention to the side. From the sound of it, Ostik and Zira were arguing again, like they did most days. Drakkal turned his head toward the disturbance.

Shay found herself studying his strong jawline and admiring the patterns in his fur. It really was quite appealing. Despite his animalistic traits, she found his appearance far more masculine than bestial. She was suddenly tempted to reach out and touch his fur to see if it was as soft as it looked.

What the fuck am I thinking?

She was reaching for the door control—meaning to shut it while he was distracted—when he turned his face toward her again. His gaze flicked to her extended hand, and he frowned. Her hand paused. Why did it fucking pause? And why did she feel a little pang of guilt over what she'd been about to do?

"I want to talk. Can I come in?" he asked.

"For real?" she asked. "You really expect me to believe that you weren't trying to buy me as a sex slave, or that you're not going to make me pay for robbing you and leaving you naked in an alley?"

He shrugged his right shoulder; she swore she could almost see the play of his powerful muscles through his coat, even though that didn't seem possible.

"I've been naked in worse places. You can keep your gun on me, and I'll keep distance between us. Whatever makes you feel safe, terran."

"I'd feel safe if you left."

He turned his head, glancing first right and then left before swinging his gaze up across the ceiling as though taking in the entirety of the apartment complex. His brows rose questioningly when he returned his gaze to her.

"Yeah, okay, so maybe I don't feel safe here at all," she said snidely, "but your being here definitely isn't making that better. You looked like you wanted to eat my face yesterday!"

His expression darkened. "That's just how I look, damn it. It's not my fault!"

"So you're really trying to tell me that this is all a big misunderstanding because you suffer from RBF?"

"I don't know what that means."

Shay snickered. She couldn't help it.

"Give me a few minutes of your time. In private. If you feel that threatened, you can always shoot me. You wouldn't be the first."

"I could shoot you now."

The azhera nodded. "But you won't."

She arched a brow. "You're so sure about that?"

"I don't doubt you're capable. But if you truly thought I was going to harm you, you would've shot me in that tunnel weeks ago."

Shay stared at him for a moment, lips pressed together. Finally, she sighed, took several steps back, and waved him in with the blaster. Her arms were burning from holding it steady for so long, but she for damned sure wasn't going to point it anywhere but at him. "Get in and shut the door."

His ears perked slightly. Though it was a relatively subtle change, Shay had the impression that it was the result of deep surprise and delight he was trying to hide. Keeping his palms raised and facing her, the azhera stepped forward, stopping to press the button and close the door behind him once he was through the doorway.

He seemed even bigger now that he was inside her apartment. Her landlord, Vrisk, was at least half a head taller than this azhera, but she'd bet the azhera could rip that scaly son of a bitch to shreds with his bare hands.

"Weapons?" she asked.

"Only two." Keeping his left hand raised, he slowly moved his right down to his belt. He flipped open a container behind the empty holster and removed a hilt identical to the one she'd found in the stolen belt. He tossed the hilt onto the floor near her feet.

"And the other?" Shay prompted. It wasn't just her arms bothering her now; her feet were aching, and that discomfort was slowly working its way up her legs. And that wasn't even counting all her now-typical pregnancy pains. Without letting the blaster waver, she backed up to the table.

The azhera's brow furrowed as Shay lifted the utility belt—formerly *his* belt—off the back of the chair, laid it atop the table, and sat down. She rested her arms on the table, keeping the blaster trained on him, and stifled the relieved sigh that threatened to escape her. How could it feel *so good* just to rest her arms and take some weight off her feet?

His expression didn't ease, and his gaze lingered on Shay as he slowly shrugged off his jacket, revealing a sleek, black prosthesis with red highlights that ended midway up his left bicep. He draped the jacket over his right arm and moved his right hand to the top of his prosthesis. His fingers pulled an unseen release. There was a soft hiss, a much louder click, and Shay's eyes widened as he slid off his *arm*. The stump beneath ended several centimeters above the point where his elbow would've been and was capped with a curved metal brace that had an open socket on the bottom.

Without looking away from her, he walked forward and gently placed his prosthesis on the floor beside his discarded knife.

Shay stared at the prosthetic limb for a few seconds before raising her eyes back to him. "I...was not expecting that."

"And I didn't expect to find you at Foltham's, but here we both are." The azhera walked toward her, his pace measured, and grabbed the empty chair.

Shay leaned back in her own chair as he drew closer. She was wary of him, but there was no flare of panic, no wave of fear. Despite everything, she believed him when he said he wouldn't hurt her.

That didn't mean she'd let her guard down, though.

He dragged the chair backward until it was several meters

from the table. He draped his jacket over the back of the chair and sat down. The chair groaned as he leaned back. Though he kept his right arm loose and relaxed, he moved the remnants of his left like it pained him to keep it still—or, perhaps, like he was uncomfortable to have it exposed. Overall, he assumed a casual posture, but his tail, which hung off the chair to one side, undulated restlessly.

"My name is Drakkal vor'Kanthar," he said. "But just Drakkal is fine. You willing to share yours yet, or do I just keep calling you terran?"

Shay tilted her head. "We'll see. How did you find me?"

"City surveillance. Used it to track you back here from the tram station."

"Why?"

For a few seconds, his features were strained, and indecision danced across his expression. "I didn't get you out of that place just to toss you into this city with nothing. I know how hard that is. I...was in a similar situation when I first came. But I had help."

"Why me? Why not any of the others trapped there? All the others?"

Drakkal's brow furrowed. "You were the only one I had the chance to save."

Shay had a feeling that his response was only part of the truth—there was something more he wasn't saying. She studied him a little closer, and when her eyes met his again, she recalled the heat, the desire, the *need* that she'd seen burning in their emerald depths. "So, you're telling me it wasn't to be your freaky sex slave? You just wanted to help a helpless female?"

That fire rekindled in his eyes, which searched hers for a few seconds before he spoke again. "You weren't helpless."

"You didn't know that." One corner of her mouth quirked. "Clearly."

"I knew you were a fighter. I saw it in you right away." He shook his head and made a sound partway between a grunt and a chuckle. "Didn't expect you to rob me, but I wasn't really surprised. You're a survivor. All you needed was the right opportunity. And I *do* want you, terran. Just not as a slave."

Keeping the gun trained on him, Shay cleared her throat and glanced away. That didn't save her from the mental image of him standing in that maintenance tunnel with his long, thick cock jutting toward her. "That was obvious."

Her gaze dipped to the tray of now cold, congealed food, and her lips pulled back in disgust before she returned her attention to him. "So after that pronouncement, why should I trust you?"

"Because you're pregnant and alone in an alien city, living in a shithole."

Though he was right, she couldn't help taking some offense. "I'm *surviving*."

"And I want to give you more than just survival." He leaned forward, settling his elbow on his thigh. "I know what was in my pockets when you robbed me. Living frugally—like you are—you might get as much as four or five months out of it before it dries up. Considerably fewer if the owner of this dump takes advantage and adjusts your rent at a whim, like a lot of these *gresh navari* do. You can't get real work because you were a slave and have no identity here. If you go for something legitimate, the authorities will be notified, and that'll cause you trouble. So if you keep working jobs like passing out flyers and getting paid off the books, you might stretch your funds out to as long as half a year.

"But your cub will come before then, won't it? And once that happens, it's only going to get harder. How are you going to work with a little one? Who can you trust to care for your cub?"

Indignation swept through her. Her hand tightened around the blaster's grip, but she kept her finger away from the trigger. The strength of the resentment burning inside her was unreasonable. He was right. Shay *knew* he was right, but that didn't make hearing it any easier. As much as she'd tried to deny it, the fact was that she was floundering. There was little hope, no help, no sign of relief.

But this azhera—*Drakkal*—was offering her help. It was tempting, and it also ratcheted her suspicions up through the stratosphere—if this planet even had a damned stratosphere.

Nobody did anything for free.

"I freed you from that place," Drakkal said, his voice low, deep, and oddly passionate. "I haven't come after you for my belongings. And I literally disarmed myself for you. I'm not asking you to come to my slave dungeon to pleasure me, terran. I can give you a safe place to live and work that pays well. A chance to build a future, to build a *present*."

"Why? You freed me, shouldn't that be enough for your conscience? Why didn't you just let me go and forget about me?" Her brows lowered as she stared at him. "You were looking for me before yesterday, weren't you?"

His ears perked and flattened, and his tail sped. "I've looked for you every day since the first. I've scoured this city. I wasn't lying when I said I want you, terran. You've consumed my thoughts."

Drakkal stood up and stalked toward her, slowly but confidently, and once again, Shay had the impression of powerful muscles shifting beneath his clothing and fur. She watched him approach, her body frozen in something like awe, the blaster forgotten. When he reached the table—standing only a meter away from her now—he placed his right hand on the tabletop and leaned forward.

His scent—leather and sweet cloves underscored by something wholly, uniquely *him*—struck her, as potent as any drug she'd ever used. That scent was familiar by now, almost soothing. It was the smell that clung to the clothing she'd taken from him, the smell that lingered on his jacket, which, despite everything, she still had tucked away in her bedding. She hadn't understood why she couldn't part with it, only that it was her only comfort in this damned city.

"I want you and your cub safe and secure," he said. "That's my priority. The rest will happen naturally."

"The rest?" she asked, mentally shaking off the effects of his nearness and scent even if her body couldn't ignore them. Her thighs were squeezed together, her toes curled upon the floor, and something had kindled low in her belly, something that hadn't sparked in months.

Was she...*attracted* to him? Attracted to an azhera?

"It's in your eyes right now, terran, even though you're resisting. That's all right. I'm patient."

Shay forcefully hardened her expression, but she couldn't stop warmth from flooding her cheeks; he'd caught her with her guard down. "So certain, azhera?"

He slid his big hand across the table's surface and settled it over hers, apparently unbothered by the blaster she was pointing at him. His palm was strong and rough but also warm and comforting. "I am."

She swallowed, remaining completely still. She knew she shouldn't have allowed him to get this close, knew she should've slipped her finger behind the trigger guard, knew she should've pressed the barrel to his chest...but she couldn't. His eyes held hers, their slitted pupils expanding until there was only a thin ring of vibrant green around them.

For several seconds, Shay and Drakkal remained like that, with eyes locked and bodies connected in that small but somehow intimate fashion. Then Drakkal lifted his hand away and stood straight. Still moving with deliberate care, he dropped his hand to one of the pouches on his belt and opened it. Shay's eyes widened, and her finger shifted toward the trigger.

He withdrew a small notepad and a pen.

Shay's brow furrowed as he set the pad on the table, fumbled to get it open one-handed without releasing his hold on the pen, and then pinned it beneath the side of his large palm. He clicked the pen open and wrote something on the paper.

When he was done, he took the top of the little pad between the claws of his forefinger and thumb and held it toward her. "My contact information. Think about what I said."

She didn't move. He lifted the pad slightly, gently urging her to take the paper. Shay finally gave up the pretense. She wasn't going to shoot him, and if he'd meant to harm her, he would've done so back in the tunnel weeks ago. She laid the blaster on the table, keeping one hand over its grip but turning its barrel away from him, and used her free hand to tear off the paper. The characters printed upon it were in Universal Speech—and in surprisingly neat handwriting, despite the size of his hand compared to the pen and pad. It was a comm ID.

Drakkal tucked the pen and pad into their pouch and closed it. Once they were away, he fished a credit chip out of his pocket and placed it atop the table. "Whether you decide to take my offer or not, this should help you keep afloat for a while longer."

Startled, Shay stared down at the credit chip. Her father had taught her from a young age to always be prepared and adaptable, to respond to unforeseen occurrences quickly and confidently. But she was caught off guard by this; her time on the wrong side of the law had taught her that people weren't kind, weren't charitable, weren't willing to help others unless they somehow benefited from it. This...couldn't be real. Nothing was given for free, not in her world.

But Drakkal wasn't asking anything of her. He was simply giving.

She looked up at him. "Is this a trap?"

"It's money," he said flatly.

"You know what I mean. You use this as bait to lure me to you, honey to attract the fly, only to spring the trap once I arrive seeking aid. Nothing is free, azhera."

To Shay's surprise, she didn't flinch away when he extended his hand and hooked a strand of her hair with his claw.

He lifted the hair gently and took it between his fingers, rubbing it between their pads. "Make no mistake, terran—I want you so much that it hurts, but I'll help you however I can whether I have you or not. I want you safe above all else. All the rest is up to you, but you have no obligations to me.

"I understand your suspicions, your indecision. I understand your reluctance to trust. But you *can* trust me. All I need is the chance to prove it to you."

He withdrew his hand—not without a hint of reluctance —and turned away from her, crossing the room to crouch over the items he'd placed on the floor. He returned the knife to its case before lifting his prosthesis. Rising, he moved the prosthesis into place. It clicked into its socket. He flexed his cybernetic fingers in the same way a person might've tried to work away pins and needles. And all the while, Shay watched him.

Drakkal twisted slightly to look back at her. Fire still blazed in his eyes, but there was something else there, too—a glint of sorrow, perhaps, or of hesitancy. It was as though he didn't want to leave. "I'm available any time. Just call."

That said, he grabbed his jacket and walked toward the door.

Before his hand reached the control, she spoke, forcing her name past her lips. "Shay Collins."

He paused and bowed his head slightly, ears turning slightly. "What?"

"My name. It's Shay Collins...but just Shay is enough."

Drakkal looked at her over his shoulder. The corner of his mouth lifted in a smile; the expression was so disarming, so *charming*, and it completely changed his whole face. The heat in Shay's belly surged through her, quickening her pulse.

"Good to finally meet you, Shay Collins." He faced forward again and pressed the control. The door slid open, and he didn't waste any time in walking through. It closed a few seconds later.

The apartment felt suddenly colder, emptier, and larger with him gone.

And she didn't like it one bit.

She didn't even know him, not really, but he'd been so gentle...and he'd made such an impression upon her, had such a commanding presence, that she couldn't help wanting him to come back. He'd turned up while she was sinking to what felt like a new low and offered her everything she needed. She knew it was too good to be true, it had to be, but the hope he'd instilled in her was undeniable. Despite her wariness, she'd felt safe with him near.

He seemed like an entirely different person than he'd been yesterday. She couldn't shake the memory of his ferocity as he'd plowed through the crowd, but was there a different way to interpret what had happened? He'd been gentle with her when he'd taken her from Murgen, too. Even after she'd robbed him for his efforts. He'd seemed a bit frustrated, but not angry. He'd even flirted while she had a gun aimed at him. Hell, he'd had an erection!

Only because he'd been perving out on me while I was naked.

Hypocrite, a voice from the back of her mind shouted.

She'd taken her time studying his body after she'd had him strip. She was just as much of a perv as he was. She'd never looked at an azhera that way before. There were plenty of his kind on Earth, and she'd worked with a couple over the years, but she'd never had a sexual thought about any of them—not that she'd found anything wrong with their appearances. Shay had just been involved in a relationship—one that had lasted a couple years too long in its two-year existence.

So why did her body react so strongly to this azhera?

There were humans on Earth who were involved in interspecies relationships, but it wasn't necessarily commonplace. Shay had just never personally seen the appeal. Drakkal was covered in fur, and some of it—especially around his shoulders and his chest—was downright shaggy. She'd never found body hair that attractive...

But it's not hair, *is it?*

Part of her wondered if his fur was softer than it looked. She could picture herself running her fingers over it, through it, could imagine herself enjoying its feel against her skin, against her palms as she grasped it while they—

Shay groaned at the insistent throbbing between her legs. "What the fuck is wrong with me?"

She needed to take her mind off this. Off *him*.

With a frown, she looked at the credit chip on the tabletop and slid her fingers to it. She pressed the tiny button on its top. Her heart skipped a beat at the number on the display.

"That can't be right," she said breathlessly, pressing button again when the display timed out. But there it was again. The amount was greater than all the credits she'd found in Drakkal's pants combined.

Why would he do this? He'd said he wanted her, and she wholeheartedly believed that; he'd made no effort to hide his attraction for her. But she hadn't agreed to anything. Drakkal had no guarantee that he'd have her. And what was the extent of his want, anyway? How deep did it run? Was he just after a quick rut to satisfy his curiosity?

Make no mistake, terran—I want you so much that it hurts, but I'll help you however I can whether I have you or not. I want you safe above all else.

That last sentence dissuaded her from believing he was after nothing more than a fuck. There was something he wasn't telling her, something that shone in his eyes as he looked at her, something underlying the way he moved that said it took everything in him to keep from pouncing on her. Something that said he was on the verge of having his way with her despite how gentle and controlled he'd acted.

More than that, it said she would've loved every moment of it.

Shay quickly pushed those thoughts aside.

Whatever his intent, she didn't believe he was out to hurt her or her baby, and that was what mattered.

Picking up the credit chip, she curled her fingers around it and glanced at the food tray. The thought of having to take another bite from one of those cheap meals—not that she could imagine anyone of any species considering this real food—sent a shudder through her. As though in agreement, the baby gave Shay's belly a little kick.

Shay smiled. "No, we'll eat good tonight. I promise."

Opening her hand, she looked at the chip in her palm, then turned her gaze to the piece of paper, her smile fading.

She had a decision to make, but she didn't need to make it

now. Drakkal was giving her time to think. And though she was tempted to call him that instant and accept whatever it was he was offering, whatever it was that would keep her and her child safe, whatever it was that would guarantee a future for her baby, she had to think rationally. She had to know he was trustworthy.

But something inside her already said he was.

SEVEN

Nostrus drew in a measured breath and clasped his hands behind his back. He fought back numerous physical manifestations of his frustration—like the way his lower jaw nearly shifted forward, the way his tongue itched to slide across the fronts of his teeth, or the way his fingers twitched to curl into fists that would tremble with a primal desire to do harm. Allowing any one of those slips would be like blasting a hole in a dam; what would follow would be far worse.

A sharp pain skittered through his right hand, a reminder of the injury he'd suffered during his moment of utter failure. Even care from the best medical professionals and equipment in Arthos—including tristeel rods to reinforce the bone—hadn't been enough to eliminate that ache.

The passage of three weeks hadn't eased his anger.

"Nonsense," Master Foltham said with a throaty chuckle. "You'll come for lunch, and we'll settle on the details face to face. I'm sure you can agree that's the best way for such matters to be resolved."

The small holographic image over Master Foltham's desk—

the xendur named Gau'cil to whom he was speaking via the commlink—shifted in Nostrus's peripheral vision as the xendur's large, flexible bone head crest stood forward. Nostrus kept his gaze fixed on one of the wall panels ahead and allowed his mouth just enough movement to clamp his teeth on his tongue.

It's not my place to interrupt.

But that was wrong, wasn't it? He was Murgen Foltham's personal bodyguard and chief of security. His job, his purpose, was to assess and anticipate risks and protect his employer from them. He had a duty to speak up and make Master Foltham aware of the security risk posed by his invitation to Gau'cil. Yet Nostrus held his tongue, focusing on the pain of his bite, because he knew Master Foltham would only be annoyed by any interruption to his *business*.

Foltham would say, *Don't mind Nostrus. He's the best in the business, but he's a touch overzealous at times.* And Nostrus would have no choice but to bite his tongue anyway because he knew even a dismissive comment like that was more praise than he deserved.

He was lucky to have maintained his position after the incident with the azhera. Hell, he was lucky to be employed here at all. He was as grateful for that as he was ashamed. It was a bitter thing to hold a position he no longer deserved.

"Very well, Foltham," Gau'cil replied. "It is wise to conclude our business in person. All matters of true importance are determined thusly."

"I've an opening the day after tomorrow," said Master Foltham.

"Then let it be so, my friend. I will bring my wares, that you may peruse them personally."

Nostrus released a long, slow breath. At least he'd have time to prepare this time. The azhera's arrival had been an unexpected thing—as soon as Master Foltham had learned that the ID chip he'd wanted was ready, he'd insisted the forger send it over at once. Nostrus's team had been informed a mere ten minutes before the azhera's arrival, leaving them no time to make the sorts of arrangements and inquiries he normally would before the arrival of any guests.

Master Foltham's decisions were often impulsive, but he demanded full compliance regardless of the difficulties his rash choices created. A former member of the security team had called such decisions *Murgen specials*. That guard had been promptly fired and blacklisted by every security firm in Arthos.

But he hadn't been wrong.

"I'll have one of my people contact you tomorrow with instructions," Master Foltham said. The glowing hologram over his desk vanished.

"Sir, I must strongly advise against inviting the xendur into your home," Nostrus said with as much care and firmness as he could manage simultaneously.

Master Foltham laughed. "You worry too much, Nostrus. Everything will be fine."

"After what happened, sir, I—"

"Come sit, my boy. No need to converse from across the room."

Nostrus pressed his lips together and nodded. He turned toward Master Foltham, walked forward, and seated himself in one of the chairs facing the desk. Posture rigid, he grasped the arms of the chair, which only renewed the pain in his right hand. Tension claimed every centimeter of his body.

"Ease yourself, Nostrus."

"With respect, Master Foltham, I find my current level of stress justified."

Master Foltham hummed thoughtfully, swelling the excess flesh beneath his chin. "For what reason?"

Nostrus only barely maintained a neutral facial expression. "The azhera, sir."

"Ah. He's certainly disrupted things, hasn't he?"

"I failed you, sir," Nostrus said through his teeth. His *qal*, the intricate markings on his skin, heated in shame. "You have graciously allowed me to continue my service, but the fact of my failure remains."

Master Foltham leaned back in his chair and clasped his hands over his prodigious gut. "Your father was my loyal protector for many years. You've filled that same role for"—he glanced at the ceiling, his thick lower lip jutting outward—"has it really been eighteen years? Longer than even your father, now. And you've been in my house much longer than that."

Nostrus nodded; he could trust himself with no other response. He'd accepted his current position upon his father's death, had accepted it as his purpose, his duty, and if he allowed himself to reflect upon the shame he'd brought upon his father's once-proud name...

"One mistake in all that time is hardly worthy of harsh reprimand. Your loyalty is worth far more than that," said Master Foltham.

Not when a single mistake on my part could mean the end of your life, sir.

Nostrus gave no voice to that thought. He knew Master Foltham understood that truth, though he sometimes seemed oblivious to reality. Perhaps, in time, the master's forgiveness would be enough.

Despite the dryness of his lips, Nostrus did not allow himself to lick them. "I will not make another mistake, sir. Which is why I must reiterate my objection to hosting the xendur here. He's a flesh peddler, sir. A criminal, just like the azhera."

Master Foltham laughed again, further expanding his

throat flesh. "Gau'cil has been my procurer for years, young Nostrus. The money he makes from me is too great a sum for him to forfeit through betrayal."

Nostrus held his master's gaze and said, "Similar thinking led to the incident with the azhera, Master Foltham."

Lifting a hand, Master Foltham absently ran a finger along one of his thick tusks. "The meeting with Gau'cil will happen here, Nostrus. But if it puts you at ease, you may make the security arrangements with any resources or precautions you deem necessary."

Suppressing a surprised smile, Nostrus nodded. This was more than he'd expected, and though he understood the risks of pushing Master Foltham further, he found himself emboldened by the success. "There's also the problem of the azhera, sir."

Master Foltham grunted. "He and I have an...understanding. He won't cause any more trouble, Nostrus."

"He has insulted you and your house, Master Foltham," Nostrus said, leaning forward. The tension in his limbs was that quickly run through with a furious energy. "He stole your most prized possession."

Features hardening, Master Foltham stared at Nostrus while absently tapping his tusk. Murgen Foltham was a being of deep intellect and keen business sense, and Nostrus knew him well enough to understand that Foltham was at his most competent—and most dangerous—while wearing this cold, calculating expression.

"I accepted his offer," Master Foltham finally said, but there was a hint of question in his tone.

"Under duress, sir."

Master Foltham released another grunt, following it with another thoughtful hum. "An offer made in bad faith. Always makes for unfair business."

"Now he's holding it over your head. Using what you

shared with him as leverage to keep you from reneging on a deal that was never valid to begin with."

"This azhera...he's plagued your thoughts for some time now, hasn't he?"

Nostrus nodded; lying would gain him nothing in this case. "He has, sir. I cannot stomach the insult he's done you."

Nor the insult he's done me...

"Yes, yes...he's been on my mind, too, if I'm to be honest. I had hoped to simply put this matter behind me and be done with it, but..."

"Great individuals like you, sir, need not take such slights in stride. Scum like the azhera would view your pragmatism as weakness and seek to take advantage again."

Nostrils flaring with a heavy breath, Master Foltham dropped a hand to his desk. He drummed his fingers in a quick rhythm—an impatient rhythm. "I had hoped to avoid the problems that might arise should he decide to share the sensitive information to which I made him privy. It wouldn't cause any issues I can't make go away, of course, but it would all be an unwelcome waste of my time and resources."

Master Foltham's fingers quickened, moving with surprising dexterity despite their size. Nostrus had seen a few such signs of agitation in his employer since the incident, but Master Foltham had remained largely silent on the matter until now.

"Such distractions and their eventual resolutions would be quite costly," Master Foltham continued, "and though the money itself is not an issue, well... There's something far more important at risk here, isn't there? It's a matter of principle. This azhera came into my home as an honored guest and betrayed my trust."

Master Foltham's normally calm demeanor crumbled with each word; Nostrus didn't need to push any more. Murgen

Foltham was already tumbling down a hill, gaining speed, and would not stop until he was fully submerged in the vengeful waters below.

"He stole from me," Master Foltham shouted, slamming his hand atop his desk. He shoved himself to his feet. "No one steals from Murgen Foltham, damn it. No one threatens me, no one gets away with trying to intimidate me, no one gets to disrespect me, especially not in my own house! This azhera is barely a step above bottom-feeding vermin on the evolutionary chain, and it's time he learned his place."

His jowls wobbled with his angry, impassioned words. As much as those transgressions against Master Foltham were marks against Nostrus, the volturian held a more personal score —the brief but agonizing twinges in his hand even now wouldn't let him forget it.

"I will have what is mine returned to me, Nostrus," Master Foltham said, brandishing his finger as though it were a terrifying, deadly weapon. "I'll not accept this loss. I won't let a meddlesome animal disrupt my plans."

Nostrus stood up, crossed his arms over his chest, and bowed. "Master Foltham, allow me the opportunity to right these wrongs. Allow me this chance to restore honor to my father's name."

Master Foltham jabbed a finger toward Nostrus. "Honor! Yes, honor, and respect! We must—" His eyes widened, but the rest of his expression slackened. He dropped into his chair with a heavy thump. "We must keep honor and respect in mind as we proceed."

"Sir, I will handle the matter personally."

Master Foltham waved his hand, eyes unfocused. "No, my boy, you won't."

Those words sparked an unsettling fire in Nostrus's heart— and pierced it with shards of ice at the same time. "Sir?"

"I've no doubt as to your ability, Nostrus, but you are openly connected to me—and that connection is quite public." Master Foltham's tone was sober now, but not defeated; it still held that note of cold calculation. "We cannot risk any of this being tied to you, because that would naturally come back on me, and then we'd be in the very situation we're seeking to avoid."

None of Nostrus's considerable respect or loyalty for Master Foltham could combat his deep, roiling frustration in that moment. He maintained his bowed position, keeping his face downturned to hide his clenched jaw and slanted eyebrows from his employer's view. Fresh heat pulsed along his *qal*.

"Sir, I know how to operate covertly," Nostrus grated through his teeth. "It will never come back on you."

"It's an unnecessary risk all the same, Nostrus." Master Foltham brought up a holoscreen over his desk and opened his contacts list. "It takes a particular skillset to hunt beasts like this azhera, a mindset that advanced beings like you and I are simply too sophisticated to comprehend. We need to call upon someone closer to his level. You may assist in coordination, but you will have no direct role in this matter, not until my terran and that thieving azhera are securely in our custody. Is that clear?"

Clenching his fists at his sides, Nostrus lifted his gaze to meet Master Foltham's. "Yes, sir."

"Good. You may go begin the preparations to receive Gau'cil the day after next." Master Foltham waved his fingers. "I'll begin orchestrating the hunt for our little fugitives."

Fortunately, Nostrus managed to catch his tongue between his teeth before he could say anything in response. This had gone far better than he could've expected, and it was best not to push his luck. He'd press the matter of personally hunting the azhera another time. With a final nod, he turned and exited Master Foltham's study.

A piercing ache radiated from the center of his hand outward to his fingertips; it felt like a metal spike was being hammered through his bones. He assured himself that he wasn't giving up—he would reclaim his lost honor, or he would die trying.

EIGHT

The scent of leather and cloves filled Shay's senses as she slowly roused. She inhaled deeply, drawing more of that delicious aroma into her lungs. It brought a sense of peace, a sense of comfort, and sparked a heat that spread through her body and pooled low in her belly. She shifted on her pallet and moaned as her shirt rasped across her tight, sensitive nipples, which sent another pulse to her already throbbing sex.

Her eyelids fluttered open to darkness as total as it had been while her eyes were closed. She didn't know how long she'd slept, didn't know how close she was to her alarm going off, and she didn't care. Her body was ablaze, aching in a way it hadn't in months. Had she been dreaming? If so, she couldn't recall those dreams, but they'd clearly sent the right signals to the right places. She couldn't remember ever feeling this aroused.

She hadn't had sex in at least five months. Between getting kidnapped by aliens, being sold as a pet and kept in a cell, and recently working herself to exhaustion, she hadn't given sex a thought. But a little self-indulgence, a little pleasure, couldn't hurt, could it?

Rolling onto her back, Shay closed her eyes again. She ignored her uncomfortable bedding and focused on the sensations as she slowly trailed the fingertips of her right hand down her chest, over the swells of her breasts, which had grown fuller and more sensitive during her pregnancy, and pinched her nipple through her shirt. Her breath hitched at the pleasure that arced through her. Her pussy clenched, aching to be touched, to be relieved, so tightly that it was almost painful.

In the past, Shay would've taken her time, would've prolonged the act as much as possible. But there was no need now. Her body demanded release.

Moving her hand farther down, she slipped it beneath the waistband of her underwear, spread her thighs, and eased her fingers between the folds of her sex. The slightest brush against her engorged clit made her gasp with a blast of pleasure. She arched her back and turned her face to the side, grasping the jacket beside her and pulling it close to her nose.

For a moment, she held perfectly still, letting the sensation ease. When she took in a shuddering inhalation, her senses were again overwhelmed with that leather and clove scent.

Her pussy was slick, and her panties were soaked with her need. Biting her bottom lip, Shay stroked her clit again, moving her fingers in gentle, circular motions. Her hips rocked of their own accord as the euphoric sensations heightened. Her panting breaths escalated in volume.

She imagined another hand—a much larger, rougher hand, its fingers tipped with deadly claws but its touch confident and gentle. A hand connected to a muscled, fur-covered arm that belonged to a vibrant green-eyed azhera.

"Drakkal," Shay cried out as she came, body seizing. Her pussy clenched around nothing, and her thighs snapped together, locking her hand in place as the sensations became too much for her to stand. Liquid heat flooded her. She pressed the jacket to her face and muffled her cries, unwilling to let the neighbors hear her release.

It wasn't until her body eased and the sleep and desire fogging her mind had cleared that Shay realized whose name she'd said.

Drakkal.

It had been him she'd imagined touching her, him she'd envisioned, and it had been *him* who'd had sent her over the edge. It had likely been his scent that worked her body to such ravenousness as she'd slept—and it was his damned jacket clutched in her fist, currently pressed against her face.

Thrusting the jacket away, Shay yanked her hand out from between her thighs and groaned as she lay back on her pallet, staring up into the darkness. Her skin tingled, her legs trembled, and her face was warm in the aftermath of her orgasm. Despite her frustration and embarrassment, she felt...good. Relaxed.

But no less needy.

If anything, she wanted *more*, and she didn't think her hand was going to cut it no matter how many times she brought herself to climax.

"Fuck."

Yes, please. A nice fucking would do. A rough, hard pounding with soft fur brushing against my ass and the backs of my thighs as clawed hands—

"Damn it!" She struggled into a sitting position and rubbed her eyes with her clean hand. "It's just...pregnancy hormones. That's all. It's making me all sorts of crazy, and now I'm fantasizing about some alien werecat with a nice big co—ah come on! Lights on."

As the lights flickered on, she got to her feet and gathered her damp sheets, muttering, "Losing my goddamned mind."

So much for the alleged stress-relieving effects of orgasms.

She carried her bedding into the bathroom, shoved it into the auto-washer, and started it. When she turned, she caught sight of herself in the mirror. Her hair was mussed, her cheeks were flushed, and her blue eyes shone. All she was missing were kiss-swollen lips and she'd look like she'd been properly fucked.

If only.

"Ugh."

She closed her eyes and sighed. "That's enough. No more thoughts about sex." Opening her eyes, she looked down at her holocom and pressed the button on the side. It was two hours before her alarm. "Fuuuuuck. It's going to be a long day."

Her gaze dropped to her bedding. "Might as well get started."

She'd take a shower, eat breakfast—without having to hurry—and, when the time came, go find out if she still had a job.

She had to think about the azhera's *offer*, after all, *not* his large, powerful body, his big, strong, hands, his green, heated stare, and his long, thick cock jutting from between—

"Damn it!"

FORTUNATELY—OR rather, *unfortunately*, depending on how you looked at it—Shay was still employed.

Pain radiated through her jaw, which she'd clenched in her effort to keep her mouth shut. She stood still, chin up, eyes forward, refusing to feel as small as she was compared to the ranting groalthuun towering over her. It was a good thing her blaster was holstered beneath her jacket, or she would have been tempted to go for it the moment her boss had looked at her and spat *terran ji'tas*.

She'd been around aliens long enough to know calling her *ji'tas* was basically saying she was a prime candidate for being made a sex slave and little else.

At some point during his ranting, which flowed freely between his native tongue and Universal Speech—all of it easily understandable thanks to her translator—the urge to pull her blaster grew so strong that she forced herself to stop listening.

I need this job, she repeatedly reminded herself.

But do I though?

Her thoughts turned toward Drakkal and his offer.

I can give you a safe place to live and work that pays well. A chance to build a future, to build a present.

Could she trust him? Was his offer real? Everything she'd learned over the last several years told her it was a setup, that she'd be stupid to trust him, especially after what she'd done to him. But if he really meant to hurt her, why had he rung her doorbell and asked to come inside to talk?

He had money at his disposal, that much was clear, and he was a capable male. She had no doubt that he could've easily entered her apartment without her knowledge whether subtly or by force, especially with that cybernetic arm. Wouldn't it have been easier for him to kidnap her in her sleep or something?

Yorgaz thrust a thick finger into Shay's face, startling her out of her thoughts and calling her attention back to him.

"One more mess up, *ji'tas*, and you're done. No more work. And maybe I call my friends and see if they have use for you," Yorgaz said.

Fire blazed in her belly, and the words burst like lava from her mouth. "You're *not* going to fucking stand here and threaten me."

Yorgaz recoiled slightly. "What did you say to me, terran?"

Shay glared at him. "You heard me. You barely pay me as it is, and I definitely don't get paid enough to listen to this shit." She stepped forward, tilted her head back, and jabbed her finger at him, poking his chest. "I don't respond well to threats. You deduct your damned lost flyers from my pay if you want—not like you would've known the difference if I tossed them in the trash and told you I passed them all out—but you're not going to intimidate me. I've dealt with bigger, badder men than you, you fucking goat, and my patience is just about worn out."

As she continued her advance, Yorgaz backed away, his dark eyes going wide. The fine scales on his face paled; clearly for all his bluster, he hadn't been prepared for Shay to stand up for herself.

"Now are you going to give me my flyers for the day so I can get to work, or are we going to have trouble?" she demanded.

He swallowed thickly and, without taking his gaze off her, slapped his hand on the counter beside him to grope around until he found the stack of paper-thin holographic flyers. He grabbed them and very nearly spilled them all on the floor as he thrust them toward her.

"G-get to work, terran."

Shay took the flyers and smiled wide. "Thank you."

Without another word, she left his office and made her way back out onto the streets toward her assigned location. She wove easily through the crowds, and was unable but to contemplate again how, despite being of different races, sizes, shapes, and appearances, despite coming from countless different worlds and cultures, everyone here shared that common, unifying trait. They didn't give a shit about anyone or anything apart from getting to wherever they were going.

Once she reached her corner, she got to work, offering flyers and calling out to passersby. Time drudged on at a sluggish pace. Several times, the hairs on the back of her neck rose, and she could have sworn she was being watched. But every time she swept her gaze over the crowd, she didn't see any faces that stood out, couldn't find the eyes that were fixated upon her. Everyone else seemed to be going about their business, so she continued to go about hers.

As was the norm, most everyone ignored her. Some cast her curious glances, a couple actually took the damned flyers, and one or two of those who took them did so only to throw the flyers back at her.

Why am I doing this?

She dropped her arm and stood there, mouth pursed and turned to one side as she seriously considered that question. She'd been offered something that sounded so much better—a safe place to live, a good wage...a future for her and her baby. Why the hell was she still out here? Why hadn't she jumped on Drakkal's offer?

Because I need to be sure. I need to know the azhera and his offer were legit. That my baby will want for nothing, that it'll be safe.

His offer has to be real though, right? If he wanted to hurt me or take me, he could have done that at any time.

That wasn't really how things worked, though. People were patient. Sometimes, they took their time in hurting you. Sometimes they wanted to soften you up before sinking in that knife. But what was her alternative? Hit the streets and find something else, knowing that almost no one wanted to hire a terran for anything but sex work, or get arrested for shooting her boss in the face?

Shay lifted her wrist and looked down at her holocom. A single call was all it'd take. She'd be off this street, living somewhere nice, somewhere safe and secure, eating food that wasn't unidentifiable slop, and—

A hand squeezing her ass brought her thoughts to a sudden, screeching halt.

"What a delicious little morsel," a rumbling voice said from behind her.

Shay whipped around, baring her teeth. *Three* eyes—blue against black—stared down at her.

The tall, horned, sedhi grinned, flashing his fangs as he stepped closer. His tail eased forward to stroke her leg. "Forget the flyers, *ji'tas*. How much for you?"

NINE

Though he'd never been a fan of crowds—a city like Arthos was the last place he would've chosen to live, had things gone differently for him—Drakkal was grateful for the mass of pedestrians today. In a less crowded setting, he would've stood out like a tralix at a volturian dinner party, but here they provided him some cover.

Some small part of him said this was wrong—or at least that Shay might see it as such—but his instincts were insistent enough to drown out that little voice of doubt. He needed to know his terran was safe. This was the only way he knew how to accomplish that—watching her. It didn't matter if she wanted him to or not, it was what he had to do. It wasn't much different than what he'd done for Arcanthus for years, was it?

Apart from Arcanthus having asked *me to do it and being fully aware of my presence and my methods...*

Though Arc did have *the cren brothers keep an eye on Samantha without her knowledge.*

He sighed and muttered, "Not sure that makes it right, Drak..."

He stood against the outside of a building, only fifteen or twenty meters away from Shay. He'd donned a long, dull gray coat, hoping it would obscure his frame a little better than the more form-fitting leather jackets he preferred. The hood was a bonus, even if he hated the feel of it over his mane and ears. Shay was dressed in a green hooded jacket, form-fitting black leggings, and boots. More than once, Drakkal found himself hoping she'd move in such a way that the hem of her jacket would rise to afford him the sight of those leggings hugging her ass and thighs—not that the thick flow of pedestrians would've afforded him a clear view.

So I'm not just a stalker, I'm an aroused stalker. Nothing at all wrong with that...

Drakkal didn't know if she'd been assigned this location for work or if she'd chosen it herself, but every time she was ignored or rebuked by a passerby, a spark of rage flared in Drakkal's chest. Violence had been a part of his life in some fashion or another for almost as long as he could remember, but he'd never been so motivated toward it for so petty a reason. He wanted to attack everyone who glanced at her in a way that could be interpreted as even mildly rude.

But he held himself back. He'd made mistakes when it came to Shay, and he intended to keep them to a minimum going forward. That meant leaning on the patience he'd commanded before meeting her. It meant drawing on the skills he'd learned as a hunter long before Arthos was anything more to him than a distant, almost mythical city he had no desire to see.

Yet despite his considerable willpower, it was a unique sort of torture to be so close to her without being able to interact with her, especially given how *good* it felt to finally speak to her yesterday. Their conversation in her apartment had eased the stress that had built in Drakkal over the last three weeks—and he wanted to capitalize on the progress they'd made. He wanted to *woo* her, as Arcanthus had suggested.

And how would that go? Hello Shay, I was just stalking you and I found myself wondering if you wanted to get some lunch?

He'd been watching her for a few hours with his tail pinned against the wall behind him to keep it still when the sedhi approached her. Though Drakkal couldn't see the entirety of their bodies—and therefore their interactions—through the constant flow of foot traffic, he knew Shay was not comfortable with the sedhi's presence by her expression.

Keeping his eyes on Shay and the sedhi, Drakkal stalked closer, shifting his ears beneath his hood to focus his hearing forward.

"How much for you?" the sedhi asked.

Drakkal hadn't wanted to punch a sedhi in the teeth that much since he'd seen Arcanthus that morning.

"I'm not for sale, so fuck off. And don't touch me again," Shay snapped. She turned away from the sedhi, her bright blue eyes spitting fire into the crowd as she raised a flyer. "Check out the Spectacular Skrudge Show!"

Drakkal's brows fell low, his fur bristled, and a growl sounded from deep in his chest. The sedhi had *touched* her? Instinct rapidly overpowered Drakkal's rational thought. He increased his pace, eyes locked on the sedhi as a red haze flooded his vision.

The sedhi reached forward and grabbed Shay's shoulder. As he spun her around, he said, "I'm talking to you—"

Were he not so experienced a fighter himself, Drakkal might've missed what happened next—it was fast, much faster than he'd expected from a terran. Shay dropped the flyers in her left hand, lifting that arm and using the momentum created by the sedhi's pull to bat away his hand. She hammered her right fist into the sedhi's chin before he could react.

The sedhi's head snapped back, and he staggered back a step, grating a curse. The crowd eased back from the terran and her foe, finally granting Drakkal a clear view.

Drakkal's heart stilled when the sedhi recovered and swung his arm in a counterattack. Shay was too small, too delicate to take such a blow from a being so much bigger than her. Drakkal charged forward, but he wouldn't get there in time.

Shay ducked beneath the sedhi's swing. Having overextended himself, the sedhi was thrown off balance by his miss. Shay thrust a leg in front of his and twisted slightly to give him a shove on the shoulder. He toppled face first onto the ground.

By the time the sedhi flipped over and started to sit up—no more than a second or two, at most—Shay had thrown open her coat, drawn her blaster, and backed away from her opponent. She stared at him, her gaze as hard and unwavering as the gun in her hand.

The sedhi glared at her, fangs bared, his third eye dipping to the barrel of the blaster.

"I *said* don't touch me. Is it really that hard to listen?" Shay asked.

"Fuck you, you—"

"I don't know exactly where your dick is, but I have enough patience and ammunition to find out. So I want you to think very carefully about the next words coming out of your mouth."

"You won't shoot me."

"How much you willing to bet?"

The sedhi pressed his lips together in a tight line, and a glimmer of uncertainty entered his eyes. Several people had stopped to watch the altercation. Drakkal halted at the edge of that crowd. Despite his fury, he'd maintained just enough control to know that his interference now had a chance of worsening the situation.

"Good," Shay said, her expression surprisingly calm. Even

if she'd been shaken up, she was fully in control. "Now you're going to get up very slowly, turn around, and walk away."

Nostrils flaring with heavy breaths, the sedhi carefully stood up. His attention once again fell to the blaster as he retreated. Shay kept the weapon aimed at him even when he turned and sprinted away, his long tail trailing behind him.

With sighs and soft conversation—some of it relieved and some of it oddly disappointed—the crowd reverted to its typical state of motion.

Drakkal couldn't take his eyes off Shay. The confidence and competence with which she'd handled the sedhi were startling, though they shouldn't have been—he'd seen hints of it in all his interactions with her before now. It was yet more evidence of what Arcanthus had speculated regarding Shay's past. This terran knew how to take care of herself.

And that fighting spirit, that warrior soul, called to Drakkal. It fanned those desirous flames she'd already woken in him, stoked them to new heights. That quickly, the fires of rage burning in Drakkal became an inferno of yearning.

Shay holstered the blaster and tugged her jacket closed to conceal it again. She looked down at the flyers on the ground, and her lips and nose scrunched endearingly.

"You know what? Fuck this," she muttered and lifted her hand, yanking back her sleeve to reveal her holocom. She pulled up the control screen and flipped through the commands.

The now lustful haze in Drakkal's mind prevented him from realizing what she was doing until it was too late to react. She detached the earpiece from her holocom, slipped it in her ear, and selected an option on the menu.

The holocom built into Drakkal's prosthesis chimed—out loud. Were he even a few steps farther away from her, she likely wouldn't have heard it over the din of the crowd, but he'd come within a couple meters during her scuffle with the sedhi.

Shay's head turned toward the sound—toward *Drakkal*—and her eyes skimmed over him briefly. Almost as soon as she looked away, she snapped her gaze back to Drakkal, eyes going wide.

Of all the times to forget to silence this damned thing...

He almost always wore the earpiece for his holocom, keeping its speaker silenced. That was part of his typical day, so much so that he rarely thought about it. But today, he'd been so focused on his task, so focused on her, that he'd not bothered with his earpiece. He'd wanted to keep his full attention on her.

Shay ended the call and removed her earpiece. "For real? You're stalking me?"

If he should've been embarrassed, the feeling never came. He'd told Shay that he wanted her safe above all else. There was no shame in following through with that.

He reached up, tugged down his hood, and shook out his mane as he approached her. "I am."

"Just like that? No excuses? No lies?" Her brows furrowed as she tilted her head. "You...you realize that doesn't necessarily help your case, right? Just makes you creepy."

Drakkal shrugged. "Creepy but honest. You hungry?"

Startled, she opened her mouth, closed it, and studied him with a furrowed brow.

He could feel her gaze on him like a physical touch, and his skin tingled beneath it as though she were looking right through his clothing. There was something inexplicably exciting about that. "Doubt you have anything better to do, terran. I heard you just lost your job."

She looked down at the flyers littering the ground and kicked one with the toe of her boot. "Actually"—she lifted her gaze to meet his—"I quit. You buying?"

One corner of Drakkal's mouth rose in a smirk. "I don't know. Heard you came into some money recently. Shouldn't it be your treat?"

"You asked. I can go eat on my—"

"Yeah, it's on me."

She grinned. "That's what I thought. Let's go. I'm starving."

As surreal as this turn of events had been, Drakkal didn't dwell on it. The only thing that mattered was that he'd found his mate, and she was both surprising and extremely capable. His want for her grew by the second.

They fell into step side-by-side, with Drakkal altering his gait to match her pace.

"Anything you're particular to?" he asked.

She glanced up at him from the corner of her eye and shrugged. "Any recommendations?"

Half a dozen options flitted through Drakkal's mind. He knew the city well—at least chunks of it—but his knowledge of terrans wasn't remotely as solid. Even living around Samantha for a year hadn't taught him enough about their species, especially because he rarely thought of Sam as a terran anymore—she was just part of his crew, part of his family.

What did Sam say? No...bugs? Nothing still alive? He wished he could remember for sure.

He turned his head toward Shay and looked her over, as though that could somehow tell him her dietary necessities. "What do your kind eat?"

She arched a brow at him. "Food."

His expression fell, and he fixed her with a droll look. "You don't get to complain if you don't like it."

"Kitty, as long as it tastes good, it's not moving, and you don't tell me what it actually is, I'll eat it."

"You call me kitty again and I'll eat *you*." The words came out with an unintended hint of lust.

"Promise?"

Based on the surprise in her expression, Drakkal guessed she hadn't intended her sultry tone, either.

Oh yes, Shay. It's a promise.

Despite a thousand other scents on the air, hers was the fragrance he noticed, the fragrance that filled his nose and rushed to cloud his mind. He longed to touch her, to feel her warm, soft skin beneath his palm, to peel off her clothing and lick her from head to toe and back again. He wanted to taste every centimeter of her body.

Just the thought of it had his mouth watering. Barely suppressing a growl, he forced himself to turn his attention ahead and keep walking. This was neither the time nor the place—though the way his body reacted to her, he knew in his heart there could be *no* wrong time or place. The only thing that would stop him was the audience. Shay was for Drakkal alone.

Kraasz ka'val, we're just sharing a meal, not rutting!

...Not rutting yet.

Drakkal led her to the closest place he could think of—a borian restaurant specializing in roasted meat. The aroma of fresh, hot, juicy meat slowly cooking in the kitchen struck him immediately when he entered, making him realize just how hungry he was. But it wasn't quite enough to overpower Shay's scent.

Not that he wanted anything to overpower her scent.

Shay slid into an open booth, folding her arms atop the table, and Drakkal seated himself across from her. For a few seconds, her eyes roamed the room, studying everything—and giving him an opportunity to study her.

Though he'd seen her up close several times now, he found something new in her features each time he looked, and her beauty only grew as he became more familiar with her appearance. He'd always assumed his mate would be an azhera—a huntress, a strong, agile female with sharp senses and steely nerves. For a little while, he'd even thought he had that...

But that had been nothing compared to what he felt now—and he hadn't even claimed Shay yet. She was simultaneously exactly what he'd imagined and nothing like it at all, but he already couldn't picture his mate as anyone other than her.

Though the restaurant was dimly lit, Shay's hair, which was pulled back into a tie at the back of her head and rested over her shoulder in a thick strand, glistened pale gold. She'd let him touch that hair when he was at her apartment; would she object now? How far could he push before she'd had enough? How fast would she be willing to move?

She hasn't agreed to anything more than lunch, stupid. Don't get ahead of yourself.

Hard advice to take when he'd already mated her in his mind.

"Nice place," she said, turning those bright blue eyes back to him. "A bit fancier than I'm used to. You trying to impress me?"

"Only if you're actually impressed," Drakkal replied, unable to keep a small smile from tugging his lips up. He reached to the side and activated the menu. A holographic screen appeared over the table between them, displaying all the available dishes and drinks, each accompanied by three-dimensional representations. "Order whatever you want."

She scanned the items and huffed a laugh. "You loaded or what?"

Her question made Drakkal think of Murgen Foltham and people of that ilk—the elite, the wealthy, the ones who looked down on everyone else simply because they could afford to. He'd never felt ashamed of the success he and Arcanthus had achieved, not until that moment.

"I'm comfortable," he grumbled.

Shay met Drakkal's gaze through the holo screen, positioning her face between two platters of steaming meat. She was, by far, the most delectable thing on the menu.

"Didn't mean to offend you," she said. "You just seem to throw credits around left and right."

Drakkal frowned and leaned forward, settling his elbows on the table. "Not offended, and I don't throw credits around. I only throw them straight ahead—lately at you."

One of her eyebrows rose, and her cheeks darkened faintly as she looked back at the menu. After a few seconds, she tapped her selections—roasted polovi meat with a side of fajetta, which was a flowering root native to the borians' homeworld. Drakkal let his gaze linger on her a little longer before he made his own choices, foregoing the plants in favor of a variety of meats. He added an order of breaded and fried glehorn meat to the order for good measure; he knew Shay had been conserving her credits, and doubted she'd been eating as well as she should. She and her cub needed nutrition. They needed protein.

Providing suitable food for her was amongst the simplest things he could do to satisfy his instinctual need to care for her.

When the prompt screen came up, he took out a credit chip and let the system deduct the bill without checking the price. It didn't matter.

"So, terran, how was the passing out flyers on street corners business?" he asked once the holo-menu closed.

"Shitty, as you already know." She leaned closer to him. "What is it *you* do?"

Drakkal inhaled slowly. "Private security."

"Which is how you hacked into the city's surveillance system to find out where I lived, right?"

He shrugged. "Something like that. I have a friend who's good with computers."

"I'm calling bullshit."

Drakkal furrowed his brow and tilted his head. "Calling *what* shit?"

Shay straightened in her seat, keeping her narrowed eyes locked with his. "You might have a friend who's good with computers, but you're not working for some standup security firm. You weren't at Murgen's talking about security, you were selling him an ID chip. If you want my trust, lies are not going to win it."

He leaned farther forward, settling more weight onto his elbows, and lowered his voice. "And I'm going to guess you weren't exactly legitimate before you wound up in his basement."

She eased closer until their faces were only a handspan apart. "Yeah. Been there, done that, and I'm tired of being hurt and getting backstabbed. I'm not going down that road again."

"This isn't like that, Shay."

"That's what everyone says. I'm not getting involved in that life again, not when I have someone who'll be depending on me."

She scooted across the seat as though to exit the booth.

Drakkal extended a hand, catching her wrist before she could get up. She whipped her face toward him, lips pressed tight.

"It's *not* like that," he said firmly. "This isn't some street gang...bulkshit, or whatever shit you said before. I trust everyone there with my life. I won't lie to you and say I haven't done terrible things, Shay, but we're not bad people."

The muscles in her arm relaxed as she lowered herself onto the seat. "Are you going to be truthful with me?"

He couldn't bring himself to release her arm, not yet; there seemed too great a chance of her running, and he didn't want to chase her through the city again. "Yes, but not here. I think you know certain matters are best not discussed in public."

She searched his face before finally saying, "At my place then. After we leave here. But all I'm agreeing to is hearing you out, that clear?"

Drakkal released her arm, but before he could answer, a tall, pointy-eared borian arrived at their table with a large tray full of food. When the borian let go of the tray, it hovered in the air beside him. He quickly transferred the plates of steaming food from the tray, along with a pitcher of water and two glasses, to the table.

Shay's attention shifted to the meal; she didn't notice the borian staring at her, didn't notice the hungry light in his eyes.

Drakkal couldn't notice anything *but* the light in the borian's eyes.

"Can I get you anything else?" the borian asked in accented Universal Speech. He didn't look away from Shay.

"No," Drakkal growled.

The borian swayed a little closer to Shay, brows falling low.

Shay, oblivious, shoved one of the fried glehorn strips into her mouth and moaned as she leaned back in her seat, arms going slack at her sides. Closing her eyes, she chewed slowly. "So. Damn. *Good*."

The server bowed, his lips stretching into a wide grin. "I'm glad everything is to the female's liking. If she would—"

Utensils clattered as Drakkal closed his cybernetic hand around the blade of one of the knives, finally drawing the borian's attention.

Drakkal squeezed the blade between his metal fingers and snarled, "*Go*." When he opened his hand, the knife—now twisted and warped into an unidentifiable shape—dropped to the table with a clatter.

"Yes sir, sorry sir," the borian said hurriedly before snatching the tray out of the air and quickly retreating.

Once the server had vanished through the kitchen doors, Drakkal carefully settled his prosthetic hand on the table and turned his head to face Shay again.

She was still chewing, but her eyes were upon him now, sparkling with humor that mirrored her crooked grin. She swallowed the food in her mouth. "Feisty kitty."

Despite the agitation of a moment ago, Drakkal smirked. "I broke the arm of the last person who called me *feisty kitty*."

Shay chuckled. "Yeah, but you didn't threaten to break my arm. You threatened to eat me."

"It wasn't a threat, terran. It was a promise."

She slid her plate closer and skewered a chunk of meat with a knife, lips curling into a teasing smile. Just before she took a bite, she said, "I know."

This female is going to drive me to madness.

And madness had never been so appealing.

Shay took another bite and shifted her attention to Drakkal's prosthesis. She pushed the mouthful of food to one cheek. "So, what happened there?"

Drakkal turned his head to follow her gaze, frowning when his eyes fell on his arm. Only his hand was visible thanks to his coat, but she'd seen the rest already—she'd even seen him without his prosthesis.

"Someone from our past showed up unexpectedly and tried to murder me and my friend—the friend who's good with computers," he said after a brief silence. "Tried to murder my whole crew. I stopped to hold him back while everyone else escaped."

The corners of Shay's mouth fell. "You're alive, so I'm guessing you took care of the fucker."

With a humorless chuckle, Drakkal shook his head. "No, I

didn't. Don't get me wrong, I got in a few good shots after he did this"—he lifted his cybernetic arm off the table for a moment—"but he knocked me out cold. *Zhe'gaash* was a cyborg. More machine under his skin than flesh and blood. Guess my hard head was all that saved me from brain damage. I got off with a concussion and a metal arm. My friend and his mate are the ones who killed him. She saved my life. He was about to finish me off before she intervened."

"Damn." For a few moments, Shay stared at him, brows raised and eyes wide. "Look, I'm glad you made it out of that okay, Drakkal, and I admire that you were fighting to save the people you care for, but... That's exactly the kind of shit I'm trying to get away from. I don't want that life anymore."

"I've been in the Infinite City for a decade, Shay, running this operation with my partner. That was the first time anything like that happened. We're not in a business that tends to garner that sort of attention."

She lifted another piece of meat. "So you say, Kitty."

Drakkal smirked. "Yeah, I do. You'll be safe with us, Shay. You and your cub."

Shay tore off a chunk of meat with her teeth and leveled that thoughtful, inquisitive stare on him again as she chewed. When she'd finished, her little pink tongue slipped out to lick her lips clean. "We'll see on that. Can that thing do any other cool shit?"

The laughter that rose from Drakkal's chest was rich and pure, and it felt good.

If this is madness, keep it coming.

TEN

As the elevator doors closed, Shay peeked at Drakkal from the corner of her eye. Though she was average height for a female human, she felt incredibly small beside him; his presence seemed to fill the entire lift. His leather and clove scent permeated the air, and heat radiated from his body. Shay was tempted to move closer to him.

Really tempted.

Spending time with him had been...nice. Nicer than she'd expected. Beneath his gruffness, he was actually quite funny, and he'd made her laugh several times as they ate. But his demeanor had changed as soon as they'd left the restaurant. He grew quieter, more alert, and kept so close to her that it should've made her uncomfortable. But she hadn't felt uncomfortable, not even a little. She'd felt protected. For once, she hadn't had to constantly look over her shoulder, hadn't had to worry about someone following her and attempting to attack or kidnap her.

While she was with Drakkal, Shay felt like she could overcome anything this city threw at her. And it was nice to let her guard down a little. It was nice to have someone watching her back. To have someone she could depend on.

Getting a little ahead of yourself there, Shay. You barely know the guy.

With a faint shuddering, the elevator began its ascent.

Regardless, she had a feeling that Drakkal was what her father had called *good people*. That he *could* be trusted. It had been a long time since she'd known someone like that.

The elevator jerked and stuttered, metal grinding and screeching. Shay threw out a hand to steady herself, but before her hand touched the wall, she found herself enveloped in azhera. Drakkal had wrapped his big arms around her and drawn her against his chest, leaning forward to shield her body with his. He was solid and steady. Warmth cocooned her, and she readily inhaled his spicy scent.

"I've got you, *kiraia*," he said, his voice a low rumble that she felt as much as heard.

Shay cleared her throat and patted his chest, barely resisting the urge to run her palm over the hard muscle beneath his shirt. *Fuck me, this male is ripped.* "It, uh, does that a lot."

The elevator stabilized, but it took Drakkal a few seconds to release his hold on her. Not that she minded. She actually... liked it. A lot. She liked his heat, his solidness, liked the way his arms embraced her and the feel of his strong, rough hands on her body. It was doing all kinds of funny things inside her. Funny, *pleasurable* things.

When he finally stepped back, she glanced up at his face to find his pupils thinned to slits and his ears forward. His tail whipped through the air behind him, its movements fluid but restless.

"Still, Shay...I've got you."

Somehow, those words found their way into her chest, sparking a warm, fluttering ache. Shay lifted a hand to rub at it.

Not a second later, she felt a little kick in her belly. She could imagine her baby giving her a nudge and saying, *Well, Mom?*

"Um, thanks," she replied.

Yeah, that was totally not *awkward sounding. What the hell, Shay?*

The lift came to a grinding halt, and the doors noisily slid open. Shay hurried out. It felt like things were moving too fast with Drakkal, but it was only her *lack* of alarm about it that worried her. Unfortunately, the move into the hallway did not bring an improvement in environment.

"Aww, hell," she muttered.

Two males were fist-fighting in the middle of the corridor, and *of course* they were between the elevator and Shay's apartment door. They were both big—something she was getting used to by now—and they didn't seem to be taking it easy on one another. The larger of the two was a naked four-armed onigox who looked to be at least a head taller than Drakkal. The other was one of her neighbors, the cren named Ostik—just as tall as his opponent, but leaner, with a pair of tusks jutting up from his lower jaw.

The onigox seemed to have the advantage, though Ostik was dishing out a good deal of punishment despite his foe's greater mass and extra set of limbs.

A female cren—Zira—stood a meter or two away from the combatants, her eyes fixed on the melee. She looked far more excited than concerned.

The two cren lived in the apartment two doors down from hers. Whenever Shay heard neighbors arguing—or fucking—it was usually these Ostik and Zira. She'd never seen the onigox before, but her gut-feeling speculation here was that Zira hadn't *only* been fucking the Ostik.

Drakkal growled and stepped around Shay.

"What are you doing?" she asked.

He turned his head to look at her. "Your apartment is down the hall."

"Yeah."

"So why would we stop here?"

"We're not. But you got all growly and stepped in front of me, so…" She shrugged, hands out, palms up.

Ostik kicked the onigox and launched himself at his larger opponent with a roar, slamming him into the wall.

Drakkal shifted his attention back to the fight, lifted his hands, and tugged off his coat. He handed it to Shay. "Yeah, because I know how situations like this usually go."

Shay accepted the coat and watched as he stalked forward, unable but to focus on his ass in those tight, black pants, and the hypnotizing sway of his tail. He really, *really* had a nice ass.

Stop it, Shay. Eyes up.

Before Drakkal reached the fighting males, Zira pushed herself away from the wall and approached him. Her yellow eyes were intent upon the azhera, and a flirtatious smile had curved her lips. She was dressed only in lingerie, similar to a baby doll nightie, its fabric sheer and glimmering—and it left nothing to the imagination regarding the body beneath. She had long, toned limbs and supple blue skin. Her tall, athletic figure made Shay feel even smaller and more inadequate, especially with the bowling ball that had taken residence in her belly.

Sorry, Baby. I don't mean that.

The female cren seemed totally unbothered by the green moisture dripping down her inner thighs.

Shay cringed.

Oh, her man definitely *just walked in on her in bed with that onigox.*

"Azhera," Zira purred, reaching out to brush her fingers down Drakkal's arm. "You look like you need a rough fuck."

What. The fuck?

Shay narrowed her eyes and took a step forward. Something burned in her chest, something hot and lethal, something she couldn't identify—but it definitely wasn't heartburn. This discomfort wasn't a result of her pregnancy.

She curled her hands into fists, squeezing Drakkal's coat. She wanted—needed—to hit something. And that something was the female easing closer to Drakkal, about to press her nasty, splooge-covered body against him.

"Bitch, back off," Shay snapped.

Startled, Zira looked at Shay as though just noticing her presence.

Drakkal glared at the female cren, who'd taken hold of his arm with both hands. Voice barely more than a low growl, he said, "*She* is my female, and I will not hold her back if you choose to disobey her."

She is my female.

An entirely different heat bloomed in Shay at the sound of his claim.

Whoa! Simmer down, Shay. No one is claiming anyone.

...Right?

Zira chuckled. "I don't mind sharing."

"Never would've guessed it," Drakkal muttered.

"Zira!"

Shay looked past Drakkal at the female to see Ostik—he was the one who'd spoken—and his onigox opponent now separated by a few meters of space. Both were battered and bloody, their postures hunched with chests and shoulders heaving. They were glaring at Drakkal now, as though his presence had given them a common enemy.

Ostik's eyebrows fell low. "I saw you here yesterday, azhera. Are you with my female, too?"

"*Kraasz ka'val.*" Drakkal shook off the female cren. "I did not come here for a fight."

Zira stumbled back and bumped into the wall.

Drakkal kept his focus on the other two males. Though he didn't assume any sort of fighting stance, Shay noted the slight change of his posture—he sank just a touch lower, shifting his muscles into a ready position, the claws on his right hand extended by half a centimeter or so, and his mane bristled.

"Damn it," Shay said. Striding forward, she grabbed Drakkal's right arm and settled her gaze on the male cren. "He isn't fucking your woman because he's fucking me. Now get the fuck back and let us through. Then you can get back to knocking the piss out of each other. Or, maybe, you accept that she's playing you both and kick her to the curb."

She gave Drakkal's arm a tug as she continued forward, past the males gaping at her and the female glaring at her. Drakkal's powerful muscles were tense, but he offered no resistance.

When they reached Shay's door, she shoved her hand into her pocket, withdrew her keycard, and held it up to the reader. The door whisked open. She stepped inside, pulling Drakkal in after her.

As soon as the door closed, she released him, glanced over her shoulder, and pointed at him. "No funny business."

His brows fell, and he frowned. "What's that supposed to mean?"

"It means behave yourself." Shay walked over to the table to drape Drakkal's coat over one of the chairs before removing her hair tie. She massaged her scalp as her hair fell loose. Putting one hand on the table for balance, she kicked off her boots. Once her feet were free, she sighed and wiggled her toes.

They'd had to stop twice so Shay could relieve herself on their way here from the restaurant. Thankfully, she didn't have to pee now. Drakkal hadn't complained, but *she* was tired of going all the damned time.

He followed her into the room, though he left a couple meters between them. "Why behave? I just heard we're fucking now."

Shay turned to face him, ready to put him in his place if he really thought her words in the hall had meant anything, but stopped when she saw the amusement—and traces of heat—in his eyes. She smirked. "You wish, azhera."

"Yeah, I do," he replied.

His gaze lingered on her for a moment before he turned away to study her little apartment, walking slowly as he examined everything—not that there was much to see. At least it spared her the embarrassment of him seeing her reaction to his words—the way her skin flushed, the way she squeezed her thighs together to ease the ache of her clenching pussy. The heat that had been in his voice, in his eyes, paired with his total lack of hesitation in answering...

I'm too damn horny for this. I'm blaming the pregnancy hormones. It has to be the hormones.

"So?" she prompted, desperate to change the subject.

"I'm willing any time, *kiraia*," he said, continuing his slow perusal of her apartment.

"Azhera, you know that's not what I meant."

When he didn't immediately answer, Shay frowned and glanced around the apartment. The place was already familiar; she knew it wasn't much to look at, knew it was a dump. That was no fault of her own. But she still couldn't stop the shame that was pulsing up the back of her neck now, feeling like flames spreading over her skin.

She cared about what Drakkal thought. She didn't want him to look at her any differently now that he'd been in her apartment, now that he was *really* seeing it.

You're acting like a teenager, Shay. Get your shit together.

She pulled out a chair and eased herself onto it. "Tell me all about your super-secret criminal career."

Drakkal leaned close to the wall and scratched at a stain with a claw—one of many that had been present when she moved in and would likely be present long after she was dead. He scowled and made a decidedly disapproving grunt before turning and walking toward the table. Before he reached the empty chair, his eyes flicked to her pallet, and he paused, tilting his head. He gave her a questioning glance and stepped over to her bed.

Her brows drew down. "What?"

He bent down and snatched up his coat from atop her pallet. He looked at her over his shoulder after he straightened, holding her gaze as he slowly—*so* slowly—raised the jacket to his nose. His nostrils flared with an inhalation, and his eyelids drifted shut. He made a low, rumbling sound that was somewhere between a growl and a purr. A damned *purr*.

I think I just came.

Shay suddenly recalled how she'd started her morning.

Eyes wide, she leapt from her chair and crossed the room, holding out a hand. "Give me that!"

Keeping the jacket raised, Drakkal turned away from her, shielding the garment with his body. "You sure you want to waste time talking, Shay?"

"It's not wasting time," she said, standing on her toes and leaning against him as she reached for the jacket. "Now give me back my jacket!"

"Can't. Smells too good." He turned toward Shay just enough for her to see him rub the fabric against his cheek and draw in another deep breath.

How could she be so mortified and turned on all at once?

"I'll give it to you if you promise to wear it for me again," he finally said.

Shay stepped back, held her hand out, and glared up at him. "Fine. Give it to me and I'll put it on."

The visible corner of his mouth lifted in a devilish smirk that displayed one of his wicked fangs. "*Only* this."

Make that mortified, amused, and fucking *aroused*.

She wasn't used to this kind of playfulness, and never would've expected it from Drakkal...but it was a *very* good look on him.

And it was also a distraction from the true purpose of his visit—he'd come to offer her work and a safe place to live. She needed to know that she could trust him, that she wasn't going to get involved in something she'd regret. She couldn't make that mistake again.

Keeping her gaze locked with his, she curled her lips in a sensual smile and leaned forward, letting her hair fall around her face. She beckoned him with a finger. "Here kitty, kitty, kitty."

Drakkal's ears perked, and he finally lowered the jacket and turned to face her. Though surprise and suspicion crept into his expression, they were overpowered by the desire still burning in his eyes. "I don't like being called *kitty*," he said as he took a step toward her, but his voice was sultry instead of annoyed.

She lifted her chin and stared up at him with hooded eyes. "Yes, you do."

He hummed thoughtfully and came to a stop immediately in front of her. "Only when you say it, *kiraia*."

Shay lifted a hand and settled it on his cheek. The fur beneath her palm was softer than she'd anticipated. His eyelids drooped, and his lips parted. She slid her hand along the back of his neck and into the thicker fur of his mane. A shudder traveled from his body into hers, accompanied by another of those rumbling purrs.

"Good," she said softly, easing closer. "Then you'll also like it when I say you'd been a *bad* kitty." Curling her fingers into a fist, she gave his mane a yank.

He winced, and the noise that emerged from him was somehow a snarl and a hiss at once. Before he could recover, she snatched the jacket out of his hand, released her hold on his mane, and retreated from him, dropping a hand to rest over the blaster on her hip.

The pain on his face quickly gave way to an amused smirk —as though he'd not really been hurt at all.

"If you don't want to rut, you shouldn't be teasing me like this," he said in a husky voice.

The tension eased from her as soon as she realized he wasn't going to retaliate. She stared at him questioningly, unable to shake her lingering wariness, before returning to her chair. She sat with the jacket folded protectively over her lap and both arms atop it, one hand clamped on the fabric.

The remembered feel of his soft fur, his heat, lingered on her palm.

"Enough playing around, azhera," she said. Things were getting too...relaxed with him. "Spill it. What do you do?"

He approached slowly; despite his leisurely pace, he put off the air of a predator confidently stalking its prey. Shay couldn't stop her eyes from dipping to the prominent bulge at his crotch —which was definitely larger than it had been a few moments ago. Her core clenched as the fires in her belly roared to new heights. She tightened her hold on the jacket.

Fuck. Me.

Focus Shay!

She wrenched her gaze from his groin and forced her eyes to his.

Drakkal's grin had only widened—fully baring his sexy fangs—by the time he reached the empty chair across from her and sat down. His expression said *I know what you're thinking, Shay. I can smell it.*

"I run a forgery operation with my partner," he said. "I handle security and logistics; he does the forging."

"Forging what?"

"Identification chips. He's very thorough. We haven't had a single chip flagged by the Consortium as fake. Which is surprising, given how often he has his head up his own ass."

Shay arched a brow. The mirth with which Drakkal had spoken told her there really wasn't any bad blood between him and his partner. "That's it? You make fake IDs?"

"Yeah, that's it as far as our day-to-day." He tilted his head and folded his big arms across his chest. The stance would've seemed standoffish on most people, but Drakkal gave it a casualness that should've been impossible given his size and appearance. "We've had to break a few other laws from time to time. It's inevitable. But the ID chips are our only criminal enterprise."

"So...no drugs, sex trafficking, or contract killing?"

Drakkal shook his head. "Never killed anyone for money."

"But you do kill people."

"I have. Probably will have to again."

"Did they deserve it?"

"Some of them did."

Shay frowned. "And the others?"

Separating his arms, Drakkal leaned forward and rested his elbows on the table. The move strengthened the shadows on his face just enough to create a faint, reflected glow in his eyes. "Depends on who you ask."

Shay lifted her arms from her lap and folded them on the table. "I'm asking you."

"Some of them didn't. Some of them were...almost friends. But the rest either threatened me or the people I cared about, so it doesn't matter to me whether they deserved it or not."

She nodded. "And the rest? The drugs and sex trafficking."

"No and fuck no."

The vehemence in his words and the disgust in his voice made Shay's lips twitch upward, but more than anything, it relieved her.

"And what are you offering me?" she asked.

His eyes dipped to take her in, and his tongue slipped out from between his dark lips for an instant. He parted those lips as though to speak but hesitated before finally saying, "Work. I don't know what you used to do, but you can clearly handle yourself."

"Not as easily as I used to," she said, dropping a hand to pat her belly. "My dad was in the military, and he taught me some tricks when I was a kid." *More than a few tricks. He taught me* everything. "There was a time in my life when I was...making bad decisions. I ended up in the middle of a lot of shit, and those skills kept me alive through all of it. But I don't want that kind of life anymore. I don't want that for my baby. It's too dangerous, and I'm trying to do things the right way."

"What I'm offering is less dangerous than your life now," Drakkal said with surprising gentleness. "I know you don't need to be reminded, but where are you now? Alone with limited funds in a shitty building in a rough sector. No ID chip. A cub on the way. I met your landlord. He'll sell you out at the first opportunity—that's how I found your apartment yesterday. And places like this are lucrative for bounty hunters who earn their livings by bringing in illegals. It's only a matter of time before one of them comes for you, or before one of your neighbors decides they want a taste of terran.

"My crew isn't like that. We trust each other, we protect each other. We're a family. I know how that sounds—"

"Yeah, it sounds like what every gang leader says before he puts a bullet in someone's head."

"But it's *not* like that, Shay." He shifted his hands toward her, one metal, one flesh, and turned his palms up. "Most of my people are former military...or were slaves who won their freedom however they had to. We all understand what it means to be betrayed, and we're not the kind who'd do it to one another."

Shay stared at his hands. His left hand was sleek black metal with glowing red highlights, its segmented pieces similar in shape and proportion to his flesh and blood hand. This wasn't the armored limb he'd been wearing when he chased her on Orcus Street. His right hand was the rough, strong hand of a seasoned fighter, its relatively dark, calloused skin crossed by a few pale scars. His three fingers and thumb were thick and powerful, each tipped with a long, hooked claw that should've instilled fear in her. He didn't need weapons to kill; he *was* a weapon. But his hands were inviting, nonetheless.

She clamped her fingers around her forearms to keep from placing her hands in his.

"I'll give you a spot on my security team," he said. "Mostly they just sit around and play Conquerors or watch sappy Volturian dramas. The pay is good, and room and board are included. I'll even buy you lunch every now and then. And I promise you, Shay—"

She lifted her gaze and met his.

"—you and your cub will be protected. You won't have to put yourself in any danger to earn your pay."

"Why?" she asked, brows dropping low. Deep down, she knew he was being honest, and that she could trust him, but doubt still whispered in the back of her mind. His offer was too good to be true. There had to be some ulterior motive here, something he *wasn't* saying. "Why are you doing this for me?"

He searched her face for several seconds, and her heart quickened beneath his intense stare. She couldn't guess what he was thinking, couldn't guess what he was going to say—and never could have anticipated the next words out of his mouth.

"Because you're my mate, Shay."

It took several seconds for Shay to register those words, for them to make any sense, because there was no way they could be true—and what did they really mean, anyway? Maybe she'd just heard him wrong. Maybe her pregnancy was fucking with her hearing, because he couldn't have just said what she thought he'd said.

"What?"

"You are my mate," he repeated. "My every instinct is drawn toward you. It started the moment I first picked up your scent in Foltham's, even if I didn't know what it meant right away."

Shay stood up abruptly, knocking her chair backward onto the floor. "The fuck you say?"

Mate? *Mate?* Like an animal sniffing out its selected female?

She retreated a few steps and pointed at him. "But you're an *azhera*! You're all...hairy and werewolfy and whatever, and I'm...I'm *human*."

He furrowed his brow. "What does *werewolfy* mean?"

"It's like...like you, kind of. Part wolf, part man, all mixed together. But that's not what we're talking about right now!"

"I thought I looked more like a cat," he muttered dejectedly.

Shay narrowed her eyes on him. "Again, that's beside the point."

Drakkal leaned back, and the chair creaked and wobbled

beneath his weight. "Doesn't matter what I am or what you are, apart from you being my mate. I haven't tried to hide that I want you. But I'm not asking you to accept it, terran. You will, eventually, but I won't force it."

Shay shifted her stance, uncertain of what to say. He was so sure that she would accept that she was...*his*. Like she belonged to him.

Would it be so bad to be his? To have him as a protector, as a provider?

Damn it, I can provide for myself!

Yeah, she could, but at what cost to her and her baby? Why make it harder when he was offering her...*everything*?

Drakkal placed his hands on his knees and pushed himself to his feet. He stepped around the table, righted the chair she'd knocked over, and picked up the jacket that'd fallen off her lap —the one she'd stolen from him. He draped the garment over the chair's backrest.

"If I don't accept?" she asked, unable to look away from him.

"I'm still going to look out for you and your cub." He took a step forward, and though it seemed such a small move for him, it devoured the distance that had served as the last buffer between them. He lifted his right hand and reached for her face, hesitating briefly as though to give her a chance to retreat. When she remained still, he tentatively settled his hand on her cheek.

His palm was rough and warm, but she couldn't let herself admit how good it felt. She couldn't let herself show how starved for affection she was by leaning into his touch.

"There were a lot of people locked away down in Foltham's zoo," Drakkal said in a low voice, "and I felt for every one of them. But when he showed me you, I *recognized* you. I had to act. I had no choice. I needed to get you out of there, needed you to be free...needed to have you. And even if you had shot me afterward, I would've chosen to get you out of there again and again."

He stroked his big thumb over her cheekbone, and the tip of its claw brushed back a few strands of her hair. "Think about my offer. Like I said, it's not contingent on you accepting that you're my mate."

All Shay could do was nod.

Drakkal lingered for a moment, an oddly sad smile on his lips, before lowering his hand. She felt its loss immediately.

"Let me know what you decide," he said as he turned, scooped up his coat, and walked to the door. He swung the coat on as he moved. "That way I know whether I can stop stalking you or not."

"Totally creepy, azhera," she said, one corner of her mouth quirking despite her inner turmoil.

He pressed the control button, and the door slid open. He paused there and glanced at her over his shoulder. "It's my job to keep my partner and our operation safe. But it's my purpose to keep you safe, *kiraia*. I'll be nearby if you need anything."

With that, he walked into the hallway. The door closed a few seconds later, but Drakkal's presence—and his intoxicating scent—lingered in the apartment long after he'd left.

She was torn. Though her instincts told her Drakkal could be trusted, her gut hadn't always been right in the past.

But this feels different.

It did, and that scared the crap out of her. She'd made some bad—*really* bad—decisions in her life, and she couldn't afford any more. She had her baby to worry about. Yet nothing about Drakkal made her feel like accepting his offer would be a mistake. This...could be her one and only chance. A chance to give her baby a good, safe life.

As for Drakkal claiming her as his mate...

That both freaked her out and intrigued her. She wasn't disgusted by him—obviously not, considering her body's reaction to him—but he was...different.

There'd been people in the gang she'd run with back on Earth who'd considered azheras nothing more than walking, talking animals. Some humans had been ostracized for associating with aliens, and the treatment was sometimes worse for those who became physically involved with nonhumans. Shay had seen people beaten, tortured, and killed, all because they'd allowed themselves to feel for something *other*.

But that wasn't the case here in Arthos, and she'd be lying to herself if she claimed she didn't feel something when Drakkal looked at her, when he touched her.

And it wouldn't have made a damn difference to her on Earth, either. She would never have let someone else dictate how she should feel or live her life, and if she wanted an azhera as her man, then she'd damn well have him.

But did she?

Shay settled her palm over her cheek, wishing that it was Drakkal's rough, scarred there hand instead.

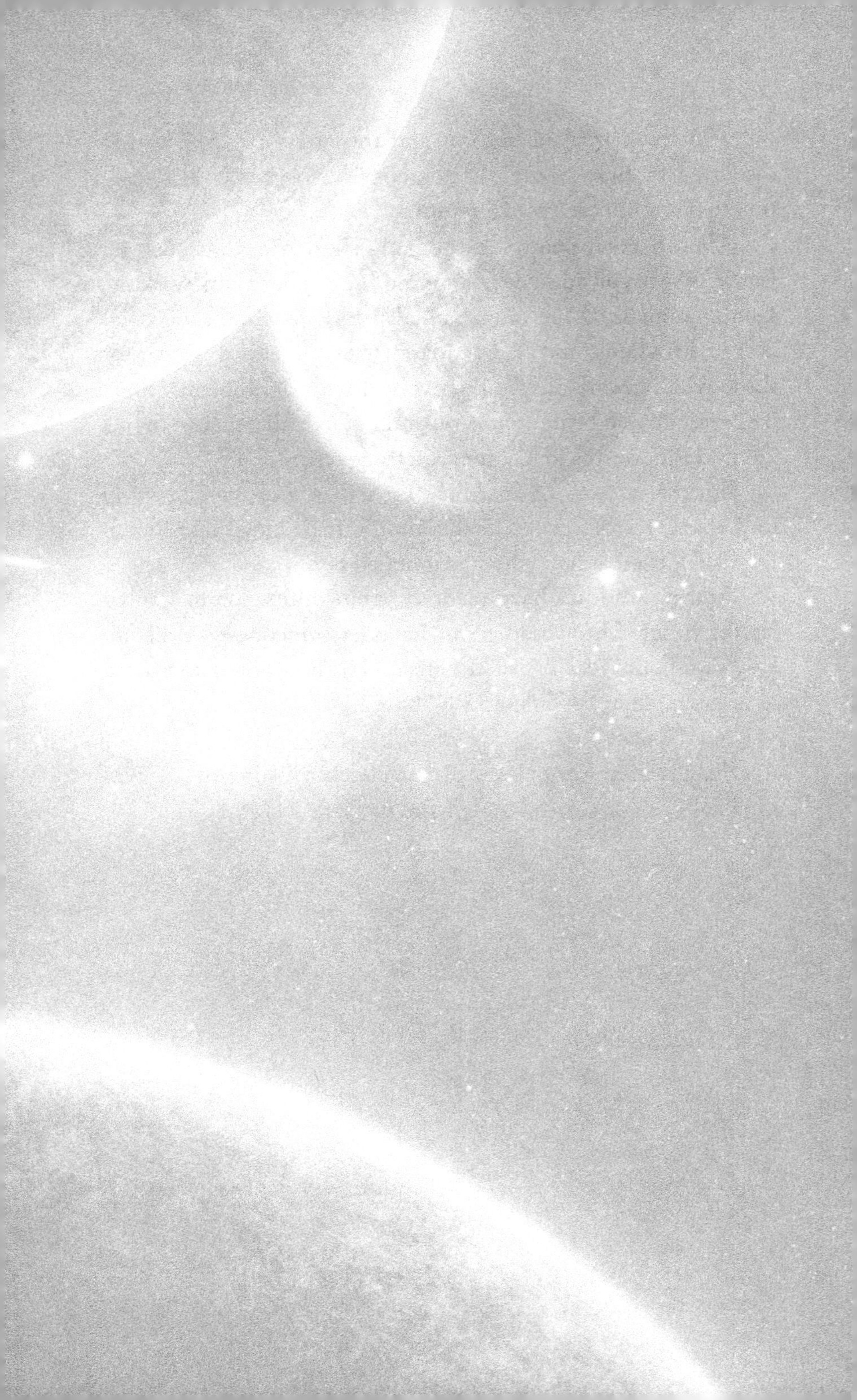

ELEVEN

Drakkal took a swig of *gurosh*, hoping the fiery-sweet beverage would help force his attention back to the here and now—if only for long enough to complete his turn and keep the game moving. He understood the rules and gameplay of Conquerors well, even if he'd never been quite as good as a few of the people he usually played with, but he was struggling tonight. The gameboard—a large holographic map depicted in hexagons of varying elevation and pattern—made little sense to him, and the colors on it, which marked the territory claimed by Drakkal and his opponents, seemed to bleed together.

It would have been easy to tell himself he was just feeling off, but he knew the real reason for his distraction.

Shay.

"Come on, azhera," Arcanthus whispered. "How are we supposed to beat Sam if your head's not in the game?"

Samantha, who was seated to Arcanthus's right, turned her head toward him and narrowed her eyes. "Is that how it is?"

Arcanthus's mouth fell open, dragging his brows down

along with it. "And what exactly are you accusing me of, my flower?"

A mischievous smirk lit upon Sam's lips. "Being bad at Conquerors and secretly plotting against your mate."

Urgand, the vorgal sitting to Drakkal's left, sucked in a sharp breath. "I'd better go get my medkit."

"Why's that?" Arc asked, frowning with exaggerated hurt in his eyes.

"She just bludgeoned you with the truth."

Warm laughter erupted around the table, even from the big cren, Razi, who never seemed to take his attention off the board when he was playing Conquerors. Drakkal joined in, grateful for anything that could take his mind off Shay, even if it was only for a few moments.

Drakkal finally selected a holographic card from his hand and placed it on the board. Two of the empty hexagons bordering the one upon which he'd played his piece changed to his color—a muddy orange brown. The majority of map, as usual, was divided between Sam's and Razi's colors.

"The *gurosh* is hitting you hard tonight, Drakkal?" asked Sekk'thi, the female ilthurii seated beside Sam.

"Just more fun to get a rise out of the sedhi by throwing the game," Drakkal replied with a smirk.

"We had a deal." Arcanthus shot Drakkal a glare as he reached out and made his own play. He set his card down without looking—directly beside one of Sam's hexes. Arc's card changed to her color, crimson.

"Maybe you should pay attention to what you're doing, Arc," Drakkal said.

Samantha, Urgand, and Sekk'thi laughed.

Arcanthus turned his head toward the board and grumbled, "Damn it. I knew I shouldn't have let you use my favorite color, Samantha. It was bad luck."

"For you," Samantha said with a snicker. She didn't take her eyes off her mate as she reached forward and placed down her own card without hesitation. Four spaces—four of *Arc's* spaces—flipped to crimson.

Impossibly, Arc's look of feigned indignation only strengthened. "Give me another *gurosh*. If I'm going down, I'm going to enjoy it however I can."

Razi produced a fresh bottle of the stuff and passed it across the table to Arcanthus as Sekk'thi assessed her options.

"She is your master in the game, sedhi." Sekk'thi tilted her head and shuffled her holographic cards, choosing one from her hand and placing it on the dwindling unclaimed space. "We must assume she is in control elsewhere, as well."

The innuendo implicit in her tone produced smirks from everyone but Samantha herself; the terran looked down, her cheeks pinkening.

"Samantha is my master whenever and wherever she chooses," Arcanthus replied smoothly, sliding a hand onto her thigh. "Hence the installation of sound dampeners in our bedroom and workshop."

"Just need them in every other room and we can all sleep in peace," Urgand said.

Samantha's cheeks darkened to a red that rivaled her color on the gameboard, though there was a soft, loving smile on her lips as she peeked at Arcanthus from the corner of her eye.

Arcanthus grinned. "I strive to please. Samantha, that is. Not the rest of you."

"I *do* lead him around by a leash, after all," Samantha said.

Though it didn't diminish his amusement, Drakkal felt for Arcanthus in that moment—and was even a bit envious. All Drakkal wanted to do was please his mate. But Shay needed to choose him first.

"About time someone put him in his place," Drakkal said with a chuckle.

Arcanthus's grin took on a fiendish slant. "Just wait, azhera. It'll be you in a collar eventually. I already picked out a nice one to gift your lucky female."

"No collar for me, sedhi," Drakkal replied, baring his fangs in a grin of his own. "My female will need a saddle." Saying those words aloud conjured a mental image of Shay riding astride him, her golden hair unbound around her pale shoulders, and her delectable breasts bared to his hungry gaze. It sent a jolt of heat straight to his cock.

Razi—looking much too large for his seat—leaned forward and continued his careful examination of the gameboard with a furrowed brow. "Where are you going to find a saddle small enough for your hand?" he asked casually.

For a moment, silence reigned around the table. Drakkal stared at Razi. Though he was sharp, the big cren rarely took part in such banter; he often caught everyone off guard when he offered insults like that.

Arcanthus broke into laughter so intense that it began almost soundlessly, and he was quickly joined by Urgand and Sekk'thi. Only Samantha restrained herself, pressing her lips together to contain laughter that shook her shoulders. At least she had the decency to cover her mouth and hide some of her mirth.

Drakkal's attempt to hold in his own laughter resulted in a snort. "*Kraasz ka'val,* Razi. If your head weren't so hard, I'd knock some sense into you," he said with a grin.

For what might've been the first time that evening, Razi looked away from the game to meet Drakkal's gaze. He was smirking around his pronounced tusks. "Afraid you'll break your hand?"

"Yeah, and I don't want to spend a night all alone," Drakkal replied.

That only intensified the laughter from the others. This time Samantha joined in, too.

Razi finally made his move, and Urgand, who'd carved out his own respectable little pocket of territory, placed a card decisively once the cren was done.

A faint buzzing ran through Drakkal's neural link with his prosthesis, and an instant later, his holocom chimed with an incoming call. He often received calls from the security team—usually to report that there was nothing to report, just the way he preferred it—so he didn't bother checking the comm ID on the display. He quickly chose a card and played it.

Two of Arcanthus's hexes flipped to Drakkal's orange brown.

"This is what all our years of friendship mean to you?" Arcanthus demanded.

"Quite whining, cub," Drakkal said as he lifted his left arm and accepted the call. "Yeah?"

"I'm in. Pick me up tonight."

The call disconnected before his distracted mind fully registered what had just happened. He knew that voice, he'd been waiting to hear it, but that didn't ease the shock of Shay calling him.

I'm in.

Was that simply an acceptance of the offer he'd made her yesterday, or was it something more? She'd looked at him several times with unmasked desire in her eyes. Had she finally decided to accept her attraction to him? Had she decided to accept...*him*?

Thinking into it too much, Drak. She's accepting the job, not me...not yet.

Silence reclaimed control of the room, causing Drakkal to

realize that he'd not used his earpiece. Everyone had overheard the brief call. All of them—even Razi, who normally *appeared* disinterested—were staring at Drakkal intently, questions brimming in their eyes.

"Who was that?" Samantha asked.

Arcanthus leaned forward, propping his arms on the table. "And what is she in on?"

Sam's eyes brightened, and her voice filled with excitement. "She's human, isn't she? She sounded human."

"Since when do females call you?" Urgand asked. "Apart from Sekk'thi."

"I do not count," Sekk'thi said.

"Oh, you count. Just not for him." Urgand grinned; for a moment, the heat in his eyes was reflected in Sekk'thi's.

Vrek'osh, what is going on here?

"Are you bringing her here?" Samantha asked.

"Yes, *are* you bringing her here?" Arcanthus echoed.

"Can I answer a single damned question before you ask twenty more?" Drakkal demanded.

Arcanthus turned to smirk at Samantha. "It must be that human Drakkal's grown fond of."

Samantha's brow furrowed. "Wait...the one who *robbed* him?"

"A terran robbed Drakkal?" Urgand asked incredulously. "You're never going to hear the end of it from Thargen, azhera."

"I'm aware of that," Drakkal grumbled. "Now if you'll all shut the fuck up—except for you Sam, you're fine—I'll tell you what's going on."

Sam flashed him a toothy grin.

For a few moments, Drakkal relished the quiet, though it didn't do much to help him collect his thoughts.

"It is the same terran," he finally said. "I freed her from a zoo in the Gilded Sector a few weeks ago, and she robbed me once we got out."

"Took the clothes right off his back," Arcanthus added, absently brushing his cybernetic fingers down Samantha's hair.

"So glad you're here to add in the juicy details," Drakkal muttered.

"So far she sounds like the kind of female Thargen would appreciate," said Razi.

An unbridled, involuntary snarl rose from Drakkal's chest, and the claws of his right hand gouged the table as tension seized his muscles. "She's *mine*."

Five sets of wide eyes stared at Drakkal; he met each of his friend's gazes one at a time.

"Just want to make sure that's clear from the outset," he said, forcing his lips into a more neutral expression and dropping his hand onto his thigh. "Her name is Shay. She's been struggling to make her way in the city."

"And she's coming here?" Samantha asked. "Tonight?"

"Yes. I offered her a job, and she accepted. She's joining the security team."

"I'm sorry, what was that?" Arcanthus leaned back and cocked his head to the side, eyebrows slanted down. "I thought we're supposed to discuss personnel matters before any decisions are made?"

"I only say that because I can't trust you to make thoughtful decisions," Drakkal replied.

"That's not fair at all, azhera. You're bringing someone into our home, someone the rest of us don't know, and—"

Arcanthus snapped his mouth shut when Drakkal pointedly shifted his eyes toward Samantha.

The sedhi looked at his mate, frowned, and drew in a deep breath before saying, "That was an entirely different situation."

Drakkal shook his head and folded his arms across his chest. "Samantha's your mate. Shay is mine."

Arcanthus lifted a finger and opened his mouth to speak, but he hesitated before any words came out. "All right. But let me point out, Drakkal, that Samantha didn't rob me when we first met."

"Point noted, sedhi. Doesn't change anything."

"Oh my God, I can't believe this. Drak has a *mate!*" Samantha pushed her chair back and stood. "She'll need a room...um, unless she's staying with you?"

Drakkal's tongue slipped out and ran over his suddenly dry lips. His ears drooped. "She, uh...hasn't exactly agreed to anything but the job, so far..."

Sekk'thi leaned back in her chair and cackled. "A terran is giving you trouble, Drakkal?"

"If only you knew," he muttered.

"I'll get a room ready for her," Sam said.

Drakkal nodded and offered Samantha a gentle smile. "Is there anything extra she'll need? She's carrying a cub."

"Huh? A cub?"

He lowered a hand to his stomach. "A...baby."

Sam's mouth dropped open. "She's... You... *Already?*"

"You azhera have strange ways if you make younglings before accepting one another as mates," Sekk'thi said.

"I'm not the cub's sire," Drakkal said. The irritation creeping into his voice wasn't because he was not the cub's father, but because he wanted to be—whether tied by blood or not.

"How far along is she?" Sam asked.

Drakkal shook his head and shrugged. "Don't know. Not really sure how to judge it with terrans."

Urgand sighed. "I guess it's a good thing Arcanthus has had me studying terran medicine."

"You should be proud that you're expanding your knowledge," Arcanthus said.

The vorgal narrowed his gaze on Arcanthus. "I believe I was promised a bonus in exchange for the extracurricular studies, *boss*."

"Isn't the work itself a reward?"

A mischievous light sparked in Urgand's eyes, and he grinned. "I suppose it can be, considering the body parts I'll get to see."

Arcanthus's expression fell. Something sank in Drakkal's stomach even as fire flared in his chest, accompanied by a tightness that threatened to seize his heart and lungs.

"*What?*" Arc and Drak demanded in unison.

Samantha cleared her throat and eased toward the door. "I'm...going to get that room ready now." She hurried out of the room, and the door slid shut behind her.

Sekk'thi shifted in her chair. There was a thump under the table, and Urgand jumped in his seat, legs bumping the table's underside and rattling everything atop it. Without betraying any emotion on his face, Razi reached out with both hands and caught several *gurosh* bottles before they could topple over.

Sekk'thi jabbed a finger at Urgand. "Behave. I will not step in if you provoke them."

"I was joking. Just didn't realize it was in such poor taste until the words were out of my mouth," Urgand said, scooting his chair away from the table—and from the end of Sekk'thi's lashing tail. "Of course, everything will be in the capacity of a medical professional. What did you think, I'm just going to coach her through birth over a commlink?"

Irrational anger, Drakkal told himself. *There's no logical thought behind this.*

The tightness and heat in his chest didn't diminish.

Arcanthus closed his eyes and ran a hand over his face.

"Why didn't I consider this before I asked you to look into it, Urgand?"

"You will both just have to get over your instincts so your females can be cared for," Sekk'thi said, sweeping her gaze from Arcanthus to Drakkal before settling it on Urgand. "And *you* will need to keep their feelings in mind as you work."

"My patients are my priority," Urgand said, frowning at Arcanthus and Drakkal, "but I understand. I'll...choose my words with more care, since you're all a bunch of oversensitive dicks."

Urgand's comment drew chuckles from the people gathered around the table, even Arc and Drakkal. Drakkal's irritation faded slowly.

"Guess this means the game's over," Razi said, shattering the silence. "You all lose again." He leaned forward and swept the credit chips piled beneath the board toward the others stacked neatly in front of him.

Arcanthus turned his attention to the cren. "Slow down, Razi. Sam had the biggest section of the board. That means she gets the biggest portion of the pool."

Razi lifted a hand, palm toward the ceiling, and shrugged. "But she left the game. She forfeits."

"Well, none of us forfeited," Arcanthus said.

Razi arched a brow. "Do you really think you have to? Might as well save us all some time."

Arcanthus sighed and threw his hands up. "When you're right, you're right. All for the best, though"—he rose from his seat and slapped Drakkal on the shoulder—"since it'll give me more time to help Drakkal look his best before he picks up his *mate*."

Drakkal leveled a skeptical gaze on Arcanthus. "Look my best, sedhi? I'm already doing that. All day, every day. That's why you can't take your eyes off me."

Arcanthus caught his lower lip between his fangs as his center eye dipped, raking over Drakkal. "Old friend, it's about time someone explained it to you—you look like something the cat dragged in."

"Fuck you, Arcanthus."

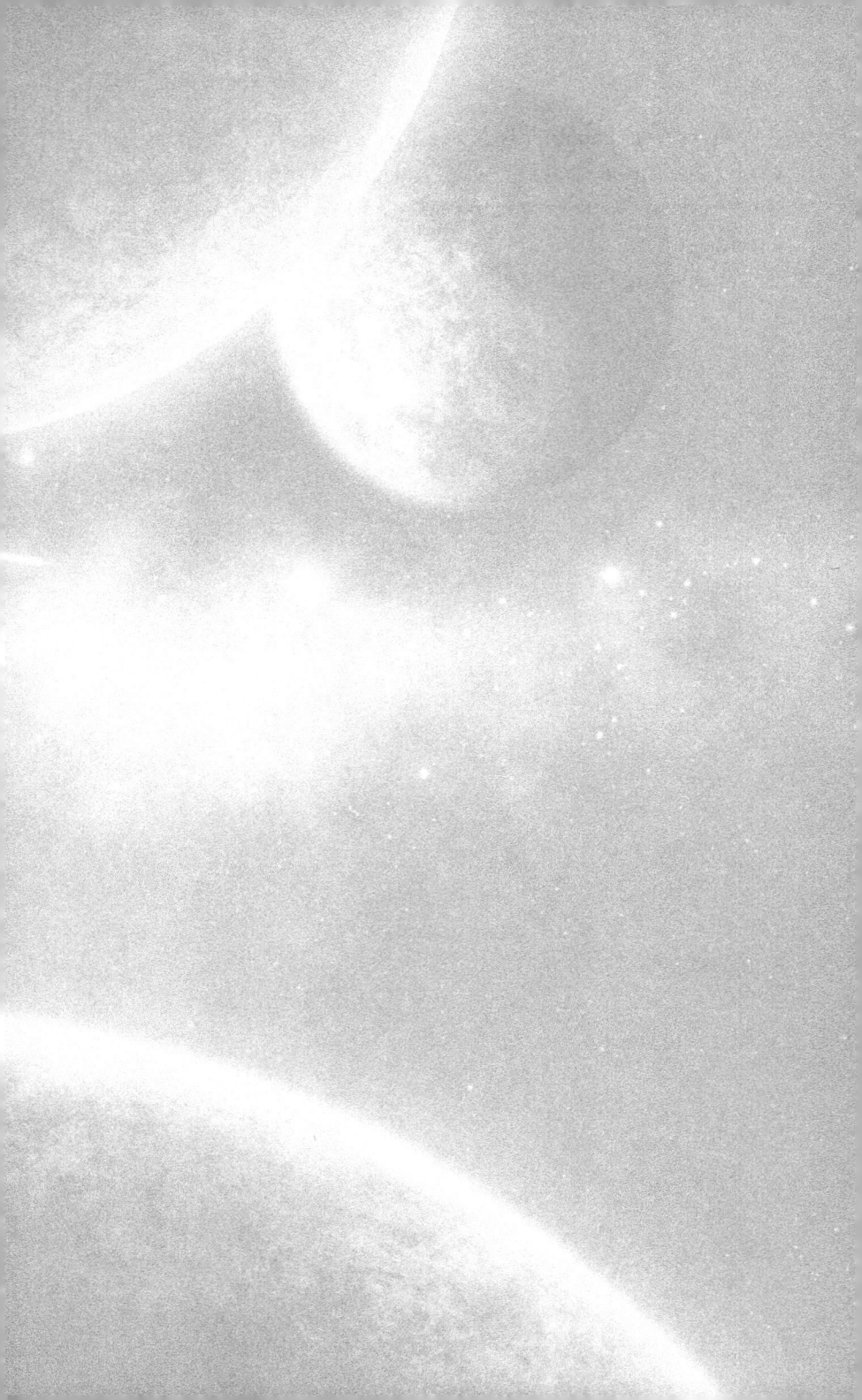

TWELVE

One bag. That was all it took to fit everything Shay owned—one measly bag. And the backpack wasn't even full; it only held clothing, toiletries, and a few other essentials. Her weapons were on her belt, hidden beneath her oversized jacket, and her holocom was securely around her wrist. But she wasn't going to let herself be depressed over it. This was her new beginning, wasn't it? Everyone started somewhere. It'd only get better from here.

For her baby, it *had* to get better.

She hadn't given Drakkal a specific time to pick her up when she'd called him earlier. It had been a hell of a wait, and she cursed at herself several times for not just saying *pick me up in thirty minutes*. It's not like she'd needed time to pack or settle her affairs. The moment he'd messaged her to say he was on his way, she'd leapt off her chair, scooped up her backpack, and left the room for the last time without a backward glance.

And now here she was, standing outside the rundown apartment building, anxiously awaiting Drakkal's arrival.

She hadn't bothered telling that bastard Vrisk she was leaving. He was a big boy; he'd figure it out on his own. If he had any complaints, he could shove the credits he'd extorted from her right up his scaly asshole.

Not that she thought he'd care. He was basically getting a month's rent—or three weeks of rent, since the fucker didn't seem to know how long a month was—for nothing, and he'd get some other desperate sucker in the room the moment he discovered she was gone. Hell, even if her room had been painted in blood, she doubted he'd ask any questions.

Shay adjusted the backpack's shoulder strap and frowned. She was familiar with feeling like her life didn't matter to anyone. It'd been like that for her on Earth while she was working amongst drug lords, thieves, pimps, and mercenaries. But she *had* mattered once.

And you threw it all away, didn't you Shay?

Her throat tightened, but she refused to let those feelings, those memories, suffocate her now. It wasn't the place or the time.

When will it be the time? When will it ever be?

Shay shook her head and looked to her left, glancing at the people walking through the dark, alien-made canyon running between the nearby buildings. They all looked different, but she recognized kindred spirits—all these people were just trying to get by and live their lives.

There was someone who claimed she mattered. Someone who was alive, someone who was coming for her right now. Why did that knowledge scare her a little?

More than a little.

Drakkal's intensity scared the piss out of her. Plenty of guys had shown interest in her, but they'd always been drawn to nothing more than her body. Drakkal... He wanted *Shay*. All of her—mind, body, and soul.

He wanted her as his *mate*.

Why did that word seem more permanent than *wife*, more powerful than *marriage*?

The air between Shay's old building and the structure across the broad alley seemed suddenly alive, vibrating with a barely perceptible hum. Shay turned her head to see a hovercar descending between the buildings to her right, its lights bathing the otherwise dimly lit space with brilliant luminescence. Its sleek body was black, polished so highly that it reflected the lights from other hovercars high above. The people outside scurried away from the vehicle, a few of them casting it annoyed glares.

The vehicle approached Shay slowly, hovering about a meter in the air, and eased to a smooth halt within a couple meters of her, where it sank closer to the ground. The drivers' side door swung open, and Drakkal drew himself out.

"Ready to go, *kiraia*?" he asked, his green eyes aglow with reflected light.

A warm, comforting sensation chased away some of Shay's anxiousness. Her baby shifted within her, giving a few swift little kicks.

Yeah. I kind of like him, too, Baby.

The corners of Shay's mouth quirked up. "I've been ready. Where have you been?"

Drakkal walked around the front of the hovercar to open the passenger side door. "Driving. In case you haven't noticed, this city's on the large side."

"Must have slipped my mind," she replied as she moved to the passenger door, tilting her head back to look up at Drakkal.

He was wearing black pants and a dark gray tank top that showed off his broad shoulders and the muscles of his arms—which were evident despite being covered in fur. His left arm ended several centimeters above his elbow; from that point down, it was a cybernetic prosthesis even more sleek than his car. It matched the size and proportions of his flesh and blood limb, but it was more graceful, run through in places with glowing red highlights.

Drakkal smirked. "Hmm. Maybe you're not a good fit for a security team, after all."

"Guess you'll have to find a better use for me, then."

"I can think of a few," he rumbled. His heated gaze moved over her, and his lips stretched wider. "Can even try some right now, if you're not ready to be on our way."

Shay laughed even as her body responded to imagined scenarios his words sparked. "I guess I walked into that one."

"I did leave the door wide open for you." He gestured to the interior of the hovercar. "Let's see where it goes, *kiraia*."

Shay placed a hand on the door for support and eased herself down into the passenger seat. It wasn't all that long ago that she could've climbed into a car without a second thought, but now every movement was a unique ordeal. Carrying a little extra person in her belly—a person who was pressing against internal organs, including her bladder—had definitely disrupted her grace. She buckled her harness and settled her pack on her lap.

Drakkal closed the door once she was fully inside. Shay studied the interior as he circled to the driver's side. The seats were big and supple, cradling her body in a loving, soothing embrace; it was easily the most comfortable seat she'd ever sat in. The hovercar's controls looked both highly sophisticated and simplistic, with a few unfamiliar symbols here and there. In some ways it was like climbing into any hovercar back on Earth, but in others it was entirely new.

She'd never been in a car this nice, for starters. He wasn't kidding when he'd said he was *comfortable*.

The vehicle swayed when Drakkal climbed into the driver's seat. He closed his door, and the ambient noises from outside—

the soft flit of hovercars high overhead, muted conversations, and a subtle but constant drone of unseen machinery—ended abruptly. There was only Shay and Drakkal now, and this felt like a moment from which there was no turning back. This was it.

Drakkal strapped in before settling his hands on the controls—one on the wheel, one on the directional throttle. Screens and displays flashed on, the most central of which was a hologram of the vehicle from the outside, depicting the locations of nearby objects. The gentle hum of the vehicle's antigrav engines pushed back the silence.

"Say goodbye to this dump," Drakkal said.

Shay turned to look at the building through her window. She raised a hand and flipped it off.

Drakkal glanced at her as he guided the hovercar into a smooth ascent. His eyes flicked to her extended middle finger. "What's that?"

Shay dropped her hand back into her lap. "What's what? The finger?"

"Yes. What does it mean?"

She chuckled. "It means *fuck off*."

The vehicle cleared the top of the apartment complex, and Drakkal turned his attention forward, lips parting in a grin that displayed his wicked fangs.

Those fangs *definitely* didn't turn her on. Nope. Not...at...all.

Shay shifted in her seat, refusing to squeeze her thighs together and give in to her body's reaction, refusing to acknowledge the sudden ache pulsing in her core. Her resistance was made more difficult when something brushed along the side of her calf. She glanced down to see the tip of Drakkal's tail running slowly along her leg, just like it belonged there.

She clenched her bag in one hand. She should've moved

her leg, should've broken the contact with him...but she didn't. She liked being touched. Liked *his* touch.

"So, what's *kiraia* mean?" she asked. "You've called me that a few times now."

"*Kiraia* are creatures from a planet I once called home. They are small, and very beautiful, but they are also dangerous predators." He looked at her from the corner of his eye, his grin falling into something closer to a smirk. "They're especially dangerous when provoked. Many hunters carry scars from underestimating a *kiraia*."

Something in her chest warmed, and her heart skipped a beat. That was...quite flattering. And wholly unexpected.

Shay grinned. "Guess I've been taking it too easy on you, then."

"I'll take anything you want to give, Shay, and ask for more when you're done."

She shook her head and laughed. As her cheeks warmed, she scrunched her nose. "You naughty, naughty kitty."

Drakkal laughed, too; the sound was deep and rich, and only warmed her further. "You can keep calling me kitty only if you let me pretend they are also powerful, deadly animals."

Unable to help herself, she reached toward him and slowly ran her finger down his furred arm. "Some are," she said in a husky voice.

His ears perked, and his tail quickened. His scent filled the cab—and so did his *presence*. It would be so easy to forget about everything else and focus solely on the azhera beside her. So easy to accept what he was truly offering. To accept...him.

"I promise you, *kiraia*, I put them all to shame," he purred.

This time, Shay did press her thighs together. He might as well have stroked her downstairs with how much his voice affected her.

Shay forced her gaze away from him and returned her hand

to her bag, doing her best to ignore the tail lingering against her leg.

They spent the remainder of the journey in silence, though she was painfully aware of his presence throughout. She attempted to occupy herself by staring out the windows—which had been dark-tinted from the outside but were perfectly clear from within. Surprisingly, the tactic almost worked. She'd never seen the city like this before.

From the air, the Undercity held a certain beauty she couldn't deny. All the lights and holograms popped against the darkness and bathed the structures with splashes of vibrant color, lending everything a sense of welcoming life and liveliness at odds with the chaotic rush on those streets and walkways. Traveling by hovercar allowed her to take in the conflicting nature of the Undercity itself—it was both a sprawling city with wide streets and tall buildings and an immense series of artificial caverns. For every free-standing structure, there were several more built directly into the walls and ceilings, with walkways and access tunnels crisscrossing throughout. Everything was tiered, but there were no definitive borders between those tiers.

Though the whole city was clearly a marvel of construction and engineering, it gave off the impression of total randomness —as though it had been approached from a more spontaneous, artistic angle than a practical, mathematical one.

The variety of vehicles in the express tunnels through which Drakkal piloted the hovercar nearly rivaled the variety of buildings around and below them. There was certainly no shortage of things to catch her eye, and yet her mind continuously returned to Drakkal. She didn't let her gaze follow it.

She had no idea where they were when Drakkal finally slowed the hovercar and drove it through a chain of winding side streets and tunnels. Shay had the impression that they were near a bustling part of the city, but the shadowed pathways he followed were largely deserted save for brief glimpses of tiny creatures scurrying between patches of darkness.

Given the nature of the route he was taking, she was rather surprised when he pulled up to a large door that opened on an immaculate garage in which several hover vehicles of varying sizes were parked.

Shay drew her legs closer and grasped her bag with both hands, sweeping her gaze over the garage as Drakkal eased the hovercar inside. They were here. The ride hadn't been nearly long enough to mentally prepare Shay for the gravity of this moment.

This was her new home.

And yet, after years of training, after years of dealing with criminals and the lowest of the low, after years of constant danger—and a couple months on display in a private zoo—she was only *now* apprehensive. In their own ways, all those things had been familiar. She'd known what to expect from the sorts of criminals she'd associated with, had known what to expect from men like Murgen. That wasn't the case with Drakkal.

She was walking into a new life for her and her baby, but everything was unknown. She wasn't sure of what to expect, didn't know the people here or what they would think of her, had no idea if they would find her wanting, or if—

A low rumbling sound came from Drakkal, just loud enough to interrupt Shay's thoughts. She looked at him.

"I've got you, *kiraia*." His lips curled into a smile much too soft to be on such a fierce, bestial face. "Not that you need my protection."

That struck her as funny. She would've scoffed at the thought of needing his protection a short while ago, but now she found that she liked the idea. She wanted it. And having him here for her was enough to push away some of her unease.

Trust him.

He told her the people here were not like the ones she used to associate with. That they could be trusted; that they protected their own.

That they were a family.

God, what would it feel like to be part of a family again? A *real* family.

Drakkal unbuckled his harness and shut off the hovercar's main engines. The displays went dark, the holograms vanished, and the vehicle settled closer to the ground. "Ready for the next step?"

"Yeah. I am."

With a nod, Drakkal opened his door and climbed out of the hovercar. Shay unfastened her harness and exited the vehicle as well, swinging the strap of her bag over her shoulder as she looked around.

She was familiar with many makes and models of hovercars back on Earth, but she couldn't identify any of the vehicles stored in this garage. Still, she didn't need to be familiar with them to know they all looked expensive, and she guessed at least two or three of them were armored—there was a certain universal look to discreetly armored hovercars that she couldn't quite define but which had become almost second nature to spot over the years.

She looked at Drakkal as he approached her. "I guess saying you were loaded was putting it lightly."

He glanced at the surrounding vehicles. "Most of these are...company assets. I'm loaded because I don't usually buy stuff like this."

Shay smiled. She hadn't missed his discomfort when they'd talked about money in the borian restaurant.

He's humble.

"So what do you buy?" She parted her jacket enough for

him to see her tactical utility belt and wiggled her eyebrows. "Toys?"

His eyes dipped to the belt, but they didn't stop there—and he took his time bringing them back up to hers. "Bought a terran recently."

Her smile fell.

I'd forgotten about that.

She pressed a finger to his chest. "I'm not for sale, azhera."

"Not anymore, *kiraia*."

"I never was."

His mouth stretched into a wide grin, and the light in his eyes seemed mixture of mirth and lust as he gently wrapped his hand around hers. His thumb brushed along the outside of hers and down to her wrist, sending tingles across her skin. "Best money I've ever spent."

She laughed. She couldn't help it. As serious as she was trying to be—okay, so maybe she wasn't trying very hard—she couldn't win against Drakkal's playfulness. "You might have buyer's remorse soon enough."

He leaned infinitesimally closer, nostrils flaring with a slow, deep inhalation that he released several seconds later as something close to a sigh. His grip on her hand tightened just a bit, and she swore she felt his body heat increase.

"Not possible," he rumbled.

She didn't know how or why he affected her this way, but Drakkal completely and utterly disarmed her when he was like this. The blasters and knives she carried were useless against his words. They couldn't shield her from the way he looked at her, the way he treated her like she really mattered. She wasn't used to this kind of flirting. There was a raw sexuality to it—Drakkal had never tried to hide that—but it was built atop a foundation so genuine and caring that part of her mind still couldn't believe it was real.

Heat suffused her cheeks. "So, uh, are we going in or what?"

"In a minute. Not ready to share you yet."

"Share me?"

Drakkal nodded. "The crew's eager to meet you."

All Shay could do was watch as Drakkal lifted her hand to his face, pressed her palm to his cheek, and rubbed it against his soft fur. Though the action reminded her of a cat leaving its scent on something—marking its territory, its property—there was something deeply arousing about it that turned up the heat inside her even further. She couldn't stop one of her earlier thoughts from surfacing again.

Would it be that bad to be his?

"You do realize I haven't accepted your other offer, right?" she asked a little breathlessly. She told herself it was because of her pregnancy, not because Drakkal made her heart flutter. And still she didn't pull her hand away.

Drakkal lowered Shay's hand, slipped his left arm around the small of her back—beneath her jacket—and drew her closer. She settled her free hand on his prosthesis. For a time, they stood with their eyes locked like they were about to start a slow, sensual dance, and Shay's heart pounded in anticipation. She should've pulled away. Should've stopped it. But as he dipped his head and grazed her jawline with his lips, she tilted her head aside, allowing him access to her neck.

Releasing her hand, Drakkal settled his right palm on her hip and brushed his cheek and mouth along her neck and shoulder, his fur a combination of soft and scratchy that sent thrills across her skin. She clutched his arms, sinking the fingers of one hand into fur and pressing the fingers of the other against warm metal. Her breath hitched. Liquid heat pooled between her thighs, and she leaned into him, relishing the slight pricks of his claws through her clothing as he tightened his hold on her.

"Yet," Drakkal purred, his voice vibrating into her through his powerful chest. "And it wasn't an offer, just the truth."

Something wet, warm, and delightfully rough trailed upward from the place where her shoulder met her neck, tracing a path to the sensitive spot just beneath her ear.

"Oh fuck!" Shay gasped, eyes widening as a bolt of pleasure shot straight to her pussy. He might as well have licked her between her legs, because she was pretty sure she'd almost come right then and there.

What would it feel like to have his tongue lapping at my pussy?

Drakkal lifted his head and released her, severing all contact between their bodies and leaving her cold, alone, and unfulfilled. He gestured to a nearby door. "This way, *kiraia*."

Shay looked at him and narrowed her eyes. "Oh, you naughty kitty. That was straight up playing dirty."

One corner of his mouth tilted up in a smirk that made her already trembling knees weak as he walked to the door. "That was just a taste. For both of us. I still owe you for calling me *kitty*."

She eyed him with exaggerated disbelief before following him to the door, which he opened and stepped through. She didn't allow herself any hesitation in crossing the threshold; it was a bit late for second-guessing her choice, and *damn* if that lick alone wouldn't have been enough to convince her to go anywhere with this azhera.

She raked her gaze over Drakkal's delectable backside and swaying tail.

And he already promised to eat me.

She barely kept herself from moaning out loud as her core

clenched in need. She really had to do something about that soon...

The corridor they entered wasn't what Shay had expected —not that she'd really known what to expect to begin with. Its aesthetic was an odd blend of industrial and tasteful luxury. Concrete and exposed ducts, pipes, and conduits were all over the walls and ceilings, but the plush carpet was wine red, divided by thick, rectangular black borders and thin white lines that cut directly across it from one wall to the other. Rectangular panels mounted on the walls at regular intervals provided the light, which had the faintest red tint to it.

"Interesting choices on the interior design here," Shay said.

"My partner has an affinity for a particular style that even his female cannot shake him from, even though her taste is objectively better than his," Drakkal replied.

They passed several closed doors, and when they reached the first intersection, they turned left into a similar hallway.

How big was this place? How many people worked for Drakkal and his partner?

What am I getting myself into here?

But the misgivings she should've had were absent. Nothing about this reminded Shay of her past experiences on the wrong side of the law, and Drakkal was nothing like the criminals with whom she'd once associated. Hell, so far, this seemed more legitimate than anything she'd been involved in since she was a teenager.

Finally, Drakkal stopped in front of one of the doors and turned to face her. "For the record, most of these people work for me, but I have no control over them."

Shay arched a brow, but before she could ask what he meant, he pressed the control button beside the doorframe. The door slid open with a quiet whoosh, and Drakkal entered without another word.

Frowning, Shay followed him into what she could only describe as a break room. There was a small kitchen area, complete with what looked like a refrigerator, in one corner, a couple round tables each with half a dozen chairs, and a pair of couches positioned in front of a huge holographic display screen. She spent only a second or two taking it in before her attention was caught by the diverse group of people gathered inside the room, all of whom had turned to watch her enter.

They were gathered around the tables, some sitting and some standing. Three cren, two of whom had the same blue-gray skin and navy-blue hair. The third, who was taller and broader than the others, had slate gray skin and snow-white hair. There were two vorgals seated beside each other, one with brown skin and the other with green. Both sported red tattoos on their right cheeks—she knew thanks to her father that it was an indication of rank in the Vorgal military, though she didn't know the specific meanings of the markings. The vorgals were accompanied by a female ilthurii with vibrant green scales.

Shay's eyes finally settled on the couple at the counter. Despite his casual stance, the sedhi was clearly tall and athletically built, with long black hair and bright yellow eyes that matched the faintly glowing markings on his gray skin. He wore a silky red robe that revealed the upper portion of his chest—and all four of his limbs looked like prosthetics similar to Drakkal's. A female sat atop the counter beside him, one leg drawn up with a tablet on her knee.

A *human*.

For a moment, Shay was frozen by surprise. It had been so long since she'd seen another human that she'd wondered if there were any in Arthos at all—but here was one now.

The woman lifted her head and met Shay's gaze. Excitement sparked in her eyes, and a bright smile spread across her face. "You're here!" the woman said, setting her tablet down on the counter.

A booming, sputtering cough cut off anything else the woman might've said. Shay looked to the source of the disturbance; the green-skinned vorgal had spit his drink across the table and was currently choking. The other vorgal frowned, narrowed his eyes, and slapped his choking companion on the back.

"*Fuck*," the choking vorgal managed. As his throat cleared, it became apparent what his coughing had been from the beginning—laughter. "*This* is the female that robbed you, Drakkal? You're getting soft."

Shay arched a brow as she regarded the green-skinned vorgal. Half his head was shaved, and the black hair on the other side hung in several braids that reached nearly to his shoulder. In addition to the tattoos, he had a few scars on his face—the worst of which was a big, jagged one on the shaved side of his skull.

"Says the guy who almost lost a fight with his drink?" she asked.

Looks of surprise spread across the faces of the others, and within a second, everyone was laughing.

"She already pushed you to the bottom, Thargen," the blue-skinned cren with short, spiky hair and green irises said.

Thargen ran his sleeve across his mouth, wiping away alcohol and spittle. His laughter still hadn't quite died down. "I like her, Drak."

"Think you found a keeper, Drakkal," said the other blue-skinned cren, who had yellow eyes and a long ponytail.

Wait. Do they all think...?

"Anyone who can put Thargen in his place the first time they talk to him is worth having around," the largest of the cren said.

"You have found a good female for yourself," said the ilthurii.

Fuck, they do.

Drakkal glanced at Shay, meeting her gaze briefly. His expression spread more of that fuzzy warmth through her—it said, *Yeah, she's a keeper, and she's mine forever.* She didn't understand how that simple look could say so much, but there it was. And she *liked* it.

"You're cleaning that up, Thargen," the sedhi said in a deep, smooth voice. His eyes were on the vorgal—save for the third one on his forehead, which lingered on Shay.

Weird.

Drakkal turned back toward the others and cleared his throat, calling their attention to him. "Everyone, this is Shay. She's one of us now."

The human woman hopped down from the counter and approached Shay. She was wearing a loose tunic and leggings, and had long, wavy brown hair and big brown eyes. Even wearing boots, she was about five centimeters shorter than Shay. The woman had a sweet, shy air about her, as though she'd rather sit unnoticed on the edge of a crowd.

She held her hand out to Shay. "I'm Samantha, but you can call me Sam."

"Nice to meet you," Shay replied, grasping Samantha's hand. Once she released it, she shot Drakkal a glare. "You didn't tell me there was another human here."

"Didn't tell you there were three cren, two vorgals, an ilthurii, and a sedhi here, either," he replied. "I'll make sure to compile a list next time."

She gave him a droll look. "I think there being another human here would've been noteworthy. We're not exactly common here, are we?" Turning back to Samantha, she smiled.

"Sorry, it seems Tiger here was a bit forgetful. It really is nice to meet you, Sam."

"She's got some claws," Thargen said with a delighted hoot. "I *really* like her."

"So do I, Thargen," Drakkal growled, "so don't get any ideas."

The female ilthurii hissed soft laughter, eyes narrowing and mouth curling into a grin. The small spines on the top of her head laid back. "This will be better than Razi's dramas."

The sedhi stepped forward—though *sauntered* might've been the better term, as he moved with a grace that might've been comical had it not been so overtly sensual. He offered Shay a roguish grin and settled one of his cybernetic arms over Sam's shoulders. "I'm Arcanthus. A pleasure to finally meet you, Shay. I'm—"

"He's my secretary," Drakkal said, "though I let him drive the car sometimes."

"If I recall," Samantha said with a grin, "it's you who always drives the car, Drak."

"Well, would you trust Arc at the controls?"

"Not really." Samantha cleared her throat, and her cheeks pinkened. "He can't seem to keep his hands to himself."

Arcanthus bent down and tipped his head to rest his cheek atop Sam's hair. "It's not my fault. Three eyes simply aren't enough with which to admire you. To not touch would be criminal."

"You *are* a criminal." Samantha, fully blushing now, smiled and leaned against Arcanthus's chest.

Shay flicked her gaze back and forth between the tall, confident sedhi and the small, shy human. They were of two different species and two wildly different, opposite personalities. And yet they meshed like two halves of the same whole.

Shay had absolutely no question of how deeply and truly

they felt for one another. Was it possible for her to have that sort of thing? Was it possible to have that with *Drakkal*?

"Don't mind him," Drakkal said, pulling her attention away from the couple. "He's like that most of the time. He manages to do surprisingly decent work when he actually sits down to do it. Enough about him, though…"

Drakkal introduced her to everyone else one at a time. The ilthurii was Sekk'thi, the blue cren were brothers, Kiloq and Koroq, and the brown-skinned vorgal was Urgand. Drakkal presented the big, white-haired cren last, calling him Razi.

Despite his intimidating size, obvious strength, and three-centimeter-long tusks, Razi's smile was warm.

"So, who is your partner?" Shay asked Drakkal.

"Let her guess," Thargen suggested. "More fun that way."

Drakkal shook his head. "Don't you have a new gun to shoot or something?"

"Yeah, but I wanted someone to shoot it at before I used it."

Shay jabbed a thumb at Thargen and grinned. "I like him."

One of those low, threatening growls rolled up from Drakkal's chest.

Urgand patted Thargen's shoulder. "It's a shame. All you wanted was a new friend. It's been fun, Thargen. Die with honor."

Those doubts Shay had long been harboring about this whole thing rose to the forefront and finally died. Drakkal hadn't been lying. This place, these people, really were nothing like anything she'd known before. Sure, she'd been in groups whose members had slung shit at one another, but never in this good-natured, familiar fashion. The people she'd run with in the past had often taken to beating each other bloody rather than laughing and moving on. It had all been about reputation and ego for that sort—if they were insulted, they had to escalate their response to save face.

This made her think of the few times she'd been with her father while he was with other soldiers, when every word, no matter how insulting or rude on the surface, had been exchanged with an underpinning respect and admiration that completely altered their meanings. Dad had often called the men and women he'd served with his brothers and sisters. Was *this* what he meant? Was this the sort of camaraderie he'd known?

Drakkal turned his head toward Shay and eyed her. "You're not allowed to like him."

She tilted her head and arched a brow. "Excuse me?"

"I'm your boss now, remember?"

Shay shifted her weight from one leg to the other, crossed her arms over her chest, and held his gaze, trying *really* hard not to let the corners of her lips twitch up. "Yeah, and?"

"And...you're supposed to listen to me?" Drakkal cringed at his own words.

"You're my *boss*, not my master. Wanna know what happened when my last boss tried to push me around?"

Drakkal scowled. His ears drooped, and his tail lashed behind him.

A few of the others covered their mouths—likely to hold in the laughter sparkling in their eyes.

"I like her too, Drak," Arcanthus said. "So glad I decided to let you hire her."

With a final glare at Drakkal, Shay turned her attention to Arcanthus. She took him in again, this time in his entirety—the confidence, bordering on arrogance, of his stance and expression; his silky crimson robes; his sleek and expensive-looking cybernetic limbs.

"*You're* his partner?" she asked.

Arcanthus's brow furrowed, and his amused grin fell. "Why did you ask like you don't believe it?"

Shay shrugged. "You just don't put out that commanding vibe."

Thargen barked laughter. "Finally, someone said what we all—"

"Time to get back to work," Urgand said quickly, cutting the other vorgal off. "Doors won't guard themselves."

Arcanthus kept his center eye on Shay while turning the other two to glare at Thargen. "Attacked in my own home. And here I mistakenly thought us all friends."

"We are friends," Kiloq said, grinning around his tusks.

"That's why we tell you these things," Koroq added, picking up where his brother left off.

Samantha wiped her eyes, seemingly unable to stop laughing.

Arcanthus leaned aside to look down at Sam, who he was still holding against his side. "You too? Is there no loyalty to be found in this place? Why do I pay all of you?"

Drakkal snickered and folded his arms across his chest. "You don't. I do."

"A technicality, azhera."

"Yeah. Anyway, Urgand's right. Some of you have work to do. Plenty of time to get to know Shay later." Drakkal kept his eyes on Arcanthus and lifted his brows. "That means you, too."

"You're not my master, either—or my boss, for that matter. I just want it to be clear that I am returning to work of my own volition, *not* because you told me to." Arcanthus turned toward Shay. "Despite your questionable taste in males"—he flicked his central eye toward Drakkal—"it truly has been a pleasure to make your acquaintance. Welcome."

Shay grinned. "Thanks."

Everyone stopped to say their goodbyes and nice-to-meet-yous on their way out until only Drakkal, Shay, Arcanthus, and Samantha remained.

Samantha extracted herself from Arcanthus's hold, who didn't appear eager to relinquish it, and made her way closer to Shay. "Would you like to see your room?"

Shay recognized the barely contained excitement in Sam and couldn't fault her for it. Samantha was the first human Shay had seen in a long time, and she imagined the reverse was true for Samantha. Shay never would've guessed how comforting it would be to see another terran face-to-face after all these months. "Actually, yeah. My feet are killing me."

"Come on, then. I'll show you." Samantha looked at Arcanthus over her shoulder. "I'll meet you in the workshop later."

"I might have to come looking for you much sooner than that, little flower," Arcanthus said with a smoldering light in his eyes.

"Focus, Arc," Drakkal said, shaking his head—but there was a similar light in his eyes when he met Shay's gaze. "I have to talk some business with him, but I will find you soon, *kiraia*. Do you need anything?"

"I'm sure Samantha can help with anything I need," Shay said, adjusting the backpack strap on her shoulder.

His nostrils flared slightly, and his ears dipped just a hair. "Whatever you need, I'll find a way. This is your home now. I'll do whatever I must to make it feel that way."

The solemnity and dedication in his voice obliterated her lingering irritation from their earlier exchange—not that she had been particularly annoyed over it. She knew things were... different for nonhumans. That he was running on some pretty strong, testosterone-fueled instincts. So long as he got her point, everything was good.

Shay smiled at him and walked over to Samantha, who was waiting by the door. "See you later, Drakkal."

Before he could respond, Shay and Samantha stepped into the corridor. The door closed softly behind them.

"Sorry if I act overly excited," Samantha said as she led Shay down the hallway. "It's just... It's been a long time since I came here, and you're the first human I've seen."

"How long has it been?" Shay asked.

"A little over a year." Sam gestured to Shay's bag. "Want me to take that?"

"Nah, I'm good. But thanks." Shay let her gaze wander over the walls and doors as she moved past them. "So...were you kidnapped and brought to this city, too?"

"No. I actually came here through the UTF's Emigration Assistance Initiative. It wasn't easy in the beginning, but I know it was nowhere near as hard as what you've gone through." Sam frowned, brows drawn low. "Drak didn't go into many details, but he told us where he found you. I'm so sorry you had to go through that."

Shay scratched at her arm uncomfortably, though she didn't feel it through her sleeve. "It's fine. Not like it's your fault or anything."

"No, I know it's not. It's just..." She took a deep breath and let out a small, nervous laugh. "I don't think I would have survived that."

Shay turned her face toward Samantha and ran her gaze over the woman. Despite Sam's timidity, there was something below the surface, something stronger than steel—something Shay's dad had taught her to recognize. In any encounter, physical strength was only one aspect that could affect the outcome. Often, it wasn't even the most important aspect. Whether Samantha had only recently found her inner strength didn't matter, because it was there now.

"I'm not going to lie and say it's easy, but I think you would've found a way," Shay said.

Samantha shrugged and looked away. "I don't know..."

Something Drakkal had said suddenly rose to the surface of

Shay's mind—from when he'd been telling her how he'd lost his arm.

My friend and his mate are the ones who killed him. She saved my life. He was about to finish me off before she intervened.

Shay found herself looking over Sam again. "Holy shit."

Startled, Samantha met Shay's gaze. "What? Did I...say something wrong?"

"No," Shay said, shaking her head and chuckling. "You're the one who saved Drakkal's ass, aren't you? When he lost his arm?"

This time, Samantha only lifted one shoulder. "I would've died, too, if Arcanthus hadn't showed up."

"No, you don't get to do that, Sam. Don't sell yourself short. You're a fucking badass, and you need to own that."

"I didn't do much, really..."

"If you went toe-to-toe even for a few seconds with a guy who could beat down Drakkal like that, you're a certified badass. There's not really any argument against it."

Sam smiled even as her cheeks flushed further. "Thanks, Shay. That...means a lot."

Shay's own cheeks warmed; it was weird having someone thank her so sincerely. It was weird having a positive effect on someone, especially someone she didn't know.

Man, I really screwed myself up after Dad died.

That thought led her to another realization, one that almost stopped her dead in her tracks—it had been almost ten years since her father's death. A whole decade, more than a third of her life, that she'd filled with what? Bitterness, anger, stupidity? Regret?

Maybe this really is my chance to finally turn it around. To finally make Dad proud...

To finally make Mom proud.

The threat of tears stung her eyes, and Shay cleared her throat. She needed a subject change—and damned fast. "So, a sedhi, huh?"

Samantha laughed. "It's a long story, but yeah. I'm...mated to a sedhi."

"How does that work?"

Though it seemed impossible, Samantha grew even redder than before.

Now it was Shay who laughed. "I don't mean *how* it works, you know, between the two of you, but how do a human and sedhi become mates? Just like..."

"Like a human and an azhera?" Sam asked.

"Yeah."

The other woman shrugged. "It's some kind of chemical thing, but it's also something more. It's hard to explain. Some species, like sedhi and azhera, have these strong mate-driven instincts that recognize that certain someone and push them toward that person. Me and Arcanthus think it might've been partly because of the mutative compound the Consortium gives to people when they come here. Even people who are smuggled in illegally usually get it, because it's basically required to survive in this place. It changes us. Terrans, anyway. Not who we are, but our bodies. Makes us more adaptable to pretty much everything."

"Yeah, I know a little about that stuff. They gave it to me, too," Shay said. "They said it allows humans to get knocked up by aliens."

Murgen had droned on and on about how he couldn't wait to breed her after she'd given birth.

"Yeah. It does," Samantha said.

"What does it mean to be someone's mate?"

"Truthfully? Everything." Sam reached up and tucked her hair behind her ear. "I know that's not really helpful, but it's like...there just aren't adequate words, I guess. It's attraction and...lust, but its friendship and affection, it's *love*...and it's so much more. Not that it's all those things right away, of course. But it became all those things for Arc and me."

"Can they sniff out more than one mate?" Shay asked.

Sam laughed, shaking her head. "I mean, I can't speak for every species, but... I don't think so. Arcanthus knew I was his before we even met. He just...saw my profile in the ID system and *knew*. And he lost interest in everyone else from that moment."

Shay pulled back and furrowed her brow. "Are you saying you're like...*soul mates*?"

"I guess that's what we are, isn't it? I know it sounds crazy but... Look at me. Do you really think someone like him would have picked me out in the crowd?"

Shay frowned. "Why wouldn't he? You're a beautiful, badass woman."

Sam's cheeks flushed. "Thank you. But I mean, he was so" —she threw her hands up and swept her arms out—"big. I mean his personality. He's so confident and smooth and so, so sexy, and when we met, I was just...me. Quiet, shy, timid. I couldn't compare. So if it wasn't instinct, if it wasn't this magical, wonderful thing that led him to me... What could it really have been other than fate?"

It was bizarre to have a stranger open up like this, to confide in Shay so soon, but in a way, it also felt good. Shay lifted her hand, hesitated, and placed it on Samantha's arm. They both came to a stop. "You were definitely selling yourself short."

Samantha laughed. "You're incredibly nice."

Shay arched a brow. "You don't know me very well. We'll see if you still think that by the end of the week."

Sam's smile only grew. "I guess we will see. But yeah, I was selling myself short. I came to Arthos to get out of an abusive relationship. Whatever confidence I had before that asshole, I had nothing left by the time I finally built the nerve to run. There's no way I would've ever brought myself to approach Arc back then. I didn't believe a man like him could even *see* a woman like me. He pushed me to believe in myself...by believing in me when I didn't. Everyone here did. Drakkal, too, even though he was leery of me at first."

Shay frowned. "Of you?"

Samantha's smile widened into a full-fledged grin. "He thought I was a dangerous distraction for Arcanthus."

A laugh burst out of Shay. "I guess he was right."

"More than you know."

They resumed walking, turning right at the next intersecting hallway. Shay's feet were hurting, and she had to pee something fierce, but she wanted Samantha to keep talking. She needed to know more. There was just something niggling in the back of her mind, something that made her feel uneasy and on edge. It was like that little voice that had kept telling her this was all too good to be true.

"So, if it's a chemical thing, do they not have a choice in the matter?" Shay asked as nonchalantly as she could.

"Yes and no. They're drawn to that mate, but it's all instinctual at first. Emotions have nothing to do with it, other than lust. They can fight it and ignore it. It's not necessarily easy, but it's possible. So they can't prevent themselves from feeling it, but they can prevent themselves from acting on it."

Which meant Drakkal really *wanted* Shay.

"What's he like?" Shay asked. "Drakkal."

"He can be...intense. I was scared of him, at first. There was the whole him not liking me around thing early on, and he's pretty hard to read."

Shay chuckled. "Resting bitch face."

Samantha smiled. "Yeah. He's...I don't know. He's trustworthy and *exceedingly* loyal. He's very focused most of the time, and he can come off as being overly serious, but he jokes around just like everyone else. Even more, when it comes to Arcanthus. They've known each other a long time, and are pretty much like brothers to each other. But Drakkal's very guarded. He doesn't like to show much real emotion, even though I know he feels it. He just locks it away and tries to show everyone the big, strong azhera.

"And he's *very* protective of his friends. Like"—her smile faded, and she dropped her gaze—"like willing to die to keep them safe."

Those words caused a deep, sharp ache in Shay's chest, so strong that her next breath was a struggle.

Just like my father.

That reminder hurt, but what hurt even more was the thought that followed—she wasn't sure if she could endure that sort of pain again. She wasn't sure she could endure another loss like that. Her fear of it was so strong, so intense, that she didn't know if she could even bring herself to take a chance on it, regardless of how small the likelihood of her fear coming to fruition was.

And is it really that small? He runs security for a criminal organization. There's bound to be trouble. That's how he lost his arm, isn't it? And just look at what happened at Murgen's.

I almost killed Drakkal down there. What would've happened if the rest of Murgen's security team had been alerted?

"Here we are!" Samantha announced.

Shay looked up to find herself in front of a door; she'd not realized just how lost she'd become in her own thoughts. Samantha pressed the button on the panel, opening the door, and stepped into the room. Shay followed; she was immediately struck by how big and beautiful the room was.

It had to easily be at least three times as big as the apartment she'd just left behind. The carpet was a deep violet, which complimented the light blue accents evident throughout the room—and both colors worked surprisingly well with the more neutral gray of the walls. A wide, square light panel hung from the ceiling directly over the large bed, casting a clear, inviting glow on the neatly made, navy-blue bedding.

Samantha moved deeper into the room and brushed her fingers over a control panel on the wall. Several wide drawers pushed out of the wall, and a door-sized section slid aside to reveal a closet. "I got you some clothes. I really hope they fit okay. I wasn't sure with..." Her gaze dipped to Shay's rounded stomach, visible between the parted sides of her jacket. "You can put your stuff wherever you'd like."

Shay smiled. "Thanks."

Sam returned the smile and pointed at the other end of the room. "The bathroom is through there. Oh, and we ordered some things for the baby. They should come soon."

Shay moved her hands to her stomach, cradling it, as her heart clenched.

There's that damned stinging in my eyes again.

Seeming to understand Shay's silence, Sam went on, her smile unwavering. "If you need anything, just let me know. And, uh...just so you know, since he basically demanded it, your room is next to Drakkal's."

Shay huffed a laugh. "Of course it is."

The other woman chuckled. "Anyway, it's late, and I'm sure you're exhausted. I'll have some food brought here so you can eat and get some rest." She moved to the door and opened it. Before she stepped through, she looked back and said, "And honestly Shay...I'm glad you're here."

Once Samantha was gone, Shay eased herself onto the bed. *Floored*—that was the word. She was absolutely floored. These people didn't know her, *Samantha* didn't know her, and yet they'd opened their arms to Shay and welcomed her into their home.

Part of her wanted so badly to distrust them, to see them as the criminals they'd admitted to being and treat them with the appropriate caution and skepticism, but she couldn't. And that left her utterly off balance. The world—the *universe*—wasn't a nice place full of nice people. It was cold, and hard, and lonely, and people were mean and selfish.

Mom and Dad weren't. I wasn't.

I'm not anymore.

Shay shrugged off her jacket and settled her hands on her belly, smiling as she rubbed it lovingly. "This could work, Baby."

Even if it didn't...she'd earn some credits and get out. She'd left bad situations before, and she could leave this one if necessary. It wasn't like she'd put permanent roots down here; this was just another stop along the way, hopefully better than the others she'd made.

But she found that she didn't want to leave. She wanted to make this work. A safe place, food, good people—it was perfect for her and her baby. This could be *home*.

Shay breathed in deeply and lifted her gaze toward the door.

There was just the matter of her *mate* to sort out.

THIRTEEN

Four days passed with impossible speed, hastened by a flurry of potential clients that required thorough background checks and careful planning. Drakkal had been afforded almost no time to spend with Shay—a frustrating issue he couldn't solve even though *he* ran this whole operation alongside Arcanthus—and each day his hunger for her deepened and grew more insistent.

Every moment he spent separated from her had been its own unique bit of agony, all of them coming together to create a mosaic of suffering that shouldn't have been possible considering the female he so desired was in the same damned building as him the entire time. The days had passed quickly, but the seconds had dragged on forever.

He'd long known that the passage of time was relative, but he'd never experienced it as so terribly fast and brutally slow simultaneously.

Kraasz ka'val, I'm losing my mind.

By all accounts, Shay was settling in well. The crew's initial assessment of her hadn't changed; they all liked her, and that admiration had only grown. She fit in perfectly, and part of

Drakkal hated that—because everyone else had spent hours and hours of time with her.

Drakkal had known his share of hardships, had faced injustices and been wronged more times than he cared to count, but this was the first time in all those years that he ever felt the universe was unfair. Why the hell had business suddenly picked up the morning after he brought his mate home? Why was he being kept apart from his female when he'd only just brought her close?

Maybe I shouldn't have been so hard on Arcanthus when he was trying to win over Samantha...

Now Drakkal stalked along the corridors, breathing deeply through his nose to pick up every scent on the air and filtering them all out of his awareness until only that sundrinker perfume with its exotic flair remained.

This was it—he was making time with her, *taking* it if necessary, and he wouldn't let anything stop him. He'd waged a ceaseless, internal war against his instincts over the last four days. Having his mate so close and knowing he'd yet to claim her was a torture unlike any he could've imagined. He'd resisted his urges to focus on work, telling himself repeatedly that said work was necessary to maintain everyone's safety.

But right now, his only concern was Shay. The others were adults; they could take care of themselves for a few hours. Mama Drakkal needed some personal time.

His search was complicated by the fact that her scent was everywhere in this building by now. After he'd checked her room—she wasn't there—he should've just pulled up the surveillance feeds on his holocom to find her, but something inside him had railed against the idea. He couldn't tell if it was a deep opposition to violating her privacy, which was an almost comical thought after he'd spent a day stalking her through the Undercity, or a more primal, instinctual need to track her.

There was a drive in him to learn her scent so intimately that he could find her even were he stricken deaf and blind.

His skin prickled, his fur bristled, and his tail lashed as he searched the likeliest places. He opened the break room door, pressed his hands against the door frame, and leaned through the doorway, sniffing the air and scanning the room. Like everywhere else, her scent was there—but she wasn't. Only Razi, watching two teary-eyed volturians profess their love for one another on the entertainment screen.

Snarling, Drakkal shoved away from the doorway and continued the hunt. He needed to claim her, yes, but she wasn't likely ready for that yet. Just being near her would be enough for now. It had to be enough.

Vrek'osh, I hope it's enough.

He stopped at the gym next. The air smelled like sweat and greased tristeel, but it was the scent of Shay's sweat that stood out the strongest to him—not just because he was actively seeking it, but because it was the freshest. She'd been here recently.

Ears flattening, Drakkal clenched his fists and continued to the only other place she might've gone while off duty. Her scent strengthened as he descended into the lower level and approached the building's training facilities, one of the only areas that had required little remodeling when the forgery operation had been relocated here. The stairs let him out in a short corridor with the door to the shooting range directly ahead and the control room for the simulation chambers to his right.

He entered the shooting range first.

The range ran almost the full length of the building— nearly one hundred and fifty meters from one end to the other —though it was only fifteen meters wide. Its dark gray walls were constructed of a material similar to that found in most combat armor, meaning they would absorb and disperse energy from plasma bolts and physical projectiles rather than deflect them.

The stalls lined up on this end of the range were empty, their control panels switched off, and the chamber was so quiet that Drakkal could hear the faint rustling of his fur against his clothing. For some reason, this room had always seemed lonely to him. Perhaps it was its size—it suggested wide open space without truly providing any, and that tease was enough to rouse Drakkal's old desires for fields and forests, for fresh, warm breezes and endless skies.

But none of that mattered now; Shay wasn't here, which only left one other likely place. If she wasn't there, he'd have to tear through the entire building one room at a time, disregarding the quiet, rational part of his mind that insisted such a search was impractical and inefficient.

He exited the range and turned left, settling his gaze on the entrance to the simulation control room. There was a sign near the entrance that indicated the individual simulation chambers with a square and a number in Universal Speech for each one. All twelve of the squares were red except for chamber one, which glowed green, meaning it was in use.

Drakkal walked forward and turned into the long corridor than ran along the shooting range's outside wall. The doors and view windows to the simulation chambers were lined up along the right side. He stopped at the first chamber and turned to look through the wide, one-way viewing window.

Shay was at the center of the chamber, standing on an omnidirectional moving floor that was currently hidden by the holographic simulation she was running—a simulation which, for her, was fully immersive and surrounded her completely on all sides. The window allowed Drakkal a clear view, cutting out the hologram that would've run along that wall from her perspective.

It was almost like watching a movie, though no movie had ever drawn Drakkal in as quickly and thoroughly as this.

His attention, not surprisingly, was consumed by her. Her blond hair was pulled up in a messy bun that barely kept the numerous dangling, rogue strands out of her face. Her skin glistened with perspiration, and her tank top—which revealed her graceful, faintly toned arms and shoulders—was damp with sweat. Its fabric hugged her body, molding to her breasts and her rounded belly. Her pants were just as form fitting.

Drakkal couldn't help but notice there were no lines denoting the presence of undergarments beneath those leggings—the generous, natural curve of her ass was his to devour with his eyes. He groaned low, and his cock throbbed, suddenly straining against his pants.

How many times had he imagined taking Shay by her hips as he pushed inside her hot, welcoming body? How many times had he imagined her skin sweat-slickened like this as their bodies joined and their breaths mingled?

Fuck, how have I focused on anything *else since I brought her here?*

The answer to that was in his heart, nestled deep but not hidden—he *hadn't* focused on anything apart from her for a month now. Since the moment he'd first locked eyes with her, Shay had been his only concern, his only goal, his only drive, and everything else he'd done since that night at Foltham's manor was lost in a fuzzy haze of memory. He knew he'd worked, knew he'd handled business, but he'd retained none of the details.

Oh, but I can recall every detail of her body beneath those clothes, right down to the tiniest blemish.

He'd seen Shay fight during her brief scuffle with the sedhi on the street corner days ago, but that had offered only a hint of her training and discipline. She'd said her father had taught her, that he'd been a military man. Drakkal believed it as he finally forced himself to watch not just her body but the way she moved.

She held a training auto-blaster at the ready, its stock tucked against her shoulder. The weapon couldn't fire live plasma bolts, but it operated like the real thing within the simulation—and it could be modified both physically and functionally to mimic the feel and characteristics of real weapons. The auto-blaster looked natural in her hands, especially paired with her confident stride.

Though she remained in place at the room's center as she walked, the holographic corridor moved around her—and now that he was paying attention, he realized that corridor bore a striking resemblance to the halls of this building.

A deep, pulsating ache ran down his arm from elbow to fingertips—down his *left* arm, which he'd lost a year ago in defense of his then-home. That place had been like this one in many ways, and Drakkal had been mistaken to think it secure. He didn't want to consider the possibility of an attack on this building, especially not while Shay was here, but he had to. That was his job. If he ignored the worst-case scenarios, he couldn't keep his people safe. He couldn't keep Shay and her cub safe.

He absently flexed the fingers of his prosthesis and returned his attention to his mate. Though her movements were occasionally awkward—undoubtedly because of her rounded belly—he could see the muscle memory behind each one, the skill that could only have come from extensive practice. She moved through the holographic hallway methodically, checking her corners and keeping alert, eliminating threats with speed and precision, often before her simulated foes could react.

And as minutes passed, her shoulders and chest began to heave, her reaction speed gradually slowed, and frustration hardened her expression.

She came to an intersection in the corridor, always a dangerous spot in combat situations, and paused for a second to catch her breath. The delay was a second too long.

Two of the doors directly ahead of her opened, and two featureless enemies stepped into the hallway. Shay raised her gun and fired. The simulated plasma bolts struck the enemy on the left side of the corridor, but the gunman on the right fired before she could take him down.

The gunman's plasma bolts—a bright green produced by no real blasters—struck Shay in the chest. She flinched, face paling, and staggered back a step.

Drakkal's heart leapt, and his body reflexively jerked toward the window, claws splayed. He stopped himself before he struck the glass. Tension had that quickly claimed his every muscle, and his thundering heart refused to immediately slow.

Just a simulation. She's fine. Wasn't real.

But it had looked real—real enough to push him to action based on instinct alone, real enough to heat his skin and twist his insides.

The holographic corridor flashed red a few times, and an alarm wailed briefly before everything faded away, leaving Shay in the center of a square, ten-by-ten-meter room with black walls and dull white overhead lights.

She shouted something Drakkal couldn't make out—though the movements of her mouth indicated it had been the terran word for *fuck*—and bent forward as far as her belly allowed, bracing her auto-blaster across her thighs as she panted.

Droplets of sweat trickled off her nose and chin and fell to the floor.

Though his heart hadn't slowed, and his chest was still tight, Drakkal's dipped his gaze to appreciate the way her position pulled the fabric of her pants taut around her thighs and ass. He didn't have adequate words to describe her beauty. And even if it had been a simulation, even if she'd technically lost, seeing her move like that—seeing her fight like that—was fucking hot.

He couldn't hold himself back for another moment; he stepped to the door and entered the simulation chamber.

Her scent permeated the air within, washing over him in a cloud of sundrinker perfume and sweet, tantalizing sweat, undoubtedly fraught with her irresistible pheromones. His cock, already erect and confined, swelled impossibly—and painfully—further.

Shay jerked her head up at the noise. As soon as her eyes fell upon him, her startled expression gave way to a grin. She straightened, letting the blaster fall to hang by its shoulder strap at her side, and raised a hand to wipe sweat from her face. "Look what the cat dragged in."

Drakkal lifted a brow. "Arc already used that one. Doesn't affect me anymore."

"Fur real? I thought it was clawver."

He jabbed a finger at her. "You're not allowed to talk to Arcanthus from this point forward. Clearly he's distracting you from your duties."

Shay laughed. "Man, he wasn't kitten when he said cat puns make you fur-ious." When Drakkal just glared at her, she waved her hand, laughing harder. "Okay, okay! I'll stop."

Drakkal tilted his head back, drew in a deep breath, and released it in a sigh. "If the Consortium knew about such puns, they wouldn't have invited terrans to Arthos. Maybe they would've gone so far as to quarantine your species on Earth."

She snickered. "You like it. Admit it."

He smirked. "All right, I can admit it. I'm feline a little better about it now that you're involved."

Shay burst into another round of laughter. "Good one."

Drakkal's amusement faded slowly, leaving only... What was it he felt for her? Attraction, lust, and desire—all slightly different nuances of the same thing—but there was much more to it. Admiration and respect, certainly. For the rest, it seemed too early to tell; the feelings were too new to identify.

He swept his eyes over her body again, drinking in her curves and her petite but enticing form. Even her stomach, swollen by her growing cub, somehow made her body lusher, adding an undefinable yet undeniable appeal. But it was the perspiration on her skin and soaking her clothing that stood out the most in that moment. It was the result of Shay pushing herself hard despite her situation, had been the result of her seeking out her limit and defiantly shoving against it.

Pride flooded his heart, and he accepted it even if it wasn't technically his to claim—because she'd not yet chosen him.

"You did well," he said.

She crinkled her nose, and her lip drew back in distaste as she approached him; the omnidirectional floor was locked in place now, having been deactivated along with the simulation. "I'm rusty as fuck and out of shape."

Drakkal took that as an opportunity to study her body again —any excuse was good enough. "I enjoy your shape."

Her cheeks, already pink, darkened further. She glanced at him briefly. There was appreciation and shyness in her gaze— and a glimmer of interest.

"That sim you were running is designed for a squad," he said. "Not many people could've made it that far alone."

When she reached Drakkal, Shay stepped around him and squatted down to retrieve a bottle of water and a towel from the floor beside the door. "Why do you have training programs for squads in here?"

As she stood up, she opened the bottle and took a long, deep drink.

Drakkal turned toward her and leaned a shoulder against the doorframe. "This place used to be the headquarters of a security company. Up until a few decades ago, the Eternal Guard used to contract out security in sectors like this, basically making private companies the peacekeepers. People liked that even less than they liked the real peacekeepers. They decommissioned all these stations and left behind anything that would've been too much trouble to haul out—like these simulation chambers."

"And how did you guys end up with this place?

"Arcanthus hacked the Eternal Guard systems and found it in their records. It hasn't been used in thirty-five years, so he updated the records to reflect that it had been sold off fifteen years ago and transferred ownership to a shell company."

Shay grinned. "So, you guys are running a criminal operation out of a *stolen* former police station?"

Though Drakkal had never heard the term *police*, the way she'd used it made it easy enough to decipher what it meant. He couldn't help but grin in response. "I thought that was funny, too."

She took another drink from her bottle and raked her eyes over Drakkal. "So, where have you been, stranger?"

"Working. Turns out I might've let things stack up for a few weeks while hunting for a certain terran."

She lowered the bottle, tucking it between her arm and her ribs, and raised the towel to wipe her face and chest. "Ah, well.

And here I was wondering if my big, ferocious protector was abandoning me."

Drakkal released a low, rumbling purr. "Call me your big, ferocious protector again, *kiraia*. I like the sound of it."

She chuckled and locked her eyes with his. "I thought you might."

Pushing off the door frame, Drakkal closed the distance between himself and Shay. He took in a slow breath, relishing her scent. "*Kraasz ka'val*, you were so close this whole time, but I've *missed* you."

To his surprise and satisfaction, she didn't move away when he trailed the pad of a finger along her forearm.

"I will never abandon you, Shay."

Something in her eyes shuttered, and one corner of her mouth lifted in a humorless smirk. "See, that's a promise you can't keep. No one can."

Once again, she stepped around him, this time to move through the open door. There'd been a somber note in her voice, as though her playfulness had been chased away by bitterness.

Drakkal turned and followed her into the corridor. "You don't believe me?"

"Everyone leaves"—she glanced at him over her shoulder—"whether they want to or not. It's not always up to you."

His brow furrowed, and he fought to ignore the nagging, dreadful pang in his chest that cropped up at the thought of losing her—or of being forced away from her. "That's not abandonment, Shay. Abandoning someone...*betraying* someone... that's always a choice."

She looked away from him, but not before he caught the regret and hurt in her eyes. "I know."

He reached forward with his right hand, took hold of her upper arm, and halted her. "Look at me, Shay."

She tugged on her arm, and for a moment, she seemed about to pull away and keep walking. But she didn't wrench herself out of his grasp—she turned toward him, eyes ablaze with challenge, and asked, "What?"

"I want you to look me in the eyes and hear me," he growled, leaning down to put his face on level with hers. "I will *never* abandon you. So long as there is life in my body, I will fight to be at your side. I swear it on my blood."

"And I believe you, Drakkal." She let out a terse laugh and shook her head. "You barely know me, but I have no doubt you'd die for me. Now hear *me* when I say that I don't want you doing that."

Frustration and helplessness welled up in him, and he railed against them. "It's not your choice."

Her shoulders sagged, and she bowed her head with a sigh. "I know that."

Drakkal exhaled slowly, sobered by her sudden change in demeanor; he'd never seen Shay look so...defeated. He loosened his hold on her to gently smooth his palm up and down her arm. "Who did you lose?"

"My parents."

Curling a finger beneath her chin, he lifted it, bringing her eyes back to his. "Tell me about them."

She pressed her lips together, looking as though she would refuse for a few moments before sighing.

"When I was little, my dad was my world," she said softly. "He was special forces, and I think his unit was attached to some branch of the Volturian military a lot of the time. He'd be gone for months and months at a time, but I always knew that when he came home, he'd spend all his time with me. He'd take me out camping and teach me to hunt and shoot and survive, teach me how to defend myself. To fight."

A soft smile touched her lips. "He used to say that by

twelve I was already better trained than most of the UTF's standing army. Sometimes he'd have friends over, other soldiers like him, and they'd teach me, too. Some of them were women, and I thought that was so *cool*...I wanted to be just like all of them.

"And when he wasn't around, it was me and Mom. She was a badass in her own way, even though I didn't fully understand it while I was a kid. She'd been active duty, too, a combat medic. She met Dad in a combat zone. Saved his life from a blaster wound. They married a couple years after that, and once she got pregnant with me...she chose me over her career and was honorably discharged from service."

Her smile fell, and a sheen of tears filled her eyes. "Dad was going to retire when I was seventeen. He'd already put in twenty-five years of service, and even though he was as tough as ever, I could tell he was tired, too. He was ready for peace. But they begged him to run one more mission, said they didn't have anyone as qualified for it as him. And my dad was the kind of guy who couldn't turn away when they asked him like that. He couldn't turn his back on his duty. So...he went. And I was so *angry*. He wasn't supposed to leave again, and Mom *let* him. She didn't fight him, didn't demand that he stay. She let him go. And...he never came back."

Shay's tears spilled, and Drakkal caught a whiff of their saltiness. Frowning deeply, he brushed away some of the moisture with the side of his thumb.

Sniffling, Shay rubbed angrily at her other cheek, as though the forcefulness of the action could stop her tears. "I despised the UTF for taking him from me after that, but I hated Mom for *letting* him go. So, I did everything I could to show her my anger. I made trouble in school, being as disruptive as possible, started a lot of fights with other kids—and it really wasn't fair for any of them, even the boys bigger than me. My dad was a damned good teacher. After I broke the quarterback's arm in three places, the school had finally had enough, and I was expelled.

"I ended up running away not long after that and got mixed up with some bad people. I guess it was pretty typical stuff, but it was all exciting at that point, and everything I did was basically a big fuck you to the government for taking my dad. Drugs and extortion at first, just street-level gang shit. But they liked me because of my skills, and I started moving past the petty stuff quick." She snickered, again without humor, and shook her head. "They wanted me as muscle. Seems pretty ridiculous when you look at me in this city, doesn't it?"

Despite everything, a corner of Drakkal's mouth lifted. "No, *kiraia*. It doesn't."

"You're a bad liar, kitty." She frowned and wet her lips with her pink tongue. "Cops brought me in a few times, mostly on little stuff. And even after everything, after all the stupid, hateful stuff I said, my mom kept bailing me out. She never said much when she did, and...and I know that she had every reason to have chewed me out or just abandoned me all together, but she didn't, and it just *hurt* when she was quiet because it felt like she was judging me, you know? And it almost made me hate her *more* that she kept helping me. Like part of me wanted her to blow up, wanted her to get pissed, wanted her to speak up like she should've done before Dad left."

Fresh tears fell from Shay's eyes, faster than before, and her voice was thick when she spoke again. "And through it all, I was blind to the pain I was causing my mother. Blind to the pain she was going through at having lost her husband...and in the process of losing her daughter, too.

"But I...I was the one who lost *her*. She was driving home after bailing my dumb ass out of jail again, and there was an accident. An automated freight hauler glitched out, and her car was the first thing it plowed into. She was gone instantly."

Shay tipped her head down, pressing her cheek into Drakkal's palm, and her tears flowed hot over his fingers. She lifted a hand and swept back loose strands of her hair toward her bun, which she grasped in her fist and squeezed until her knuckles were white.

"I didn't even get to say I was sorry," she said in a small, broken voice. "Didn't get to say goodbye. That I *loved* her. She died thinking I hated her, died knowing that her daughter was a criminal, a fuck-up, a walking, talking piece of garbage."

Drakkal put his left arm around her shoulders and drew her against his chest. Shay offered no resistance; she buried herself against him, her shoulders shaking as her quiet tears became full-bodied sobs that wrapped around Drakkal's heart and squeezed it. He rested his cheek atop her head and moved his right hand to the back of her neck. Her tears soaked his shirt, but he didn't care. He just held her.

He held her as though it were the only way to keep his heart in one piece.

When her crying finally began to ease, he said, "My people have long believed that our ancestors watch over us from some place beyond death. That is what I meant when I swore not to abandon you by my blood—by the blood of the generations who walked before me. Their legacies shine on in our lives, and they watch to see what legacy we will make. Your mother and your father watch you, Shay. They've seen your shame, and your guilt, but they've seen your strength, too. And they know, even more surely than I do, that you have it in you to make them proud.

"I know that you've already made them proud. You're here, and you're alive, and you're fighting for your cub. No matter what happened, they loved you, *kiraia*, and they love you still in their place beyond the stars."

She sniffled loudly. "You think?"

"I do."

She pressed her forehead to his chest and drew in a deep, shaky inhalation. "Some humans believe the same. I was never the religious sort. But it...it would be nice if they were."

"I haven't been to my home planet in decades, but I haven't forgotten all our ways," he said, running his right hand down her spine and back up again. "Thank you for honoring me by sharing the memories of your ancestors, Shay. I will hold them along with my own."

She drew away from him then, and though he was reluctant to release her, he did. His arms fell to his sides, suddenly useless. She looked up at him, her pale blue irises vibrant against the irritated red around them, and her expression became uncharacteristically self-conscious. "Sorry for blubbering all over you. It, uh, must be the pregnancy hormones making me all emotional." She took another step back and wiped her cheeks with the towel. "But thanks. For listening."

Drakkal's palms—both of them, impossible as it was—itched with a want to move, with the desire to wrap her in a tight embrace and draw her against his chest again. He could take some satisfaction in having comforted his mate in her time of need, but *he* needed more. He needed to give her more. To give her everything.

But all he managed to do was say, "Any time, *kiraia*."

She removed the water bottle from under her arm and stared down at it, fiddling with its cap. "I just really don't want to fuck up with this baby. I'm all it has. Everyone else is gone."

Drakkal stepped forward and settled a hand on her shoulder, drawing her gaze back up to his. "Even if that were true, Shay, nothing on this world or any other would get through you to harm your cub. But you're *not* alone. I'm here for both of you."

She stared into his eyes for several seconds, unspeaking, and Drakkal's heartbeat increased in volume to fill the silence. Her skin was warm and soft beneath his palm, her scent as sweet and alluring as ever, and the color on her face only made her seem more radiant. But none of that mattered now; all that was important was making sure she *knew*, without a doubt, that she could always rely on him.

The little crease that formed between her eyebrows and the downturn of her lips told him that she was torn, that she hadn't quite accepted what he was offering, that part of her didn't believe him. And it felt like...rejection. It sparked frustration and hurt deep inside Drakkal, though he knew in his heart and soul that she had every reason to doubt after the life she'd lived.

She had every reason to doubt him because of her guilt regarding her own perceived betrayals.

Finally, Shay dropped her gaze, shrugged off his hand, and said, "I'm pretty tired and sweaty. I'm sure I stink too, which I rubbed all over you. So...I'm gonna take a shower and get some rest."

Drakkal frowned. All his instincts demanded he pursue her, stop her, and show her physically just what she was to him. Every cell in his body demanded he show just how much he wanted to protect her. Every molecule urged him to worship her body and ease her worries. He needed to make Shay *his* in every way...and to convince Shay that he should be *hers*.

But he only offered Shay a tight nod before she stepped back, turned, and walked away. He clenched his jaw as he watched her go and clenched his fists once she'd entered the stairwell and was out of sight.

Arc never had this much difficulty with Samantha.

That thought, rising unbidden from the recesses of his

mind, only made Drakkal's irritation flare. Partly because it was right—despite her initial timidity, Samantha had taken to Arcanthus quickly—and partly because it was a shitty thing to think. Arcanthus wasn't at fault here, and neither was Sam or Shay.

Drakkal was the one who needed to act, he was the one who needed to figure this out. There must've been something more he could've said or done just now to prevent her from pulling away. She'd opened up, had shared old, painful memories, and he'd *almost* forged that connection. He'd almost infiltrated the inner walls she kept up so much of the time.

Should've pushed harder. Could've broken those walls down without breaking her. My Shay is tougher than that.

And on top of all that, his balls ached like they'd been kicked by a tralix. It wasn't just his instincts drawn to Shay, it was his entire body, and that desire was quickly becoming a frenzied need. He had no idea how much longer he could contain it.

His body thrummed with a desperate, restless energy that had suffused him down to the bones, a feeling reminiscent of the effects of enhancing drugs that were sometimes given to slave gladiators before a fight. Drakkal hadn't felt like this in years, and he knew his hand wouldn't be enough to assuage his desires. It hadn't been enough for weeks.

Digging his claws into his palm, he forced himself to count to one hundred before finally heading upstairs. He needed to find a way to vent this energy before seeing Shay again, and that likely meant pushing his body to exhaustion in the gym.

But deep down, he suspected there was only one way to be rid of it for sure—there was only one person who could help.

FOURTEEN

Drakkal growled and shoved up the chest-press machine's bar, which locked in place when he released the grips. He sat up, wishing the burn in his abdomen—the same burn radiating from all the muscles of his upper body—meant something. Wishing that it had made a difference. He hadn't worked out with this intensity in a long time. Normally, it would've felt good. There would've been an underlying satisfaction to it, a euphoria sparked by whatever chemicals his brain normally released during hard physical activity.

That wasn't the case now. His muscles ached, but still pulsed with restless energy, as though it could only be released in a very specific way.

But Shay didn't want that. Not yet.

He leaned forward, meaning to rest his elbows on his knees and take a steadying breath, but the shifting of his weight only reminded him of the tenderness in his groin. Groaning, he dropped a hand to his hard cock and pressed down on it. His balls felt swollen, ready to explode. Yet he knew that nothing he could do—at least on his own—would provide any relief.

He growled again and stood up. This time the growl was prolonged, lengthening into a snarl through his bared fangs. He stalked toward the running platforms positioned along the far wall. As tired as he was after nearly an hour of lifting heavy weights, his body refused to quit, and his instincts...

They were even stronger than before.

How did *that* work?

He was throwing himself into this physical activity, pouring all of himself into it, and yet his mind constantly shifted back to Shay. Every thought led back to her no matter how tenuous the bridge seemed; she was unavoidable.

Because our mating is inevitable.

"Vrek'osh," he grumbled as he stepped onto one of the running platforms—a two-by-two-meter square topped by an omnidirectional tread.

A holographic control screen appeared in the air in front of him. He slashed the *on* command with the tip of a claw, wishing there'd been something physical there just so he could feel his claw tear through it.

He started walking, and quickly increased his pace to a jog and then a run. The platform's surface moved in accordance with his speed, keeping him centered. His ears flattened, his heart thundered, and his blood flowed hot as lava through his veins. Shay's face, her lips tilted in a smirk and her eyes flooded with heat, flashed in his mind's eye. Drakkal's cock strained against his pants. For an instant, it seemed as though it'd be strong enough to break free.

Releasing a sharp, annoyed breath through his nostrils, he pushed himself faster, tilting his upper body forward as he pumped his legs. The platform trembled under his weight, and the ache in his groin deepened, spreading to his lower abdomen. He welcomed the discomfort. Soon, his breath was ragged. Heat radiated from his core and skittered across the surface of his skin.

The lingering smell of Shay's sweat wafted from his fur and shirt. Drakkal spat a curse, torn between his appreciation of that scent and his wish that *he* could sweat, too, if only to overpower her aroma and shift his mind away from her for a few seconds.

He pushed himself harder still, intensifying both his internal heat and the beating of his heart. There was a limit to how much of that heat his body could handle, but he didn't care about it now. It didn't matter. He needed the exhaustion it would eventually bring.

When he squeezed his eyes shut, he meant to do so for only a moment—just long enough to center himself—but his imagination seized the opportunity offered by that brief darkness. Against his will, he pictured himself chasing Shay—not through the streets of the Undercity but through a forest on his home planet, following her scent between the trees. Hunting her. Instinct drove him to claim his prize, and the longer she ran, the more determined he grew. The more excited he grew.

In that impossibly vivid imagining, he passed between two large tree trunks and entered a clearing to find his mate awaiting him. She was naked, bent over on her hands and knees with her delectable ass in the air, presenting herself for the taking—for his claiming. And she was staring at him over her shoulder with that maddening fire in her eyes.

His cock throbbed, and suddenly the friction between it and his pants had him on the verge of spilling his seed.

"*Kraasz ka'val,*" he rasped, forcing his eyes open. His breath sawed from his lungs, burning his throat, each exhalation underscored by a growl. He slowed his pace and straightened, lifting his hands and clenching his fists as though he could catch all this frustration and discomfort between his fingers and squeeze it down into something manageable.

Drakkal's chest and shoulders heaved as he turned off the platform and stepped down. He felt his heartbeat in every centimeter of his body, a frantic pulse that refused to quiet, refused to slow, and each of its rapid, heavy thumps increased that internal heat just a little more. It felt as though there were a furnace burning in his chest.

He walked forward, lifted an arm, and braced it against the wall, leaning his forehead against his wrist. His insistent pulse strengthened the ache in his groin, pronouncing the agony of his need, and created a new discomfort behind his eyes. He'd never built this amount of heat without pushing his body to brink of collapse, and yet his limbs hummed with fresh stores of strength.

Swallowing thickly—his mouth was dry, his tongue as rough as hard-packed sand—he pushed away from the wall and left the gym. He'd been a fool to think he would find relief here. He'd known from the beginning that there was only one means of release, only one thing that could satisfy him.

His fur, already tousled from his exercise, stood on end in agitation as he strode down the corridor toward his room. His tail whipped ceaselessly as though fighting off unseen attackers, and his ears restlessly lifted and fell, over and over. Despite the pace of his walk—which was glacial compared to his all-out sprint a few minutes before—the heat in him continued to build.

He paused as he reached the door just before his own— Shay's door. His chest swelled with a deep inhalation; for several seconds, he could not release it. The pressure within him grew along with the heat, and it was all too much, it was impossible to bear, and he had to act, or it would tear him apart. She was on the other side of that door, probably in her bed. Her scent was fresh in this hallway, and it lingered on him; he wanted that scent embedded in his fur forever. He wanted her slick oils coating his cock.

Drakkal reached toward the door's control panel. He stopped himself before he touched it, curled his fingers into a tight fist, and pressed the side of his hand against the door. Tension gripped his every muscle. He'd been in low places before, had faced more struggles over the years than he could count, had known consuming rage and sorrow. Nothing in his life compared to this. Nothing in his life had been this hard; that was the truth, as absurd as it seemed when held against the challenges he'd faced in the past.

Gritting his teeth so tightly that he swore they would shatter, he pushed away from Shay's door and walked the most harrowing six meters in all the universe to reach his bedroom. The sound of his door sliding shut behind him once he was inside was a soft and fleeting—and it was *mocking*, questioning his devotion to his mate, doubting his strength, needling his pride.

"Fuck you," he growled at the door before hurrying into the bathroom.

He didn't allow himself to consider the implications of snapping at inanimate objects as he tore off his clothes. Once his pants were down, his cock sprang free, fully erect, to throb in open air. He shuddered at the relief—though that relief was miniscule, and even the gentle caress of air along his shaft was nearly too much to bear.

Precariously balanced on the edge of explosion, he clamped his right hand around the base of his shaft just beneath the knot, squeezing mercilessly to alleviate the discomfort, and moved to the shower. His thighs brushed his oversensitive balls, which were tight and heavy with unspent seed.

He turned the water on cold and entered the shower,

immersing himself. The chill was jarring but welcome, immediately chasing away the heat crackling across the surface of his skin, but it didn't penetrate deep enough, didn't extinguish the source of the fires raging within him. Shay's scent remained strong in his nostrils despite the water streaming over his face.

Releasing his cock, he grabbed his soap and scrubbed his fur to a furious lather, wishing more with each second that it was her hands touching him. When he washed his throbbing cock and aching balls, it produced an immense wave of pleasure-pain unlike anything he'd experienced. He clamped his mouth shut and willed himself to hold it together. If he came by his own hand now, it wouldn't provide him any relief. He'd only be hungrier.

Have to ride this out. Have to hold myself together.

He used the internal shower control to make the water colder still, shuddering beneath the stream as it rinsed the lather from his fur. He just needed to cool off. Needed to relax.

As though in response, the instinct-fueled flames at his core roared to new heights, blasting back at the icy water sluicing over his body.

Drakkal slapped his left hand against the wall and grasped his shaft with the other, growling as his cock twitched and its knot swelled further.

Fuck riding it out. I need her now.

He clawed the controls to shut off the water, shook the excess moisture from his fur, and exited the shower. Despite the scent of soap clinging to him, he still smelled Shay's sundrinker perfume and sweet sweat.

Without the need for conscious thought, he entered the hallway, went to her door, and banged on its face with his metal hand. His heart beat thunderously enough that he wouldn't have been surprised had its sound echoed along the corridor.

He was about to pound on the door again when it opened.

"What do you—oh." Shay's eyes flared as they dipped to his pulsing cock.

Drakkal raked his gaze over her greedily. She wore only an oversized shirt, the hem of which hung around the middle of her thighs, and her pale golden hair was loose and disheveled. Her cheeks pinkened, and the color of her irises darkened.

She slowly trailed her eyes up his body until they locked with his; desire burned in those piercing blue depths. Her breath quickened, and her breasts strained against her shirt, making the points of her hardening nipples visible through the fabric.

"You want to fuck?" she asked. "Then fuck me."

He stepped into the doorway, drawing close enough to feel the heat radiating from Shay, close enough to smell her arousal.

She lifted her hand and pressed her palm to his chest. "No strings attached. No commitments. We're just two people getting it out of our systems."

Fuck that.

He knew it wasn't possible—and suspected that she, deep in her heart, understood it, too. But he'd let her lie to herself if that was what it took for her to give in, if that was what it took to convince her that she was his—that this was inevitable.

Drakkal took another step forward, crossing the threshold, and Shay stepped back, keeping her hand on his chest. He blindly slapped the control. The door shut behind him.

"Did you hear me, Drakkal?" Shay asked.

"I heard you, female," he growled.

She narrowed her eyes. "And?"

He lifted his right arm, placed his hand on the back of her head, and took hold of her hair. Before she could react, he angled her face toward his and bent down to slant his mouth over hers.

Shay's breath hitched, and her body tensed, but Drakkal

gave her no respite as he tasted her. His mouth covered hers hungrily, desperately. A soft moan escaped her, and her lips parted, granting him access to her mouth. Her hand slid up his chest before her fingers curled in his fur. She pulled him closer.

This taste of her sweetness after weeks of being teased by her scent was beyond anything he could've imagined, so powerful and overwhelming that it left room only for one thought—*more*. Drakkal wrapped his left arm around her and cupped her ass with his hand. He tugged her body against his, pressing his throbbing cock to her rounded belly. He made no effort to suppress his groan as a fresh wave of pleasure-pain flowed outward from his groin.

Shay grinned against his mouth before pressing her forehead against his, breaking the contact between their lips. "You want me?"

"*Need* you."

She looped her arms around his neck and stepped backward, leading him deeper into the room. "I've wanted you too." Her tongue flicked out and teased his lower lip. She sucked it into her mouth briefly and nipped it with her teeth, causing Drakkal to growl and bare his fangs at the jolt that swept through him. "Did you know that I touched myself while thinking of you after you found my apartment? I imagined what your hand would feel like stroking my pussy. What your *tongue* would feel like."

Though it seemed impossible, her words further stoked the fires inside him and made his cock stiffen more than ever.

"*Pussy*," he rumbled, sliding his left hand around her thigh from back to front to press his thumb over the top of her slit. Heat emanated from her. "Is that what you call this?"

Lashes fluttering, Shay moaned and rocked her hips forward, causing his thumb to slip between her folds and stroke a tiny, hard nub. "*Yes.*"

"I thought of you, too," he said as the backs of her legs bumped the edge of her bed. He brushed his thumb over that nub again, coaxing another gyration from her hips. The sweet musk he'd picked up within her scent was stronger now, fogging his mind in the best of ways. Keeping his gaze locked with hers, he lifted his left hand to his mouth, extended his tongue, and licked her oils from the metal. If his first taste of her lips had been ambrosial, this was something else entirely, something that could not be encompassed in words, and he needed more, forever more. "Mmm...but I'm done imagining."

"So don't imagine," she said. "Take me. Fuck me." Her eyes fell to stare at his cock. "Cause I fucking want you, too."

Drakkal stepped back from Shay. Her arms fell from around his neck, but he would not mourn their loss—he'd feel her touch again soon enough. With both hands, he grasped the collar of her shirt and pulled it in opposite directions. Shay inhaled sharply. The fabric tore down the middle, exposing her full, lush breasts and their budded pink nipples.

Instinct demanded he press her onto the bed and shove inside her, demanded he ravage her body and make it known, without a doubt, that she was his.

Instinct had driven him to her, had brought him to this point. But he would not allow those instincts to ruin this moment. He would not allow instinct to diminish his enjoyment of her—or hers of him. He would take his time no matter how much it hurt to hold back, because she deserved nothing less, and what was the point of the chase if he ended it all so quickly now?

Drakkal stalked closer to her. Shay held his gaze as she moved back onto the bed, shrugging off the tattered remains of her shirt. Once she was fully atop the bed, she propped her arms behind her and spread her knees, baring her sex to him.

Drakkal stared down at the glistening pink petals of her sex, and his nostrils flared as he drew in her ever-strengthening fragrance. His mate was ready for him, wet and waiting, inviting him in, but he didn't want a quick, simple fuck. However primal his need for her was at heart, it was anything but simple. No, he would please his mate. He would bring her to heights of pleasure that no one of any species had ever experienced, would push her to beyond her limits, and would not be satisfied until she was helpless but to breathe his name in a desperate plea for more.

He stepped forward, dropped to his knees, wrapped his arms around her legs, and dragged her to edge of the bed. Before he'd even completed those movements, he lowered his mouth to her open sex and groaned. He ran his tongue along her slit from bottom to top, flicking that little, hidden nub. Her flavor burst upon his tongue, dominating his awareness. She gasped and bucked her hips; Drakkal growled and tightened his grip on her. More of her nectar coated his tongue.

His craving, his *need*, finally overwhelmed his self-control. There was no turning back. There was no escape—not for Shay, and not for Drakkal. She was his.

And he was going to make her understand it in every possible way.

STILL PROPPED ON HER ELBOWS, Shay stared down at Drakkal's head between her legs, unable to look away from the erotic sight as she trembled with the sensations flooding her. Her lips parted with her panting breaths. Drakkal's rough, flat tongue dragged over her sex, lapping at her like he'd been dying of thirst. Every time it reached her clit, spikes of pleasure shot through her—each stronger than the last—and her breath hitched. The tips of his claws pricked her flesh, but the small amount of pain they produced only enhanced her excitement.

Biting her lower lip, Shay reached out to grasp his mane and pull him closer, to guide him to where she wanted him most, but he lifted his head and snarled through bared teeth, knocking her hand aside. That might've scared other people, but Shay found it sexy as all hell, and it sent a fresh rush of liquid heat to her core.

Drakkal's nostrils flared, and he dropped his face between her legs again. This time, his tongue slipped *inside* her.

"Oh fuck!" Shay collapsed onto the bed and spread her thighs wider, arching her pelvis up as much as his hold allowed. She felt the roughness of his tongue within her, stroking firmly, before he withdrew it and flicked it over her clit again.

"Right there. Please, right fucking there," she begged, squeezing her eyes shut and undulating her hips against his mouth as spirals of ecstasy swirled within her, coiling tight.

He huffed, blasting her with warm breath as his mouth hovered over her sex. Her anticipation grew, increasing her arousal in accordance, and her core clenched. Finally, his tongue dipped, lapping at her clit in quick, steady strokes. Reveling in the sensations, Shay moaned and clutched fistfuls of bedding. She forced her legs wider still.

She opened her eyes and looked down to see Drakkal's predatory stare over her stomach; he was watching her, his gaze aflame with pure want. Though it was difficult, she kept her eyes open as much as she was able, staring back at him as her pleasure climbed and her breathless moans became increasingly short and shallow.

Drakkal closed his mouth around her clit and sucked.

Rapture cleaved through Shay, blinding and deafening her as she came with a choked cry. Her back bowed off the bed, and she squeezed the bedding while the already overwhelming pleasure rocketed into something so intense that it nearly shattered her mind. Everything returned in a rush—the cascading waves of bliss crashing through her, her scream, Drakkal's rumbling growl as he greedily drank from her pussy, the rasp of the bedding against her bare skin as she writhed atop it, the press of the claws of his right hand against her thigh.

She was still riding those waves when Drakkal moved faster than she could quite comprehend. His hands were suddenly on her hips, and he flipped her over. Reflexively, she caught herself on hands and knees. Even if she'd had time to react, to resist, she never could've overcome his strength—but she didn't *want* to. She knew what was coming and she craved it. Though her pussy was still spasming from her last orgasm, she needed more.

Drakkal spanned his big hands over her hips, angled her ass up, and thrust into her.

Shay gasped at the sharp sting of his entry, rocking forward with the force of it. She felt herself stretching around him. Before she could draw another breath, he drew his hips back and yanked her ass toward him as he pumped forward, plunging his thick cock into her again, shoving deeper and forcing her body to accommodate him, to accept him, to take all of him. And it did, ravenously—greedily.

She closed her eyes and moaned, shoving back against him as he sank into her again and again, his entry eased by her slick. His claws pressed into her hips as he thrust, until finally, she had accepted all of him except the thickest part—his knot. With each gyration of his hips, he released a heavy grunt, their volume increasing along with his pace.

Drakkal bent forward, pressing his huge body over hers to surround her with his heat and soothe her with his fur. He moved his left arm over her left shoulder and wrapped his metal hand around the underside of her jaw while he slid his right hand down to her sex, pressing the pad of a finger over her clit. She was trapped by his body—trapped in a cage from which she never wanted to escape.

She felt his lips and his warm, ragged breath on the side of her neck as he lowered his head.

He unleashed himself in that moment.

His pace became frenzied, wild, relentless, and the slide of his big, hard cock struck that perfect spot inside her repeatedly, sparking new blasts of pleasure before the prior sensations had faded. His scent invaded her senses, along with the combined smell of sex. Breathy, needy moans tore from her throat as he plunged in and out of her. The overwhelming pleasure building inside her made her mindless. She grasped the bedding in her fists, helpless but to submit to the beast holding her body captive.

Guttural, feral sounds escaped Drakkal, and though his hold on her was firm, he did not hurt her. The minor pain she'd experienced in the beginning had faded, leaving only blistering pleasure.

With every thrust of his hips, he rocked her pelvis upon the finger pressed to her clit. Soon, the prickles of sensation spreading through her strengthened into an electric pulse that crackled along her every nerve, searing her with white-hot pleasure from head to toe. Another rush of heat flooded her core.

"Oh, fuck! Oh fuck! *Nngh!* Drakkal," she cried as her muscles locked and spasmed, and her pussy contracted around his shaft. The ecstasy was so staggering that she would have fallen were it not for his hold on her.

Drakkal snarled next to her ear, and his pace grew impossibly faster, sending her straight into another orgasm. She squeezed her eyes shut and let it take her.

He flattened his hand on her pelvis, pulled her toward him, and drove into her one last time, tightly wedging their bodies together. She gasped as the knot near the base of his shaft was forced into her sex. Her flesh stretched, and she felt the burn, but she just as clearly felt the throbbing of his pulse and an immense, unbelievable fullness. And then he *expanded*.

His body tensed around her, and Drakkal roared—a sound that would've sent a lion running with its tail tucked between its legs. The roar ended when he clamped his fangs over the place where her neck met her shoulder, their tips producing pricks of delightful pain. Hot seed burst from his cock an instant later, its force and heat triggering another climax for Shay. Her awareness narrowed, leaving only the sensations coursing through her, the feel of his body over hers, the sting from his teeth, the twitching of his cock inside her.

Shay panted; her ragged breath lifted her hair away from her face in little bursts. She remained utterly still as her pussy continued to spasm and contract around Drakkal's shaft. She had no choice, not with the way he held her immobile—which only turned her on more. Her flushed, sweat-slickened skin was made only hotter by the living furnace covering her.

Drakkal's left hand loosened and fell away from Shay's neck. He pressed it down on the bed, bracing his weight atop it, while shifting his right hand to the outside of her thigh. A low, rumbling sound emanated from his chest and vibrated into her as he widened his jaw and withdrew his fangs. Not a moment later, he pressed his mouth down over the wounds and caressed away the lingering sting with his lips and tongue.

With his arm no longer holding her up, Shay sagged down, and Drakkal followed. From this position—with her ass still pressed against his pelvis—he felt even bigger inside her. The rumbling in his chest continued as he rubbed his face up and down her neck and along her shoulder, occasionally lapping at the spot where he'd bitten her.

Exhausted and floating on a lusty, satisfied haze, it took

Shay a few seconds to realize what was happening. "Are you...*purring*?"

"I'm enjoying you." There was unmasked contentment in his voice. He ran his rough tongue behind Shay's ear, sending shivers through her.

His cock pulsed, and another burst of warmth flooded her. Drakkal tightened his arms around her, shuddering, and released a low growl.

"Are you... Did you just... *Still*?" Shay asked, shocked. She attempted to push herself up, to pull away, but Drakkal kept his arms locked around her, holding her close to his body.

"Can't yet. You'll just hurt both of us." He teased her with his tongue again, this time along the underside of her jaw.

She wasn't quite sure what to do with this loving, cuddly side of Drakkal, but if she was perfectly honest with herself... she liked what he was doing. *Really* liked it. "What do you mean?"

"I'm knotted, *kiraia*. You know we cannot separate until it's done." He pressed his lips against her neck and groaned, his body seizing as yet more seed pumped out of him. This time, it sent a pleasurable thrill through her, nearly pushing her over the edge again.

Shay shook her head, trying to think through the thickening fog of pleasure. "Uh, yeah, this isn't something that happens with humans."

As soon as he eased again, he asked, "Are you saying *that's* as big as your males' cocks get?"

She laughed, but the way it made her body shake sent fresh waves of pleasure through her, making her toes curl as she and Drakkal groan in unison.

"I should have known sex with an alien would have some weird aspects to it." She pressed back against him and waited until the intensity of the sensations diminished before speaking again. "So you mean...we're stuck together?"

"Until I'm spent." His purring strengthened, and his right hand shifted to cover one of her breasts. "Fortunately, I don't have anywhere else to be." He tweaked her nipple.

Shay gasped as a bolt of pleasure flowed through her; his touch was like a live wire connected straight to her clit. "Lucky me," she said breathlessly.

Drakkal chuckled deeply; the sound flowed into Shay, only heightening her pleasure.

When his cock twitched and poured more liquid fire into her, it was too much for Shay to bear; she came again, filling the room with raspy moans. Drakkal gyrated against her, creating just enough friction to prolong her orgasm and turn her moans into a cry of ecstasy.

Her body went slack when it was done. She closed her eyes and rested her cheek against the bedding, panting. She wanted nothing more than to sleep. She couldn't remember ever being so well and thoroughly loved—couldn't remember being sexed to the point of exhaustion.

Because she *hadn't* been. Not until now.

Drakkal rubbed his face against her neck and placing a gentle kiss over the place he'd bitten. "Your pleasure is beautiful, *kiraia*."

Shay's lips curled into a dreamy smile; she could only hum in response to him.

They remained that way for a while, his lips, tongue, and right hand lovingly stroking her body, caressing her skin, her breasts, her belly, and her clit. No part of her was left untouched. It was strange being physically tied to him like this. Had she known about his *knotting* before, she might've said no, might've resisted a little more, might've—

Oh, who the fuck was she kidding? This gave new meaning

to after-sex cuddling; it was more intimate than anything she'd ever experienced. Besides, she'd wanted the big azhera too damned badly, and she was enjoying this more with each passing moment. But she worried that this was more than just an itch being scratched. That it was *so much* more. That scared her; she was already growing too attached to him.

Drakkal's spasms spread farther and farther apart, and Shay soon felt full near to bursting. Just as she swore she couldn't take any more, his cock began to soften, pulsing gently in time with his heartbeat—which she could feel, steady and strong, against her back.

He groaned as he withdrew. Moisture spilled from her, pouring down the insides of her thighs. There was no question as to what it was.

Shay's sex contracted, suddenly feeling emptier, and she moaned as he eased her onto her side. Her every muscle was strained and worn; it was a delightful burn that couldn't have been accomplished through any exercise save for what they'd just done.

Drakkal settled his warm hand on her hip and his stroked her skin with his thumb. "Be right back, *kiraia*."

Shay could only muster another contented hum as he pulled away. She barely registered his absence before she succumbed to her weariness.

DRAKKAL LIFTED his hand from Shay's hip, looked her over —*kraasz ka'val, there is no sight more beautiful than my mate*— and turned away to walk into the bathroom. Her scents were in his fur, both that exotic sundrinker-kissed fragrance and the smell of her arousal, and he was reluctant to dilute those smells by washing, but it would need to be done eventually. He'd still detect those scents even after he bathed, he would still be carrying the mark his terran had left upon him—just as she'd be carrying his. That would be enough.

For now, his mate was weary. He would bathe with her when she was ready, and not a moment before. But he needed to drink.

Though he could still feel its flicker low in his belly, the lustful fire that had turned his body into a living furnace had finally subsided. Shay had done what his own hand could not. Her body had fit his perfectly, her oils had been a balm to his aching cock, and her *pussy* had granted him the release he'd so long craved. He was not so foolish as to think his hunger ended —even now, he craved more of her—but he'd be content for a while. He'd finally joined with his mate. He'd finally laid claim upon her.

And she'd accepted.

When he reached the counter, he turned on the water, bent down to shove his face beneath the faucet, and drank deep. The cool water eased the lingering heat inside him and fought back the dryness in his mouth. He stopped only when his belly was full.

He stood straight, braced his hands on the countertop, and glanced at himself in the large mirror set behind the counter. His fur was tousled, damp in places due both to her sweat and her oils, and the green of his eyes was darker than normal. His gradually receding cock still protruded from its sheath. All it would take was a single look from Shay to coax it back out fully.

Drakkal ran his fingers through his mane, tugging it back. He'd never knotted inside a female.

That's not quite right—I've never let *myself.*

Even when he was young, when he'd first *thought* he'd found his mate, some part of him had known it wasn't real. Something had always held him back, something more than simply not being ready to bring a cub into existence. Though it felt a little foolish to think it, he told himself now it was because his body had always been awaiting Shay, even if his brain hadn't known it.

And that felt...*right*. It felt true. She was the only one to get all of him, and he gladly gave it.

Tonight was only the start. She will have everything. She... and her cub.

Shay hadn't changed her position when he returned to the bedroom; she was fast asleep. He couldn't hold back a pang of disappointment, but it was accompanied by a swelling of pride—he'd pleased his mate to exhaustion. He gently moved her, only to stop as he discovered her thighs were sticky with his seed. His cock twitched, and a rumble rolled up his throat. She was his, and he wanted to have her again—right now.

He forced himself back to the bathroom instead and fetched a warm, damp cloth before returning to the bed to carefully clean his mate's legs and sex. She barely stirred.

After he finished, he tossed the cloth aside and took a few moments to appreciate her body again, sweeping his eyes over her slowly from bottom to top. She looked so beautiful, small, and delicate, but he knew that appearance of fragility belied the immense strength she harbored inside. His gaze lingered longest on her shoulder. The spots where his fangs had broken her skin were still red, but his saliva had stemmed the blood flow.

Without modern medical attention, the bite would likely scar, and that thought only further swelled his chest with pride. It would be physical proof of his claim—a sign to all that she was *his*.

Drakkal gently slipped his arms beneath Shay and lifted her, moving her up to rest her head upon one of the pillows. He climbed onto the bed once she was settled, rolled onto his side, and drew her against him, tucking her back along his front. The combination of her body heat and delectable scent had his cock stirring again.

Not now, he grumbled in his head.

He shifted his head forward, pressing his lips to her sweet, soft hair, and draped his right arm over her middle to palm her rounded belly. Something small but surprisingly strong pressed against his hand for an instant.

Drakkal lifted his head and stared toward her stomach, his heartbeat marking the passage of time in the otherwise silent room. Seconds passed, creeping toward a minute.

The push came again, lingering a little longer this time.

Drakkal's lips spread in a wide smile, and he gently brushed his palm over Shay's belly. Pride and protectiveness tightened his chest; he finally understood his purpose, finally knew what all this meant. The deep emotions he felt toward Shay and the unborn cub strengthened, bolstered by new dedication, and he embraced them even if he couldn't fully identify all of them.

"Your mother is my mate," he whispered, "so you are my cub. Mine to protect." He caressed Shay's belly again. "Neither of you will want for anything again. Because you are both mine...and I am yours."

FIFTEEN

Shay awoke to a painfully bloated bladder and something tickling her nose, but despite how much she had to pee, she really, *really* didn't want to get up. She hadn't been this comfortable in longer than she could remember—she was warm, cozy, languid, and she knew if she changed her position at all, she'd never find this comfort again.

She could ignore her bladder for a little longer, but the sensation on her nose was too irritating. The last thing she needed was to sneeze and pee herself. She wrinkled and wiggled her nose. When the tickle persisted, she made a discontented sound and turned her face, rubbing her nose against what was somehow both the hardest *and* softest pillow ever.

But pillows didn't rise and fall with deep breaths, and they didn't have heartbeats, and they most definitely didn't *purr*.

The scents of leather, cloves, and unbridled masculinity surrounded her. Shay tensed and opened her eyes. The room was dark, too dark for her to see, but she knew. Oh, she *knew* whose chest her face was buried against.

I slept with him. He stayed in my room, slept in my bed...with me.

Drakkal was pressed against her, front to front, with his arms wrapped around her securely and one of her legs between his. Heat radiated from him.

My very own warm, fuzzy furnace.

No. No. Not my anything. He isn't supposed to be here!

It was just supposed to have been sex, no strings attached. They were supposed to have enjoyed themselves and gone their separate ways. Not...not...*sleep* together! He wasn't supposed to be holding her like she was the most precious thing in the world, wasn't supposed to be purring contentedly, and she wasn't supposed to love it so damn much.

"Awake already, *kiraia?*" Drakkal murmured huskily, shifting to nuzzle his cheek against the top of her head. "Guess I didn't do as good a job as I thought."

His voice sent a jolt of desire straight to her core.

Fuck!

Shay jerked away from him. Drakkal released his hold on her without struggle. If she hadn't needed to pee so bad, she would've been annoyed at herself for feeling immediately so cold outside his embrace.

"Lights on," she snapped.

The lights flared to life. She flinched from the brightness, narrowing her eyes to slits and groping blindly for the blanket as she scooted—with some difficulty—toward the edge of the bed.

"You all right, Shay?" he asked, sounding far more awake, alert, and concerned.

She yanked the blanket around her to shield her nakedness from him and stood, only to go deathly still.

Something—*a lot* of something—warm and viscous spilled from her, running down her inner thighs.

For a moment, Shay thought she might have actually peed herself, but that thought fled as quickly as it had formed. No, this was the aftermath of being cock-locked with an azhera as he blew his load into her over and over and over and fucking over again.

Shay clutched the blanket to her chest. She turned and glared at Drakkal, who was sitting up in bed, totally naked himself, his features strained with worry. He looked like he was about to jump to his feet and come to her.

She jabbed a finger at him and said, "Stay. There."

He stilled, ears perking.

Without waiting for a response, she turned her back on him and waddled—fucking *waddled!*—to the connected bathroom. As soon as the door closed behind her, she released the blanket and looked down at herself. It was difficult to see with her belly in the way, but she could *feel* his come dripping out of her, soaking her inner thighs.

Where'd you think it'd all go? That it'd just magically disappear?

Despite the situation, Shay snort-laughed.

Magically disappearing spunk. Would sure make clean up easier.

Shay sighed and moved farther into the room, stopping abruptly when she caught sight of herself in the mirror. Her hair was in complete disarray, hanging in tangled strands down her back and over her shoulders, and her eyes were bright and sleepy, but it was the marks on her skin that she stared at the longest. She turned slightly to the side. There were bruises on her hips in the shape fingers—thick *azheran* fingers. The memory of the way Drakkal had held her rushed to the forefront of her mind, accompanied by faint echoes of the sensations she'd felt while he thrust into her.

There was another bruise where her shoulder met her

neck, barely visible through her hair. She swept her hair aside. There were several dark red spots within the bruise—scabs where Drakkal's teeth had penetrated. She gently probed the spot with her fingers. The wound was tender, and its shape, along with its origin, was distinct and unforgettable. Drakkal had bitten her right before he came. And despite the brief flash of pain, she'd *enjoyed* it.

That had been, hands down, the best sex she'd ever had in her life.

Then why am I so pissy? Isn't sex supposed to give you all those feel good feelings? I should be floating blissfully on a cloud of oxytocin.

Shay placed her hands on the counter and leaned forward, staring into her own eyes.

"I should still be in bed with the azhera," she said quietly. Just like that, her irritation bled away.

Who cared if he'd stayed after sex? That didn't mean anything. They'd shared pleasure—*intense* pleasure—and had worked themselves to exhaustion; it made total sense that he would've just crawled onto the bed beside her and slept. And after the way he'd made her feel, after the frenzy of their lovemaking, it made sense that she'd enjoyed being held by him so calmly and tenderly.

So perfectly.

Did I really just think of it as lovemaking? *Nope, no, wrong word. It was just sex.*

But had it been? Had it really been *just* sex?

As much as she wanted to tell herself it'd been casual sex and nothing more, she knew that was a lie. She'd *wanted* Drakkal to stay, and he'd clearly wanted to stay, too. He'd made it clear what she was to him. Shay was the one holding him at arm's length. Drakkal would gladly shelter her in his arms all night long, every night, and she...longed for that, too. She longed for *more*, but it scared the hell out of her. What if she allowed herself to care about him only to lose him? She couldn't open herself up for that kind of hurt.

I already have.

Shay's eyes stung. She grasped the edge of the counter and pressed her lips together, willing the sensation away.

I can take care of myself.

Yeah, Shay, you can. Nobody's questioning that, you've got nothing to prove. But why make yourself and your baby struggle just to say you did it alone when there's someone who gives a damn about you and the baby, someone who's more than willing to help? Why be so damn stubborn when he wants you, and you know you want him, too?

Drakkal was *nothing* like her ex, Anthony. Drakkal wouldn't betray her, wouldn't abandon her; only death could keep him away, though she had the impression that even death would be leery to test its strength against Drakkal's willpower. The Shay of a month ago would've called her a stupid, naïve little girl for believing in anyone so thoroughly. But Drakkal wanted her *and* her baby.

"Am I really considering this?" she asked herself. "Am I really going to take an azhera as my...boyfriend?"

The word *boyfriend* sounded so damn absurd, and she knew it wasn't the right word.

Mate. He'd be her mate.

Shay let out a long, slow exhalation, and, unable to stand the pressure any longer, finally waddled to the toilet to relieve herself. Once she was finished, she stepped into the shower and washed, scrubbing her hair and body clean. When she probed her sex, she almost moaned at its tenderness—it was a pleasurable tenderness. She smirked.

Damn, he loved me good.

Once she finished and used the convenient glowing panels

on the floor and ceiling to dry herself, she carefully squatted to retrieve the blanket from the floor and wrapping it around her body again. As she reached up to touch the door panel, her hand stilled.

What if I fuck this up? I've done so much stupid shit, hurt the only person left who loved me...

But she'd learned from those mistakes, hadn't she? She'd grown since then, and she was determined to make this new life with her baby one worth living—one worthy of the parents she'd lost too soon. And of all the people she'd met, who better to try and build that life with than Drakkal? He was the sort of man who Shay's dad, Captain Ryan Collins, would've liked—and that went a long way with her.

It helped that she really liked Drakkal, too.

Before she allowed doubt to rear its ugly head again, she pressed the control button, and the door whooshed open. She stepped back into the room. Drakkal was sitting on the edge of the bed, hunched forward with arms resting on his thighs. He met her gaze and lifted his brows in question.

"Last night was supposed to be no strings attached," she said, moving closer. "You agreed."

He sat up straight, bracing his hands on his knees. "No, I didn't."

Shay's eyes dropped to his lap, where his cock—its deep red making it hard to miss against his tan and brown fur—protruded from his sheath, growing harder the longer she stared. She jerked her gaze back to his only to find the corners of his mouth curled upward in a knowing smirk; he'd already caught her looking.

"You did," she said. "I told you what this would be when you came in, and you—"

Shay snapped her mouth shut as she reviewed her memory of their brief conversation, fighting through the haze of lust and pleasure that entirely overshadowed her recollection of yesterday.

No. He hadn't agreed at all.

She narrowed her eyes but couldn't stop the grin that spread across her lips. "Oh, you sneaky, sneaky kitty. You played me good."

"Didn't play you, terran. I just chose not to agree...and you didn't stop me." His eyes dipped, and though she was wrapped in the blanket, Shay felt his gaze penetrating the fabric, producing a trail of heat on her skin as it moved. He slowly smoothed his hands along his thighs, toward his pelvis.

"So you want this, then?" she asked, forcing her eyes up to his again—it was much harder this time. "You want me? As a...a mate?"

Drakkal nodded. Fire sparked in his emerald gaze, intensifying as his pupils expanded. "Fuck yes."

"And this baby? Even though it's not yours?"

"*You* are mine," he said with unwavering surety, "so your cub is mine, also."

Shay's heart clenched, and her throat constricted around the sudden, heavy emotion flooding her. She tightened her grip on the blanket and dropped a hand to her belly.

Hear that, Baby? He wants you. He wants us.

Shay had been furious when Anthony had declared the baby wasn't his and that he'd never have anything to do with it. He'd even said *get rid of it*. A painful sense of abandonment had come after her initial rage. She hadn't cared about losing Anthony—he'd shown her once and for all how much of a deadbeat, cheating asshole he was—but she'd mourned the fact that her daughter wouldn't have a dad. Shay's father had been so wonderful, so loving, and she'd stupidly hoped that somewhere, buried deep in Anthony's body, there'd been at least one selfless bone. She'd hoped that he would've given a shit about his own kid.

But none of that mattered now. What mattered now was the male in front of her—the male who *wanted* Shay and her baby.

Taking a deep, shuddering breath, she closed the distance between them, stopping only when she stood before him. Drakkal tilted his head back, ears perking. There was an eagerness in the way his tail moved atop the bed, an anticipation—and it mirrored the way Shay felt.

She reached out with one hand and ran her fingers through his mane. "So...we're really doing this? We're really giving it a shot?"

Drakkal covered her hand with his, stilling it, and stared into her eyes. "I want nothing more than I want you, *kiraia*. Maybe I've been stupid lately, but I'm not dumb enough to pass up a chance to have you."

Heat flooded her core and overflowed to suffuse her body, right down the tips of her fingers and toes.

I want this. I want him.

She smiled and released her grip on the blanket, letting it slide down her body to pool on the floor. "Then have me."

The hungry gleam in his eyes intensified as he raked them over her. He inhaled deeply, nostrils flaring, and fixed his gaze on her pussy. She knew he could smell her desire. He extended both arms, settling his hands on her hips—over the bruises he'd left the night before. That only turned her on more. With an oddly gentle firmness, he drew her closer until she stood between his thighs.

He slid his right hand up, his calloused palm gliding over her skin until he was cupping one of her breasts in his big, strong fingers. He leaned forward and sucked her nipple into his mouth. Shay moaned and delved the fingers of both hands into his mane, using it to pull him closer. His rough tongue abraded her nipple, sending strong currents of pleasure straight to her center. She tilted her pelvis toward him.

Drakkal slid his metal hand around to grasp her ass. Like the rest of him, that hand was a contradictory blend of hard and soft—the unyielding metal plates contrasting the thick padding on its fingers and palm, which had the slightest give to it.

Only after her sensitive nipple was tender and red did he release it, shifting his mouth to the other to lavish it with equal attention. The delicious torment left her quivering in need. Her breath quickened and grew ragged, and her pulse pounded as her arousal grew. She squeezed her thighs together, but it wasn't enough to alleviate the hungry ache between them.

He withdrew his mouth from her breast, leaving her bereft and desperate for more, and moved his hands to her hips. When he guided her backward, her instinct was to resist—she only wanted to be closer to him—but he was too strong.

Drakkal drew his legs together. His cock was fully erect now, throbbing in the open air, with its head aimed directly at her and the knot at its base thickening.

He hooked his hands behind her thighs and lifted her suddenly, forcing her legs apart. Despite how awkward she felt with her rounded belly, Drakkal had plucked Shay off her feet with no apparent effort. He guided her legs to either side of his thighs as he pulled her toward him, positioning her astride his lap. His shaft pressed along her slit, hard and hot, and she felt his pulse through it; its every faint beat and tiny twitch produced a new twinge of pleasure low in her belly.

Shay looped her arms around his neck.

"You're already mine, *kiraia*," Drakkal growled.

He cupped the back of her head with his left hand, twining his metal fingers in her hair, and pulled her down into a scalding, claiming kiss. She parted her lips, and Drakkal readily accepted her offering. He ravished her mouth, demanding everything she had to give, and she succumbed to his savageness. Their lips molded to each other, their teeth nipped tender flesh, and their tongues moved in an intricate, sensual dance.

The kiss was reckless, punishing, masterful, and consuming.

It was everything.

Shay rocked her hips, sliding her slick pussy along his cock. Whispers of pleasure rippled through her. With every undulation, the head of his shaft stroked her clit, building her desire higher and higher and making her belly flutter.

Gripping his mane, she wrenched his head back, breaking the kiss. Drakkal snarled, but the sound ended with a grunt when Shay dropped a hand and clamped it around his shaft. Locking her eyes with his, she lifted her hips, guided the head of his cock to her entrance, and bared her teeth as she sank down upon him. "And you're fucking mine."

SHAY'S SEX welcomed him into its hot, tight embrace, taking him in so deeply that her folds were touching the uppermost portion of his knot. Drakkal hissed through his teeth, trembling with the immense wave of ecstasy that had erupted within him. The words she'd spoken—paired with the way she'd just taken him into her body—could be interpreted as nothing but a claim.

He'd claimed her last night. Now, she was claiming him, accepting their bond as mates. That alone was almost enough to make him come right then and there.

He curled his metal fingers in her hair, tugging her head aside to expose the bite mark on her shoulder while he kneaded the supple flesh of her thigh with his right hand. An approving rumble sounded in his chest.

"Leave your mark on me, female. Show me your words are

true." He lifted his chin and tilted his head to the side, baring his neck and shoulder as he guided her face closer.

Her little teeth clamped down over his flesh, and, though she didn't have fangs, he felt her bite. The flash of pain sent a jolt straight to his cock. He growled and moved his hands to her hips. He refused to climax without giving her anything in return, and he was already dangerously close.

Without releasing her bite, she lifted her hips and dropped back down on him, again and again, and he used his arms to grant her movements new force. Each of her downward strokes brought a maddening blast of pleasure, and each upward slide of her pussy nearly stole his breath.

Her panting breaths were hot against his neck, and small moans tore from her throat each time he entered her. She slid her hands to his chest, clenched his fur in her little fingers, and, finally, released her bite. Drakkal shuddered, groaning as feeling flooded back to the mark she'd made. The resurgence of pain only heightened his pleasure.

"Look at me," he growled between heavy, ragged breaths.

Shay drew back, and her half-lidded, lust filled eyes met his. She was beautiful. Her golden hair flowed around her, brushing over her radiant, flushed skin, and her pink lips were kiss swollen. Her full breasts bounced with her movements, teasing him with her well-loved, hardened nipples, and her muscles quivered all around him. Her oils coated his cock and thighs.

He lifted his hips as she came down on the next stroke, driving his cock deeper still.

"Oh, fuck—*mmh!*" Shay shuddered. Her eyelids shut, and her head fell back.

Drakkal caught her neck and jaw in his right hand, pressing the pads of his fingers and thumb against her cheeks, and forced her face back to his. "*Look at me.*"

Panting, she opened her eyes and met his gaze again.

"Do not look away, *kiraia*," he said, punctuating his words by repeatedly driving her down upon him. "See me, and know I see you."

"I see you," she rasped, her body shuddering as her sex contracted, hungrily sucking him deeper. Her grip on his fur tightened. "And I fucking *feel* you."

Drakkal's breaths became erratic as pleasure rocketed outward from his cock, racing along his every nerve to set his body alight with overwhelming sensation, but he would not yet give in. "Who do I belong to?" he demanded.

Her eyes bore into his, glassy with desire but equally fierce as she bared her teeth. "Me."

He quickened his pace, keeping his jaw clenched for several seconds before grating, "And who do *you* belong to?"

Her motions stuttered, and her moans escalated with every thrust of his cock. Her sex constricted around him, and her inner walls quivered as she came, producing a hot flood of her oils.

"You," she cried. "Oh, fuck me. *You!*"

With a roar, Drakkal slammed her down a final time, forcing his bulging knot into her tight pussy. She gasped at the intrusion, her body tensing. He didn't allow her to look away—didn't allow himself to look away—as he came undone. He ground his thickening cock deep inside her as his seed burst from him, grunting and growling his satisfaction with each powerful spurt.

As the frenzy of their lovemaking died down, Shay relinquished her hold on his fur, glided her hands up to his shoulders, and slid her arms around his neck. Panting, she leaned forward and pressed her forehead to his. Her spasms eased into delightful shivers. Drakkal wrapped his arms around her and held her close.

Shay hummed contently, her eyes drifted shut, and her lips curled into a smile. She and Drakkal maintained their positions as they slowly descended from the new euphoric pinnacle they'd reached, as Drakkal's body pumped all its seed into her —and as her body milked it from him. Warm and sated, Drakkal lapsed into thought.

He would never have believed this degree of contentment possible were he not feeling it now. Certainly, he'd longed for it since his youth, but life had suggested early on that it was unattainable, that he'd have to settle for whatever he could find instead—that he'd have to settle for what was realistic. Twenty years ago, he'd mistakenly thought he'd found that. He'd thought he'd found a mate...or at least as close to a mate as he'd ever have.

It was different with Shay, so different that there really was no comparison; *this* was it. This was what he'd truly craved, what he'd always needed. *She* was what he'd always needed.

Shay's acceptance of his claim had been rapturous. Knowing that she was for him—and he for her—had so strongly cemented Drakkal's purpose that it cast his entire life before finding her into doubt.

Long ago, he'd been forced to walk a path he'd never wanted any part of, and he'd spent a long time lamenting the choices stolen from him. He'd found friends along the way. Better than that, he'd found a brother he would never otherwise have known. But he'd never had reason to be grateful for the way things had gone. Not until now.

Not until Shay.

Each step he'd taken had brought him here, to her. He wasn't certain of what he believed as far as ancestors and spirits, wasn't sure of the truth behind reality and fate, but he could see now that all the hardships, all the suffering and pain, had made him into the person he had to become to find Shay. A month ago, all of it had seemed random, the results of an uncaring universe without discernable pattern, without any sense of justice, morality, or purpose. Now it all made sense.

Shay had given his past meaning it would otherwise never have held. She'd given *him* meaning. The years had shaped him into exactly what he needed to be for her—a protector, a partner, an equal.

For the first time in two decades, he had peace.

He had his true mate.

And if anyone tried to take her from him, he'd rip them to fucking shreds.

SIXTEEN

Shay stared at the security feeds and blindly dipped her fingers into the bowl of Kalatharian nuts Kiloq had left on the desk during his shift. She knew he'd done so out of kindness rather than forgetfulness—after trying them for the first time in the break room five days ago, she'd developed a crazy craving for the pale green nuts. Lately, the rest of the crew had taken to leaving bowls of them everywhere, making sure she always had access. She was touched by their thoughtfulness. It was especially appreciated while she was working—the nuts made a perfect movie snack, and her job had her staring at screens for hours and hours at a time.

Though she was forced to sit in one place for long periods of time, her job, thankfully, wasn't *always* a boring one. The surveillance feeds from inside and immediately around the building were slow and uneventful, their monotony broken only by the occasional shift change or the arrival of a client, but the screens covered much more than that—Drak and Arc had eyes on all the surrounding streets, too, and those were always bustling no matter the time.

She'd seen fistfights and street performances, a foot chase or two, and had even spotted a couple pickpockets working their trade on the crowds. People watching had proven endlessly entertaining, especially when Shay didn't even know the species of many of the people she was watching. Hell, she could have even had free porn if she wanted, given the frequency of unsuspecting couples who ducked into nearby alleys for quickies—though she suspected Drakkal wouldn't have appreciated her watching those encounters. None of them could have compared to her mate, anyway.

My mate.

It'd been a week since she and Drakkal had made that claim, and though the word still felt strange—especially coming from a world of boyfriends and husbands—it was *right*. Happy wasn't adequate to describe how she'd felt since then; it didn't seem strong enough. She was exhilarated, contented, blissful...*complete.*

Even when she and Drakkal were apart, he found ways to let her know he was thinking about her. Leaving little gifts in places he knew she'd be, having food sent to her when he couldn't join her for a meal, or sending holocom texts—some of which left her so horny that she was ready to leap at him the moment they were together.

Drakkal doted on her when they were together. He didn't treat her like glass, like she was some delicate little thing that would shatter at the slightest touch, but he made her feel cherished, worthy, important.

Loved.

They didn't spend *all* their free time in the bedroom, though. She especially enjoyed when he'd head down to the simulation chambers with her. They'd load into sims together—though they were in separate rooms, the system loaded in holographic avatars of the other participants—and engage in competitions that began as friendly contests and always ended in fierce rivalries. He'd topped her on kills and accuracy the first few times, but she'd finally begun shedding the rust and rediscovering her groove.

Shay had won the last time, if only just barely. She hadn't passed up the opportunity to gloat—and to warn him that he wasn't ever going to win again once she had her baby and got back into shape. Many of the men she'd known on Earth would've had their egos bruised by that. The crowds she'd run with during her rebellious, misguided years had been filled with males who'd carried their heavy but fragile masculinity on their shoulders, and many of them didn't like to be outdone by a woman.

Drakkal had only grinned, emerald eyes twinkling with pride, and told her to bring it.

She plucked a nut from the bowl and popped it into her mouth. Its sweet and salty flavor reminded her of cashews, but these were a little sweeter and had a hint of vanilla. She hummed appreciatively and ate a few more.

"I'm getting so fat," she said just as the door opened.

"Pfft. You're a runt, terran," Thargen said as he entered the room and approached her. He reached over to snatch a few nuts from the bowl, tossed them into his mouth, and chewed noisily. "Anyway, all the flavor's in the fat."

Shay leaned back in her seat and chuckled. "Do you even realize how messed up some of the stuff you say is?" She narrowed her eyes and tilted her head. "*Have* you eaten a human before?"

"Don't think I have." He plopped down on the empty chair near hers and turned on the extra screen—the one Razi used to watch his shows while he was on surveillance duty. "Hard to say. Memory ain't what it was. At least I think it isn't." The vorgal reached up and tapped the scar on the shaved side of his head.

She used her toes and shift her chair from side to side. "Well, if someone's going to eat me, I might as well taste good."

"Probably best for me if you don't tell Drakkal about any of this," he replied with a laugh. "And I say why be tasty when you can be tough? Make them work for it, and let the fuckers choke when they try to swallow you."

Shay laughed. It hadn't taken long to find her place in the crew. They'd accepted her without question, had treated her as family from the beginning. And even though they were all breaking the law just by being a part of Arcanthus and Drakkal's operation, they reminded her much more of her father's military buddies than any criminals she'd associated with.

"Those tattoos on your face...they're military, right?" she asked.

Thargen nodded. He absently flicked through different entertainment feeds on the screen. "Vorgal tradition. Rank and honors for everyone to see."

She studied the markings on his cheek. They were blood red, centered around a symbol that looked like an axe or a similar ancient weapon, radiating outward from that center. She flung her mind back to things her father had shown her long ago; the vorgals had been allies of the United Terran Federation for a few decades, and Dad had been familiar with their military system. She'd seen that symbol before.

"You were infantry, right?" she asked.

"Yup." He lifted a finger, indicating a spiked symbol above the central axe. "Vanguard. First in. We got to do all the fun parts."

"That how you got the scar?"

"Yeah. Don't really remember much of what happened. I'm

sure I killed plenty of the bastards, though, because I was covered in a lot of blood that wasn't mine afterward." He turned his head toward her and grinned, fully displaying his pronounced canines and tusks; it should've been an unsettling expression, but Shay had come to appreciate it.

"The healers said I should've died," he continued. "Severe brain trauma, or something like that. But Urgand fixed me up right there, knee-deep in mud and blood. He dragged me off that field." His gaze dipped briefly to her belly. "My head's kind of...foggy, most days, and I can't pretend I understand all the medical shit Urgand goes on about sometimes. Don't know if I ever really did. But I know you and your youngling are in good hands with him."

It was a rare moment of comfort from him, and honestly, Shay had really needed to hear it—especially today. She'd tried hard not to think about it, had tried to suppress her nervousness, to occupy her mind, but it had all been festering just under the surface. She trusted Urgand, there was no question about that. It was just... What if something was wrong? What if *she'd* done something wrong?

Thargen's grin stretched wider. "And growing up around here, your youngling will be a little ass-kicker for sure."

Shay returned the grin. "There's no question about that."

Knowing that her baby would be so loved here made Shay's heart feel like it was near to bursting; her child would be as loved and accepted as she'd felt among her father's friends.

The door opened, and Shay and Thargen turned their heads to find Samantha standing in the doorway.

She had a warm smile on her face as she met Shay's gaze, and her voice was brimming with excitement when she said, "They're ready."

Shay's heart leapt, and her anxiety returned with vengeance. She wanted this. She *needed* this—the *baby* needed this—but that didn't stop the worry that was making it difficult for Shay to fill her lungs with air. Was it better to know or to remain ignorant? Was it better to be aware of potential problems and complications, even if they couldn't be solved, or to carry on blissfully unaware?

She felt like that should've been easy to answer, but she couldn't figure it out. She'd been in shoot outs with dangerous people, had felt bullets and sizzling plasma bolts zip by within centimeters of her face, had partaken in deals that could've erupted in terrible violence at any moment...and none of that had been as scary as the prospect of a simple medical exam was now.

Circumstances—like being a wanted criminal on Earth and then being abducted by aliens—had prevented her from getting the medical attention she should've sought after first discovering her pregnancy. Things hadn't been much different here on Arthos—at least not until recently. Even if it made her uncomfortable to know they must've spent a big chunk of money on it without asking her for anything in return, Arcanthus and Drakkal had purchased medical equipment specifically to assist in prenatal, birthing, and postnatal care. Urgand had been setting it all up over the last few days.

Shay had no more excuses, no valid reason to hide. Her fears didn't matter—this was for her baby.

Shay pushed herself out of the chair and patted Thargen's shoulder. "Looks like you're on your own now. Don't have too much fun."

"I always have too much fun, terran," he replied, finally stopping the entertainment feed on something unexpected—a Volturian drama.

Samantha grinned. "Did Razi finally corrupt you?"

Thargen chuckled and shook his head, settling more

comfortably into his chair. "This shit's funny. Even funnier when I tell Razi that to his face."

As Shay moved toward the door, she lowered her voice and said to Sam, "He totally has a hard-on for that Volturian actress."

Thargen barked laughter. "Damn right I do, terran!"

Shay thrust a finger at him, narrowing her eyes. "Hey! I work in here. You'd better clean up after yourself."

He waved a hand dismissively. "Only time I mix work and pleasure is when I have to kill someone. Now get to the infirmary before your kitty gets anxious."

Both the women laughed.

"Arcanthus has the whole place calling Drakkal kitty now," Samantha said as they stepped out into the hallway.

Shay smirked, falling into step beside Sam as they walked down the corridor. "He doesn't seem to mind when I do."

"You're his mate. Of course he doesn't mind." A smile played on Samantha's lips. "Arc does just about everything he can to needle Drak, but Drak retaliates in kind. Seems to be their way of showing affection for each other."

Chuckling, Shay nodded. "Sounds about right."

Comfortable silence stretched between the two of them for a few moments. Shay glanced at the other woman, who, along with Thargen, was fast becoming her closest friend. The two humans were complete opposites, but Shay suspected that had they met under different circumstances, had their lives not taken the bad turns that eventually led them here, they would have met some other way and formed a friendship all on their own. Samantha was a caring, compassionate woman with a great sense of humor she only revealed to those close to her.

Were they still on Earth, Shay would've loved to teach Samantha's abusive ex a lesson after Arcanthus was done with him—if there was anything left.

"Sooo, out of curiosity, what's it like with a sedhi?" Shay asked. "I mean, we're both mated to some pretty *alien* aliens, and well...there's some differences between sex with a human."

Eyes going wide, Samantha stopped and turned toward Shay. "Oh my God, you have *no* idea how badly I wanted to ask you the same thing! I just...didn't know how to."

Shay chuckled. "You just ask. Easy."

A blush stained Samantha's cheeks. "Not so easy. It's a little...embarrassing. Other than Sekk'thi, I was the only female here, and well... I just didn't know how to really...bring up sex, you know? And it's pretty clear that her experience with it is pretty different from mine..."

"Yeah, Sekk'thi sure isn't shy about it. Though at the same time, neither am I."

Samantha peeked back and forth down the hallway before meeting Shay's gaze again. "When you and Drak have sex, does...anything weird happen?"

"Other than getting cock-locked for extended periods of time? Nope. It's some pretty amazing sex, and if I were to say it gets intense...well, that'd be an understatement."

"Oh God, yes. The sex..." Sam's expression turned curious. "Cock-locked?"

"As in, we're locked together. You couldn't pry us apart with a damned crowbar."

Sam's eyes widened. "*You too?*"

"Me too? Okay, back up a second there. Now I need the deets."

To Shay's astonishment, it was possible for Samantha to get redder still. The poor girl was far too self-conscious, but Shay found it endearing.

"I, uh...thought I broke it when I first saw it," Samantha said, the corner of her mouth quirking sheepishly.

"Wait. *Broke* it? As in his cock?"

The shy woman nodded. "It...split."

Shay stared at her, unable to process what had just been said. "*Split?*"

"Split."

"Like..."

"Like into four parts."

"*Holy shit!*"

Samantha laughed. "I was horrified. I mean, not by him. It was a shock. But I swear his ego has never taken a hit like it did then. Can you imagine how a guy would feel when his mate recoils from his...you know, the first time she sees it?"

Shay curled her lips in and bit them, trying to contain her mirth, but failed. Laughter burst from her, so hard that she had to catch herself on the wall. "I would have loved to see the look on his face."

"In hindsight, it *was* pretty funny." Sam grinned. "*He* still hasn't laughed about it."

"I can't imagine he would."

Samantha tucked her hair behind her ear and smiled. "It does feel nice though. *Really* nice."

Shay's thoughts immediately turned to Drakkal. "Yeah, they do. And Arc also...locks?"

Sam's tongue slipped out to run over her lips. "It kind of more...*latches.*"

"*Latches?*" Surely it couldn't be bad if Samantha said it felt nice, but just the thought was... Shay shuddered and cringed. "Do I want to know how that works?"

Shaking her head, Sam chuckled. "It doesn't hurt. Well, it does if you try to pull away before it's done implanting."

"*Implanting?*"

"Well, it like, grabs...the walls..." Samantha caught her lower lip between her teeth, leaned closer to Shay, and raised a hand, fingers and thumb pressed together. She opened her fingers slowly. "And pries them open. To, uh...well to make sure all the, um, the *you know* gets in there."

Shay recoiled, dropping a hand to cup her groin as though she could shield it from the mental image Sam's words and demonstration conjured. "And you saw it before he stuck it in you?"

Samantha nodded. "Yeah. I did. I mean...*look* at Arc. He's..." Her eyes shut and a dreamy smile curled on her lips. "Perfect. He's so perfect."

"Freaky cock and all, huh?"

Sam laughed again. "Yes. Freaky cock and all."

"Yeah," Shay agreed, her lips twitching into a smirk. "I love my knotty kitty, too."

"Your *knotty* kitty?"

"Cause, you know, he *knots*." Shay held her fists one atop the other, as though an invisible cylinder were in her grasp, and expanded the lower hand.

Laughter burst from Sam. "Oh my God! That's a good one."

When they reached the infirmary a little while later, Shay's cheeks hurt from how much she'd been smiling and laughing. As soon as they entered the sterile, white room, her unease returned. The center of the room was largely open, but most of the wall space was taken up by cabinets, counters, and medical machinery for which Shay had no name. It'd been so long since she'd been to a doctor—a trustworthy doctor, anyway—that everything looked only familiar enough to be unsettling.

Drakkal and Urgand stood beside a large chair that looked like something out of a dentist's office. Though with just a little spattered blood and dimmer lighting, it would've made a perfect horror movie prop.

This is not the time to let that imagination run, Shay.

Samantha placed her hand on Shay's arm and smiled gently. "I can't wait to hear the results."

Knowing full well she was failing to keep her concern from showing in her expression, Shay smiled back at the woman. "Thanks, Sam. I'll let you know."

"You'll be fine. Both of you." Sam gave Shay's arm a gentle squeeze before releasing her hold and exiting the room.

Drakkal grinned and walked over to her. "Was about to come looking for you myself, *kiraia*."

She looked up at him and smirked. "Sam and I were having a little female bonding time. There were some...interesting discussions."

"You were talking about cocks, weren't you?"

Shay's grin widened.

Drakkal chuckled. "And you reached the conclusion that mine's the best, of course."

She looked him dead in the eye, serious as could be, and said, "Yes."

"Good."

Her lips twitched and she lowered her voice so only he could hear her. "I quite enjoy my knotty kitty."

He drew in a slow, deep breath and lifted a hand to his temples, covering his eyes. "That's another pun, isn't it? *Kraasz ka'val*, what is wrong with you terrans? Do *not* tell Arc that one."

Shay snickered. "Better hope Sam doesn't tell, either."

Drakkal's hand fell, and his brows were low as he stared down at her. "You said that to Samantha?"

"Maaaaybe."

His lips trembled and peeled back to reveal his fangs, and he drew in several breaths as though he meant to speak but had failed to find the words before finally saying, "You're lucky I like you, terran. Get on the fucking chair."

Shay laughed as she moved to the chair. "Oh, I love it when you talk dirty."

Though she was sure there'd be no fucking on that chair...at least not while Urgand was present.

Urgand manipulated a control, lowering the chair to a more comfortable height for Shay to sit. He wore a long white coat that might've looked right at home in a hospital or lab back on Earth were it not for its collar, which fit snugly around his thick neck. She'd also never imagined a doctor quite as broad shouldered and clearly well-built as him...or with face tattoos and short tusks protruding from his lower jaw.

"This won't take long," Urgand said. His voice was deep and gravelly, but it possessed a decidedly professional tone that eased a bit of her nervousness.

More of her anxiety faded when Drakkal positioned himself beside her, not quite close enough for them to be touching, but close enough for Shay to feel his body heat.

Urgand used the controls to raise the chair, simultaneously lowering its backrest to smoothly lean her back. Components of the chair shifted as her position altered, cushioning the new points of stress on her body at her lower back and neck. Without thought, Shay reached out and grasped Drakkal's flesh and blood hand, clutching it.

"Got you, *kiraia*," Drakkal said softly, giving her hand a squeeze.

In that moment, she loved him. She loved him more than she'd thought possible so early in their relationship, more than she'd thought possible at all, but there it was. She really, truly, deeply loved her gruff, sweet, persistent *azhera*.

She held his gaze, unable to voice the emotions swelling within her, until movement on her other side drew her attention away.

Urgand had pulled up a holographic display in the air

beside the chair and was working through options on it. "Just going to scan you, Shay. Nothing invasive, nothing painful." His lips moved as though he were muttering to himself as he perused the display in front of him. "How's your wrist feel? Any tenderness or pain?"

Shay lifted her right hand off her belly and turned her arm to look at the inside of her wrist. There was a small red mark there, evidence of the new ID chip she'd received yesterday. Getting a body scan for that had been interesting. Arcanthus had been startlingly professional during the process earlier that week, which had involved Shay stripping down to her birthday suit and stepping onto a glowing platform.

Despite Arc averting all three of his eyes, Drakkal had been more grumbly than usual—which said a lot considering how grumbly he tended to be. There was no question about his trust in Arcanthus, but when it came to Shay, instinct was in control of Drakkal. He was quite...beastly. And Shay wasn't embarrassed to admit that turned her on, especially once they'd returned to their room and he turned that beastly nature on her.

She twirled her hand around. "No pain, doc."

"Good. Boss has never had an issue getting those in, but it never hurts to be sure." Urgand highlighted something on the holographic menu.

The chair hummed faintly beneath her. A moment later, several curved metal objects floated up freely from the chair's base to hover over Shay. Blue circles sparked to life along the undersides of the objects, bathing her in a soft glow. Her hand tightened around Drak's.

Two more screens appeared in the air beside the first. Urgand turned his attention to them. "Give me a minute to get my bearings. Things are in weird places in your kind."

"I'm sure *things* are all in the right places," Shay said drolly.

"I haven't had any problems," Drakkal offered.

Urgand glanced to Drakkal and then Shay before returning his attention to his displays. "Yeah, anyway...the youngling."

His fingers manipulated an image on one of the screens, turning and resizing it; from her angle, Shay couldn't really make out what it was. The light from the displays reflected in Urgand's dark eyes, making them seem aglow.

"How do you want to do this?" he asked, glancing at her again. "You want to see?"

Trepidation and amazement filled her. See her baby? She'd actually, for the first time, get to *see* her baby? She settled her hand on the side of her belly. Countless times, she'd felt the baby moving and shifting inside her; that alone had been astonishing. There was a life growing inside her, a tiny little person. But even knowing how advanced medical technology had become—even back on Earth—she'd somehow never realized it was possible to see her child before it was born.

"Yes," she replied, shifting her eyes from Urgand to the holographic screen.

"Just a second." He muttered to himself again as he returned to the initial control menu. "This is Volturian tech. They always make their shit so damned complicated."

"Should we call Razi?" Drakkal asked. "He's an expert on all things Volturian, isn't he?"

Urgand smirked. "An expert if you want to know the appropriate gifts to bring to a Volturian wedding, maybe. Here it is." He moved a hand to one of the other screens and made a motion like he was grabbing something with his fingers.

A three-dimensional hologram formed in the air near his hand. When he cupped his hand around it and moved his arm, the hologram moved with it. He positioned the hologram over the floating scanners, leaving it to hover over Shay's belly.

She knew what she was looking at instantly, but it took several seconds for it to truly settle in. "That...that's my..."

"Your cub," Drakkal said, awe in his voice as he leaned closer.

The image was so clear, so crisp, showing more detail than Shay had imagined possible. Her eyes roamed over her baby's features, from its closed eyes to its little nose and mouth, from the rounded curve of its ear to the dark hair on its head. It shifted, kicking, and Shay felt it from inside at the same instant.

She laughed, and tears welled in her eyes. "Running out of room, aren't you, Baby?"

"Guess it's a terran trait to be so small and frail-looking," Urgand said.

Frail. That one word was enough to tear Shay's eyes away from her baby to look at Urgand. Her heart quickened, and something on the machine beeped, flashing red for an instant. "Frail?"

Oh God, what'd I do?

Drakkal growled menacingly; Shay didn't have to look at him to know he was glaring at Urgand.

The vorgal frowned. "Calm down. I said *frail-looking*. Just like Shay and Samantha. As far as I can tell, this youngling is healthy. She looks perfect."

Relief flooded Shay, and it took her a moment to register what else Urgand had said. "She? It's a girl?" Her eyes turned back to her baby, moving along its body, and sure enough, the proof was there. "I'm having a girl?"

"You're having a girl." Urgand fiddled with something on one of his readouts. "Looks like you're about thirty-two weeks along. About eight more to go." He pressed another option, and a sound began to play—it was like someone rapidly banging a sheet of metal. "She may be tiny, but her heart is strong."

Drakkal gave Shay's hand another squeeze and leaned down further, nuzzling her neck. "Like her mother's."

Shay laughed thickly, struggling to hold back her tears. She turned her face toward Drakkal and closed her eyes, pressing her forehead to his. "A little girl. And she's perfect."

"Also like her mother."

She opened her eyes and drew back to look at Drakkal. Her heart constricted at what she saw in his eyes. They were focused on the hologram of her daughter, bright with wonder and adoration but also hard with the same savage protectiveness he'd shown toward Shay. That one look was enough for her to know without a doubt that Drakkal would always be there for Shay—and, more importantly, that he would always be there for her baby.

She released his hand. The action caused him to turn his attention toward her. There was a brief question in his eyes before she grasped his face and pulled him down, pressing her mouth to his. An answering rumbled vibrated from his chest. She kissed him firmly, fiercely.

"I love you," she rasped against his mouth, kissing him again and again.

"*Kraasz ka'val, kiraia*," he growled between kisses, "I love you, too."

Urgand grunted and muttered a curse. "This is new equipment. Clean up your damned mess when you're done."

Neither Drakkal nor Shay paid any attention as the vorgal tapped the control, dismissing the screens and sending the scanners back to the base of the chair, and exited the room.

Their lips caressed and nipped, their tongues flicked and stroked. Shay's fingers delved into Drakkal's mane, and she drew him closer; she needed more of him. Drakkal settled his big hand—his flesh and blood hand—over her belly. As though sensing him, Shay's daughter stretched, reaching toward him.

Drakkal lifted his head, separating their mouths. His intense green eyes locked with hers.

"She is *mine*. You're both mine, *kiraia*." His hand curled protectively, though gently, around her belly as he cupped her jaw with his prosthetic hand and tilted her face up toward his. "May the ancestors hear my vow, made by my bone and my blood—I will allow nothing to harm you or your cub so long as I draw breath." He pressed his forehead against hers, his voice gruff as he said, "You are mine to love, mine to protect, mine to keep."

SEVENTEEN

"Come, my boy, and sit down," Master Foltham said, waving Nostrus over to the desk.

Nostrus closed the door and strode across the study. He sat in one of the chairs and settled his arms over the armrests.

Master Foltham leaned forward, propping his elbows on his desk. "Well, have we made progress?"

Careful to keep his expression neutral, Nostrus nodded. "I believe we've found a...suitable candidate, sir."

"All this time and only one candidate?" Master Foltham huffed and shoved away from the table to lean back in his seat. "The cost is of no concern, Nostrus. If I need to hire a small army to have justice, I will!"

"I understand, sir." Nostrus drew in a steadying breath. He knew he'd been overly sensitive regarding this matter, but he couldn't let it go. He couldn't allow another stain to cling to his father's name, couldn't allow his own reputation to remain tainted. "But, as you've said, we must go about this delicately. Your security is my foremost concern, and putting out an open contract risks drawing too much attention."

Master Foltham's throat skin swelled for a moment. "The best, Nostrus. This *candidate* had better be the absolute best available."

"Everything we've been able to dig up so far, sir, points to that. This hunter's reputation has been earned over many years of work."

"Hmm. And yet you sound trepidatious."

"Most bounty hunters who are willing to go after runaway slaves, sir, are barely a step above criminals," Nostrus said carefully. "Regardless of reputation, I have difficulty bringing myself to trust their ilk."

Nodding thoughtfully, Master Foltham settled his hands over his belly. "Perhaps. But I imagine a generous bounty is enough to curtail any thoughts of betrayal."

Just like a high payout was supposed to keep that azhera from stealing from you in your own home?

"I can't pretend to understand the motivations of such individuals, Master Foltham."

"No, of course not. You're a cultured being, young Nostrus. But if there's one thing I know, if there's one secret to my success, it's the understanding that you ought to turn elsewhere when something falls outside your own areas of expertise, especially when acquiring those skills is impractical. We need animals hunted down and dragged home, so we must seek out one well versed in dealing with such creatures—someone barely removed from animals themselves."

The rage that had been simmering within Nostrus for weeks flared a little at that; he was deemed unfit to perform this duty, but someone Master Foltham considered barely more than an animal was qualified?

Nostrus realized in that moment that he'd been gritting his teeth. He forced his jaw to relax. "Sir, I will dedicate my every moment to hunting them down. I'll bring them back to you. I've scores to settle with both of them."

"I'll not discuss that matter with you again, Nostrus. You know my mind on it. You'll have your revenge, rest assured, though it will not be in the terms for which you're so desperate." Master Foltham lifted a hand a few centimeters and waved his fingers lazily. "Now then, do you have the contact information for this bounty hunter?"

"I do, sir."

"And have you made any inquiries regarding the arrangement of a contract?"

"A member of my team has made contact. The hunter was willing to discuss the matter further."

Master Foltham reached forward and brought up a holographic display over his desk. With a flick of his fingers, he turned the screen to face Nostrus. "Call the hunter now. I want this set into motion."

"Sir, it would be—"

Master Foltham slapped his hand down and shifted his considerable bulk forward to loom over his desk. "I want my terran back, Nostrus, and I'll wait not a minute longer than necessary. It's been what? Forty-nine days? *Fifty?* I have always exercised patience in all things, but the limits of my patience have been hard-pressed by this situation. Call the hunter. Now."

Pressing his lips into a tight line, Nostrus turned his attention to the screen and accessed the secure, encrypted commlink. He entered the bounty hunter's commlink ID and pressed connect to engage an audio-only call.

The connection opened after a few seconds.

"Yeah?" asked a raspy voice.

"An associate of mine contacted you regarding a contract," Master Foltham said.

"You the one with a couple lost pets?"

"Indeed. From what I understand, your record is impeccable."

Nostrus clenched his teeth and clutched at the armrests. He couldn't ignore the persistent ache in his hand any more than he could forget the reason it was there to begin with.

"Yeah," the bounty hunter replied.

Master Foltham leaned back again, turning his gaze toward the ceiling. "Are you interested in the work?"

"I'll need details before I commit to anything."

Smirking around his thick tusks, Master Foltham nodded. "Naturally. I'd prefer my pets returned to me unharmed, if possible. They are a male and female. An azhera and a terran, respectively. It's only prudent that I mention they are both dangerous."

"Most people are once they're being hunted. I'll need some more specifics."

"The male managed to overcome my head of security and escape an extremely secure compound with the female in tow. And she has caused serious injuries to several members of my staff despite her deceptively petite size and build."

The ache in Nostrus's hand intensified, becoming a rapid, piercing throb. He forced himself to lean back, hoping that the few extra centimeters it put between himself and the call screen would help him keep his mouth shut. He didn't need to dishonor himself any further than he already had.

"I should add that the female is pregnant," Master Foltham continued. "I want her offspring returned as well—alive and unharmed, if she's birthed it when you collect her."

"Price?"

Master Foltham turned his head toward the screen. "I would prefer to work out that detail in per—"

"Price," the bounty hunter repeated firmly.

Master Foltham's lips peeled back in distaste. He preferred a manner of doing business that struck many as old-fashioned or unnecessarily prolonged, but Nostrus saw the wisdom in it—it provided further opportunity to reveal the true nature of the people with whom the master was dealing.

With a disapproving grunt, Master Foltham said, "Two hundred thousand each, but they must be alive."

"One azhera, one breeding terran, and possibly an infant, presumably hiding out on Arthos. Adults both dangerous enough to overcome trained professionals," the bounty hunter said flatly. "Five hundred each."

Master Foltham's throat flesh swelled, and his heavy brows fell low over his dark eyes. "Preposterous!"

"It's nothing for a person like you."

"How dare you presume anything about me after demanding such an outrageous sum? I am the one who was insulted and stolen from, the one who was attacked in my own home. Have I not paid price enough already?"

"If you owned a terran," the bounty hunter replied in a measured tone, "you've paid handsomely. Which is exactly why you're going to pay what I'm asking to have her back. A half million is nothing compared to what you spent to have her."

Master Foltham clenched his teeth and leaned forward again; for a few moments, he looked as though he were contemplating trying to strangle the holo screen in front of him. "And how soon will you deliver?" he asked tightly.

"Have your people send me the rest of the information. Images. Names. Everything in your possession. We'll talk timelines once I've been able to review it all."

"I don't typically deal in such vague terms," Master Foltham grated.

"You also don't typically deal with locating two individuals in a city of billions, or you wouldn't have contacted me. I'll be in touch."

The call disconnected abruptly.

Master Foltham's nostrils flared with several deep, heavy breaths, his throat flesh swelling and deflating with them. He didn't look at Nostrus when he said, "That will be all for now."

Nostrus stood, turned away, and walked toward the door. He told himself that his burgeoning sense of satisfaction at seeing Master Foltham so irritated by dealing with the bounty hunter was both immature and inappropriate, but he couldn't dismiss the feeling. Part of him—a part to which he would never give voice—thought it served Master Foltham right.

If this was the path they had to take to make Master Foltham see the folly of outsourcing a contract for something Nostrus would've gladly done by his own hand, so be it. One way or another, they'd get their hands on that azhera. One way or another, Nostrus would right his failure.

And it will all be worth it just to see the look on the azhera's face right before he dies.

EIGHTEEN

Drakkal drew in a deep breath through his nostrils, closed his eyes, and turned his face toward the sky. The surface air, though as fraught with clashing scents as that in Undercity, was sweet and fresh, and the light of the quasar was pleasantly warm. He hadn't been topside in a long time—not since the day he'd driven Arcanthus and Samantha to the Ventrillian Mall over a year ago. The abundant plants and fountains on the upper city streets *almost* created the sense of being back in the wilds, far from the troubles of cities and civilization.

He opened his eyes and glanced at Shay, who was walking beside him, her left hand in his right. She held her other arm beneath her belly for support; it had grown noticeably larger in the month since Urgand had performed her first medical scan, and the cub had grown along with it. The time was fast approaching. She'd give birth soon enough, and his excitement and anxiousness increased with each passing hour.

He had dedicated himself to being a father for this cub, and nothing would make him waver from that. He only hoped that he would be a worthy father.

"It's *so* much nicer up here," Shay said, turning her head to look at him. "Why didn't we do this sooner?"

Drakkal shrugged, sweeping his gaze around to take in the shining buildings, well-tended gardens, and countless pedestrians in their varied clothing. "Never really had a reason to."

"No reason to? The air up here is reason enough." She closed her eyes and inhaled slowly. "It's so sweet I could take a spoon to it and have it for dessert."

Drakkal's eyes fell upon her again, and he smiled. "I'll keep that in mind, *kiraia*. We do have to be careful, though. We're not exactly law-abiding citizens."

"Ha! Speak for yourself, kitty. I've turned over a new leaf, remember?"

"Should I remind you that the first thing you did once you were free was rob me?"

She grinned up at him. "It was self-defense."

"Oh. No problem, then." He flicked his gaze to her stomach. Over the last several weeks, she'd often grabbed his hand and pressed it to her belly so he could feel the cub within shift and kick. "How are you feeling? Have the cramps eased?"

She shifted her hand to the top of her stomach. "They come and go, some stronger than others. But I'm okay. Urgand said it was normal for how far along I am."

Whether it was normal or not, Drakkal didn't like it. Shay's discomfort had only increased lately, and her pregnancy was clearly impacting her in many ways. She couldn't move as easily as she had when they first met, she often seemed fatigued, and she struggled to find comfortable positions in bed no matter how she and Drakkal contorted their bodies—or how many different pillows and blankets he obtained to accommodate her. And there was nothing he could do about it. He hated that feeling of helplessness, hated that his mate was suffering, and that he couldn't do anything to diminish her suffering.

Over the last few days, she'd taken to moving ceaselessly, even when she looked otherwise exhausted.

Shay stepped in front of him, causing him to stop, and raised her hand to cup his jaw. "You suck at hiding your thoughts."

Drakkal frowned and furrowed his brow. "According to you and Arc, I just look grumpy all the time."

"A hot grumpy." Her lips spread into a wide, teasing smile. "A *sexy* grumpy."

He stared into her eyes, and warmth spread across the surface of his skin. His tail swung around to brush along the outside of her leg. "I just wish I could do more for you, *kiraia*."

Her smile softened as she stroked her thumb across his cheek. "You do everything already, Drakkal."

"Everything will never be enough," he said, unable to keep his lips from stretching into a grin; he knew she considered such sentiments sappy, but it was the truth. He'd never been one to share his feelings—and had never been accused by anyone of *sucking* at hiding his thoughts before her—but it came naturally in Shay's company.

Shay's cheeks pinkened. She opened her mouth to speak, but quickly snapped it shut, lips pale and thin. She released his hand to clutch the sides of her belly, drawing in a sharp breath. "Oh. That was a rough one."

Drakkal's frown swiftly returned. He placed one hand on her shoulder and cupped her cheek with the other. "We're going back to—"

He was silenced when a voice—a husky, feminine voice that was entirely too familiar—said, "Drakkal?"

For an instant, Drakkal's past, stretching back twenty years, was laid bare at the forefront of his mind. All the pain, hurt, and heartache flooded back, as raw and potent as it had been back then. He turned his face toward the person who'd spoken.

The female azhera gasped. "It *is* you."

Vanya looked largely unchanged by the years. Her fur was the same rusty brown, her eyes the same gold—and just as cold as they'd been the last time he'd seen her. She was tall and athletically built, standing with the confidence she'd always displayed; as much a natural, beautiful huntress as ever. Even her attire harkened back to their younger days—a leather harness on top, little more than a series of straps and buckles that crossed over her mounds, a broad belt with pouches, a knife, and a blaster, and a skirt formed of swatches of drab cloth and strips of tristeel-reinforced leather.

It was the same sort of clothing she might've worn on one of their hunting trips two decades before.

Drakkal's old pain faded quickly, but it left an emptiness inside him, likely the result of shock. He should never have seen this female again, and he wasn't sure what to think, what to feel. Drakkal's arms fell away from Shay. "Vanya."

She smiled and stepped closer. "You remember me," she purred, reaching out to touch his face.

Shay smacked Vanya's arm away. "Don't fucking touch him."

Drakkal hadn't seen Shay move, but there she was, standing between him and Vanya like a small but terribly formidable wall, every bit as confident as the female azhera—and infinitely more beautiful.

Vanya reared back in surprise for an instant before her features contorted into a snarl. She growled at Shay, baring her fangs and spreading her claws.

That was more than enough to spark something in Drakkal, something he hadn't allowed himself to feel toward Vanya in all this time, something he *should* have felt long ago. Fury. It wasn't only about what she'd done, it was about what she was doing. Drakkal would not tolerate threats to his mate.

He growled and wrapped his arm around Shay's shoulders from behind, drawing her back against his chest and twisting to turn her away from Vanya.

"Who the hell are you?" Shay demanded before Drakkal could speak.

Vanya's expression remained hard and cold as she moved her eyes over Drakkal. Her gaze shifted to Shay and dipped; she undoubtedly noticed the swell of Shay's stomach. Envy flared in Vanya's eyes.

"His lover," Vanya said, raising her chin and sensually rolling her shoulders. "Who are you?"

"I'm his *mate*, so you better fucking back off."

Vanya laughed, her grin wide and mocking. "His mate? Hardly." She leaned down so her eyes were level with Shay's. "You're nothing but a weak, soft-skinned terran. Easily...*broken*."

Shay lunged for Vanya with startling strength. "Bitch, I'll show you who's easily broken!"

Grunting, Drakkal wrapped both arms around Shay and held her back. Despite the disparity in their size and weight, he was losing that struggle until he lifted her off her feet—but even then, she didn't stop.

"You're about to have your ass kicked by someone who has to waddle to the bathroom three times a night!" Shay shouted.

"It would be too easy to take you apart, terran," said Vanya.

Drakkal's ears flattened, and his fur bristled. His muscles tensed with another wave of rage that coaxed a fresh growl out of his chest. He turned fully, giving Vanya his back, and set Shay on her feet. "Stay," he grated through his teeth.

He barely registered her glare before he turned toward Vanya. She had a mirthful spark in her eye and that smirk on her lips that had once lured in a young, lonely, naïve azheran male. It had been too late by the time Drakkal had recognized the cruel, icy void lurking behind her humor.

"You ought to put a leash on your pet, Drakkal," Vanya said, sauntering a little closer.

Were they in the Undercity, he might've killed Vanya right then. His old feelings for her didn't matter—they were long dead. He would not abide insults and threats to his mate, and Vanya herself was a walking threat. But his surroundings stayed his hand; violence here would be noticed, and the peacekeepers would act. He could not bring that sort of attention to himself or Shay.

"She is my mate, and I will not allow a traitorous *zhe'gaash* to speak ill of her," he said in as slow and measured a tone as he could manage. "I know you for what you are now. Leave, or I'll treat you accordingly."

Her ears dropped briefly before they rose again. "Time changes us, Drakkal. I'm not what you remember."

He stared into her eyes, his shoulders rising and falling with deep, heavy breaths. He made no effort to mask his bitterness and hatred. "Neither am I."

She sighed. "Oh, Drakkal, you loved me once. Surely you haven't forgotten everything." She eased closer still and flicked her tail out to brush his leg. "We were fierce lovers."

That reminder only further agitated the maelstrom within him. There'd been something there once, something he'd mistaken for love even for years after she betrayed him...but it had never been that. She knew it as well as he did.

"I remember all of it." Though he kept his hands lowered, he flexed his fingers, extending his natural claws and forming his prosthesis' hardlight claws. "You have three seconds, Vanya. Walk away, just like the last time."

Her voice lowered and grew huskier as she said, "Mmm.

When you strike, Drakkal, you strike *deep*." She reached out despite his warning and caressed his cheek.

He snarled and batted her hand away.

Pain and anger flashed across Vanya's features for an instant, but she recovered quickly, and the smugness returned to her expression. "Seek me out again when you're *alone*."

Dropping her hand, she turned and sauntered away, her tail lazily swaying behind her. Drakkal didn't remove his eyes from her until she was gone, but Vanya being out of sight offered him no comfort. Her scent, woefully familiar, lingered in the air—and on his cheek. Once, he'd longed to have that scent in his fur, had craved it, had thrilled in it. Now he wanted nothing more than to scrub it off.

He turned to Shay and froze.

Her skin was pale, too pale, and her lips were pressed into a tight line. She stood with her feet wide apart, posture stiff. The angry fire that had burned in her eyes moments before had vanished, replaced by a gleam of fear. He knew immediately the change had nothing to do with Vanya.

"I fucked up, didn't I?" she asked in a shaky voice.

Drakkal's brow furrowed, and his heart quickened. "What's wrong, *kiraia*?"

"I...I think my water broke."

He tilted his head and lowered his gaze. There was a dark stain beginning at the crotch of her pants and continuing down her leg, but he couldn't detect even a hint of the distinctive scent of terran urine. "I...don't understand."

"The baby, Drak. The baby is coming," she said, speaking quicker and quicker with every word, her voice rising as tears filled her eyes. "It's too soon. She's not supposed to come yet! Oh, God, I fucked up."

For a second, perhaps two, Drakkal couldn't process what she'd said. It *was* too soon. Wasn't it? And how could the cub possibly come *now*, after what had just happened? But even if his logical mind was slow to catch up to the situation, his instincts roared up from his subconscious.

He scooped her off her feet, cradled her in his arms, and ran back toward the hovercar. "You're all right. You're both all right. We're going back now."

She wrapped her arm around his neck and sniffled as the tears ran down her cheeks. "I messed up like I always do. I-I shouldn't have tried to attack that woman. I did this."

"Quiet, female." He maneuvered through the surrounding foot traffic, which fortunately wasn't as thick as in many places in the Undercity—the upper portion of Arthos had nothing if not abundant pedestrian pathways.

He roared at the people in his path regardless, unwilling to risk even the slightest delay.

"It's her time to come," he said to Shay in as calm a voice as he could muster between those roars. "You didn't do anything wrong."

Shay gasped and hunched forward, body stiffening. She grasped a fistful of his mane, pulling his fur, as she clutched her belly with her other hand. Drakkal barely felt the pain. He increased his pace as much as possible without jarring her.

When they reached the hovercar, he wasted no time in opening the passenger side door and settling her on the seat. He fastened her safety harness and closed the door without allowing himself even an instant to fret over her condition—every second was precious now. Urgand had warned them that this could happen at any time, and that there was a chance she'd have little warning. The data he'd found on terran pregnancies suggested that no two were quite the same.

He vaulted across the front of the hovercar, tugged open the driver's side door, and climbed in. The vehicle swayed under his weight. He activated the engines before he even had the door fully closed and ascended the moment the hovercar was ready.

Keeping his left hand on the controls, he held the right out to Shay. "I'm here. We're going to get back, and everything will be fine."

She grasped his hand and nodded, breathing heavily for a few moments before some of the tension left her. "Okay. Okay," she said, still holding her free hand over her belly. "Hear that, baby girl? Everything...is going to be fine."

As much as Drakkal disliked voice commands, this was exactly the sort of situation in which they were useful.

"Call That Horny Prick," he said.

Shay huffed a laughed despite everything. "*That's* your contact name for Arc?"

"Tell me it doesn't fit," he replied with a fleeting smirk.

The vehicle's center control screen switched to a commlink array, displaying a pending connection with a commlink number. The connection was accepted almost instantly.

"Pussy Cat," Arcanthus said smoothly. "I thought you were on a date with Shay. Were you—"

"I will claw your fucking eyes out if you make one more cat joke," Drakkal growled. "Cub's coming. We'll be there in ten. Have Urgand ready."

"Baby's coming right now?" There were muffled voices in the background, too low and garbled to understand. "We'll all be ready. Drive safe."

The call disconnected.

"Oh fuck, fuck, fuck." Shay's grip on Drakkal's hand tightened again as her breaths shallowed and quickened.

Drakkal glanced at her from the corner of his eye even as he increased the speed of the hovercar. Beads of perspiration had begun to gather on her forehead.

"Breathe, *kiraia*. You're in control. And soon, you'll be holding your cub with your own hands."

"Who was she?" Shay asked when her body eased.

"Who?"

"That female azhera."

His expression tightened at the mere thought of Vanya; she was a threat to Shay, and his instincts didn't appreciate that he'd let her walk away. "Someone who doesn't matter."

It had taken them nearly twenty minutes to drive to the starting point of their upper city walk. Drakkal completed the return journey in eight—and those eight minutes were the longest of his life. Shay's flares of pain were frequent, coming and going at random, and all he could do was let her squeeze his hand and drive. The former felt ineffective, the later too slow.

The garage door was already open when they arrived home. He swung the hovercar around and pulled up directly to the interior door so it was only a meter or two from Shay's side.

Arcanthus, Razi, and Samantha were waiting. They helped Shay out of the car as Drakkal rushed around to her. He swept her into his arms again and hurried for the infirmary. Urgand was standing in the hallway as they approached.

"Her water broke," Drakkal said. "Can you fix it?"

Urgand preceded him through the door and gestured to an adjustable bed with a pair of stirrups. "Probably just the amniotic sac rupturing."

Sam followed Drakkal in, closing the door behind her.

"That sounds worse," Drakkal growled as he carefully lowered Shay onto the table.

"Messy but normal," Urgand said distractedly. He was hurriedly moving equipment into place around the bed and pulling up floating holo screens. "Take off her pants."

Drakkal's ears slapped down. He clenched his jaw and

reminded himself—more than once in rapid succession—that this was necessary. She couldn't very well push her cub out into her pants.

"It's fine, Drakkal," Shay said, dropping her hands to her waistband.

Drakkal scowled and tugged off her boots before helping remove her pants. He tossed them onto the floor, turned his head, and glared at Urgand.

"Do I need to have Razi and the boss hold you back?" Urgand asked, pulling on a pair of gloves.

"Why?"

Shay grunted and closed her eyes, her face strained as she gripped the sides of the bed. Fluid seeped from her and wet the bedding.

"I need to check how far along she is," Urgand said.

"So turn on the scanner and see," Drakkal replied.

"He has to *feel*," Sam said, easing up beside Drakkal at the foot of the bed with a sheet. She draped the sheet over Shay's legs and waist.

Not for the first time, Drakkal's instincts warred with one another. The most rational of his impulses was to question the necessity of *feeling* anything. All this damned equipment, all this expensive equipment, and for what? What was the point of it? But he was not so lost to instinct as to crumble to those impulses.

He loved Shay, and—though he'd yet to meet her—loved the baby, too. Whatever was the best for them. Whatever was the safest.

Drakkal nodded tightly.

"Get her feet up," Urgand said as he pulled on a pair of thin gloves.

Samantha and Drakkal took opposite sides of the bed and did as Urgand had commanded.

"Let us know when your contraction is over, Shay," Sam said.

Shay nodded, features tight. After a few seconds, her expression relaxed slightly. "Okay. I'm ready."

With an uncertain, concerned glance at Drakkal, Urgand slipped one hand beneath the sheet and placed the other over Shay's pelvis.

Drakkal growled long and low, forcing his full attention to Shay. "I've got you, *kiraia*."

She kept her eyes locked with his, and though she didn't speak, she lent him strength through her gaze. He loved her more than ever in that moment, even if this was backwards—he should've been able to hold his shit together without needing to draw comfort from her. *He* was supposed to be supporting *her*.

Urgand stepped back and removed his gloves. "Five centimeters. The terran charts say that's halfway there." He frowned and looked at Shay. "How long you been having contractions?"

"You mean the cramps?" she asked. "Since yesterday."

"You've likely been in labor since then," Samantha said.

Urgand's frown deepened. "I'll get you something for the pain."

"No!" Shay hissed as soon as the word was out, her body tensing. She shook her head several times. "No drugs."

Drakkal's stomach churned. He caught her hand in his and gave it a squeeze. "You don't need to suffer like this, Shay."

"No drugs," she repeated firmly, breathing in and out through her teeth until her body eased again. "I don't want anything that could hurt my baby. I don't want to chance it. I won't chance it. I've dealt with pain before...and this pain will be worth it because it'll result in something *good*."

Samantha placed her hand on Shay's shoulder and smiled. "It's your choice, Shay. I can't wait to meet your daughter. And just think, you could be helping me with my baby someday soon."

A short laugh escaped Shay between her deep, even breaths.

Drakkal leaned forward until Shay was his entire world and stared into her piercing blue eyes. "Whatever you need to do, *kiraia*. Give me as much of that pain as you must."

She nodded, and despite the strain on her features, despite how exhausted she already looked, the strength he'd seen in her from the beginning remained evident in her eyes.

If the eight-minute hovercar trip to bring Shay home had felt like an eternity, Drakkal had no adequate words to describe the time he spent in that room—he'd learn later that it had been just under twelve hours, but he felt like it stretched beyond the age of the universe itself.

She squeezed his hand and dug her nails into his flesh; she gasped, moaned, and occasionally cursed—never at anyone in the room—but she did not scream. Drakkal admired her strength even as he felt weaker and more useless than ever. Watching his mate, the female he loved in a way he'd never dreamed possible, go through such agony tore him apart inside. He could do nothing for her but be there, and he couldn't help feeling that was inadequate.

But when Shay gave that final push, fueling it with defiance for her exhaustion and for the universe that had forced so much hardship upon her, and the first cry of her little cub hit the air, time stopped.

Drakkal's ears perked, and he watched with a strange, fluttering warmth in his chest as Urgand carefully lifted the cub, who looked so tiny and meek in the vorgal's big, rough hands. Her cries were high and piercing and *beautiful*. Though she was so small and so young, though she seemed so helpless at a glance, Drakkal could already sense the fighting spirit within her.

Urgand looked from the cub to Shay. "You terrans cut the birthing tether, don't you?"

Shay nodded, her tired, bright eyes meeting Drakkal's. "The father cuts it."

The sensation within Drakkal's chest intensified and expanded with a swelling of pride. His entire body thrummed with excitement and nervousness, so much so that he felt like he should've been trembling with it, but his hands were steady as he accepted the small surgical laser cutter from Urgand and sliced off the birthing tether where the vorgal had indicated. The cutter cauterized the wound, and the tether fell away.

Samantha stepped forward with a small, soft blanket, which she gently wrapped around the cub. An instant later, the cub was placed on Shay's chest and cradled in her arms. The cries ceased.

Shay stared down into that tiny face, her own face full of wonder and love. Tears shimmered in her eyes as she smiled.

Drakkal positioned himself beside his mate, slipped his left arm around her shoulders, and stared down at her cub. *Their* cub. As gently as he could, he reached out with his right hand and cradled the back of that delicate little head.

The cub's skin was ruddy and smeared with blood and fluids, and thick, dark hair was plastered to the top of her head. She looked nothing like an azheran cub—which only made sense, as terrans didn't look much like azhera. But she was *his*. "Sorry, *kiraia*," he said softly, "but you might only be second most beautiful now."

Shay laughed, glancing up at Drakkal briefly. She brushed the tip of her fingers over the cub's cheek, nose, and forehead. "She is beautiful, isn't she?"

"What are you going to name her?" Samantha asked.

"Leah." Shay looked up at Drakkal again, her smile widening. "Leah Audrey vor'Kanthar."

Hearing that name—vor'Kanthar—from Shay's lips produced a new sort of pride in Drakkal, one he'd not felt in a long while. Though he'd introduced himself to her as Drakkal vor'Kanthar, he'd left that name behind many years ago, during his time in the slave arenas. He'd thought his capture and enslavement had left him unworthy of the name of his tribe, and he'd never sought to truly reclaim it.

But his oldest memories came rushing back now, memories from his time as a cub, hazy but powerful, nonetheless. He'd been a part of a tribe, a *family*, and he'd forgotten how good that felt. He'd forgotten what it meant. Shay had just given that back to him.

These terrans before him, they were his people. They were his family. They were *his*. Perhaps he'd not felt any right to the vor'Kanthar name for a long while, but it had always been his. And now it belonged to Shay. Belonged to Leah Audrey.

A few moments ago, it had seemed his chest couldn't get any tighter, but it did now, flooded with a fresh surge of pride, of protectiveness, of belonging. Everything he'd given up or been forced to lose in his youth—things he hadn't known would be so hard to reclaim—he'd found again. A place. A home. A family. But he had so much more now.

He had his tribe.

NINETEEN

Shay lay in bed, staring at the sweet, sleeping face of her daughter, who rested on her chest. It was surreal that Leah was here now. After nearly nine months of more struggling, fear, and anxiety than Shay could've ever imagined possible, after all the pain of the last day—the worst physical pain she'd ever experienced—she had this baby. This little person. All of it had been worth it. Even now, the memory of that pain was fading, unimportant compared to the love she felt for her daughter.

She'd spent a few more hours in the infirmary after Leah's birth. There'd been a little more work for Shay to do; she hadn't realized that the baby wasn't the only thing that had to be pushed out, but she'd happily never think about the aftermath again. Sam and Urgand had cleaned Leah, fitted her with the cutest, tiniest diaper, and swaddled her in a soft blanket. Shay had been cleaned up, too, before she and Leah were scanned. To her immense relief, everything came up perfectly normal and healthy. Finally, she'd fed her baby and got some sleep.

Now she was back in the room she shared with Drakkal, enjoying the comfort and privacy—the former helped by the spectacular pain suppressants running through her system, which Urgand had guaranteed would not affect Leah through Shay's breastmilk. Leah had fallen asleep again after another feeding and a diaper change, but Shay wasn't ready for more sleep yet. She was tired, that was for sure—it felt like she'd strained every damned part of her body, right down to her eyeballs—but that was physical exhaustion. Mentally, she just wanted to stare at this beautiful wonder in her arms.

As she brushed her thumb over Leah's soft, dark hair, tears stung Shay's eyes. Had her mother felt this deep, immediate bond, this unconditional, undeniable love for Shay when she was born?

Shay knew the answer to that. Audrey Collins had felt it, even when Shay was at her most difficult, even though Shay had hurt her time and time again. Her mother had still loved her. Shay blinked, and warm tears slid down her cheeks.

"Grandma would have loved you, Leah," she whispered, but even those quiet words were a struggle to get past the tightness in her throat. She sniffled as more tears fell. "I wish I could tell her how sorry I am. How wrong I was to blame her. So, so very wrong."

"We all have our regrets, *kiraia*," Drakkal murmured from beside her.

Shay turned her head toward him. He was sprawled on his belly with his arms wrapped around a smushed pillow and his face turned toward her. Though his eyes were half-lidded, they were as bright and alert as ever. His tail swept over her leg slowly.

Lifting her hand, Shay wiped the tears from her cheeks. "Sorry. I didn't mean to wake you."

"You didn't. I've been awake for a while. I liked hearing you hum while you fed Leah."

Shay wrinkled her nose, but her cheeks warmed, and her heart fluttered at his words. "So, you were spying on me?"

Drakkal made a sound that was half chuckle and half snort, scooted closer to her, and propped himself up. He rubbed his cheek against Shay's neck and shoulder. "Making up for your mistakes isn't about what you say, Shay. It's about what you do. Even if you can't tell her, you can show her spirit that you've changed. That you've learned from your mistakes."

She smiled, closed her eyes, and tilted her head to allow him more access, reaching up to absently stroke his mane. "I've tried to do the right thing. After she died...I tried to leave that life of crime behind. I didn't want to do it anymore, *couldn't* do it anymore, not after..." She drew in a deep breath and released it slowly, willing away the stinging in her eyes. "But I couldn't cut myself off from everyone I used to associate with right away. That makes them real suspicious, you know? And Anthony...he just happened to be there at the right time, at the exact moment that I needed someone, and—"

Drakkal's low growl reverberated through her.

Shay chuckled. "Sorry. Life with him was shit, anyway. I don't know why I didn't just walk away, why I didn't just move on. It's not like me to put up with that. I guess I was just desperate to not be alone, you know? Somehow, I didn't even realize at the time that he was dragging me back down into that life I wanted to leave behind." She sank her fingers deeper into his mane and turned her face toward him until she was able to look into one of his eyes. "Then I found out I was pregnant. And when he told me to just get rid of it, enough was enough. I realized that I was being so, so stupid. I left him, left everything I'd known, and started new. I lived in a shithole of an apartment, worked two jobs that paid under the table and didn't require background checks because I wanted a better life. I needed a better life...for her. For Leah.

"Do you think my mom was proud of me then? Because I thought about her. Every day, hoping that she was seeing me, listening, knowing that I was trying to make up for all the fucked-up shit I did."

"I think that even when she wasn't proud, she loved you," Drakkal replied gently, lifting a hand to cradle her face. "Your efforts to do better wouldn't have gone unnoticed by her."

Shay leaned into his touch. That simple, uncomplicated contact between them was so powerful, so overwhelming, and yet so grounding; she'd never realized how much could be communicated through touch. Having someone in her life again who cared so much was...wonderful. She wasn't usually the sort to get all mushy and sappy—though she could still use the pregnancy hormones as an excuse for now—but she cherished these quiet, tender moments with Drakkal. She was learning more and more that it was okay to let her guard down with him. It was okay to be vulnerable.

"What are your regrets?" Shay pulled back to meet his gaze again and moved her hand to the side of his face. "Who was that female azhera, Drak?"

That spark of fury reignited in her belly as she remembered what the female had called herself—Drakkal's *lover*.

He released a huff through his nostrils and smirked. "Not sure if I should be turned on or afraid when you make that face, *kiraia*."

Shay's brows furrowed. "What face?"

"You look like you want to rip something to shreds. Don't know if it's a threat...or a promise."

She arched a brow and gave his cheek fur a gentle tug. "Guess it'll depend on what you tell me."

"Should I go stand on the other side of the room first?"

Shay scowled. "You're not making this any better. Aren't you supposed to like, I don't know, calm your mate down when she gets all jealous and stuff? Not rile her. *Especially* after she just had a baby."

The humor on Drakkal's face faded, giving way to something more solemn—but his eyes maintained their loving light. "Told you she wasn't important, and she's not. Not anymore. But...I won't lie about who she was to me a long, long time ago. You willing to hear me out before you kill me?"

Sighing, Shay let her head rest on the pillow, keeping face turned toward Drakkal, and stroked his cheek with her thumb. "I'm not going to kill you. You're too big for me to dispose of the body by myself." She smirked, but it faded quickly. She drew her hand from him to settle it gently upon her sleeping baby. "Won't be able to help my mad jealousies, though, considering she was your lover and all."

His expression darkened. "*Lover* isn't the right word. Vanya never loved anything apart from herself. I think... You've shared a lot of your past with me, Shay, and I haven't really told you anything. I need to tell the story from the beginning, so you understand. So *I* can understand...because I don't think I've had the chance to truly put it all behind me until you came along."

"So, start from the beginning. I want to know, Drakkal. The good, the bad, everything. It's not going to change how I feel about you now."

He nodded and lay down, rolling onto his back. His eyes swung up toward the ceiling, but they had a far-off gleam, as though he were looking well beyond the physical. "I was born on Jakora, the azheran homeworld. Big cities everywhere, billions of people...kind like how Sam describes your Earth. And it never sat well with me. My parents were historians, basically, so I spent my youth learning about the culture and traditions of my people, our history, and I felt like we'd strayed so far from what we were. I wanted something different.

"I met Vanya a year before reaching my majority. She seemed to feel the same as me—she wanted a simpler life, a life more in touch with the roots of our people. We wanted to know what it was like to live off the bounties of nature, to hunt and fish and survive, to make things with our own hands. She was... beautiful, confident, strong. A huntress even then. Everything I thought I wanted.

"I fell for her. For a long time"—his brows fell low, and his lips turned down in a deep frown—"I even thought I loved her."

Shay pressed her lips together and lifted a hand away from Leah, curling it into a tight fist at her side. She turned away from Drakkal to look at the peaceful face of her baby. It calmed some of the violent impulses inside Shay.

Everyone has a past, Shay. Get over it. Drakkal didn't go bat shit crazy when you mentioned your ex, who you created a baby with.

Not that she was angry with Drakkal—she just wanted to knock a few teeth out of that bitch Vanya's smug face. Shay was sure Drakkal had to suppress similar thoughts when her ex came up.

"Once we were of age," Drakkal continued, "we left Jakora. Went to one of the fringe worlds, a frontier planet with abundant wildlife and few people. We stocked up on supplies at one of the few permanent settlements and headed out to find our piece of the wild. Built a house, built a life. And it was good, for what it was. Or at least I *told* myself it was good. It wasn't ever easy—we had to work for everything, and there were stretches where we were pretty hungry—but it felt good. Satisfying. At least for me.

"And I was still taken by Vanya. We had sex. Often. But any time I pushed for more, she pulled away. Guess I was blind to the signs. She didn't want anything official, didn't want any real commitment beyond what we already had. And I figured what we had should've been enough for me, right? She was living with me, sharing a home and a bed. Wasn't it greedy to want anything more?

"She started taking longer trips away from home. I thought she was pushing to find new animals, new hunting spots, or maybe scouting for valuable resources so she could sell the information in town. That was a good way to bolster our supplies sometimes. I was either too dumb or too naïve to realize the truth of what was going on. Figured she just needed space, and I wanted to give her everything she wanted.

"During the last of her *trips*, I was outside chopping wood. I looked up and see this big, ugly ship come over the mountains. It looked like some kind of modified military transport. There were some rough ships—and rougher people—who went to planets like that one to lie low and hide from the authorities, but I'd never seen one like that."

Drakkal settled his hands over his abdomen, intertwining his fingers. "Thing flies right up to the house, opens a drop ramp, and a dozen slavers hop out with guns and shock staffs. I didn't give myself time to think. I ran inside, grabbed my rifle, and prepared to defend myself. When they came toward the house, I shot at them.

"My people...we have this old warrior tradition that everyone on my homeworld liked to point to with pride, but few people are willing to follow anymore. The right thing to do, the honorable thing to do, was to fight to the death in defense of my home. Because what if I failed, and they were still there when Vanya came home? I was ready for it. Can't say that I was some skilled warrior or that I had much experience fighting, but I was ready."

Tension formed a crease between his brows and made the muscles of his jaw briefly bulge. "Turned into a gunfight right there. They were covering each other, forcing me to duck away so they could advance toward the house, but I know I hit at least a couple of them. I was a decent shot, at least. The whole time, they were yelling at me to come out, to surrender. And then I hear the back door open, and I spin around, ready to shoot...only it was Vanya.

"Stupid me sees her and doesn't wonder how she managed to show up right at that moment, doesn't wonder why the slavers hadn't already surrounded the place...and I guess there was no reason to. I just thought to myself *now we have a chance*. And she looked me right in the eye and nodded like she was there for me, *with* me, like she was in it until the end, too.

"She strode toward me, and I turned around to shoot back at the slavers, actually *excited* about the fight since she was there. I didn't hear her activate the stun gun. Didn't even have a chance to face her again. My whole body seized up, and I fell. Stayed conscious—guess I'm a lot tougher than I am smart—and tried to resist as she pulled out this big set of manacles. She had to hit me with the stun gun twice more before she could get me restrained.

"Then she called to the slavers, and they strolled right up to the house like that had been the plan all along. Because it had been. They dragged me to my feet and pulled a hood over my face, but I heard them talking. Heard *her* talking. And even then, even as they were hauling me toward their ship, I just couldn't fucking believe that she'd done that."

Pain radiated along Shay's jaw; only then did she realize that she'd been clenching it for some time. She worked it loose, but tension still gripped the rest of her. "If I'd known about all this before, Drak, I would have shot her in the fucking face the moment she showed it."

Drakkal's chest rumbled, and he reached out to brush the backs of his fingers along her arm. He smiled. "My fierce *kiraia*. You're a hundred times the warrior she could ever hope to be. I was tempted to kill her...but she's not worth the trouble it would've caused. The Eternal Guard wouldn't care what she did in the past, only that we shot her in the middle of an upper city street.

"But like I said, I heard them. I was the last target on the list Vanya made for them. It was her passage—her price to become part of their crew. Guess she'd had enough of the frontier life. Wanted a change."

"Dirty, cowardly, bitch," Shay muttered.

"Yeah," he growled. "She's a fucking *zhe'gaash*."

Shay could help it; she laughed. She bit her lip, holding as much of that laughter in as possible to keep from disturbing Leah, and flicked her eyes from the baby to Drakkal. "You totally upgraded. I may have done some bad shit, but least I never backstabbed anyone."

Drakkal lifted a thick strand of Shay's hair and curled it around his metal finger. "Shay, there is *no* comparison between the two of you. She is nothing. You are *everything* to me."

Warmth bloomed in Shay's chest, spreading outward. The high created by Drakkal's love was better than any drug could provide, and it pushed aside her jealousy; Vanya really was nothing to him anymore.

"What happened after they took you?" she asked.

"They brought me and all the other people they'd captured to Caldorius, capital of the whole damned slaver universe." He shook his head, and his tongue briefly slipped out to run over his lips. "Guess I have the sort of physique they like to see in the slave arenas, so I was bought by someone who wanted to make me a fighter. And that's what I did. They trained me hard, and they were mean bastards, but it was a good distraction from my despair.

"Had some dark, dark days there." He rubbed her hair between his thumb and finger and stared at it for few seconds before releasing it. "Spent a long time on the verge of just... giving up. Being done with it all. Good fighting slaves were a big investment for the owners—the crowds and gambling brought in a lot of money—so they kept most fights nonlethal, but when those death bouts came up...sometimes I really thought about just losing.

"I met Arc the day I had to fight him. It was nonlethal, and he was such a pretty, delicate thing, so"—his mouth twitched up in a small smirk—"I let him win. He'll tell it differently, but that's what happened."

Shay chuckled softly. "And here I thought you were being honest with me."

He turned his head toward her and scrunched his face as though in pain. "Ouch, terran. I could've put Arcanthus in his place if I'd wanted to. Like I said, he was just too pretty. Seemed a shame to damage that."

She grinned. "And I guess I was just too pretty when I robbed you?"

"Well, you *did* have a gun pulled on me..."

"You had other weapons. You weren't a helpless little kitten."

"Could've fooled me on that lately," he grumbled.

Shay knew he was referring to her pregnancy in general—but her labor more specifically. Her big, strong, fierce azheran mate had felt powerless when it came to her pain.

"You were with me the whole time, Drak. That means more than I can say."

He shifted a little closer and brushed a kiss on her forehead. "I'll always be with you, *kiraia*."

Shay smiled and settled her hand upon his chest, over his heart. It pounded beneath her palm. "Keep going. What happened after you supposedly threw your match with Arc?"

"We had a few minutes to talk. I'd seen him around before,

knew of him. He was building a reputation—I was his thirty-second win in thirty-two fights. An undefeated fighter was a big deal. And he was...not what I'd expected, considering how well he fought. He's egotistical and insulting, but he's charismatic, and at heart...he's genuine. He was the one who told me about the rule on Caldorius—survive a hundred and fifty matches and you earn your freedom. Said he had some plans for after he earned his, and that he'd need good fighters like me. *Don't die, azhera.*

"Like I said, I'd never really been a fighter before I was enslaved, but I took to it well, and I *was* good at it. And up until that point, I'd been running on anger. Didn't really have direction. Arcanthus gave me direction. He gave me something to work toward."

"And you've been together ever since," Shay remarked. "I was wondering how the two of you met. You're both so different...but at the same time, similar in some ways."

Drakkal grinned. "He has a few admirable qualities. Picked most of them up from me. But all that...it's well in the past now. It's been almost twenty years since I saw Vanya, and it wasn't nearly long enough. I never told anyone the truth of what she did. It was just easier to say she died when the slavers attacked. Easier to try to convince myself she was dead."

Shay's brows drew low. "Not even Arc?"

He shook his head. "Not even Arc."

"But I thought you two are like"—she lifted a hand and crossed her fingers—"tight and all that. Like you had some bromance where you didn't keep secrets from each other."

"A *bromance*?"

"Yeah. It's when two dudes are really, really close. Like... best friends and brothers and *almost* a couple at once?"

"Oh. Yes, we have a bromance," he said flatly. "Whenever we go out, we twine our tails together."

Shay narrowed her eyes. "There shall be no twining of tails. Your tail, and everything attached to it, belongs to me."

Drakkal chuckled and purred, "It certainly does, *kiraia*."

She groaned. "God, I love it when you purr. It's going to kill me waiting until I'm healed up before I can jump your bones again."

She didn't even want to know the extent of the damage to her poor vagina.

That produced a low growl from his chest that sent tingles all the way down to Shay's toes.

"I'm already feeling it, *kiraia*."

"I'll have to take care of you later then."

It would be torture for her, but she'd enjoy pleasuring him *immensely*.

Drakkal took her hand and brought it to his face, rubbing his cheek against the top of it before turning it to lick her palm. The roughness of his tongue sent another tingling wave through her.

"Not until I can take care of *you*, too. The wait will be worth it."

Shay smiled and stroked his jaw. It *so* would be.

"So anyway, why haven't you told Arc?" Shay asked.

He released a long, slow sigh. "I don't know. Part of me thought he might try to find her if he knew. Arc doesn't tolerate betrayal, even when he's not the direct victim, and when he latches on to something it can be hard to distract him from it. We had other things going on that needed his focus. And another part of me felt like I had to say she was dead because it was the only way I could free myself from the whole mess."

"But now she's here. And she knows *you're* here. You should tell Arc, Drakkal. You can't keep shit like that secret."

"Yeah. And I should've learned by now how the past has a

habit of trying bite you in the ass if you ignore it." He angled his head to the side a little more, shifting his gaze to Leah, and gently brushed the pad of a finger along her little back. "Vanya can't be trusted. After what she said to you, about you...she's a potential threat. Need to make sure we're all aware so we can keep an eye out. The odds of running into her again are slim, but I won't take the chance. Not when I have so much more to lose."

After a few seconds of silence, Drakkal leaned toward Shay and kissed her forehead again. "I'm going to talk to him now. Do you need anything?"

Shay wrapped her arms around her slumbering baby. "No, I'm good."

"All right." He rolled away from her, sat up at the edge of the bed, and stretched as he stood up. His fur was rumpled and sticking up all over, but he was still sexy as hell, especially with those tight pants hugging his toned ass. He walked toward the door. "Get some more rest. I'll be back soon."

"Remember, no tail twining," Shay said with a smirk.

Drakkal snort-laughed. "If you don't see it, it doesn't count."

Shay scoffed playfully. "So much for trust."

"I'll think of you while I do it, *kiraia*," he said as he reached the door.

"Bet you wouldn't like it if I said the same thing about Thargen."

The playfulness vanished from his expression. "That's different."

"But he's my friend."

"Are you saying you have a *bromance* with Thargen?" he asked, lifting a brow.

"In a manner of speaking. I'm just missing the thing swinging between my legs."

"Hurry up and heal, *kiraia*, and I'll fill in that emptiness as much as you want."

Shay grinned. "I love it when you talk dirty."

With another chuckle, he opened the door and stepped out into the corridor, leaving Shay alone with Leah.

Shay's smile lingered. "Hear that, body? You better hurry up."

She turned her face back toward Leah and leaned down to press her lips to her daughter's head. She inhaled deeply, taking in the sweet scent of her baby, and closed her eyes. Weariness poked at the edges of her consciousness. There'd been more exhaustion, anxiety, discomfort, and pain over the last several months than Shay had thought possible. Drakkal had made it so much easier to bear, but he couldn't eliminate it, couldn't shield her from all of it. And she knew there was more to come.

"But you are worth it," she whispered. "And so is he."

DRAKKAL FELT LIGHTER as he walked the quiet corridors in search of Arcanthus. He'd never shared his past with anyone but Arc, and that had only been in pieces—and had included the lie about Vanya. Telling Shay the story—the full, true story—had been like shedding a crippling burden he'd never realized he'd been carrying.

He'd been described by others as guarded and hard to read, and he'd never disagreed. His emotions had always been just that—*his*. The same for his past. It had always seemed like sharing either could only have unfairly burdened the people around him. He'd never wanted them to worry about his problems.

But while Shay—his beautiful, fierce, strong Shay—had talked about her regrets in the training area downstairs weeks ago, Drakkal had realized that sharing those things with a mate wasn't a matter of burdening someone else, wasn't a display of weakness. It was a sort of strength beyond any he'd known before. It was a courage he'd long been unable to muster. Drakkal had always been there for Arc and the rest of the crew, but he'd never allowed them to be there for him.

Vrek'osh, I am getting sappy.

That was all right, though. Having his true mate and a newborn cub had altered Drakkal's perspective for the better. He wanted to share everything with her, and he could see that allowing himself to lean on her sometimes would only strengthen both of them—and their mating bond.

He turned a corner and entered the hall leading to Arcanthus's workshop. He wasn't going to shy away from what he meant to do now. The little spark of anxiousness and uncertainty in Drakkal's gut meant nothing. He'd correct the one lie he'd told to Arcanthus years ago, and then everyone could move on with their lives aware of the possible threat posed by Vanya.

They could reclaim normalcy—not that Drakkal knew yet what *normal* meant after the birth of a cub.

Drakkal pressed the entry button beside the workshop door, walking through the moment the door opened.

Arcanthus and Samantha were reclining together on one of the couches, her body tucked against his in a languid embrace. Sam was watching the holographic flames in the flame bowl, which were constantly changing color, while Arc fiddled with her hair, weaving a trio of strands into a thin braid.

Samantha turned her attention and offered Drakkal a warm smile. "Evening, Drak."

The sedhi glanced up at Drakkal with his center eye as his fingers continued their work. "What, you don't even use the buzzer anymore?"

"You want privacy, lock the door," Drakkal replied. He

walked to the unoccupied couch and plopped down. His eyes ached, and his eyelids were heavy; despite having had a few hours of sleep and having not done much physically over the last day, he was exhausted. He couldn't imagine how Shay felt. But he wouldn't complain—his weariness was the result of something more amazing and beautiful than he could express.

"You spent all that time whining *because* I locked the doors, and now you're telling me to lock them?"

Drakkal released a huff and tilted his head back, leaning it against the backrest. "Figure it out, sedhi. I don't have time to be your mother right now."

"How's little Leah?" Samantha asked.

A wide grin stretched across Drakkal's lips. "She's perfect. Sleeping with Shay right now."

Kraasz ka'val...I'm a father.

That thought had struck him several times since Leah was born, and each time had been just as surreal as the last. A few months ago, the idea of Drakkal having a cub would've been absurd—but only slightly more so than the idea of him finding his mate.

Perhaps the reality of the situation would eventually set in, but he didn't think his awe would fade any time soon.

"Shay still doing okay?" asked Sam.

"Yeah," Drakkal replied. "She's exhausted, but I think all she's really wanted to do is stare at Leah. Can't blame her. Painkillers Urgand gave her are helping her get comfortable, at least."

Drakkal could hear the warm smile in Sam's voice when she said, "Good."

Silence settled over the room; it was a comfortable, companionable sort of silence, but it increasingly reminded Drakkal how much he missed his mate and cub as the seconds passed. Finally, he lifted his head and looked at his friends.

Samantha's eyes were on Drakkal, bright with shimmering, reflected firelight. The joy on her face was unlike any Drakkal had seen there before—and Sam seemed happy just about all the time. Arcanthus had finished with her hair and was staring at her face. Though his expression was subtler than hers, it was beaming with love, adoration, and something...*more*.

Drakkal understood the look on Arc's face—it was the same way Drakkal looked at Shay. He smiled to himself and let a few more seconds trickle by. It had been good to see his oldest, dearest friend, his brother, so content over the last year. The bouts of darkness and depression to which the sedhi had long been prone to had been absent in all that time. Arcanthus wasn't a different person because of Samantha, but he was certainly the best version of himself.

That made Drakkal want to get back to Shay and Leah even more.

"Sorry for interrupting," Drakkal said, "but I need to borrow Arc for a few minutes. Need to talk to him about something."

"No problem, Drak. Just don't rough him up too much, okay?" Picking up her tablet from the couch beside her, she tucked it against her side, disentangled herself from Arcanthus's embrace, and patted the sedhi's thigh as she stood up. "I'm going to take a shower. Don't take too long...cause I'll be waiting."

Arcanthus grinned and ran his tail down her leg. "I could just come now. I'm sure Drakkal would understand."

Sam's cheeks flushed, and she smiled.

"Yeah, I would understand," Drakkal said with a chuckle. "But it won't hurt to wait a little, sedhi. Build some anticipation."

"I'll leave you guys to it," Sam said. She hurried to the door and out into the hallway.

Arcanthus stared after her, and even when the door closed and she was no longer in sight, his gaze lingered on the place she'd been. His expression was almost wistful, and Drakkal couldn't recall if he'd ever seen Arc look like that in all the years they'd known each other.

"You all right?" Drakkal asked.

Laughing softly, Arcanthus shook his head, keeping his gaze on the closed door. "Seeing Samantha hold little Leah earlier, seeing that joy and wonder on her face..." He sighed and finally turned to face Drakkal. "I didn't think my instincts could get any stronger regarding Sam, but they're going crazy right now."

Drakkal tilted his head, studying Arcanthus closely. "You saying you want a cub, Arc?"

"I..." Arcanthus's mouth hung open for a few seconds before he chuckled and smirked. "Yes. I think that's exactly what I'm getting at."

"Just to be clear, sedhi, Leah's *mine*. Get your own."

"That *would* be the plan, azhera...whenever Sam's ready, that is. Strange how I'd never even considered the notion before Samantha. Even now, I have a hard time imagining myself as a father."

"Me, too."

"But you are one now."

Drakkal grinned. "Meant I have a hard time picturing you as a father, too."

Arcanthus's brows rose. "Oh? Well then, you can go fuck yourself." He leaned back, crossed one leg over his opposite knee, and spread his arms to either side along the backrest. "What was it you wanted to discuss?"

Drawing in a deep breath, Drakkal leaned forward and settled his elbows on his thighs. "Need to tell you the truth about something I haven't been honest about for a long, long time."

"This ought to be interesting."

"Just...let me tell you before you give me any shit, all right?"

Arcanthus lifted a hand, gesturing lazily for Drakkal to continue.

"I told you I was living with a female before I was enslaved," Drakkal began.

"Yes, and that she died in the raid."

"Well...I altered some of the details."

Drakkal told Arcanthus the real story, the whole story, just as he'd told Shay. The words came easier than he'd expected, and Arcanthus—surprisingly—refrained from comment until Drakkal finished describing the upper city encounter with Vanya.

"Hmm," was Arcanthus's only reply for several seconds. He brought his hands together, pressing the tips of his pointer fingers against one another and tapping them on his lips. "I *could* go on for some time about how, despite all your talk of trust and openness and honesty between us, you've been keeping the truth of this from me for...what? Fourteen years? Fifteen?"

Drakkal nodded. "At least. And you could go on. I wouldn't blame you."

"All this time, and I thought you'd simply loved and lost."

Shrugging, Drakkal turned his palms toward the ceiling. "I thought the same, in my own way. But I never really loved Vanya. I loved the idea of her. Thought she was the ideal female."

"I know for a fact that thinking that way didn't ease your pain."

"No, it really didn't. I was young and dumb. Had my head

full of these old azheran ideals that probably never really meant much to begin with."

Now Arcanthus shrugged. "You were young, and you didn't have the older, grumpier version of yourself to tell you *don't be stupid*."

"Sure didn't. But what I have with Shay now...it's real, Arc. There's no question of it. She's my mate, and Leah's my cub, and I love them both." Drakkal's chest tightened with another surge of longing. He still didn't know how he could miss his terrans so thoroughly knowing they were only a minute or two away, but he felt their absence fiercely.

"I know." Arcanthus moved a hand up to sweep a few rogue locks of dark hair out of his face, tucking them behind one of his horns. "And for some reason, tossing all this in your face feels...wrong. You must've caught me on an off night. You get off easy this time."

Drakkal laughed; the sound released a little of his tension. "Lucky me."

Arcanthus's tail shifted restlessly over the couch cushion beside him. "Answer a question for me."

"What?"

"Is there a particular means by which you'd like Vanya killed?"

Perhaps it was the directness of the question that threw Drakkal off-guard; he certainly shouldn't have been surprised, knowing Arc as well as he did.

Drakkal sighed heavily and considered the question closely. He couldn't be sure whether thinking about it was a good thing or a bad thing. "She doesn't have to be killed."

"You're allowed to disagree with me," Arcanthus said, "but that doesn't make you right."

"Arrogant bastard."

Arcanthus grinned. "Maybe. But"—his expression fell into

something hard and unforgiving—"what she did to you is just as bad as what Vaund did to us back on Caldorius. No...even worse."

Drakkal nodded, dropping his gaze to the carpet. "You're right, but the circumstances here are different. Can you see if there's anything to dig up on her? I want to know what she's been up to since the last time I saw her."

"She's in Arthos, Drak. That alone makes her dangerous."

"She's just another fucking slaver," Drakkal growled. "That'd be reason enough for me, even without the rest."

"I can make all the arrangements. I'll even take care of it personally. What she did is unforgivable."

"No. Not *yet*. We need to know who she is now before we make a move, or we might end up starting another damned war we're not prepared to fight."

"Come on, azhera. Make a decision based purely on emotion for once! A rash, bold decision."

Drakkal laughed, but it was only half-full of humor. "Oh, I have, sedhi. And those risks have paid off so far. I'm cashing out before my luck runs dry."

"I understand that. You said she threw in with the slavers when they took you, right?"

Drakkal nodded.

Arcanthus leaned forward, reached across the open space between the couches, and patted Drakkal's shoulder. "All right. If there's anything to find on her, I'll find it. Slavers can be hard, though. They don't usually stay in one place long enough to leave much of a record behind. We'll play this one safe."

"I've been waiting so many years to hear you say that."

Arc grinned. "I like to make my sweet little kitty happy."

"You don't deserve it, but I'm going to say it anyway, even after that. Thanks, Arcanthus. And... I'm sorry. For lying."

Arcanthus gave Drakkal's shoulder a squeeze and pushed

himself to his feet. "We've learned some hard lessons in our time, Drakkal. And through all of that, you were the only constant, the only thing I could depend on. This doesn't change any of that. Now, if you'll excuse me, I have a mate awaiting me—hopefully still in the shower. Get back to your Shay and Leah."

"Don't have to tell me twice." Drakkal stood up and dragged his fingers through his mane, tugging out the tangles, as Arcanthus walked toward the door.

"Night, Drak."

"Night, Arc."

Drakkal entered the hallway a bit behind Arcanthus and started back toward the room he shared with Shay. She and Leah were both sound asleep when he entered, the cub tucked securely into the little basket-like nest standing beside the bed—Shay and Sam had called it a *bassinet*. Drakkal gently brushed the pad of a finger over Leah's forehead, touching soft skin and softer hair. She was so tiny—he could easily hold her on one hand.

"Sleep well, little one," he whispered before carefully climbing onto the bed beside his mate.

When he eased an arm beneath Shay's neck and around her shoulders, she stirred just enough to turn onto her side, facing him, and snuggle against his body.

Drakkal eased himself down fully and held Shay close. Despite his weariness, he didn't allow his heavy eyelids to drift shut. Instead, he watched Shay sleep, studying her face and admiring her beauty. He felt the serenity displayed on her features in his own heart, nestled deep and radiating warmth.

Right here, right now, there was no outside world. There were no threats, no dangers. Everything was peaceful. Everything was right.

Everything was *perfect*.

TWENTY

Drakkal watched warily as the female kaital dipped a hand into her pocket to withdraw a credit chip. Her long, pointed ears were downturned, accentuating her frown which nearly spanned her narrow face. She pressed the chip's display button, producing a hologram displaying the credits loaded onto the device. The total was exact; so far, so good.

He nodded to her and willed the small secret compartment on his prosthetic forearm open. He removed the IDR—ID recoder—that had been hidden within, taking the small, thin, cylindrical device between the thumb and forefinger of his right hand to show the kaital. He placed it on her open palm and plucked up the credit chip.

"This is really it?" the kaital asked, staring down at the IDR with wide, black eyes. Even in the dim alleyway light, her skin was a vibrant teal, contrasted by patches of pink on her neck and the insides of her long, pointed ears.

"Yeah." Drakkal tucked the credit chip away. "Keyed only to the ID you specified. Hold it to the wrist and press the button. Green light means it altered the chip's info."

Moving with care and a touch of awe, the kaital curled her fingers around the little device, closing it in a loose fist. "Thank you. My mate...he must become someone else for a while, to be safe."

Something in Drakkal's heart warmed at the loving tone in the kaital's voice. He didn't let that show in his expression. "One successful use and the internals will self-destruct. Destroy whatever's left over."

The kaital nodded, clutching her closed fist to her chest and bending her long, graceful neck to bow her head. "I will do as you say. Thank you, azhera, thank you a thousand times over. May the stars watch over you favorably for the rest of your days."

Though he'd heard such sentiments before, they always made Drakkal uncomfortable. This time, the work he and Arcanthus had done had a chance of protecting someone's life. He wanted to believe that someone was worthy of protection. At the very least, it was someone this female cared for very deeply. But all the same, this had been a business transaction. They'd turned a profit off someone in need, off someone in danger. They'd monetized someone's desperation.

There was as much chance that this kaital's mate deserved whatever was coming to him.

Drakkal wasn't sure how he felt about all this anymore. He was realistic enough to understand that he and Arcanthus couldn't run their operation for free, but...weren't there people in this city who needed the sort of help Arcanthus's skills could provide but who couldn't afford the price?

Vrek'osh, I'm going soft.

No, he wasn't going soft. He was just sympathizing with Shay's sentiments a little more every day—he was tired of being on the wrong side of the law. Tired of having to worry about it.

"Good luck," he said. "You need us again, you know how to get in touch with us."

After a few more thanks from the kaital, Drakkal turned and exited the alleyway.

Should've given her back the credits.

But what would Arcanthus have said? *We're not running a charity.* Those words might've seemed cold or callous on the surface, but they were right. It was impractical to delve into the story of every client, and in many cases, getting involved beyond the usual background checks to avoid making a deal that risked peacekeeper intervention was a liability. Drakkal and Arcanthus couldn't risk catching the attention of a larger, more powerful organization again, couldn't chance calling more danger to the family they'd formed.

We can't help everyone.

But Drakkal was immensely, eternally grateful for the one person he *had* risked himself to help. Given the chance to do it all over again, he wouldn't have changed a thing; he'd been fortunate enough to win Shay and earn her love and respect. The struggles he'd faced in the process only made her infinitely more precious to him.

As he returned to his hovercar, he forced aside his thoughts of work; he'd express his growing dissatisfaction to Arcanthus sometime after he'd had a chance to figure out the true depth of his feelings. For now, there were happier things to occupy his attention.

Drakkal climbed into the vehicle, started the engines, and took off. Leaving home earlier had been a struggle for him, to no one's surprise—he'd spent the last two weeks with Shay and Leah, rarely separated from one or the other for more than a few minutes at a time, and it had been both the happiest and most exhausting period of his life. That tiny cub had claimed a huge chunk of Drakkal's heart. He yearned to return to them now, but he guided the hovercar toward the upper city instead.

The delay would be worth it when he arrived home with the gifts he'd ordered.

Once he was above the surface, he couldn't help but let his eyes wander a little. The abundant plants and fountains—many of the latter designed to resemble naturally occurring features—always put him in a mood that made the Undercity much less appealing.

Would Shay ever want to leave Arthos? Could Drakkal bring himself to give up all his friends for a chance at quiet and solitude?

Oddly enough, he knew the answer without having to think on it. Arthos had become his home. Everyone important to him was here, and despite his grumblings, the city had grown on him. He'd follow Shay anywhere she wanted to go, but the life they had here wasn't bad. Hell, it was actually really good.

He left the hovercar at one of the many public parking complexes situated across the surface. He pulled on his nicest jacket, covering his sleek prosthesis but for the hand, and shifted his holstered blaster toward the back of his belt. Many people openly carried weapons in the Infinite City, but the key in places like this—places with high concentrations of peace-keepers—was to carry it so casually as to seem oblivious to its existence. The high-class people who often frequented places like the one for which he was bound tended to be somewhat more skittish than their Undercity counterparts, who weren't even guaranteed to scatter when blasterfire erupted in the street.

He'd seen the Ventrillian Mall before, and though he'd always found it nice looking—in an overly manicured, too-orderly-to-be-natural sort of way—he wasted no time in taking in the sights. He didn't deviate from his path, and within a few minutes of entering the mall, he'd arrived at the specialty tailors.

The place was owned and operated by volturians, all of whom were dressed in what Drakkal assumed were the latest fashions—he'd never paid enough attention to such things to know for sure. The female volturian at the counter eyed Drakkal up and down as he approached, arching one of her thin brows.

"Can I help you?" she asked, though her tone said, *Are you lost?*

Drakkal had dealt with such attitudes often enough that he wasn't bothered by them anymore—especially not now, when his life was good, and he felt whole. "I had an order come in. Here to pick it up."

Somehow, her expression became more skeptical. "There are several tailors in the Undercity. You probably have an order with one of them."

Grinning to display his fangs, Drakkal shook his head. "This is the place. Figured I'd have my measurements taken while I'm here, too. Just a warning—I've been shedding lately."

The distaste that wrinkled the female's face was deeply satisfying. "What's the name on the order?"

"Lion."

When she only stared at him blankly, Drakkal sighed and slowly—*very* slowly—spelled it for her in the Universal Speech alphabet.

She rolled her eyes and input information on the holo screen in front of her. After a few seconds, she sighed. "I need to scan your ID."

"No, you don't," Drakkal said. "You just need to give me my order. It's already paid for."

"Still need to confirm you are who you say you are."

Drakkal leaned forward, bracing his hands on the countertop, and said in as overly pleasant a voice as he could manage, "The order is paid for. Twenty outfits for a newborn terran and three pairs of terran *leisure pants*, ordered ten days ago. Would you like me to tell you the total on the bill and how much I paid over that number? Maybe I could go to the back and find it. Wouldn't want you to have to do your job or anything."

Though there was a glimmer of fear in her eyes, the volturian didn't back away. Drakkal, still refusing to let himself be annoyed—undoubtedly a failing endeavor—had to admire her courage. Of course, it could've also been a matter of arrogance.

Perhaps next time he *would* use one of those Undercity tailors.

The female took in a slow breath. "I need to scan your—"

Her words were cut off by an older female volturian, who hurried over saying, "Vyri, go fetch Master Lion's order, *now!*"

The intricate *qal* markings on Vyri's face darkened, and her skin blanched. She rushed into a back room with a muttered, "Yes, mother."

The older volturian took Vyri's place. "Please, Master Lion, accept my deepest apologies. My daughter is young, and like many youths, is prone to bouts of unnecessary rudeness. She has much to learn. I am Arae. Welcome to my shop."

"Thank you," Drakkal said with a nod. He stood up straight and stepped back from the counter. "All's forgiven. I'll collect my order and be on my way."

"Of course, of course."

When Vyri emerged from the back with a stack of neatly folded clothing, Arae waved her over. "Hurry girl, hurry. You've already wasted too much of this gentleman's time."

Head down, Vyri placed the stack on the countertop

between Drakkal and Arae before retreating and clasping her hands together.

Arae lifted a tiny garment from the top of the stack and unfolded it, displaying it to Drakkal with practiced ease. It was what Shay had called a *onesie*. "As you specified, only the finest fabrics. We used terran patterns as reference, but gave them a more modern and tasteful flair."

Drakkal barely suppressed a chuckle; he couldn't help seeing humor in the knowledge that his newborn cub—who wouldn't even be able to crawl for another five or six months, at least—would be better dressed than him.

Better dressed than Arcanthus, too.

What am I thinking? Arcanthus barely counts as dressed most of the time.

That thought nearly shattered his self-control; it was amusing enough to make him forget the difficulty Vyri had caused.

"Would you like to inspect the rest?" Arae asked as she deftly folded the garment.

"No. Just a bag."

Arae snapped her fingers, and Vyri hurriedly stepped forward, pulled a large, tailored cloth bag from beneath the counter, and loaded it with the folded clothes. Her *qal* remained dark, her skin pale, but she worked efficiently and precisely. She placed the loaded bag on the counter.

Even the bag looked nicer than most of the clothes Drakkal owned.

"If you are interested, Master Lion, I could make room in my schedule for some custom fittings," Arae said as though reading his mind. "We have styles that can accent all your powerful features."

At that, Drakkal did laugh. Back on Caldorius, they'd often dressed slave gladiators to make them look more imposing—

which usually just meant making them go shirtless. He lifted the bag off the counter. "I'll have to think about that."

"Very well." Arae dipped into a bow. "Please, let me know if there are any problems. We will do all we can to ensure your satisfaction."

"Yeah. I will." Drakkal offered Arae a nod, turned, and exited the shop without a backward glance.

Drakkal's amusement didn't fade—now he was picturing himself stuffed into a form-fitting Volturian suit with tufts of fur sprouting from the neck and sleeves, and it looked hilarious. But that humor was underscored by thrumming excitement. He was finally going back to Shay and Leah. He'd only been gone for two hours, but it felt like ten times as long.

He breathed in deep, filling his lungs with air redolent with the perfume of a dozen alien flowers, and turned onto the foot path that would take him toward his hovercar.

His gaze locked with a pair of sickeningly familiar golden eyes set in a brown-furred, feminine face, and Drakkal's good mood perished in an avalanche of hatred and bitterness.

Vanya smiled that old, sultry smile he'd once found so enticing and sauntered toward him, hips swaying seductively and tail swinging languidly. Drakkal tightened his right fist around the straps of the bag he was carrying. He wasn't sure whether he should've been grateful or angry that his blaster hand was full—he might've drawn the weapon otherwise.

And gunning someone down in public tended to cause problems in this part of town.

"Hello, Drakkal," Vanya said, stopping in front of him.

Drakkal released a low growl. "Following me now?"

She sidled a little closer and placed her hand on his flesh and blood forearm, slowly sliding it upward. "I've missed you. I got tired of waiting for you to come find me, so I took matters into my own hands."

He tugged his arm away from her and very nearly formed the hardlight claws on the tips of his cybernetic fingers. It would've been easy to slash them across her throat. "Fuck off, Vanya."

Her features tightened into a scowl for an instant before they fell into an exaggerated pout. "I was wrong, Drakkal. Is that what you want to hear?"

Drakkal's nostrils flared with a heavy exhalation; if it were possible to breathe fire, he would've been singing her fur that very moment. "Wrong? You threw in with slavers and fucking handed me over to them. We lived together for years. We shared a bed. But you were *wrong*? Did you suffer a traumatic headwound sometime after you sold me out?"

"What do you think would have happened to me if I hadn't helped them? I'm female, Drakkal. My life would have been infinitely worse than yours. But I knew *you* would have a chance. You were always strong." She eased a little closer. "I wish it hadn't come to that. I wish things could have been different. That *I* had been different. I just didn't realize what I had until you were gone."

He squeezed his fists tight enough to make his arms tremble —even the metal one. "Too little, too fucking late. *Kraasz ka'val*, Vanya, you really think I'm going to buy that you were in any danger? You helped them round up everyone within two hundred kilometers of us!"

Her brows fell. "I wasn't given much of a choice, Drakkal. But they didn't kill you. Isn't that enough?" She reached for him again, placing her palm on his chest. "You loved me once. I want that again. I want to try again, with you. You were such a worthy mate, and I was wrong not to see it. I want to make amends, to earn your trust, your forgiveness. I want cubs—"

"Take your hand off me," Drakkal said in a low voice,

glaring at her, "or I will tear it off and shove it down your traitorous throat."

Vanya's eyes flared and her ears perked. She dropped her hand.

Pulses of heat swept throughout Drakkal's body, flowing just beneath the surface. His ears were flat, his fur bristling, his tail lashing in agitation. "I would have done anything for you back then. I would have died for you—I was ready to. But I never loved you. I cared for the person I *thought* you were. The person you *never* were. We talked about honoring the old ways before we left home. Do you remember any of that?" He took a step toward her, and she took one back. "Do you remember who you pretended to be?

"If your life was in danger, you should've told me. But it wasn't. You're just giving me another fucking lie. You were meeting with them for weeks before they took me—that's where you were disappearing to. If it was a matter of your life against the lives of all our neighbors, you should've done the honorable thing, the noble thing. But that was never you, was it? Every choice you've ever made has been for *you*. You're not going to find forgiveness, you're not going to make amends. You're going to scurry back to whatever sewer you crawled out of and never come near me or my family again, or I will show you what it means to be azheran. I will avenge the wrong you have done me."

All traces of softness left Vanya's features as she bared her teeth in a snarl. "This is because of that *ji'tas* terran, isn't it? Your newly acquired pet?"

"My *mate*," Drakkal growled. "And you don't fucking speak of her. You're not worthy to."

"I wanted things to go differently for us this time." The corner of her mouth quirked. "You don't know the mistake you just made, but you will soon."

"I'm going to kill you the next time I see you, Vanya."

She smiled, sparking a wicked light in her eyes, turned, and walked away from him.

As Drakkal watched her go, the thundering of his heart drowned out the sounds of the mall around him. He maintained his tight hold on the bag's handles; even now, his fingers itched to draw his blaster and fire a few plasma bolts into her back. It was a cowardly way to end things, but it was no more than Vanya deserved for what she'd done.

The wisdom of hindsight had made Vanya's nature apparent to him over the long years since she'd betrayed him, but now it was clearer than ever. How had he ever been so foolish as to not see it? How had he ever believed she possessed the qualities that had drawn him in?

He'd dealt with enough criminals to understand now that she'd been manipulating him from the beginning. She'd only ever seen him as a means to an end, and as soon as she'd decided he was no longer useful for achieving her goals, she'd turned on him. He didn't doubt that she was jealous of his mate—he'd practically worshipped Vanya when he was young. It wasn't likely that her ego could handle the blow he'd dealt it now. In her mind, Drakkal was supposed to always worship her, because she *was* ideal. She was everything he should've wanted.

But even back then, he'd never taken her as a full mate. He'd never filled her with his seed—some instinctual part had known it wasn't right, that *she* was wrong.

"Fuck," he grumbled. He forced himself to walk.

The day had been so good.

Drakkal carefully monitored his surroundings as he left the Ventrillian Mall, searching for any sign of pursuit, for any sign of Vanya. If she'd followed him here, where else had she tailed him to? Did she know about the building he and Shay called home?

Pulled an Arcanthus and got careless.

Fortunately, Arcanthus's voice, as smug as ever, chimed in from the back of Drakkal's mind. *Don't be stupid, Drak.*

Seemed like it was too late for that.

TWENTY-ONE

"So Urgand finally give you the okay?" Samantha asked as she sat down beside Shay on the couch.

Shay lifted her head and grinned. "*Yes*. Finally. I've been dying, Sam. *Dying*."

It'd been a month since Leah's birth, and Shay was so done waiting. While she'd felt healed and ready to go for at least a week now, Urgand had urged her to wait, to be cautious, just in case. Terrans and their physiology were still new territory for the vorgal, and Shay was basically his test subject.

It'd been torture to do nothing but lie next to Drakkal every night as he kissed her, held her, and lovingly explored her body with his hands. And that body had changed; Shay was still getting used to it herself. Her hips were a little wider, and there were stretch marks and some loose skin on her belly, but Drakkal worshipped those changes, telling her she was beautiful with words and kisses. She saw the truth of it in his eyes every time they settled on her. So, she embraced those changes. And why shouldn't she? Her body had created *life*. It had sheltered, nurtured, and birthed their daughter.

As much as Drakkal had wanted release, he'd adhered strictly to Urgand's orders, sticking to loving caresses and kisses—and had stood by his vow to go without release until he could pleasure her fully, as well. Even when she tried to instigate it, he'd refused. Shay wanted to feel him inside her again. She wanted to feel his girth, his length, to feel him filling her completely, to have her body locked with his. She wanted that physical, bonding connection again.

She'd been horny as hell these last couple weeks. Whether it was caused by some pheromone from Drakkal that was driving her wild, her hormones still being out of whack, or his raw sex appeal, it didn't matter. She'd turned that pent-up energy toward her training, working off the baby weight and pushing to regain the strength she'd had before she was taken from Earth.

Samantha laughed and reached out to brush a finger over Leah's tiny rounded ear. "I wonder if Arcanthus would change his mind if he knew how long he'd have to wait for sex after I gave birth."

Shay grinned and looked down at her daughter, who was cuddled against her chest, nursing contently. Though Leah had a healthy appetite and fed often, Shay seemed to be producing an overabundance of milk. She'd often had to express a little milk before each feeding, or it'd be too much, too fast for Leah.

Shay hadn't bothered with a blanket since it was only her and Samantha in the break room, but she had one on standby just in case one of the males walked in—not for the sake of modesty, but to avoid a potential fist fight if Drakkal found out someone saw some nip.

She gently ran her fingers through the dark hair on Leah's head. Leah's eyes fluttered open and stared up at her. They were blue, a few shades darker than Shay's, surrounded by long, dark eyelashes.

"I'm sure he already knows. I don't see Drakkal being quiet about it," Shay said, easing back and returning her gaze to Sam. "Is Arc considering it?"

Samantha lifted her feet off the floor curled her legs beside her on the cushion. "It's like...an inner battle with himself. He's always had these instincts to reproduce—it comes from his tretin side—but neither of us were really ready for that yet when we first met. But now, seeing the baby, seeing *me* with her, it's like his mind and body are finally aligning with those instincts."

"What about you? What do you want?"

Sam dropped her gaze to Leah and smiled. "I've always wondered what our baby would look like. If it'd have horns, claws, and a tail. Even that extra eye. And how beautiful it'd be. And when I saw Arc holding Leah, I understood how he felt seeing me hold her." She looked at Shay again, her smile widening into a grin. "Why is it such a turn-on to see men holding babies?"

"Beats me. But it is fucking hot watching Drakkal hold Leah. Like ovary explosion hot. Seeing that big, rough male being so gentle and careful with something so small and fragile, with such adoration in his eyes..." Shay groaned and let her head tilt back as that familiar spark of arousal bloomed low in her belly. "I'm telling you, Sam. It's been *torture*."

Samantha laughed and patted Shay's leg. "Not for much longer. Now you can claim your man at your earliest convenience."

Shay lifted her head and smiled, but there was something on Samantha's face that gave Shay pause. "What's wrong?"

"I was just thinking about what happened last year. With... Vaund, and Arc's old place."

"That's in the past now, Sam. You guys took care of him."

Samantha met Shay's gaze. "What if something like that

happens again? What if it happens after Arc and I have a baby? That's two innocent little lives caught in the crossfire. This life... I've never been so happy as I am here with Arcanthus. Everyone here has become my family. But it's still dangerous. They're still criminals working with other criminals."

Leah unlatched from Shay's nipple and turned her head away. Shay pulled her bra up, tugged her shirt down, and rested Leah over her shoulder, gently patting the baby's back.

Samantha was voicing the same concerns Shay had harbored from the beginning. Drakkal, Arcanthus, and the rest of the crew were good people, but they were still criminals working a dangerous job, always toeing the line, always taking risks. At heart, it was still the sort of life Shay had wanted to escape. Drakkal himself had talked to Shay about it a few times over the last couple weeks. He was conflicted, but he was starting to see things the same way. They were making good money, but Arc and Drak already had more money than they could spend—though Arc sure seemed keen on trying to sometimes.

Shay hadn't pressed Drakkal on it. Gears were turning in his mind, and she was fine with letting him sort it all out on his own for now. He already knew where she stood. If there was a way for them to go legit, she'd support it wholeheartedly. She wanted Leah's life to start out *right*.

"Have you talked to Arcanthus about it?" Shay asked.

Samantha frowned. "I haven't, but I think it's on his mind, too, when he looks at Leah and me. *Especially* when he looks at me."

Shay was just about to tell her it'd all be okay when the door opened and Thargen entered, followed by Drakkal. Drakkal's gaze met Shay's; her heart fluttered, and her pussy clenched in immediate want.

Down, girl. I know you've been thirsty, and you'll drink your fill soon.

Thargen spread his arms wide. "Our three favorite terrans!"

"Going to guess they're also the only terrans you know," Drakkal said with a smirk, though he didn't take his eyes off Shay.

The vorgal flashed a toothy grin. "Doesn't change the fact that they're my favorites."

"The real test would be for him to choose which of us is his most favorite," Shay said.

Thargen barked laughter and dropped into one of the breakroom chairs. "Might be crazy, but I'm not stupid."

Shay grinned. "Good answer."

Drakkal moved to stand in front of Shay and held his hands out. Shay's smile softened as she lifted Leah off her shoulder and placed her in the big azhera's arms. Despite the immense size difference, Drakkal was delicate with the baby, cradling her on his right arm and leaning down to nuzzle her forehead.

"She just eat?" he asked.

"Yep. She's been changed and has a full belly."

He lifted his left hand and gently tickled Leah's belly with his forefinger. The baby's little hands latched onto it, and she stared up at Drakkal in wonderment. Drakkal smiled down at her, and suddenly, Leah smiled back. Drakkal's ears perked and his eyes widened.

"She smiled!" Despite her excitement, Shay couldn't help feeling a little bit jealous that Drakkal got the first one.

Drakkal's smile stretched into a grin. "Guess I'm the fun one, *kiraia*."

"She probably just realized how funny looking you are," Thargen suggested.

Leah smiled a big, gummy smile again.

"That is too cute," Samantha said.

Shay sat back and swept her eyes over Drakkal, who was beaming with love and pride. "Now we know she's a daddy's girl for sure."

"Was there any question of that?" Drakkal asked. After a few more seconds of staring down at Leah, he finally looked at Shay again. "How'd it go earlier? What'd Urgand say?"

Shay caught a loose strand of her hair and twirled it around her fingers. "I'll have to tell you in *private*."

That fire she'd come to love so much sparked in his eyes, giving his grin an entirely new meaning. "Is it almost nap time?"

Shay sighed dramatically. "Unfortunately, she just woke up from one."

"Oof. Cock-blocked by a newborn," Thargen said with a chuckle.

Drakkal turned his head toward the vorgal. "Looks like we have a volunteer."

Thargen's face sobered, and his eyes rounded. "*What? What the fuck you talking about, Drak?*"

Samantha brought a hand up to cover her mouth and stifle her laughter.

"You just volunteered to watch the cub for a little while. About an hour"—Drakkal glanced at Shay again, and eyes smoldering—"maybe two."

Fuck yes.

Shay grinned at Thargen. "How thoughtful and sweet!"

Drakkal walked over to the vorgal, who was staring at him with a look of confusion and terror. Without missing a beat, Drakkal placed Leah in Thargen's arms and stepped back. "Good luck."

Thargen's eyes dropped to Leah before returning to

Drakkal with a pleading gleam in them. "What am I supposed to do with it?"

"*Her*," Drakkal corrected.

"What am I supposed to do with *her*?"

Shay pushed herself up from the couch and walked to Thargen. She leaned forward and pecked a kiss on Leah's head. As loath as she was to part from the baby, even for a short time, she needed this time with Drakkal.

"Hold her, rock her. She'll probably fall asleep again soon," Shay said, smiling down at Leah. "Be good for Uncle Thargen."

The vorgal was holding Leah carefully but uncertainly. Shay guessed he would've looked more comfortable if someone had handed him a live grenade that had already had the pin pulled.

Samantha walked over and took a seat beside Thargen. "Go on, you two. I'll help keep an eye on Leah."

"You owe me," Thargen grumbled.

"I'll up your hazard pay the next time you collect your wage," Drakkal replied with a chuckle. When he turned to face Shay, all humor had fled from his expression—he wore a hungry grin beneath those fiery eyes.

Before she could say anything, before she had enough time to even admire his tall, powerful body, he bent forward, wrapped an arm around the backs of her thighs, and stood up, hauling Shay over his shoulder.

Shay laughed and flattened her hands on his back to prop herself up. She looked at Thargen and Samantha as Drakkal stalked toward the door. "If she needs—"

"She'll be fine!" Samantha called. "Have fun."

Drakkal slapped the control button. The instant the door was open, he crossed the threshold. The door whooshed shut behind him.

Grinning, Shay smoothed her hands down toward his ass. "I haven't told you what Urgand said yet."

"Oh, you did, *kiraia*. It was in your eyes."

"Really?" She grabbed his ass with one hand and clutched the base of his tail with the other, tugging it. "I thought that look has been there for a while now."

His chest rumbled with a deep purr. His right hand settled over her ass and squeezed appreciatively. "Why don't you tell me now, then."

Shay moaned when his finger delved between her thighs to stroke her sex though the seam of her pants. Liquid heat flooded her, and she reflexively tightened her hold on both his backside and his tail. "Basically, you're allowed to fuck me as hard and as deep as you want."

His only response was a growl—and an increase in pace.

They reached their room in what must've been record time. As soon as they were inside, Drakkal had her off his shoulder and pressed up against the wall with his mouth on hers before the door had even closed.

His mouth was bruising and hungry, and Shay returned the kiss in full, unable to get enough of his firm, warm lips and rough tongue. She buried her hands in his mane and pulled him closer. His right hand curled around her neck and cupped her jaw, tilting her face up more as he slanted his mouth, deepening the kiss. His tongue moved ruthlessly, possessively, as he devoured her. Shivers of desire spiraled through her.

He pressed his hard body against hers and used his thigh to force her legs wider apart. She felt his hard cock on her belly, separated only by her shirt and his pants, and arched into him, desperate to feel *more*.

Drakkal clutched her tighter and growled again. The sound reverberated from his mouth and chest and flowed into Shay—she felt it in their kiss, vibrating against her breasts, teasing her nipples. The sensation traveled straight to her pussy, which contracted in need.

He broke the kiss to trail his mouth down her jaw and neck. His lips and teeth left a blazing trail in their wake as he worked his way toward her front, following her clavicle and kissing the hollow of her throat. He grasped the collar of her shirt and pulled it apart. The garment tore down the middle like it were made of paper.

Shay laughed. "I'm going to run out of clothes if you keep doing that."

"I'll buy you more." He sliced through her bra with his hardlight claws next, baring her breasts to his hungry gaze. She barely had time to feel the air on her skin before he put his mouth on her again to kiss her breasts and curl that oh-so-tantalizing tongue around her sensitive nipples.

Drakkal's hands—one metal, the other rough and calloused—smoothed down her sides as he leaned closer, took her nipple into his mouth, and sucked.

A surge of lust speared her straight through her core.

Shay gasped, tightening her grip on his mane as her hips bucked against him. God, his mouth felt so *good* on her; the scrape of his rough tongue, the gentle suction, the *relief*.

Drakkal started, pulling his mouth away and lifting his head. Shay opened her eyes and looked at him. His tongue darted out, licking moisture from his lips, and it took Shay a moment to realize that there were droplets of her breastmilk beaded on his fur.

She glanced down. Sure enough, another drop of milk had formed at the tip of her nipple.

"Shit," she said, releasing his mane to cover her breasts, suddenly feeling self-conscious. She hadn't even thought about this. It had just felt so good to have his mouth on her again for real.

Before she could cover herself, Drakkal lifted his hands and caught her wrists. He pressed her arms against the wall and slid his palms up to lace his fingers with hers. The position forced her shoulders back, shoving her breasts out even further.

"Didn't think you could taste any sweeter," he rumbled, "but here you are."

Drakkal dipped his head and latched onto her breast, sucking her nipple back into his mouth. They groaned in unison. Shay's eyes fluttered shut against a flood of desire that heated her core as he took draw after draw from her breast. He released her nipple to move to her other breast, nuzzling it before he sucked the hardened tip into his mouth and drank from her again.

This was different from when her daughter nursed. The relief he was providing was immense, but he was also providing her overwhelming pleasure. This was...erotic. An experience unlike anything she'd ever imagined.

Shay ground her pelvis against his thigh. The soaked material of her pants pulling taut over her sex provided some stimulation, but it wasn't enough. It was nowhere near enough.

"Drakkal," she rasped, "I need you."

A hot, heavy breath flowed from between his bared teeth just before he released her arms. For a few seconds, he became a force of nature—a hurricane or a tornado, fast and powerful and relentless—as he tugged down her pants, underwear and all, and ripped off his own clothes. His cock sprang from the confines of his pants, thick and throbbing, just as hungry as the male it was attached to.

He hooked his hands behind her thighs and lifted her. Shay looped her arms around his neck. She felt the press of his blunt tip against her slick entrance as he angled her over him. Their eyes met, and Drakkal pulled her down, plunging into her eager sex.

Shay gasped as his cock filled her. It didn't matter that she'd just had a baby; he felt as big and thick as always. Her pussy clenched around him as a pulsing shudder ran down her spine. That shudder seemed to flow into him. He bared his teeth and clutched her ass with both hands, digging the tips of his natural claws into her flesh. His pulsing knot expanded against her folds as he ground against her, threatening to push into her fully.

"*Kraasz ka'val, kiraia,*" he said reverently. "I've missed this."

"I did too." Shay slid her hands along the backs of his shoulders and into the thick, soft fur of his mane. "Fuck me. Unleash yourself on me, Drakkal. I need to *feel* you."

As he stared at her, his already dilated pupils expanded further, almost obliterating his green irises. But that darkness wasn't empty—it was filled with desire, with lust, with the beast she'd just asked him to release.

That moment of eye contact was all he allowed before he obeyed her command.

Drakkal pulled his hips back, and Shay shuddered at the slide of his hot, hard shaft inside her. He slammed his mouth over hers, swallowing her cry as a powerful thrust of his hips forced his cock back into her. Before she could recover from the burst of pleasure it caused, he pounded into her, again and again, each thrust a little harder and deeper than the last.

Shay gripped his mane, her panting gasps mixing with his grunts as he rutted her.

He tore his mouth from hers with a snarl. An instant later, his teeth latched onto her flesh where her shoulder met her neck. The sharp pricks of pain only heightened the thrill building within Shay, and her body wound tighter and tighter with pleasure.

He squeezed her ass and quickened his pace. The frenzy of

motion, sensation, and pleasure was so strong it bordered on pain. All Shay could do was hold on as the gathering storm clouds within her neared their breaking point. She felt Drakkal's breath, felt his teeth, his claws, his fur, all on her skin —she felt every bit of him, both inside and out. He was wild, untamed, raw.

He was her mate.

He was *hers*.

Drakkal snarled. The sound's vibrations pulsed into her body and sent her over the edge. That pressure inside her, that gathering storm, exploded with a bolt of lightning that pierced to her core and shattered her being into a thousand pieces.

Body tensing and spasming with blasts of utter rapture, Shay cried out. Her pussy greedily clamped down on Drakkal's cock, throbbing as liquid heat flooded her.

He released a growl that became a muffled roar against her neck and, with one more merciless thrust, buried himself inside her, forcing his knot past her entrance. A choked gasp escaped her, breaking up her moans, but that flash of pain was worth the pleasure that followed as his knot expanded. Seed burst from Drakkal's cock. He shuddered but didn't ease his hold with either hands or teeth; somehow, he pressed only deeper.

He slapped his left hand against the wall beside her head, pinned her in place with his hips, and curled his fingers. Their tips scraped the wall, but the sound was overpowered by a ragged growl as he came again. The force of his seed flowing inside her pushed Shay's climax to new heights. Powerful tremors tore through her.

She and Drakkal clung to one another as the strength of their passion ebbed, panting heavily, bodies quivering in the aftermath. When he released his bite, a rush of sensation flooded the spot he'd marked. She knew without looking that he'd broken the skin, but she didn't care. She *wanted* to bear his mark.

With a tenderness belied by his size, strength, and the savagery of a few moments ago, Drakkal licked the spot he'd bitten, soothing away the pain.

Shay loosened her hold on his mane and opened her eyes to meet his gaze. An instant later, he bared his teeth, features contorting as his cock pulsed, and he released inside her once more. He ground his pelvis against her, and Shay moaned.

She brushed her hand down the side of his face. "I *so* missed this."

"Me too, *kiraia*," he purred and nuzzled her cheek.

She wrapped her arms around him, holding him close and brushing her face against him in turn. As much as she missed her daughter, Shay and Drakkal had needed this time. Though they were now parents, they were still mates, and their bond with one another was just as important as it had been before Leah—perhaps even more so. It would take time to figure out what life was going to look like going forward, but these moments with Drakkal would *always* be part of it.

TWENTY-TWO

Drakkal frowned when the terran embassy came into view through the hovercar's windshield. The building was smaller than many of those surrounding it, and it was plainer too—the terrans seemed to have favored function over form in its construction. It was surrounded by stretches of green grass and neatly trimmed shrubbery that he assumed were from Earth. At least two dozen colorful flags flew from tall posts, the central one being the largest. For the first time, he found himself wondering what his mate's homeworld—his daughter's ancestral point of origin—looked like.

He made a mental note to look it up later, but there were more pressing concerns to occupy him now.

"You're sure about this, *kiraia*?" he asked, well aware that he was repeating himself.

Fortunately, Shay took it in stride—even though she had every reason to be annoyed with him by now. "I'm sure. Like I said, I want her to start off right. This is where that happens."

Drakkal nodded and followed the hovering markers toward the parking complex beneath the embassy. He trusted Arcanthus's work as much as he trusted Arcanthus himself—unquestionably—but it was always best to avoid putting forgeries to the test whenever possible. Their ID chips would be scanned here, and those scans would be run through both Terran and Consortium systems. Even the slightest discrepancy could be enough to rouse suspicion.

He glanced over his shoulder to see Leah, smiling and wide-eyed, staring out the windows in wonder. She'd grown so much in the four months since her birth. She was still tiny, but she was on track to have doubled her birth weight within another month or two, and he couldn't help but find her chubbiness—dubbed baby fat by Sam and Shay—adorable. Every day, she grew a little stronger, advanced a little further.

She could already push her chest up and hold her head high when she was lying on the floor. She'd be crawling before long. His pride for Leah was already immense, and it only grew along with her. Though some might've said she was too young to display it, Drakkal saw her mother's strength in the little cub just as clearly as he could see the blue of her eyes.

His concerns about coming here were justified, he knew, but Shay's concerns were equally valid. Leah deserved a chance at a normal life. Whatever Drakkal could do to ensure that was the case, he would. Right now, that meant having her officially added to the records of her people. That meant having her legally obtain her citizenship.

They entered the parking complex without incident, and Drakkal pulled the hovercar into an open spot. He turned his head and met Shay's gaze. She smiled at him. The gratitude in her eyes made him forget his worries, if only for a few seconds.

She'd been growing stronger over the last few months, too. They were fortunate to have people around them who, despite their professions and backgrounds, were eager to help with Leah, allowing Shay and Drakkal some time to themselves.

Shay had been working out regularly and often trained with Thargen—both in the simulation chambers and in hand-to-hand combat. Drakkal's grumblings hadn't been enough to stop the latter, but he knew Shay wasn't in any real danger.

Thargen could be a bit unstable sometimes, but he was a good person at heart. And his friendship with Shay was rivaled only by his friendship with Urgand.

But the gym and training rooms hadn't been the only places Shay had been exercising. Though it wasn't always easy to find time together, she and Drakkal couldn't keep their hands off one another when they were close. The more they mated, the more they craved one another, and sometimes the wait between those wild encounters was more unbearable than those weeks after Shay had first run from Drakkal.

He suspected it was another of his instincts at work. Once she'd healed from giving birth, Drakkal's body seemed to have recognized her readiness to breed and had worked itself into a frenzy over it—apparently unaffected by the fact that she'd received a contraceptive shot to prevent pregnancy until they'd deemed themselves ready for another cub. That drive to mate with her hadn't diminished even slightly.

"It's going to be fine," Shay said, settling a hand on Drakkal's thigh.

Even now, her touch lit a fire in him, and he squeezed his eyes shut for a few seconds to steady himself. "I know."

But as he killed the engines, his stresses reintroduced themselves, poking in from around the edges of his conscious mind. It had been a little more than three months since his last run-in with Vanya—three quiet months. He and Arcanthus had tried to track her down numerous times, and each attempt had come up with nothing. There was no record of her anywhere, not even on the surveillance feeds in which she should've appeared —the recording from the Ventrillian Mall showed Drakkal speaking to nothing but a barely perceptible distortion in the holo.

That was troubling. There was technology that could cause such effects—that could essentially erase people and objects from surveillance feeds—but it was expensive, and it was rarely used outside of military operations and well-funded criminal organizations.

Who was Vanya working for to have had access to that kind of equipment?

The possibilities had kept Drakkal awake long after lying down in bed on more than one night, but they were too numerous to narrow down. It was most likely that she was still working as a slaver. That provided no comfort. The Inner Reach Syndicate, the powerful crime organization that had caused so much trouble and suffering for Arcanthus and Drakkal in the past, was immensely influential and wealthy, and they had several large slaving operations on their payroll.

Drakkal had no desire to tangle with the Syndicate again, especially not so soon after the incident with Vaund. Just the thought of it made his missing left arm ache.

Something was going to happen. Even if it had been twenty years since he'd lived with Vanya, he knew her well enough to understand that she didn't make idle threats. She would act. But when, where? And what would she do?

He covered Shay's hand with his own, giving it a little squeeze before he opened his door and climbed out of the vehicle. Shay exited on her side and collected Leah from her harnessed safety seat.

"All right," Drakkal said as he met his females at the back of the hovercar, "let's go be law-abiding citizens for a little while."

Shay grinned. "The first step in a new chapter, right Kitty?"

Leah smiled up at her mother and giggled—it was her new

favorite sound and remained the sweetest thing Drakkal had heard since the first time she'd made it.

Heart swelling, he wrapped his arm around Shay's shoulders and smiled down at his cub. "It is, *kiraia*."

They walked to the elevators together and rode them up to the embassy's main lobby, a space with a high ceiling around the edges of which hung the same flags as outside. Drakkal didn't allow his nervousness to affect him outwardly, but he didn't breathe easily until they'd cleared the security checkpoint and entered the embassy proper. Their IDs—including Shay's previously untested alias—passed the terran inspection and scan, and the Eternal Guard peacekeeper working with the terran security team waved them through with a look of disinterest on her face.

One of the guards pointed Shay in the proper direction, and she and Drakkal walked down a long hallway into an office with a big waiting room. The real challenge began after Shay had checked in at the desk—the waiting.

Even though there were fewer than a dozen other people in the waiting room, hours crawled by. Soon enough, Leah was fussy and restless, and Shay had no choice but to take the cub into the corner to feed her. Drakkal loomed beside her, glaring at the few other terrans who dared eye his mate judgmentally. Those who made that mistake once did not repeat it after hearing the azhera growl.

Eventually, Leah fell asleep on Drakkal's shoulder. He sympathized with his daughter; he was restless, but it was mixed with weariness from a long, boring wait. Not long after Leah had succumbed, Shay leaned against Drakkal's arm, slipped an arm around his middle, and closed her eyes.

He remained alert, watching as more people entered the room; they arrived much faster than they departed. How did the terrans get anything done like this? Did they all have an infinite amount of time to waste?

Drakkal didn't realize that he'd been bouncing his leg impatiently until Shay pressed her hand on his knee.

"We only have to do this once," she said, rubbing her cheek against his arm. Her voice conveyed the grin she must've been wearing. "You'd think you never sat around for hours before. You'd make a lousy security guard."

"Good thing I'm *head* of security then, isn't it?" he replied.

When someone finally came to lead them to the back, Drakkal's holocom had marked four hours and twenty-six minutes since their arrival, and Leah had already woken from her nap.

"About fu—uh...reaking time," Shay muttered, glancing sheepishly at Drakkal and Leah as she stood up and accepted the baby from him. She held her daughter up to eye level and grinned. "Mom *so* didn't cuss. Nope. I caught that one."

They followed the terran who'd come to fetch them through a door and along a hallway with offices on either side. He left them in a room with an examination bed, medical equipment, and a tired-looking female terran behind a desk who introduced herself as Misses Levitsky.

Misses Levitsky walked through her duties with an odd sort of jaded warmth; it was clear she'd done this enough times for it to be almost automatic for her, but she somehow remained personable despite that. She asked a series of questions about Leah, her birth, and Shay's arrival on Arthos, and followed up those questions with a few quick tests, including a full body scan of Leah. But it was the final two steps that caused the only issues—the first was a quick blood test to confirm Shay was Leah's biological mother, which resulted in tears from the cub, and the second was the implantation of Leah's ID chip in her wrist.

Drakkal couldn't be sure if Leah even felt the chip implant, but she was already so upset by having her finger pricked that it didn't matter. He collected her in his arms once it was done, and she grasped his fur with both of her little hands, tugging on it as she cried and hiccupped. Drakkal winced at the sting of his fur being pulled, but it was nothing compared to what seeing Leah's pain made him feel. When he looked at Shay, her eyes were watery, and she was frowning helplessly toward their daughter.

"All done," Misses Levitsky declared.

Drakkal checked his holocom; they'd been in the exam room for only twenty-one minutes. He patted Leah gently and followed Shay out of the room and back to the lobby, not allowing himself to consider the disparity between the amount of time they'd waited versus the time it took to conduct their business.

Leah Audrey vor'Kanthar was officially a citizen of both the United Terran Federation and the city of Arthos—and Drakkal was on record as her legal father, if not her biological one. That was the only matter of importance right now.

Leah finally settled as they rode the elevator down to the parking area. Her bright smile paired with her teary eyes was one of the sweetest, saddest sights Drakkal had ever seen. He gently brushed the teardrops away from her cheeks.

When they reached their hovercar, Drakkal opened the back door and carefully strapped Leah into her seat.

Shay took gentle hold of his arm, calling his attention to her. Her eyes were still a little watery. "I'm going to ride in back with her, okay?"

The vulnerability on her face pierced straight through Drakkal's heart; for all her considerable strength, for all her self-control, seeing her cub in pain was almost more than Shay could bear. She rarely showed that side of herself. He suspected that no one save himself and Shay's parents had ever seen it.

Drakkal leaned down and pecked a kiss atop her head. "That's fine, *kiraia*."

She placed her hands on his chest, stood on her toes, and kissed his lips before climbing into the car to sit beside Leah. Drakkal made sure his mate was buckled in before he walked around to the front of the car. He pulled off his jacket, tossed it onto the passenger seat, and got into the driver's seat. As he powered on the engines and fastened his seat straps, he finally allowed some relief to flow through him; they'd accomplished what they'd set out to do. Now they could go home and be at peace. The way forward would be a long one—lately, he and Arcanthus had been discussing ways to convert their operation into a legal one and whether they *needed* an operation to begin with—but Shay had been right.

This was a first step in a new chapter. Leah marked a new beginning.

They were traveling through the Undercity—about halfway home—when alarm signals and warnings flashed across every holo screen on the dashboard. Drakkal's brows fell low. A moment later, the controls seized.

"Fuck," he growled. He struggled against the unresponsive control wheel with one hand as he frantically tapped the screens with the other, trying to override the alarm, trying to take control somehow.

"What's going on?" Shay asked, restrained worry in her voice.

The vehicle pitched down, dropping out of the flow of hovercar traffic. Shay gasped.

"Lost control," Drakkal said through clenched teeth as he took the controls in both hands again. His muscles strained against the wheel, but it refused to move—and the foot pedals were locked in place, as well. "Hold on."

The hovercar plummeted, and Drakkal's insides rose up into his throat. His family was in this car, his mate and child, and they were at risk, but the fury that poured into his blood didn't help against the locked controls.

After falling at least a hundred meters in only a second or two, the hovercar leveled out over a busy street. Leah was crying in the back seat, her voice almost swallowed up by the blaring alarms. Tilting and pitching wildly, the hovercar made a series of sharp turns along several side streets, moving farther and farther from the main street they'd been flying over.

"*Someone* is controlling this thing!" Shay turned to Leah and spoke to the cub in soft, soothing tones; Drakkal could barely hear her over the other noise.

The hovercar made another sudden, tight turn, this time into an alley. Its rear end swung out and slammed into the side of a building. Though its external energy shield prevented the vehicle's body from making physical contact, the impact was jarring, and Leah's cries became terrified screams.

Drakkal's rage surged, staining his vision red. He needed to fight, needed to protect his family, needed to destroy whoever or whatever was threatening them. But how was he going to destroy the vehicle in which they were traveling?

You know this isn't the hovercar, Drakkal.

The vehicle righted itself and darted down the alley, gaining speed rapidly. Drakkal dropped a hand to the throttle and tugged it back, but the speed kept increasing, and the alley only narrowed, causing the vehicle to bounce and jitter as its energy shield struck the walls. It wouldn't hold out long at this rate.

"Oh God," Shay said, voice trembling.

Drakkal glanced back to see her half out of her harness and

leaning over Leah, enveloping the cub with her body like a living shield.

The hovercar dropped five meters in an instant, making Drakkal's stomach lurch. Before he could recover, it dropped again, and again, and the ground was suddenly much too close. The vehicle's nose pitched down.

Drakkal turned toward Shay and Leah, driven only by his instinct to protect them with his own body.

The hovercar hit the ground with a slam that jolted through Drakkal from head to toe and made his teeth crack together. The vehicle bounced up; when it came down again, the shield had failed. The hovercar's metal underside hit the ground with a deafening crash, thrashing the vehicle's occupants violently. Drakkal's head struck something—he couldn't tell whether it was the window, the dashboard, or something else in the chaos—and his world became a blur of flashing red alarm lights, screaming metal, and cries from his cub.

When the hovercar finally slid to a halt, it took Drakkal several seconds to blink his vision clear. His body ached vaguely, but that ache permeated him, and his head felt both too light and too heavy. He twisted slowly to look into the back seat as he fumbled to release his harness; the latches refused to come undone.

Shay was slumped to the side, her forehead leaned against the cracked backdoor window.

Drakkal's hands froze for an instant. "Shay?" When she didn't respond, cold, slithering dread gathered in his gut. "Shay!"

Shay groaned and slowly sat up, leaving a smeared streak of red on the window. Blood oozed from a gash on her forehead. Furrowing her brow, she reached toward the wailing cub beside her. Her eyes were concerned despite her wound. Relief eased some of Drakkal's fear.

As much as he hated the terror in Leah's desperate cries, as much as he hated to see her face so red, it was heartening in a way—she was well enough to scream. That was *something*.

A bright light came on somewhere in front of the hovercar. Drakkal turned toward it, lifting a hand to shield his eyes from the glare. A dark figure seemed to materialize from the light, clad in black from top to bottom, and sauntered toward the vehicle.

Drakkal knew that walk. He knew the sway of those hips, knew the self-importance in that stride. He knew their assailant despite the helmet obscuring her face.

Vanya stopped at the front passenger side window and lifted a bulky, gun-shaped device to the glass. When she flipped a switch on the side, a spike punched through the window, creating fractures all around the point of entry.

Drakkal wrestled his seat harness, but it still wouldn't come undone. He growled and formed the hardlight claws on his left hand. There was a hiss from Vanya's device. Drakkal glanced at it to see thick, white gas swiftly flowing into the cab.

"Drak? What's going on?" Shay asked, the pitch of her voice rising with every word.

He glanced back to see her struggling to free herself from her remaining shoulder strap. The concern on her face deepened as awareness lit in her eyes. Leah continued to scream, taking in shallow, shuddering breaths.

"Cover your mouth, *kiraia*." Drakkal sliced away the strap over his right arm and shifted forward, pulling on the remaining strap. The gas, pungent and bitter, filled his nostrils as he drew in breath, making his head swim. He coughed and bent his left arm, hooking his fingers beneath the strap. The hardlight claws sliced into his skin as he tore the strap; he barely felt the pain.

Behind him, Leah's cries had given way to a coughing fit, and Shay was coughing along with her. Finally free of the harness, Drakkal tugged on the door handle, but the door wouldn't open—it was stuck against the alley wall. He gritted his teeth against the aches in his body and swung his left fist at the windshield. It struck with a heavy blow, but only a small chip appeared in the glass. The gas, which had made the air in the vehicle hazy, stung his eyes, making them water and further obscuring his vision.

"She stopped crying," Shay said between coughs; Leah had gone silent. "Oh my God...Drak. She...she stopped—" By the time she, too, fell silent, her words had been heavily slurred.

Drakkal twisted to look back again. A sudden wave of dizziness threatened to overtake him, but he forced his eyes to stay open, forced himself to see. Shay was slumped over, one arm stretched out with her hand on Leah's belly. The baby's head was tipped to the side, eyes closed. Neither were moving.

"Shay!" he roared as a wave of panic, protectiveness, rage, and terror blasted through him. Instinct overtook conscious thought, leaving only a simple list of issues to address—air, Vanya, family.

He turned back to the windshield and struck it again, this time leading with his hardlight claws. The hardlight pierced the blaster-proof glass; he swung his arm aside, opening long cuts across the center of the windshield. When he drew his hand back and struck the glass again, it exploded outward.

Drakkal's head spun. His vision cleared for an instant before blurring again. He grabbed a hold of whatever was in front of him and hauled himself out of the cab, ignoring the chunks of hard glass on the hood beneath him as he emerged. The white haze wafted out around him and began to disperse, caught on a barely perceptible air current in the alley.

Shaking his head sharply, he struggled to get his feet beneath him and turn toward the second item on his list—Vanya. She was still standing beside the hovercar, hands no longer on the device she'd planted in the window, her hidden face turned toward him.

"You always were stubborn," she said. The speaker on her helmet made her sound digitized.

Drakkal roared. Rage flowed up from his chest and clawed its way out of his throat, and his hazy vision took on a crimson tint again. He dropped his left hand to the mangled hood of the hovercar, buried his claws in it, and used it to launch himself at Vanya.

She dodged him, and Drakkal slammed into the alley wall. He faintly registered pain on his face, head, and shoulder as he crashed to the ground, but he shrugged it off and grabbed the side of the car to haul himself up again. He shook his head sharply, but it was like the gas had gathered in his brain to blanket his every thought in a fog.

"I *really* wanted things to go different this time, Drakkal," Vanya said with enough acid in her voice to melt bone, "but you let this *ji'tas* get in the way."

His legs wobbled, unwilling to support him for much longer. He lunged toward Vanya anyway. Drakkal's claws slashed through the air as he pushed himself forward, and Vanya danced backward. He poured all his remaining strength into his every swing, but each time he swung, she seemed to be a second ahead of him.

It was only a few seconds before he overextended himself, and his missed swipe threw off his balance. He fell forward and barely caught himself on his hand.

"I gave you another chance," Vanya continued, "and you chose a terran. A *fucking* terran! People pay small fortunes to own them, but for what?"

Drakkal forced his head up and settled his gaze on her. She'd backed away a couple meters, and he had to concentrate to clear his vision enough to make her out clearly. There was a long weapon in her hands—a shock staff, crackling with a beam of white energy from one end to the other.

Vanya's tail lashed back and forth behind her. "They're small, soft, and weak. Ugly, useless animals. And you chose one of them over me! You chose *that* over *this?*"

Breath ragged and burning in his lungs, Drakkal staggered to his feet and growled, "Fuck you, *zhe'gash.*"

"Soon enough you'll be *begging* to," she snapped.

Drakkal's body swayed unsteadily, but he wouldn't stop, couldn't let her win. He slid his left leg forward, meaning to charge at Vanya. But when his weight came down on his knee, it buckled. He lashed out with his left hand, burying his hard-light claws into the nearest surface—likely the alley wall—to halt himself. He lifted his gaze in time to see Vanya swinging her shock staff.

He had no chance to react, no chance to think; there was only his driving need to protect his family, to save them from this threat, and then a flash of white and a burst of pain that seized his every muscle.

Drakkal's world went black, and he knew no more.

TWENTY-THREE

Shay's head was going to explode. She was sure of it. Pain radiated from the base of her skull, pulsed in her temples, and stung her eyes. But her suffering didn't end there—her shoulders screamed, and her entire body felt like one big bruise, like she'd been strung up and beaten with a bat for a few hours.

Or had been thrashed around in a crashing car.

Memories of the crash flooded back to her; the most vivid of them were the terrified cries of her baby.

Leah!

Shay started, lifted her head, and opened her eyes. She immediately regretted it; a spear of pain pierced her skull at the swift movement. She closed her eyes again, panting softly and willing away the nausea turning her stomach as she assessed the situation.

She was standing up, her body weight hanging by her arms and head bowed. She twitched her fingers; her wrists were fastened to the wall behind her by a set of thick, metal manacles, and something just as cold, hard, and terrifyingly familiar was clamped around her neck.

No. Oh no, no, no, no.

"He certainly takes his time," growled a rough but feminine voice.

"So do you," snapped another voice—one that Shay knew well. The rage that voice sparked inside her fought back some of Shay's terror.

Nostrus.

"A hunt takes as long as it takes," the female replied. "But you'd think he'd be eager to get his hands on them by now."

Shay slowly openly her eyes and peered through the curtain of tousled hair hanging in her face. Her heart sank and nearly froze with dread when she caught sight of Leah lying still—so still—inside a box on the floor about a meter away. The box's sides and top were clear, with a few airholes on each. The only thing that kept Shay calm was the subtle rise and fall of Leah's little chest.

"Master Foltham takes as long as he takes," Nostrus replied. "You'll have your pay soon enough, azhera. I've no wish to see you here any longer than necessary."

Azhera?

Vanya?

Was that why the female's voice seemed familiar, too?

Shay lifted her head slowly. Her hair fell away to either side of her face, allowing her to take in her surroundings. She was in the back of some sort of transport—bigger than what would've been considered a van back on Earth, but along the same lines. The two doors at the back were open, and Vanya and Nostrus were standing just outside of them. Manacles lined the walls, the same kind that Murgen had used on Shay—they didn't physically attach to anything but could be manipulated to allow different lengths and ranges of movement. Drakkal was standing beside Leah's box, head slumped forward and body held up only by his wrist bindings.

Vanya snorted. "The feeling is mutual, volturian."

Drakkal drew in a sharp breath and winced, lifting his head slightly. His ears flattened, and his nostrils flared. When he exhaled, it came out in a groan that stretched into a low, pained growl.

"Seems the marks are waking," Vanya said.

"Drakkal," Shay said, keeping her eyes on her mate. "Drakkal, wake up."

He grunted, brows dropping low as his eyelids fluttered open. His pupils expanded from slits to large circles and back again before his eyes finally met Shay's and focused. "*Kiraia?*" he rasped.

There was a snarl from the back of the transport. She turned her face toward the sound to see Vanya step into the transport. The azhera stalked over and backhanded Shay across the face. Shay's head whipped to the side, the sharp pain—caused primarily by the inner flesh of her cheek breaking against her cheek—receding quickly to a tingling numbness that was somehow even worse. The irony taste of blood washed over Shay's tongue.

Vanya grabbed a fistful of Shay's hair and yanked her head back as far as the wall and collar allowed. "Silence, *ji'tas!*"

Drakkal roared. The sound was deafening within the confines of the transport, rocking the entire vehicle.

Shay glared up at Vanya and spat. Bloody saliva splattered on the azhera's face. "Fuck you!"

Vanya recoiled, shock briefly claiming her features. An instant later, her lips pulled back to reveal her pointed fangs, and she raised a clawed hand high as though to strike.

"Master Foltham wants the terrans unharmed," Nostrus called from outside the vehicle.

Halting her hand, Vanya stared at Shay. The female azhera's chest was heaving, her nostrils were flared, and her eyes were burning with rage. She curled her fingers, extending her claws further. After a frustrated growl, she dropped her arm and stormed away from Shay.

Just removing herself from temptation, Shay thought, carefully tonguing the sliced flesh of her inner cheek.

"Then he best hurry before I change my mind," Vanya said as she stepped out of the transport. "He isn't the only buyer seeking terrans."

Nostrus looked past Vanya into the vehicle. For a moment, his hate-filled eyes fell on Shay.

Yeah, fuck you, too.

Shay flipped him off.

"You made an agreement with my employer," Nostrus said, turning back to Vanya.

The female azhera laughed; there was little humor in the sound. "Until we make the exchange, they're my prisoners. I can do whatever I want with them."

"Ah, my wayward bounty hunter has finally returned," Murgen boomed from somewhere outside the transport. Vanya and Nostrus turned to face the direction from which his voice had come.

"Are you all right, *kiraia*?" Drakkal asked.

Shay looked at her mate. His hackles were raised, and there was a wild, furious gleam in his eyes. He looked like a beast barely in control. And could she blame him? Shay was afraid—especially with her still unconscious baby locked up in here—but she was angry, too. No, not just angry. She was fucking pissed.

"I'm fine," Shay replied quietly.

Murgen and Vanya were speaking now, but their voices were too low for Shay to make out their words.

"We're going to get out of this," Drakkal said. His features tightened, and his muscles strained as he fought against the restraints. The wrist cuffs slowly moved away from the wall, a millimeter at a time, trembling with the stress he was putting on his body. Then the breath he'd been holding burst from his lungs, and his arms slammed back into the wall.

Drakkal's chest heaved as he panted through his bared fangs. "We're *getting* out."

"Yes, you are," Vanya said, again calling Shay's attention. The female azhera climbed back into the transport, followed by two of Murgen's burly guards. Vanya lifted her left wrist and input a command on her holocom. Simultaneously, Drakkal's and Shay's arms dropped away from the wall, only to be swung behind their backs, where the cuffs clanked together and locked tight.

The guards moved to Shay and Drakkal, grabbing the couple by their upper arms. Drakkal growled, opened his mouth wide as though to bite, and lunged toward the guard holding him; a light flashed on the collar around his neck, and his body seized. He dropped to his knees, held up only by the guard.

Shay clenched her teeth against the ache in her heart at seeing her mate in such agony.

"Behave yourself," Vanya said, patting Drakkal's cheek before she turned away from him and leaned over Leah's box.

Red filled Shay's vision. She snapped her head backward, smashing her skull into the face of the guard behind her. He staggered back, his hold loosening enough for Shay to break free.

She dove for Vanya. "Keep your fucking hands off my baby, you goddamned jealous bitch!"

Shay's shoulder rammed into Vanya's chest. The female azhera stumbled into the wall. Pressing her advantage, Shay lifted her knee, slamming it unto Vanya's middle and knocking the wind out of the azhera. Before Shay could strike her again, the guard grabbed her shoulders and dragged her away from Vanya.

"I do hope everything's all right in there," Murgen called from outside.

Shay struggled against the guard's hold, lips peeled back to bare her teeth; she was ready to tear Vanya to pieces. "I'll fucking kill you if you touch her! I swear I'll—"

An electric current blasted through Shay's body, locking all her muscles and sparking a white-hot flash in her brain, more intense than any migraine. Though it must only have lasted an instant, the fiery agony beneath her skin felt like it had persisted for hours and didn't immediately fade when the current ceased. Her knees buckled, and her muscles spasmed in the aftermath of the shock collar's pulse. The guard grunted and held her upright by her biceps.

Arms drawn in close to her stomach—with one hand at her holocom's control screen—Vanya straightened and snarled, "Get that *ji'tas* out."

The guard dragged Shay toward the open doors. She had no control over her twitching limbs, no feeling in her fingertips. She understood now why Murgen had never used such force on her while she was his prisoner—there was no doubt in her mind that it would have caused her to lose her baby.

She slitted her eyes as she emerged from the transport; the lights outside were bright and pure, possessing a quality that was dreadfully familiar to her. Once they'd adjusted, she was unsurprised to find herself in a large room—a loading bay or garage—with the same sleek, clean walls that made up most of Murgen Foltham's zoo.

Murgen himself was standing a few meters away from the transport, grinning around his big stupid tusks with his hands folded over his gut. He was flanked by Nostrus and several security guards.

"Give me a hand in here," called the guard still inside the transport.

Two of his comrades, dressed in the same suits as all the guards—a strange blend of military and upper-class fashion—hurried into the transport. The vehicle shook, and the guards cursed and shouted amidst Drakkal's snarls, which halted abruptly after another pained growl.

A few seconds later, the three guards dragged Drakkal's limp form out of the transport. His eyes were open, and his fangs were bared, but he was unable to resist them; what could he have hoped to do, anyway?

What had *she* hoped to do?

Vanya stepped out of the transport carrying Leah's box. She set it on the floor before Murgen. Leah was still unconscious.

Cold, nauseating fear slithered through Shay as she stared at her daughter, who looked far too pale. Leah was so small, so fragile. Had that gas harmed her? If it'd been potent enough to put down Shay and Drakkal, what had it done to Leah?

Murgen's grin widened. He placed his hands on his thighs and ponderously squatted to examine Leah. "Fascinating. I wonder, are terran infants usually so lethargic?" He frowned and swung his gaze up to Vanya. "You didn't damage it, did you?"

"It'll wake eventually," she replied nonchalantly. "Needed a stronger dose of gas for the other two. It always hits the small ones harder."

Murgen glanced down again and tapped a thick finger on the glass. "You certainly achieved results, even if you were slow in delivering. I must admit to having had my doubts about you, azhera. These months have been troubling. I wondered if I had made a mistake hiring a being like you to hunt your own." He straightened with a soft grunt and glanced at Drakkal, his lips dropping into a displeased scowl. "I've not been impressed by the trustworthiness of your people before now."

"You hired me to do the job, I wanted to do it right. Your cargo is delivered, more-or-less unharmed, and there's no trail linking you back to it. That takes time. You got what you wanted in the end."

"Yes, I did." Murgen's grin returned, and he approached Shay.

She glared up at him as he reached for her hair. He took several strands of it in his meaty hand and forced Shay's head to one side, then the other.

He touched the raised scars on her shoulder. "Bite marks, hmm? Has that azhera already been breeding with you? I suppose I shouldn't be surprised; he had that desire in his eyes the day he stole you away. Perhaps we'll be lucky, and his seed will have taken root already. If not, we'll just have to find another suitable specimen."

Vanya growled, but it was cut short when she said, "I want the male."

Murgen's eyes widened, and he shifted his gaze back to the female azhera. Shay froze.

No!

"No," Nostrus snapped; Drakkal snarled at the same instant.

Without looking at the volturian, Murgen lifted a hand and waved his fingers, as though to quiet Nostrus. "The male azhera was part of the deal. Changing the agreement at the last moment is not something I'm inclined to accept. It's...rude."

"I'll make it worth the insult I've caused," Vanya said.

Shay pressed her lips together and bit back her words. *Nothing*; there was nothing she could do. Vanya would only shock Shay into compliance the instant she spoke out. She looked first at Leah, then at Drakkal, who was on his knees with two guards holding his shoulders forward so he couldn't straighten. Her mate and her daughter were her world, and she was completely helpless. She couldn't save them.

Nostrus stepped forward and opened his mouth, but another sharp wave from Murgen silenced him.

A thoughtful sound rose from Murgen's throat, and his neck flesh expanded. "I'm intrigued enough to hear what you have to say. Please."

"He's an escaped slave, wanted on Caldorius," Vanya said. "Big reward for this one. I'll waive the fee for capturing him and split the profit I make from hauling him back to his masters with you."

"A lying *zhe'gash*," Drakkal grumbled. "You two are well matched."

Murgen snorted; he didn't so much as glance at Drakkal. "I hardly see how that benefits you. No Caldorian slave master would pay as much as I've agreed to in this case, and that doesn't even take into account the expenses you would incur for transporting him all the way to Caldorius. It would be far easier for all of us for me to simply pay your fee and dispose of him as I see fit."

"It benefits my reputation. I bring him back all the way from Arthos, and it'll impress the right people back on Caldorius—people with powerful ties. That results in more work for me." Vanya shifted her gaze to Shay and smirked; it was an arrogant, hateful expression filled with gloating. "I'm trying to think of the larger picture, Master Foltham. I consider it a long-term investment that will pay off very well over time."

I am going to fucking kill her.

Nostrus glared at Vanya before turning to face Murgen. "Sir, we have him here now. Just let me—"

"Enough, Nostrus," Murgen said. "I'm well aware of what

you want, but I didn't agree to pay that exorbitant amount just to fulfill your need for revenge. I agreed to fulfill *mine*."

"And what better revenge than what I'm proposing?" asked Vanya. When Murgen tipped his head toward her, she continued. "He'll go back to Caldorius and receive harsh punishment from his owner. When—*if*—he recovers from that, they're going to throw him into the fighting pits or set him to some back-breaking labor. Either way, he'll suffer until his very last breath, knowing all along that *you* won, and that his...*mate* is here, part of your collection."

Shay clenched her hands into fists.

Drakkal's already furious expression darkened with Vanya's every word, and the guards grunted, straining to hold the big azhera down as he swayed. With a growl, Drakkal got one of his feet beneath him and pushed up with his leg.

Stop, Drakkal. Please, just stop!

A third guard hurried over. It took all three to wrestle Drakkal back down; they forced him face-first onto the floor and knelt on his back to keep him pinned. His tail lashed stiffly.

Murgen thoughtfully tapped one of his tusks, taking in the display as though it were nothing important—and Shay didn't doubt that he saw Drakkal as just another animal, no different in his eyes than Shay and Leah.

"He has cost me a significant sum through his actions. Buying the terran to begin with and then paying *again* to retrieve her has been quite expensive," Murgen muttered loudly enough for everyone to hear. "Recovering a portion of it would be preferable, though the amount itself is not what's important. And I must admit, the level of suffering you've described...well, it is certainly tempting..."

Nostrus's jaw ticked as he glared at Drakkal, squeezing his fists at his sides.

A sudden, soft cry filled the garage.

Shay snapped her eyes toward Leah, who fidgeted and kicked as she woke, her cries growing louder. Shay's heart pounded; she needed to go to her daughter, to hold her, to soothe her, needed to take her out of this goddamned place.

Murgen's throat swelled again as he looked down at Leah. "What an unpleasant noise it makes."

Drakkal growled and thrashed on the floor. One of the guards swore as he was nearly thrown off. Vanya calmly lifted her wrist and flicked a command, triggering Drakkal's collar again. His growls took on an agonized tone as his body locked up, limbs straightening, for a second.

Stay still, Shay. Don't move, don't yell. There's nothing you can do right now.

Though she knew that was the truth, seeing her proud, powerful mate brought so low and in so much pain wrecked her. Her body itched to move, to fight, but she knew it was a losing battle. She needed to bide her time. Gut reactions would get her nowhere.

"We in agreement or not?" Vanya asked.

Leah's cries grew more frantic, her face reddening as tears streamed from her eyes.

Murgen frowned at the baby and slowly folded his hands over his gut. He nodded curtly. "Fine. You brought the youngling back unharmed, so we'll consider that enough in lieu of the azhera. Nostrus, pay her the bounty for the terran. I want these two examined immediately. Have the medical team assembled." He turned his head to look at Drakkal, and his lip curled. "Make sure he suffers. Profusely."

Vanya grinned. "I'll see to it."

Nostrus strode forward, making no effort to mask his displeasure as he tossed a credit chip to Vanya. Her grin didn't falter as she caught it. For a few seconds, they stood staring at each other, Nostrus brimming with cold fury, and Vanya with smug triumph. The tension in the air between them was palpable; Nostrus seemed ready to reach for the blaster undoubtedly holstered under his jacket, and Shay wanted nothing more than to see it happen.

So long as the prick didn't shoot Drakkal, too.

Vanya finally dropped her gaze to the controls on her holocom and tapped a selection. "Her manacles are open for you to interface with now."

Nostrus produced a small remote control from his pocket. Still scowling, he held it up to Shay's collar and pressed a button. The device beeped softly, and he tucked it away.

Vanya swung her attention to the guards restraining Drakkal. "Mind tossing him in back?"

Murgen motioned to the guard behind Shay and another beside Leah. "No more standing around. Get the terrans inside, and the rest of you get that beast into her vehicle so we can be rid of him." As he turned and walked away, he grumbled, "And someone quiet down the youngling!"

The borian guard beside Leah bent down to pick up her cage, a distinct look of distaste on his face. The guard behind Shay shifted his hold to her biceps, lifted her onto her feet, and forced her to follow the borian.

Shay turned her head, her eyes locking with Drakkal's as he was hauled off the floor and dragged toward Vanya's transport. His teeth were bared, and the light on his collar was on—that bitch was shocking him again—but the guards were still struggling to move him as his powerful legs fought for purchase, claws scraping the floor.

Though he didn't speak—probably *couldn't* speak—his eyes said everything.

I will get back to you, kiraia.

Then the guards dragged him into the back of the transport, and he vanished from her sight. Shay shifted her gaze slightly aside to see Vanya staring at her, still wearing that arrogant grin.

Though she didn't know how she'd do it, or when, Shay was going to knock that bitch's teeth out before this was all done.

TWENTY-FOUR

Despite his resistance, the effects of the shock collar were too strong for Drakkal to resist for long. After a couple minutes of struggle, Foltham's guards finally managed to stand Drakkal up against one of the transport's interior walls, and Vanya swiftly locked the manacles against it, forcing his hands up and to either side of his head. Growling through his teeth, Drakkal strained against the bindings and kicked at his captors. The panting guards stumbled backward to avoid his clawed feet.

"I'll take it from here," Vanya said, appraising Drakkal with smoldering, half-lidded eyes.

The guards wasted no time in exiting the vehicle, smoothing their rumpled suits and attempting to don an air of dignity and composure along the way. The doors closed behind them. The space was plunged into darkness but for the faint blue glow of instrument panels from the cab, which was through an open entryway up front. That light granted Vanya's features a fittingly sinister cast.

Drakkal wished he'd seen her in such a light when they'd first met.

She sauntered toward him, and the raging fires in Drakkal flared with the intensity of an exploding star. He threw his weight forward, ignoring the pain in his shoulders and chest as the muscles were stretched beyond their normal range of motion, and snapped his jaws shut on the air a few centimeters from her face.

Vanya reacted only by widening her grin. Her eyes moved over him from top to bottom. "You always were big, Drakkal, but you've filled out *very* well over the years."

Her scent, old, familiar, and despised, filled his nostrils; Drakkal focused past it, shifting his attention to the lingering scents of his mate and cub. His instincts thrummed with wild energy. He'd never wanted so badly to taste someone's blood, to feel it running warm over his lips and down his throat, to watch it drip from his claws.

She tilted her head, and her tail flicked forward, brushing his leg. "We'll talk soon. I'm sure you don't want to be here any longer than I do."

"Should've killed you already," Drakkal rasped. The words were raw and abrasive in his throat, as harsh as his festering regret.

Her grin receded into an almost wistful smile more genuine than he'd thought her capable of. "But you didn't. And that was always the difference between us, wasn't it? You may be big and strong, but you're soft on the inside. You're weak. Even now. Your terran *ji'tas* is a prime example of it."

"Don't talk about her!" Drakkal lunged forward again. This time, the transport rocked, and the cuffs lifted away from the wall, albeit for a fraction of a second and barely a few millimeters.

This time, Vanya did flinch back, surprise flashing over her features. She recovered quickly, and her expression fell into something dark and dangerous. Her voice was low but had a sharp edge when she spoke again. "She's gone, and you're *mine* now. You'll learn to put that ugly little terran behind you soon enough. Once you accept that you're never going to see her again, you'll start thinking clearly. You'll see that having me back really is the best thing for you. It's what you always wanted."

She took a step closer and leaned her face as near as possible without entering his reach. "Either you can reach that conclusion on your own, or I can break you and force you to it. You may be bigger and stronger, Drakkal, but you're just as weak as your *ji'tas* at heart."

"If I'm even half as strong as her at heart, *zhe'gaash*, you should be afraid right now."

"Do not speak to me that way again," Vanya warned.

"You're a disgrace to our people," Drakkal snarled. His entire body tensed as he pulled against the bindings again. "An honorless, cowardly traitor."

Vanya scowled and swung her arm, slamming her fist into Drakkal's mouth. The flare of pain it caused came with a metallic tang of blood.

She raised a clawed finger and pointed it at Drakkal's face. "You don't call me that. Everything I've done was to survive. *That* is the true way of our people, not your inflated sense of honor and overvalued courage."

"Truth sting, *zhe'gaash*?" Drakkal forced his lips into a grin, displaying his bloody fangs.

"You're the one who picked a fucking terran," Vanya roared. "And you're the one who's locked up. You're a failure, Drakkal. You couldn't fulfill me when we were young, and you couldn't protect your *ji'tas* and her ugly little beast now. You couldn't even succeed at dying like your blind honor dictated. But you'll learn soon enough. I'm going to shape you into something better."

Drakkal tugged violently against the cuffs around his wrists, making the transport shake. "Release me and let's test your confidence, you fucking *zhe'gaash*!"

"I suppose that's another difference between us. You always were stupid, Drakkal. Never knew when to give up. Now shut your mouth, or I'll knock you out again."

"*Kraasz ka'val*, killing you once will not be enough," he growled.

Vanya tugged something off her belt and flicked her arm to the side. The object extended and clicked as it locked at its full length, and a pulse of energy crackled on its tip. A stun baton.

Without a word—and without breaking eye contact with Drakkal—she jabbed him in the chest with the tip of the baton.

The flash of white that overcame Drakkal's vision caused all his muscles to seize and made thunder boom in his ears. The pain of it was gone so quickly that he barely registered it; instead, it was his battle against the aftereffects that occupied his focus.

But his willpower was not quite enough; oblivion rose over him, dark and foreboding, and crashed down on Drakkal like a tidal wave.

When he sucked in a sharp breath and returned to awareness, he had no idea how much time he'd lost. He was sagged forward, shoulders sore, arms stiff, head bowed, and right hand numb. His eyes were closed, and the dull throbbing of his split lip was only one of the many aches and pains throughout his body.

After the pain, he was next aware of the slight swaying of the floor, which carried up through his body, exaggerated by his hanging posture. Panic burst inside him, speeding his heart and constricting his lungs. Had they already left Foltham's? How long had he been out? How far had they traveled?

How far away were Shay and Leah?

He forced his eyes open. His eyelids did their best to resist the command, but he won the fight.

Drakkal's neck protested as he lifted his head and turned it toward the front of the transport. The entryway was still open, allowing that pale blue light to spill through. His angle prevented him from seeing Vanya, who was presumably at the controls, but he could see through a section of the windshield.

Even from that limited view, he knew they were somewhere in the Undercity by the ambient neon glow contrasting the otherwise dominant darkness.

He gritted his teeth and reached internally for that still-burning rage, but he stopped himself.

Need to think clearly for a minute, Drakkal... You're banged up already, and all you're going to do like this is wear yourself out. Can't rely solely on instinct here.

He needed a different approach, a more direct approach, and he needed it quickly. So far, he hadn't been able to move the manacles more than a few millimeters away from the wall; he didn't have enough leverage to pull beyond that. Hell, he didn't have enough leverage to even maintain that tiny gap. But if that wouldn't work...then what?

Drakkal turned his head toward his left hand. He curled the fingers slightly and formed long, red hardlight claws at their tips. This was his sleeker prosthesis, the model he could easily conceal beneath his clothing, and he didn't have quite the same degree of control over its claws that he did with the armored prosthesis Samantha had designed for him. He couldn't control their length or shape—there was only on or off.

He bent his left wrist as sharply as possible, but the thick manacle blocked the angle he'd hoped to achieve. When he bent his fingers, only the claw of the smallest one could touch the manacle. He could only generate enough force to etch a small gouge in the metal—not nearly enough damage to deactivate it, much less cut it off. The small hardlight blades *could* penetrate the material, but they'd need a bit more strength behind them.

Dismissing the hardlight claws, Drakkal let his gaze fall as he desperately sought a fresh idea, a better way, anything that had a chance of producing results. His eyes stopped on the portion of his prosthesis that connected it to the socket on his bicep.

It took him several seconds to realize what he was staring at, but once he understood, his heart leapt.

Freedom. Vanya. Back to the manor. Murgen and Nostrus.

Those were the priorities; he had to deal with them in that order if he wanted Shay and Leah safely in his arms again. This time, he would eliminate *every* threat to his family. The time for mercy had long since passed. The time to be passive, if there'd ever been one, was gone.

Drakkal bent his left arm at a sharper angle and leaned toward it, his right arm straining as it straightened and stretched. The ache from his shoulder pulsed all the way up the side of his neck. He grunted and bent farther, ignoring the pain and discomfort, until his cheek touched his bicep. He'd done this countless times with his hands. How hard could it be with his mouth?

He felt with his lips and tongue for the latch, and when he finally found the little lip that marked the outer release, he had to strain even more—to the point of restricting the flow of air through his throat—to hook a fang beneath it. He paused for a moment to release a harsh breath through his nostrils before jerking his chin up and wrenching it to the side.

The latch offered a bit of resistance, but popped open, nonetheless. Drakkal relaxed his body, allowing his countless aches to lose some of their immediacy, before dipping his head to his arm again. He shoved his nose into the open groove, seeking the right angle to press the release. He felt like an animal rooting through the dirt in search of some elusive buried morsel, snorting and snuffling quietly. The tip of his nose pressed over the release button, but the groove was too narrow and his nose too short and soft to trigger the release.

He angled his chin upward again and extended his tongue, forcing it into the groove. The muscles along the underside of his jaw tensed and cramped as he pushed as hard as he could with his tongue. He would not relent to pain. He would not lose his family today.

A low growl rumbled in his chest. He eased his head slightly away from his arm, maintaining contact between it and his tongue, and swung it back hard.

The release button sank inward. There was an audible click and a soft hiss as the prosthesis disconnected from its socket. Drakkal forced himself to straighten, pushing past the stiffness in his neck, and turned his head toward the front of the transport.

"Everything all right back there?" Vanya asked, leaning into the entryway to look back at Drakkal. Her features were obscured by shadow save for the faint blue reflections glowing in her eyes.

"I hope you piss yourself right before I kill you, *zhe'gaash*," he said.

Her eyes narrowed, and she stared at him for another second or two before disappearing behind the wall again.

Drakkal took in a few slow, deep breaths. On his third exhalation, the collar around his neck activated. He snarled in pain as an electric current coursed through his body. The snarl died when the current ceased, diminishing to a slow, hissing release of air through his teeth.

"You'll learn some manners," Vanya called without looking back again. "You'll learn to show me the respect I deserve."

I'll show you the respect you deserve when I spit on your lifeless body.

Despite knowing better, Drakkal nearly responded to her aloud. But giving voice to his hatred would only make it more difficult for him to accomplish his objectives. Provoking her further would only bring more pain. Though he'd not reached the limit of what he could endure, he could not say the same of Shay. Foltham had indicated that he'd held back on punishing her during her prior captivity only because of her pregnancy. What would stop him now?

And regardless, Drakkal couldn't afford to lose any more time to unconsciousness.

Hold on Shay, hold on Leah. I am coming for you.

"I'm going to give you a break this one time, Drakkal," Vanya said, "and make it easy on you—because I'm not in the mood to hear more of your disrespect."

A moment later, loud music with heavy drums and bass came on in the cab, sweeping back to echo through the holding area.

I'm making an offering of thanks to my ancestors when this is all done.

Drakkal waited until his breathing had steadied and his heartbeat had eased before he let himself act. He agreed with Vanya's self-assessment—she wasn't stupid. But neither was Drakkal. Everyone had a flaw, and hers had been the same for as long as he'd known her, even if he'd been too close to realize it early on. The music was just another demonstration of it.

She was overconfident, and it seemed that overconfidence had blossomed into something closer to outright arrogance over the years.

Keeping his gaze on the cab's entryway, Drakkal forced his breathing to slow further still. This was his chance. If it didn't work, he doubted he'd have another anytime soon. It relied entirely too much upon luck for his liking, but the realist in him said he had to take whatever he could get.

Carefully, he withdrew his stump from his prosthesis, bending his legs to alter the angle of the elbow and slide off the metal limb. Once the prosthesis was freely dangling from the wall, Drakkal glanced to his flesh and blood arm. He pressed his lips together and slowly turned his right wrist within the manacle, shifting his body around with it. The metal pulled his fur and scraped his flesh, offering more resistance than he'd hoped to encounter, but it wasn't enough to stop him.

He paused once he was facing the wall fully with his palm toward him. He could see the right edge of Vanya's body from his new angle; the movement had taken him a step or two closer to the cab. Her attention was fixed on the traffic around the vehicle—they were traveling along one of the many lanes of traffic that cut through the air over the streets and walkways of the Undercity.

Drakkal looked at the manacle around his right wrist and flexed his fingers. Their tips were tingling, resulting from a combination of the exertion, his position, and the manacle's tightness. Once some of their feeling had returned, he offered a fleeting glance to the cab to ensure Vanya was still otherwise occupied and clenched his fist.

Sliding his feet forward, he braced them against the place where the wall and floor met. He drew in a deep breath and threw his strength into moving his right arm toward his prosthesis.

The muscles of his legs, arm, chest, and abdomen bunched, trembling with the strain. The cuff held firm for a second, two seconds, three. With a light shake, it slid a centimeter to the right.

Drakkal snapped his head toward the front again. Vanya was facing forward.

He returned his attention to the manacle and repeated the process, leaning more of his weight back this time. Each time he took in a heavy breath, he tugged the manacle aside another centimeter or two, moving it at a crawl toward his inert prosthesis. He dared not try for more with each movement; though the music drowned out many of the sounds in the vehicle, Vanya had sharp senses. The smallest out of place sound could alert her.

The already intense heat in his body increased rapidly with his exertion, but he couldn't spare the time to cool down. Eventually—it might only have been a minute or two later, but it felt like years—he'd maneuvered his right arm to the opposite side of his prosthesis, with the manacles set about twenty centimeters apart. He leaned forward, opening his jaws wide enough that they felt close to unhinging, and clamped his teeth around the metal arm. Slowly, he turned the prosthesis so the pin would be better aligned to his new position.

He brushed his thumb across the external sensor on the cybernetic wrist. A small holographic screen rose from the projector; the holocom was the only component of the artificial limb that didn't require an active neural link to operate. He flicked through the options quickly, eyes constantly darting toward the cab to check for Vanya, and attempted to send a quick message to Arcanthus after ensuring the holocom was silenced.

The holocom displayed an error message—connection failed. Drakkal wasn't surprised, and he wouldn't allow himself to be frustrated. Vanya likely had a signal blocker somewhere in the vehicle to prevent this very thing. He dismissed the holocom screen.

Releasing his hold on the prosthesis, he shifted his body, lifted his stump, and slid it up to the metal arm. He stopped the instant he sensed that neural link with the prosthetic; it was far enough to allow him to control the arm, but not so much to lock it into the socket. It would be foolish to lock in while he had no means of releasing the arm from its restraint.

He formed his hardlight claws. Eyes flicking between his hand and the cab—Vanya was out of his line of sight again—he extended his metal fingers and swept the claws down. The hardlight blades bit into the metal of his right manacle, slicing through it cleanly—and causing a faint pain on his wrist.

The manacle deactivated, and his arm fell away from the wall—along with a couple chunks of metal that had been separated from the whole. Drakkal sucked in a sharp breath and flattened his chest and arm against the wall, catching the loose bits on the inside of his elbow. He stared wide-eyed toward the cab, not daring to breathe again. The thunderous pounding of his heart filled his ears. Were it any louder, he swore Vanya would've heard it despite the music.

But she didn't look back, didn't speak. The heat that had built within Drakkal spread beneath the surface of his skin, crackling, tingling, consuming. He finally released the breath he'd been holding; the air stung his damaged lips as it passed between them.

Soon, Shay. On my way soon.

Carefully, he turned his head to his right and bent his neck to move his mouth down. He raised his arm at the same time. Lowering his lips over his fur, he took the metal bits into his mouth.

Once that was done, he took a firm hold of his prosthesis and pulled it down along the wall so his fingers could comfortably reach his neck. He tilted his head back, watching the cab from the corner of his eye, and set his hardlight claws to the shock collar. Their tips bit into his flesh more than once as he worked, but the cuts seemed shallow enough to ignore for now.

He tugged his stump away from the prosthesis as he

reached up with his right hand and pried off the damaged shock collar. The hardlight claws vanished with the severing of his neural connection with the limb.

One item down. On to the next...Vanya.

Drakkal willed his rage back to the surface as he moved to the opposite side of the transport—which would keep him directly behind Vanya—and stalked forward. That inner heat intensified, and his chest tightened, but his mind was clear, just as it always was leading up to a fight. He'd faced worse odds, had been in situations he considered more dangerous—as though there could really be many more degrees of danger once you reached *life-threatening*—but this, more than anything, felt like *the* fight for his life. Not just to determine whether he lived or died, but whether he could reclaim the life he'd made with Shay and Leah.

He reached the wall separating the cab from the hold. He'd only have a fraction of a second to act; Vanya was fast, and he was in bad shape.

For Shay and Leah. For my family.

Drakkal charged through the entryway.

His arm was already mid-swing when Vanya turned her head toward him. Her eyes widened, and she leaned away, throwing up her own arms to shield herself. Two of Drakkal's claws sank into her right forearm.

She hissed in pain and tugged on her arm, but Drakkal spat out the metal chunks in his mouth, curled his fingers to hook his claws deeper, and pulled her toward him. Vanya tipped to her right and ducked, narrowly avoiding Drakkal's snapping jaws. She jerked her head backward. The back of her skull smashed into Drakkal's chin. It wasn't enough to knock him away, but it gave her enough time to tear her arm free of his hold. The smell of her blood filled the air.

Vanya dropped a hand to her belt and tugged her collapsed

stun baton free. She swung it at him wildly, activating the weapon as it extended, and Drakkal stumbled back to avoid the blow. She overextended, nearly falling off her seat. Drakkal kicked her. The pads of his foot struck her left shoulder. The baton fell from her nerveless fingers, clattering away on the floor, and Vanya slammed back into the door, bumping the controls.

The transport pitched its nose down.

The sudden change of angle and direction threw Drakkal against the cab's rear wall. His left shoulder took the brunt of the impact. Alarms blared and flashed on the instrument panels. Vanya recovered first, launching herself across the cab.

She hit him hard, and their struggle devolved into a flurry of slashing claws, gnashing teeth, and kicking legs, all punctuated by wordless snarls and growls. Even if Drakkal was far stronger, he was short a limb, and his body was already battered. Her claws caught his flesh more than once, but her attacks were *too* frenzied; she didn't follow through enough with anything to cause real damage.

All the while, the transport was plummeting toward a busy, neon-bathed Undercity street.

Drakkal twisted and drove his knee into Vanya's ribs. She grunted as the blow crushed her between his knee and the rear wall. He capitalized on the lull in her attacks and forced his other leg up against her other side, catching her torso between his thighs. He squeezed.

Vanya cried out and rained blows upon him. Drakkal clenched his teeth and squeezed tighter, blocking and parrying as many of her attacks as he could with one arm.

The transport suddenly righted itself, its front end swinging back up—likely a safety feature engaging the autopilot to avoid a crash. The vehicle rattled. Drakkal slipped backward, reflexively throwing his hand behind him to catch himself. His fumbling fingers brushed over the controls on the door, lowering the window and disengaging the locks before finally stopping on the door handle.

Vanya renewed her attacks. Drakkal twisted his hips to swing her aside, his only defense against her onslaught in those moments, but he knew it wouldn't work for long. He needed to end this.

Sometimes, stupid's all you have to work with.

He tugged on the handle and threw his weight backward.

The door swung open. Air rushed into the cab through the opening, making the vehicle tremble. Drakkal thrust his arm through the open window and caught the door between his bicep and ribs. Gritting his teeth, he dragged himself out of the transport—bringing Vanya with him. She fought and kicked and clawed, latching onto the doorframe. Drakkal roared and poured the fullness of his fury into his strength. Vanya's hold broke. She screamed.

Drakkal's legs swung down and away from the transport, and all his weight, along with Vanya's, was suddenly supported on his right arm, making the window frame dig into his armpit painfully. For a second, time seemed to drag. He looked down to see Vanya caught between his legs, reaching desperately for the vehicle. Below her—at least thirty-five meters below—an Undercity street sped by, the pedestrians crowding it reduced to featureless blurs by the speed and height. His gaze met Vanya's in that instant. He'd once looked into those eyes longingly, with such admiration.

"Drakkal! Don't do this!" she begged, clawing at his legs.

He never wanted to look into those eyes again. His legs reached the apex of their outward swing.

He released his hold on Vanya.

Her limbs flailed as she soared through the open air, her eyes rounded in terror. The transport pitched to the side, dragged along by Drakkal's weight, and he growled at the fresh agony in his armpit. Just before he swung back toward the vehicle, he saw Vanya smash into a ledge protruding from the one of the buildings along the street. Blood sprayed from her body. Within a second, he'd lost sight of her.

His thighs struck the lower portion of the doorframe. Grunting, he instinctually reached for a handhold inside the cab with his left arm, managing only to slap his stump against the passenger seat. He could almost feel the fingers of his left hand clutching at the cushion, but the ghost of his hand could not prevent him from swinging away again.

His legs dangled beneath him, clawing at empty air as though he'd find an invisible ledge or ladder rung to provide some stability. He needed to move quick; even in the Undercity, this was going to draw the attention of the Eternal Guard before long. The spectacle had to be too much for them to ignore.

You're not nearly done yet, Kitty. Next item. Back to the manor.

Gritting his teeth, Drakkal bent his abdomen and legs at the same time. The transport wobbled as he swung his legs up once, twice, thrice, his every muscle burning as his shins and knees repeatedly bumped into the doorframe.

He roared and tried a fourth time. Finally, he managed to bend his body and lift his legs high enough to plant his feet on the base of the doorframe. He straightened his legs immediately, locking his knees and bracing his shoulder against the top of the window frame. The cuts Vanya had inflicted upon him—along with the few he'd managed to inflict himself—stung anew, and he could feel blood trickling through his fur, but none of that mattered.

Breathing raggedly, he used his entire body to work himself up into a position that would allow him to enter the cab without falling—a process that would have been far quicker, easier, and simpler with the use of a second arm. After a heated struggle, he finally fell across the passenger seat. It was so tempting to stop there and rest. It would've been so easy to do. His eyes longed to drift shut, his body to lie in peace and stillness awhile.

He didn't even allow himself a moment's respite. He scrambled over to the operator's seat, grasped the controls, and tilted the transport toward the driver's side. The passenger door slammed shut. When he righted the vehicle, he reengaged the autopilot and turned his full attention to the central control panel. A brief search uncovered the signal jammer control, which he promptly disabled, but there was nothing for the manacles. Vanya must've controlled the restraints solely through her holocom.

After turning off the obnoxious music, Drakkal entered Murgen Foltham's sector into the navigation panel, activated the navigation program, and pushed himself out of the seat. As the vehicle began a smooth climb to join the usual flow of traffic, Drakkal staggered into the holding area, keeping his hand against the wall to steady himself until he reached his prosthesis. It was still hanging where he'd left it.

Spreading his feet wide to afford himself better balance, he reached up and touched the forearm of his prosthesis. A holographic control screen appeared in the air.

He unmuted the holocom, opened his contacts list, and called Arcanthus. The call connected almost instantly, and the control screen changed to a three-dimensional holo of Arc's head and face.

"Drak! Everything okay? You've been gone—" Arcanthus's eyes widened. "You look like shit. What the hell happened?"

Drakkal turned his head and spat. His saliva still tasted of blood. "Vanya. Murgen Foltham hired her to capture me, Shay, and Leah."

Arc's features darkened instantly. "Where are they? Are Shay and Leah okay?"

Drakkal opened his mouth to reply, but the words, hot as molten metal, lodged in his throat. He pressed his lips together and flared his nostrils with a heavy exhalation.

"No, Drak. *No.* Tell me they're okay."

"Murgen has them," Drakkal finally grated. Getting those words out was like blasting apart a dam, releasing the bitter, fiery rage that had built up behind it. "Bring the crew and every fucking gun we own. I'll send you coordinates to meet me."

In the back of his mind, he knew the things that Arcanthus should've said. *Murgen Foltham is well-connected and powerful. This will garner a lot of dangerous attention. The Gilded Sector is crawling with peacekeepers. We should stop and really think about this before we do anything; there must be another way.*

But Arc said the only thing Drakkal wanted to hear—the *right* thing. "On our way."

"Bring my arm," Drakkal said.

"Your arm?"

Drakkal nodded. The nonexistent fingers of his left hand flexed and stretched restlessly; they weren't tired, and they shared his desire for bloodshed. "The one Sam designed. The armored one. I want that hand to be the one that rips out Murgen Foltham's throat."

TWENTY-FIVE

Shay snapped her legs together as soon as the guards released her ankles from the straps on the exam table. It wasn't anything new; Murgen's medical aids had examined her a few times during her last stay. But that didn't make it any less degrading, any less violating. She took comfort only in the fact that they treated her like an animal. Their hands—and eyes—were always cold and clinical. There'd been no sense in fighting during the process—her captors had made clear they wouldn't hesitate to use the shock collar to incapacitate her. And she needed to remain clearheaded for Leah.

As soon as her arms were free of the table's restraints—though the manacles were still locked around her wrists—Shay sat up, covered her chest, and sought Leah. Her daughter was on an exam table on the other side of the room, unconscious and surrounded by four examiners who were conversing and taking notes as they touched her like she was nothing more than a test subject. The fury roiling within Shay burned hotter.

Murgen was standing with the examiners, nodding and grinning that stupid fucking grin of his.

"We're done here," said the pink-skinned female volturian beside Shay's table without looking up from her tablet.

Her voice caught Murgen's attention. He walked over, stroking a finger thoughtfully over one of his yellowed tusks. "And?"

"Healthy, Master Foltham," the female volturian said, "apart from some contusions and a cut. She should be healed within a couple weeks, even without treatment. As requested, we've removed and destroyed her ID chip."

"Excellent. I want that custom tracker implanted in her the moment it arrives. Is she ready to breed?" Murgen asked, running his eyes over Shay's naked body.

Shay glared at him, bit her tongue, and pressed her lips into a tight line. It was the only way to hold in the harsh words welling in her throat. She longed for Drakkal, for his steady, strong presence, to be away from this place and these people. She longed to be with her mate and daughter.

"This terran is in even better shape than she was before escaping, sir. No damage to her reproductive organs...though she did have a birth control compound present in her system. Now that we've neutralized the compound, she will be ready to breed and is more than healthy enough to carry offspring to term."

Murgen frowned and let out a huff. "Unfortunate. I was hoping she'd been impregnated by that azhera. *That* would be a child I'd like to see. Can you imagine?"

Shay would've liked that, too—but not now, and *not* for Murgen's benefit.

"There are traces of semen inside the terran," the volturian said. "There's a chance it will take. Or, if you'd like, we can extract some of the samples and artificially inseminate her when she's ovulating."

Throat swelling with a thoughtful hum, Murgen folded his

hands over his gut. "Take the samples and store them. I'll have to decide how I want to proceed...there are so many possibilities, after all, and I've had little opportunity over these last few months to consider them all accordingly."

"Of course, sir."

The guards stepped forward at Murgen's instruction and forced Shay to lie back down as the volturian woman took her samples. Shay stared up at the ceiling, trying to turn her mind away as the volturian worked, but the cold, hard, invasive instruments were difficult to ignore.

"All finished, sir," the volturian finally said.

"Nostrus, have the terran escorted to her cell," Murgen said. "There's still much to be learned through her offspring, and I'm eager to participate."

Shay's eyes widened, and she jerked upright. "No! I need to be with her. She *needs* me."

The guards came forward again, grasping her arms to hold her still.

Nostrus approached slowly, his eyes, burning with hatred, fixed on Shay. "Your old room is waiting, terran. Don't make this difficult."

She'd remained calm for Leah's sake, had been so sure they'd keep her and her daughter together. But she'd been *wrong*.

Shay looked at Murgen. "*Please*. I'll behave, I swear, just please let me keep her. She'll need to feed. She'll need warmth, need her mother." The words felt like acid in her throat, but it was desperation that drove her to beg. She didn't know what they'd do to Leah.

Murgen snorted. "Perhaps, but that will be determined by my medical professionals—not by an animal."

"Let's go," Nostrus said. He lifted his right hand, which had a small device in it—the remote he'd synched with her collar and manacles. When he pressed a button on it, Shay's wrist bindings swung together in front of her as though drawn by powerful magnetic force.

The guards lifted Shay off the table and set her on her feet.

She wrenched out of their grasps, bumped back into the exam table, and turned, ready to jump over the table and race across the room to reach her daughter. "No! You can't take her away from me!"

Grunting, the guards reached for her, fingers biting into her bare skin. Shay barely felt the pain. She threw an elbow back and struck one in his diaphragm, making him double over and breaking his hold.

A burst of electricity from Shay's collar seized her muscles and nearly made her bite her tongue. The pain was immense, but she didn't take her eyes off Leah, even as fresh tears welled in them. The shock lasted for a second, two, three; it lasted *forever*, but Shay refused to let pain overwhelm her only goal. She needed to be with her baby.

Her body seemed to disagree. When the shock finally ended, she sagged forward, limbs limp. The guards shoved their arms beneath her armpits to hold her up. Her legs, partially dangling, refused to accept any of her weight, and her lungs were ablaze. For several moments, the pounding throb of her pulse at her temples was the only sound she was aware of.

Nostrus stepped closer. Shay couldn't lift her head to look him in the eyes; she was stuck staring down at his boots. But she still had a voice.

"Fuck you, you cold-hearted fuck," she rasped.

He slowly lifted his right hand and pressed a button on the little remote. Another shock—this one briefer but no less painful—blasted through her. This time, her eyes squeezed shut. Her limbs trembled when the shock subsided.

There was a soft chiming sound—like the call tone of a holocom.

"Yes?" Nostrus said. There was a pause. "Get one of the techs on it immediately and notify all the security staff."

"What's the problem, Nostrus?" Murgen asked.

"Surveillance system is down, sir," Nostrus said tightly. "It's probably just a glitch, but I would like you to head to the safe room until we receive word that it's corrected."

"Nonsense, my boy. I've too much work to do here. I've waited months for this, and I'll not be delayed another moment."

Nostrus sighed heavily and leaned close enough that Shay could feel his breath against her ear when he whispered, "You don't have that baby in you anymore, terran. I'm not allowed to kill you, but I have *many* ways to hurt you. Behave yourself."

"I will kill you," she vowed, forcing the whispered words out of her constricted throat.

Her body jolted as another wave of lightning swept through her. The fiery pain was followed by sudden, frightening numbness. Though her eyelids were closed, her vision turned white for an instant. She was vaguely aware of Murgen speaking before utter darkness chased away that terrible white, snuffing out her awareness.

Shay awoke to a gentle swaying motion, just like one would experience while riding a boat over calm, deep waters. It was soothing, but it was also *wrong*. She wasn't near the ocean, or a lake, or even a pond. She wasn't even on Earth.

She took in a slow, deep breath. The twinge of hurt it caused rippled through her and triggered a chain reaction during which every one of her aches and pains made itself known. Every tiny bit of her body was sore, even parts she had never realized existed. That agony was more than enough to remind her of what had happened and where she was.

Leah.

Shay stopped herself from sitting up, but only barely. She needed to act, yes, needed to get to her baby and get out of this place, but she knew from experience that acting rashly here would not accomplish her goals. She was too disadvantaged in her current state to act purely on rage. Her father had taught her long ago that you had to assess a situation before you reacted to it—whenever possible, at least. That meant remaining calm. That meant thinking.

Either she'd find an opportunity, or she'd make one.

She was lying on her back atop a hard, flat, swaying surface, and could feel the hum of antigrav engines beneath her. Gentle *whooshes* from around and above suggested she was moving past recesses in a tunnel or passageway. The simplest and most likely explanation was that Shay was on one of the small, open transport carts they'd used to bring her and Leah to the examination room.

Her wrists were still bound together by the heavy cuffs, but they were at her front, and they weren't anchored to the floor of the transport. That was better than she could've hoped for—Nostrus was usually more cautious than that.

"You think they were exaggerating?" someone asked from beyond her feet; the voice had come from the front of the vehicle, or at least the front-facing portion.

"Who knows?" someone closer responded—someone right near her feet, by the sound of it. The first speaker had likely been the driver. Both had deep, masculine voices, neither of which belonged to Nostrus.

Is Nostrus not here?

"She's pretty scrawny," the nearest male continued. "They probably just say she's so dangerous to save face. I bet she got the drop on them a couple times and they're embarrassed about it, so they play her up."

"Maybe," said the driver, "but best not to take any chances, right?"

The males fell silent. The vehicle's easy swaying continued; it neither knew nor cared about Shay's current plight. Moving as little as possible, she tested her limbs; she had feeling throughout her body, which was a good sign even if most of what she felt was discomfort and pain.

"She isn't bad looking," near-voice said.

Shay couldn't make out the driver's reply.

"It's not impossible, right?" As near-voice continued speaking, the volume of his voice diminished, like he'd turned his face away from Shay. "Master Foltham said himself that he wants to breed her. Means there's a chance."

Shay took a chance of her own; she opened her eyes to slits and bent her neck, angling her head toward the talking guard.

He was sitting at the front of the transport's bed on a low bench, legs spread and one elbow on his knee. His torso was twisted, head turned toward the driver as he conversed. Shay took a bit more of a risk and farther lifted her head to get a better look at him.

The guard was a borian, big and broad-shouldered, and his suit was tailored to show off the impressive physique beneath. The hand dangling between his legs—almost directly above her feet—loosely held the control for Shay's bindings and collar.

Finest security, huh, Murgen?

Shay drew in a deep breath. Though they rarely displayed their weapons openly, she knew Murgen's guards carried blasters. If she could get her hands on one of those weapons, there'd only be what? Twenty or thirty armed guards to fight through? She'd faced odds like that in training simulations, and though she'd yet to overcome any of those sims successfully on her own, she had to try. She had to get her daughter back. Leah was *not* going to grow up in a place like this.

Only have one shot at this. Better make it count. They get me into that cell, and its game over.

Slowly, she bent her left leg, planting her foot firmly on the floor to better brace herself, before swinging her right leg up. Her foot struck the borian's hand. The small control flew out of his grip and clattered against the corridor wall.

The guard spun to face Shay, his eyes wide, and glanced down dumbly at his empty hand. Brief as that look was, it afforded Shay enough time to reverse the direction of her kick. She used her left leg to thrust her backside off the floor and toward him—probably looking like a flopping fish in the process—and straightened her right leg, slamming her heel into his groin.

The borian doubled over with a pained grunt and grabbed a hold of Shay's ankle in an unforgiving grip. She gritted her teeth, locked her hands together, and clenched her abdominal muscles, throwing herself forward into a sitting position; the motion was sped by the vehicle suddenly braking to a halt.

She swung her arms down with all her strength, hammering her wrist cuffs into the top of the borian's head with a dull *thwack*. As he sagged forward farther, she jerked her left leg up. Her knee struck his nose with a wet crunch. Warm liquid flowed over her bare skin. The borian's head snapped backward, and his torso tipped back along with it. Blood streamed from his nostrils.

Shay could see the other guard now—a goat-faced groalthuun. He'd stood up in the driver's seat and turned toward her with legs bent as though he meant to jump. She reached into the borian's jacket and grasped the handle of the blaster holstered under his armpit as the groalthuun leapt over his companion.

The groalthuun's hands struck her shoulders, and his momentum knocked her back. She desperately clutched the blaster, which was tugged out of the holster by her backward motion. Shay tumbled onto her back. She swung the blaster's barrel up, pressing its tip against the groalthuun's stomach while he came down atop her, and fired.

The blaster made its high whining sound three times, and the guard jolted, features contorting in shock. He released a short, harsh breath that sprayed spittle onto Shay's face, and sagged forward. She quickly raised her thighs, squeezed the guard's midsection between her knees, and heaved him aside before he could fully collapse atop her. She slid herself aside as she did so, opening some space for his larger body to land.

Once she had the room, she angled the blaster toward his chest and fired two more plasma bolts into him.

The borian groaned. Shay sat up and turned the blaster toward him. He had a hand clasped over his nose as he lifted his head, blood trickling through his fingers.

His eyes fell on Shay's blaster and rounded. "Fucki—"

Shay silenced him with three plasma bolts through the chest.

He slumped to the side, twitched once, and went still, lifeless eyes still wide. Smoke curled up from the holes in his chest.

"Fucking hell," Shay muttered, wiping the spit from her face. She allowed herself a moment to breathe only after she'd ensured the corridor was clear in both directions. Her arms trembled, as did her exhalation, and a wave of nausea clenched her stomach, which threatened to force its contents back up her esophagus.

The simulations she'd run so often back at the compound had been visually realistic, but her dad had been right all those years ago—nothing, not even extensive, intense training, could prepare you for the first time you took a life. Nothing could help you anticipate your reaction to the smell of plasma-scorched flesh and blood, or the absurd amount of adrenaline pumping through your veins.

"Fuck," she said breathlessly as she shifted first to her knees and then stood up. The transport wobbled beneath her.

Adjusting her hold on the blaster, she stepped down from the transport's bed and surveyed the corridor, seeking the little controller. Not three seconds had passed before her stomach cramped, and she spun back toward the transport. She slapped a hand against the vehicle for support and bent forward as her body again threatened to purge itself.

"Puke if you're gonna puke," she said between ragged breaths. "Don't have time to stand here undecided, damn it."

She needed to hurry, needed to get to Leah before Murgen and his people did something harmful to her in the name of *science* or *curiosity*. She needed to get her baby before they moved Leah somewhere beyond Shay's reach.

Bile rose in her throat.

No, you had your fucking chance.

She swallowed it back down, spit out a mouthful of bitter, acidic saliva, and shoved away from the transport. Her first few steps were stumbling and unsteady, but she refused to accept that. She regained confidence and stability quickly, and within ten or fifteen seconds had spotted the small controller lying on the side of the hallway about five meters from the stationary vehicle.

Checking behind again—the corridor was eerily quiet now, and that unsettled her—Shay walked to the control and crouched over it. She set down the blaster and picked up the little device. Fortunately, it appeared undamaged. The buttons were labeled with tiny pictures; she pressed the one marked with a broken circle.

As one, the cuffs around her wrists and the collar around her neck clicked and unlatched. She shook them off immediately. The sound of those heavy metal restraints hitting the floor was more satisfying than she could ever have imagined.

She snatched up the blaster and checked its charge level. Ninety-two percent. It would likely hold out long enough for her purposes, but she couldn't afford to take the chance. She turned and rushed back to the dead guards. Without allowing herself to acknowledge the fact that she was stealing from men she'd just killed, she wrestled off the borian's blood-stained suit jacket, pulled it on, and loaded spare energy cells—along with the groalthuun's blaster—into the pockets. She buttoned the jacket and hurried down the corridor in the opposite direction from that which the cart had been traveling.

The corridors were big and quiet. Now that she was moving, she guessed that this place was under the effects of sound dampeners that prevented noise from carrying very far—otherwise, there would've been echoes of every little sound bouncing up and down these halls. The place was terribly lonely despite the numerous display windows through which various alien animals could be observed, not that she had any interest in any of those displays. Murgen meant for her and Leah to be held in similar cells, waiting to be gawked at by him or his guests.

She adjusted her two-handed grip on the blaster and growled.

Not again. Never again.

Shay increased her pace, bare feet padding over the cold floor. Her imagination flashed an image in her mind's eye of Leah, so small and helpless, alone and lost in these corridors, still too young to crawl away. Shay shook the imagining away. Nothing like that was going to happen. She would fight her way to her baby, and once she had Leah, she'd fight her way out of this place. After that...she'd hunt down Vanya and kill the *shit* out of her to win back her mate.

God, I hope Drakkal is okay.

If Murgen and Nostrus had considered Shay dangerous before, they were in for a surprise now. She'd never pulled her punches here, but the odds had always been stacked against her, preventing her from inflicting real damage.

Now the odds didn't matter. These motherfuckers had Shay's baby, and they'd sold off her mate to a psycho azheran bounty hunting bitch. Even if she had to kill a hundred more guards, a thousand, Shay would not stop until Leah and Drakkal were *both* safe and secure.

Shay slowed as she approached an intersection. She'd only been moved around this facility a few times during her prior captivity, and that had usually been while restrained in the back of a cart, under the watch—and sometimes the pinning bodies—of Murgen's security guards.

She paused before crossing into the intersecting corridor, uncertain of which direction to go. Wasn't she supposed to have some kind of...mom super sense or something to lead her toward her baby? She didn't want to spend any more time in these corridors than was absolutely necessary—they were too long and lacked any practical cover apart from support frames every twenty or thirty meters, and those only jutted from the walls about thirty centimeters. Perfect if she wanted to get a tit shot off.

There was no choice but to move on.

"So what?" she muttered. "Eenie, meenie, mi—"

Nostrus walked around the corner from Shay's right, bumping into her shoulder before either of them could act to avoid the collision.

Shay reeled back and simultaneously swung her blaster up. Nostrus's eyes—rounded in surprise an instant ago—narrowed. He raised his arms and caught her wrists in his hands, stopping her before she could aim the blaster at him.

"You're going to regret this, terran," he grated through bared teeth.

Shay bared her own teeth in a wild grin that would've made Drakkal proud as rage dulled all her aches and pains. "You turned down the wrong hallway, motherfucker."

TWENTY-SIX

"*They know their surveillance system is compromised,*" Arcanthus said over the commlink.

Drakkal made a final adjustment to his earpiece and grunted his acknowledgment before returning his hand to the foregrip of his auto-blaster. Urgand had tended to the worst of Drakkal's wounds, but it had been impatience and rage that chased away his pain, leaving room for little inside him beyond that persistent heat and his thundering heartbeat.

He was in a large, dimly lit access tunnel deep below the Gilded Sector with one shoulder against the wall, standing just to the right of a wide blast door. Urgand and Thargen were positioned to the left of the door, and Sekk'thi was at Drakkal's back with her eyes and weapon trained on the large bay door a few meters away. Both entries were closed.

"Cren, you three in position?" Drakkal asked.

"*Yeah,*" Kiloq replied through the commlink. "*Initiating attack in three...two...one...*"

Blaster fire crackled across the comms.

"All right. Security team's taking the bait, already shifting guards to the main entrance," Arcanthus said.

"Good. Get this door open," Drakkal grumbled. Shay and Leah were somewhere beyond this entrance, within a few hundred meters of him, but he couldn't smell them out here. It was maddening to know they were so close and yet so completely separated from him.

"Two on the other side," said Arc. "When you breach, they'll be ahead and to your right."

Drakkal's holocom flashed on, projecting a small screen that showed a high-angle view of the garage's interior, presumably from above the bay door. A pair of guards flanked the wide interior doorway at the far side of the garage. One of them had his head bowed slightly and a finger up to his ear—he was likely listening to something over his commlink.

Thargen's grin widened. "Haven't had this kind of fun in a while."

"Focus," said Urgand, who was standing behind Thargen.

Drakkal rolled his shoulder and settled the butt of his autoblaster against it. "We're all focused."

"Those fuckers took my friend and my niece," Thargen said, fire sparking in his eyes. "They get to meet the real me today."

Perhaps at most other times in most other situations, Drakkal would've been hesitant to release *real* Thargen on anyone. But he had no qualms about it here and now. Fuck this place, fuck Murgen Foltham, and fuck the people who willingly worked for him.

"*Kraasz ka'val*, Arcanthus, if you don't open this door now..."

The keypad on the doorframe flashed, and the blast door slid upward with a faint whirring of unseen machinery.

Drakkal lifted his auto-blaster and hurried through, turning the weapon immediately toward the far doorway. Thargen and Urgand's boots sounded on the floor behind him.

One of the security guards had time enough to look toward the open blast door, eyes wide, before Drakkal fired. The auto-blaster sprayed hot plasma bolts at the guards, joined an instant later by bursts from the two vorgals accompanying him.

Both guards went down within a second, each with at least half a dozen smoking holes in his body.

"*Getting a map onto your holocoms,*" Arcanthus said. "*I'll do my best to keep enemy positions updated on it, but I'm working with an uncooperative system here.*"

Though Arcanthus was the most skilled fighter in their bunch—and very likely the strongest, thanks to his cybernetic limbs and reinforced body—this was one of those situations during which he was best used outside of combat. Drakkal trusted Arc with his life, but Arcanthus's skills as a hacker were far more valuable now. Only Arc could compromise the manor's entire security system, turn it against the occupants, and ensure that no communications left the premises. Arcanthus had complained, but he'd ultimately agreed to stay in the armored vehicle they'd parked in the tunnels outside—especially because it meant keeping Samantha, who'd refused to be left behind at home, close. She could watch Arc's back while he worked, and he'd watch out for everyone going inside.

Drakkal's holocom screen, which had automatically rotated around his wrist to remain visible when he'd raised his weapon, changed again to display a two-dimensional map of Murgen Foltham's zoo.

"Just get me to Shay and Leah," Drakkal said.

Two flashing dots appeared along the edges of the map.

"*Leah's in some sort of examination room. Shay's being*

moved on a transport cart. I think they're both unconscious," Arc said.

Drakkal's heart sped as he advanced across the garage—the same garage Vanya had taken him from less than two hours ago. The soft clicking of claws on the floor behind him meant Sekk'thi had moved up to join them.

"Who's closest?" Drakkal asked when he reached the entry at which the now-dead guards had been posted.

"Shay. She's being moved toward you," Arcanthus replied.

It wasn't a choice Drakkal had wanted to make, and the weight of the decision was almost crushing. What if he picked wrong? He knew Murgen wouldn't kill the terrans, but what if Drakkal made a mistake, and his choice placed one of his terrans in more danger? If he took too long going for Leah and Shay was harmed because of it...

Shay would want me to go for Leah first...but if Shay is closest...

No. Can't do that now, Drakkal. No time to go back and forth on this decision.

"Only one way forward for now, anyway," Arcanthus said, "and it's going to take you right past a whole mess of guards."

"Hope they're better than these two," Thargen muttered, kicking one of the bodies.

Drakkal pressed onward through the entryway, flanked by his companions.

"Odd tastes on the air," Sekk'thi whispered. "Alien tastes."

"Foltham has all manner of creatures down here," Drakkal said, moving with his auto-blaster raised and ready. He smelled all of it, and those clashing scents almost overpowered the only fragrances that mattered to him, the two scents that were so similar and yet so unique—Shay's and Leah's.

Fury roiled in his gut. The scents of his mate and cub didn't belong in this place—never had and never would. But thanks to Murgen and Vanya, here they were.

"*Turn right where the corridor splits in two. There'll be two doors on the left*"—the projected map zoomed out as Arcanthus spoke to display what he was talking about— "*that lead into a damned barracks, Drak.*"

Drakkal clenched his jaw and asked through his teeth, "How many?"

"*Ten,*" Arcanthus replied.

"*Twelve,*" Samantha corrected, her voice soft over the commlinks. "*There's two back there, Arc.*"

Drakkal could almost imagine Sam leaning over Arc's shoulder to point at the screen they were looking at. It only made him long even more to have his Shay back. His heart ached for those simple, peaceful moments, for those tastes of a life like he might not have deserved but would damned well reclaim. He'd never believed he could love anyone as wholly and fiercely as he loved Shay and Leah.

He stuck to the corner when he reached the end of the corridor, peering cautiously into the perpendicular hallway. The doors Arcanthus had indicated were visible on the left, both closed.

"*They're suiting up now,*" Arc said. "*Probably mobilizing to help fight the cren upstairs.*"

"Going to be a nasty fight," Urgand said, "but we can't just leave them at our backs."

"At least they're vulnerable now," Drakkal growled. "Urgand, Sekk'thi, take the first door. Thargen, on me."

Drakkal rounded the corner and resumed his advance, splitting his attention between the closed doors and the far end of the corridor. The map updated, displaying twelve red dots in the large room to the left. Drakkal flattened himself against the wall beside the far door and glanced back to see Urgand and

Sekk'thi already in position. He nodded to them, briefly met Thargen's wild gaze, and slapped the door control button. The door hissed open, sliding aside into the wall. Drakkal charged through the opening with Thargen immediately behind him.

Startled shouts filled the air as several guards—some of whom were only partially dressed—snapped their gazes toward the intruders. Shay and Leah's faces flitted through Drakkal's mind's eye, followed by the faces of some of the other beings he'd seen imprisoned down here during the *tour* Foltham had given him. All enslaved, all having been robbed of their freedom, just like Drakkal and Arcanthus long ago. Just like countless people throughout the entirety of time and space.

And all these guards were complicit in that by working here, by working for Murgen Foltham.

Drakkal opened fire. Thargen's auto-blaster joined in, adding its own thumping whines to the cacophony as it filled the air with sizzling blue-white plasma bolts.

Chaos ensued, exasperated by the crimson haze that had settled over Drakkal's vision. Several of the sturdy beds lining the walls were toppled over to provide the guards makeshift cover, and plasma bolts—return fire from their foes—darted back toward Drakkal and Thargen.

"*Check your fire,*" Urgand called through the commlink. "*Nasty crossfire in here.*"

A plasma bolt struck Drakkal's combat armor and dissipated, producing a faint burst of warmth that was nothing compared to the fires blazing inside him. He released the trigger of his auto-blaster—acknowledging somewhere in the back of his mind the danger it posed to his companions—and charged forward. He didn't know how many of his enemies were dead or wounded, nor did he care. He'd fight so long as there were foes still moving.

Drakkal slammed the stock of his auto-blaster into a guard's face and turned toward the next enemy before the first had fallen. Two more blaster shots struck him, one on his breastplate and the other on the armor plating extending from the top of his prosthesis. He let his auto-blaster drop to hang over his shoulder by the strap and tackled the shooter. The struggle was brief, fierce, and bloody, ending when Drakkal rose on his knees and slashed his hardlight claws through the guard's face and throat.

He looked up to see three more guards in front of him, two of them holding smoking blasters; they were facing Drakkal with their backs pressed against an overturned bed. Drakkal snarled, baring his fangs, and tensed to launch himself toward them.

A big, heavy foot came down on Drakkal's back and pushed him forward as the weight bearing down upon it increased. Thargen leapt over Drakkal, wielding a tristeel knife in each hand, and loosed a guttural roar just before he crashed bodily into the trio of guards. His blades flashed and darted in the tangle of limbs, and blood splattered the floor and nearby bedding.

Drakkal rushed into the fray as the guards grabbed, clawed, and kicked the wild vorgal in their midst. He landed on the heap of thrashing bodies and set his claws and teeth to work. Blood soaked patches of his fur and ran sticky over his hands. Blaster shots sounded from nearby, providing a beat for the melody of grunts, growls, shouts, and wet, crunching sounds. When a strong arm looped around his neck from behind and dragged him backward, he hurriedly planted his feet—one firmly on the floor and the other on meaty, unresponsive flesh—and kicked off, forcing himself back hard.

The increased momentum knocked his assailant down, and Drakkal landed atop him heavily. The hold around his neck loosened. He angled his chin down, sank his teeth into his opponent's forearm, and brought up his left hand. A slash of his hardlight claws nearly severed the guard's arm at the elbow; a hard jerk of Drakkal's head to the side finished the job, tearing apart the remaining tissue.

The guard screamed and thrashed. Drakkal rolled aside, landed on his knees, and lifted his left arm high over his head. He swung it down like a hammer. His metal fist struck the guard's face, which crumpled like it was made of cloth. The screams ended with a choked gurgle.

"All clear," Urgand declared from nearby.

"They are dead," said Sekk'thi. "May they meet their ancestors in shame."

Growling, Drakkal tugged his hand away from the guard's caved-in face and shoved himself onto his feet. He shook his hands, flicking off excess droplets of blood, and surveyed the room.

The guards' bodies were strewn across the floor and over the beds, with blood and scorch marks everywhere. Taking in the carnage, Drakkal felt...little different than before. His bloodlust wasn't sated, his rage hadn't diminished, and his worry for Shay and Leah had only intensified. He ran his gaze over his companions. Urgand and Sekk'thi sported a few new blaster burns on their armor, but seemed otherwise untouched. And Thargen...

Thargen was covered in blood of at least two different colors, so much of it that Drakkal couldn't tell whether any of it belonged to the vorgal. His lips were stretched into a wide grin that fully displayed his short, pointed tusks, and his eyes still gleamed with that wild light.

"Everyone all right?" Drakkal asked.

All three of his companions answered affirmatively.

"There are a few updates, now that you have a moment," Arcanthus said. *"The guards are aware of intruders in the lower*

levels, according to their chatter, the cren have pushed into the manor, and...Shay escaped, but she's run into a volturian guard."

Drakkal's heart thumped, sending a wave of heat outward through his arteries. He wasn't sure whether that feeling was relief or terror. He lifted his wrist and said, "Show me."

His holocom's display gave way to a surveillance feed depicting the intersection of two corridors. Shay stood near one corner, dressed in an oversized jacket of the same style the guards wore. And she was locked in a physical struggle that had her face-to-face with Nostrus.

Drakkal's eyes widened, and everything inside him went suddenly still and silent. "Guide me to her. *Now*," he barked, but his voice sounded distant to his own ears. He was already running into the hallway, though he couldn't remember telling his legs to move, and no matter how much strength he put into the movement it felt too slow, like he was running under water.

He raced down the corridor, following the directions as Arc relayed them, and saw nothing and no one even though his companions must've been right behind him. Shay was all he could focus on in those moments.

Almost there, kiraia. Almost there.

TIGHTENING his grip on Shay's forearm, Nostrus swung himself around and slammed his right shoulder into her left. The impact was hard enough to drive her aside and into the wall. Before she could react, he'd twisted his hips so his right leg was in front of both hers.

Guess I'll have to wait for a chance to kick him in the balls.

He leaned into her, wedging his hip against her midsection, and bashed her hands against the wall. Shay growled in pain. Nostrus's face was so close to hers, and his hate filled eyes and *qal* markings glowed as though alight with spiteful fire. He forced her hands away from the wall only to slam them against it again.

The blow was painful enough to break her grip; the blaster fell from her nerveless fingers and hit the floor with a heavy thud.

For all her training, she couldn't deny the facts—Nostrus outweighed her by at least twenty-five kilograms, stood at least ten or fifteen centimeters taller, and he was stronger than her. She was at a disadvantage.

So all-in-all, no different than any other fight I've ever been in.

She sure as hell wasn't going to lose her first—and only—real fight with him. This time, she wasn't held back by shock collars, heavy restraints, or an unwieldy pregnancy belly. And now she was fighting for something more powerful than ever before—her daughter.

She turned her face toward his and spat in his eyes.

Nostrus snapped his head aside and leaned away, swearing. Shay used the tiny amount of leeway that afforded her to brace her leg against the wall and shove away from it, throwing her full weight into Nostrus.

He stumbled backward, maintaining his hold on her arms, and growled through his teeth. He quickly regained his balance and halted, blinking away moisture from his eyes. His torso pitched toward her again, threatening to force her back and negate the ground she'd gained.

He snarled. "You little fucking—"

Shay snapped her head forward. Her forehead struck the bridge of his nose with a satisfying crunch.

Nostrus reeled away, losing his hold on her arms, and Shay staggered back simultaneously. Her head throbbed dully, and little black spots floated across her vision. She shook it off and dropped a hand toward her pocket.

Growling again—and releasing a ragged breath that sprayed the blood running from his nose—Nostrus charged at Shay.

His hands hit her upper shoulders and immediately slid toward her neck, but Shay lifted her hands to grasp the front of his jacket and threw herself backward, adding her weight to his momentum. She brought a leg up as she fell into a roll, planting her foot against Nostrus's stomach, and flipped him over into a somersault. He crashed down behind her, striking the floor on the back of his head before tumbling onto his back.

Rolling aside, Shay hurried onto her knees. She reached for her pocket again—for the spare blaster inside it—but Nostrus recovered too quickly. He sat up, planted a hand on the floor, and swung his leg around, spinning on his hip.

His shin struck her upper arm before her hand had even reached the pocket. The pain swept up to her shoulder and down to her fingertips, and the force of the blow knocked her aside. Gritting her teeth, she tucked her shoulder and went with the momentum he'd created, moving away from him.

She stopped herself on one knee and shoved onto her feet, raising her left arm in a partial fighting stance as she shook the tingling and stiffness from her right.

Nostrus sprang to his feet. He smiled a joyless smile as he assumed a fighting stance of his own. "I've waited a long time for this."

He was too close for her to go for the spare blaster again; all the attempt would accomplish was to lower her defenses. She knew Nostrus was carrying a blaster in a shoulder holster beneath his jacket. There was also a collapsible stun baton dangling from his belt, and she'd seen him carry knives in the past.

Guess I should be happy he hates me just enough to want to use his fists.

"Me too," she replied. "Been too long since I've seen your blood."

Nostrus's smile twisted into a scowl, and he lunged forward. His strikes were quick and controlled, conveying discipline, experience, competence, and a touch of caution. Shay refused to give him any ground. She defended herself from his blows, blocking and dodging, and offered her own retaliatory strikes—but none of her attacks landed.

Nostrus held the fight at the edge of his reach, using his longer arms as his primary means of defense.

His fist clipped her right ear. Though the damage was negligible, it hurt like a bitch. Her head snapped to the side, and heat thrummed through her ear and spread across her face. He launched an immediate follow-up, kicking at her head with his right leg. Shay bent her left arm and raised it to protect her head; the impact was still strong enough to knock her off-balance. She staggered aside, and Nostrus followed relentlessly, planting his right foot on the floor and spinning into a reverse heel kick with his left leg going high.

Recovering her balance, Shay ducked his left leg as it cut downward at a diagonal angle like a scythe. She surged forward immediately, grabbing hold of his jacket with both hands, and drove her knee into his groin. Nostrus grunted and leaned toward her; Shay hammered her knee into his stomach twice in quick succession. Face pale, he doubled over and stumbled backward a step, but Shay held on, unwilling to let him open that distance again.

Halting his backward momentum, he swung his right arm around as though to wrap it around her neck. Shay dipped under it, letting his arm slide over her back, and punished him with several fast strikes to his ribs. His right hand fell to her shoulder and grasped her jacket while his left took hold of the fabric near the center of her back. He shoved her down and thrust his knee up to meet her.

Shay dropped her arms and slammed them against his leg, robbing that first strike of enough of its power to keep him from blasting the air out of her lungs. Holding her in place, Nostrus drew his leg back and brought it up again, growling when she blocked the second blow with her forearms. As he drew his leg back a third time, Shay lifted her left foot off the floor and thrust it down, driving her heel onto the inside of his left ankle.

Nostrus's leg buckled. He dropped his other leg to catch his balance, spitting a curse, and swung both his arms to the side while twisting his hips to throw Shay away.

She stumbled aside, remaining upright only because her shoulder struck the wall. "You never been in a fight before?" she asked as she straightened. "Maybe I should put the cuffs back on."

Nostrus snarled and, despite a visible limp and the sickly pallor of his skin, moved toward her, keeping his weight off his left foot as he unleashed a flurry of punches. Shay raised her hands to defend herself, weaving and swaying to avoid as many of the blows as possible. Several still struck, hitting her sides and head, though most were glancing blows that hurt little compared to her other pains.

He was fighting sloppier now, but it wasn't quite enough; she wanted him wild, wanted him making mistakes, wanted him reckless.

She grinned. "Maybe if you go whine to your space walrus daddy, he'll pay to get you some real training."

He leaned back and, with a wordless shout, launched a haymaker at her with his right hand. Shay ducked and bobbed to her left, avoiding the blow. His fist struck the wall.

Nostrus cried out in pain. Shay punched him in the kidney —if that was where a volturian's kidney was, anyway.

He grunted and swung his elbow around, clipping Shay with it on the back of her head. The sound of the blow was a jarring bone-against-bone thud. Her vision darkened for an instant, and she stumbled away. Several huge, clumsy steps carried her to the center of the corridor before she finally caught her balance. She spun to face Nostrus.

He turned toward her, stretching and flexing the fingers of his right hand and shaking it as though to work out a deep ache.

"My azhera fucked up your hand, huh?" Shay turned her right side away from him and moved her hand toward her pocket. "Must suck to have such dainty fingers."

Eyes aflame, Nostrus ran at her and tore the stun baton from his belt.

Shay's fingers closed around the grip of her blaster. She stepped back, tugging up on the weapon. Nostrus swept his arm up, and the stun baton extended to its full length, crackling to life.

The blaster snagged on the fabric of the jacket pocket.

Fuck. Stupid fucking goddamned jacket!

Shay leapt backward as Nostrus swung the baton at her in a wide arc. She angled the blaster in her pocket and squeezed the trigger, firing from the hip. A blue-white plasma bolt cut through the air only a few centimeters from Nostrus's left elbow. She shifted the weapon toward his body and fired again, but she'd overcorrected for her second shot—it darted past his right hip, burning a hole through his jacket. The stench of singed fabric stung her nose.

That quickly, Nostrus was too close. Shay hurriedly pulled her hand out of her pocket, leaving the blaster behind, as Nostrus advanced with the baton swinging wildly. They both knew how it worked—he didn't need to hit anything vital. He just had to touch her with the active end of the device.

Shay ducked and dodged frantically as the baton cut

through the air around her; it moved fast enough to produce soft *whooshing* sounds, came close enough to make her little hairs stand on end and produce a static tingle across her skin.

Nostrus punctuated his swings with frustrated grunts and snarls. His attacks came as fast as ever, but they lacked the discipline he'd demonstrated earlier. At heart, Shay knew that was to her advantage, but it was hard to keep that in mind while a pulsing lightning stick was flying toward her head.

Jaw clenched, she kept up her gradual retreat, grateful that he was telegraphing his movements so clearly. The baton hissed and crackled, its sounds mingling with Nostrus's in a harsh and hateful symphony. Shay's heartbeat eagerly backed that music with its frantic drumming.

Her aching muscles renewed their protests, joined by a chorus of pain both new and old. God, it would've felt nice to lie down and rest, even for just a few minutes. She could keep this up for a little while longer, but there were hard, physical limits she was bound to slam into soon.

Hold on, Leah. Mommy's on her way.

Shay's backpedaling seemed to urge Nostrus on; he pressed his attack, picking up the speed and savagery. But he was still favoring that left foot.

He swung down from overhead. Shay dodged to her left, grabbed his extended right wrist with her right hand, and slammed her other palm into his elbow. She felt a *crunch* in his arm. Crying out, he dropped the baton. A barely audible scrape of metal on leather was Shay's only warning before his left hand darted toward her face, the tristeel blade in his grasp glinting under the bright overhead lights.

Eyes rounding, Shay grasped his elbow with her left hand and wrenched his arm up, diverting his knife attack to the side, prompting a scream from Nostrus. His blade sliced across her cheek rather than striking her eye. The hot blood that oozed from the wound a second later felt like molten lava.

Nostrus pulled the knife back and stabbed again, this time under his right arm. Shay jumped aside, moving toward his back. The blade cut through the fabric over her ribs and bit into the flesh beneath.

Shay growled through her teeth and pulled his right arm outward, using it for extra leverage as she swung her left knee into the back of his right. Nostrus collapsed onto his buckled knee with an agonized yell. He reversed his grip on the knife and stabbed it backward at her blindly. The blade caught her left hip. She felt it strike the bone; the impact diverted the blade's path, angling the tip away from her body.

"Fuck!" Shay twisted quickly to plant her hip against his shoulder and throw her weight against him, simultaneously wrenching back on his arm.

He pitched forward, crashing face first to the floor. The knife clattered away. Shay landed atop him, back-to-back, and pulled harder on his arm. Something cracked and popped. Nostrus screamed and thrashed beneath her, jerking his head up. The back of his skull slammed into the back of Shay's with jarring force. Darkness skittered across her vision again, and the spot he'd struck with his elbow flared with new, intense pain.

She rolled off Nostrus and away from him, clamping her left hand over the back of her head. Her tangled hair was wet and sticky with blood—undoubtedly the result of that earlier elbow shot.

Swearing again, she turned toward Nostrus and braced her right hand on the floor, struggling to push herself to her feet. She didn't trust the two meters of distance between them. She didn't trust the way his right arm hung limp, or the way he breathed heavily and groaned as he fought to rise. She didn't trust that his back was turned toward her.

"When I'm done with you," he said, words slurred like they were being forced through mashed lips, "I'm going to hunt down your azhera"—he grunted and planted his right knee on the floor—"and skin him alive."

Shay's head throbbed. She staggered once she was on her feet, assailed by sudden lightheadedness. She sucked in a deep breath through her teeth and lowered her hand into her pocket. Several drops of liquid spattered audibly on the floor; she didn't know if it was her blood, Nostrus's, or both, but it didn't matter.

Her fingers closed around the blaster's grip.

Nostrus shifted his left leg, moving himself onto his knees, and sank back to sit on his calves. His head lolled forward. He raised his left arm, bent at the elbow, as though clutching his chest. "You are going to regret every moment of this, terran."

Shay lifted the blaster. It felt like it weighed a hundred kilos, but it didn't snag on the jacket this time, and her arm was steady as she raised the weapon.

"You," Nostrus spat, swaying as he tugged on something, "and your fucking vermin offspring—"

Shay pulled the trigger. The blaster's high, thumping whine was diminished under the corridor's sound dampeners. It was a muted, anticlimactic sound, an unimportant sound, an inconsequential sound.

It was the perfect sound to mark Nostrus's death.

"You don't get to talk about my mate or my baby," she said softly.

Nostrus remained on his knees, unmoving, for several seconds. Faint wisps of smoke drifted up from the neat, dark hole on the back of his head. The smells of charred flesh and burned hair were strong in the air. There was no nausea this time, not even as Nostrus finally pitched forward and collapsed unceremoniously on the floor. A blaster fell from his left hand.

Shay's arm trembled as she lowered her weapon.

No such thing as a pretty fight, Shay, her father said in the back of her mind.

She chuckled humorlessly as warm blood flowed from her numerous cuts, as every muscle and bone in her body ached, as her head throbbed. She wished she hadn't had to go through this to hear her dad's voice so clearly again. She wished that his lessons had never proven necessary. But more than all that, she wished that her daughter would never have to learn such lessons firsthand.

From somewhere far away, a voice called her name.

Don't have time to go crazy, Shay. Need to get to Leah.

The voice sounded again, a little louder. Furrowing her brow, Shay lifted her gaze, tentatively raising the blaster along with it.

A big, beautiful, dun-colored azhera was sprinting down the corridor toward her, the vibrant green of his eyes clear even from forty meters away. An equally big, stupid grin stretched across her lips.

Drakkal?

"What a good, pretty kitty," she muttered. She stumbled backward, feet slipping on the blood-slick floor. Her arm fell limply to her side once she'd caught her balance, and the blaster slipped from her fingers. All at once, her body felt weak, sapped of every ounce of energy.

"Shay!" Drakkal called, his voice sounding so, so *real*.

Tears stung her eyes.

The last time she'd seen him was when Murgen's guards had hauled him into Vanya's transport. He'd been taken away from Shay. He'd been *stolen* from her. As he drew nearer still, she noticed the people running behind him—Thargen, Urgand, and Sekk'thi. But they didn't know anything about any of this. There was no way they could be here.

Guess I really have lost my mind.

This wasn't a convenient time or place to lose her shit—not that *any* time or place was convenient—but the evidence was right there. Full-blown audio-visual hallucinations.

Drakkal skidded to a halt in front of her, his toe claws scraping across the floor. It seemed a very specific detail for a hallucination. Her legs trembled, and she sagged toward him. His arms were around her in an instant, strong and warm, pulling her against his body. Heat wafted from him, warming her too cold skin. He was wet and smelled strongly of blood, but beneath that, she detected the leather and cloves scent that was all him.

"*Kraasz ka'val, kiraia,*" he breathed, hugging her tighter.

She must have made a sound, a whimper or a grunt of pain, because he immediately drew back, dipping his gaze to take her in. She swept her eyes over him slowly, as though he'd vanish any second; her brain still couldn't quite believe what she was seeing, feeling, and smelling.

There was blood splattered in his fur and over his armor, but he hadn't been wearing armor before. Hell, he hadn't been wearing that *arm*, either.

Drakkal's features were strained with worry as he turned his head to look behind him. "Urgand! Over here now!"

"You're really here," Shay breathed, placing a hand on his chest. She knew she wouldn't be able to make sense of his presence right now. She knew, also, that it didn't matter. He was *here*.

He looked at her again and frowned, lifting his right hand to her face. He delicately brushed the pad of his thumb beneath the cut on her cheek. "I'm here. Everything's going to be fine now."

Drakkal guided her to sit on the floor, easing himself down behind her and slipping his right arm around her middle. She leaned back against his chest as Urgand knelt in front of her.

Wearing a frown as deep and concerned as Drakkal's, Urgand quickly set about examining her wounds.

Shay's sense of surrealness didn't diminish. She felt Urgand's gentle pokes and prods, but the pain was distant now. She tipped her head back against Drakkal's shoulder and stared up at him. Impossible as it seemed, he was here, here for her, here for...

Leah.

As much as she wanted to close her eyes and let the overwhelming relief coursing through her in that moment lull her to rest, she couldn't. Not when Leah was still in Murgen's grasp. Her heart beat rapidly against her ribs, and her breath quickened.

Shay placed a hand on Drakkal's arm and squeezed it as desperation chased away her relief. "He still has Leah, Drak. She's in that examination room with him now."

"I know," Drakkal said. "Arcanthus has eyes on them. We'll get her."

She tightened her grip on his arm, and it had nothing to do with the flare of pain as Urgand peeled the jacket's fabric away from the cut on her hip. "I'm going with you."

Drakkal's brows fell, and he glanced at Urgand.

Urgand gently guided Shay to lean on her right hip, frown deepening. "These are going to need some work. More than I can do here. But I can get you patched up enough to stop the bleeding, at least."

"Do it. Quickly," Drakkal rumbled.

"I know, I know." Urgand reached back to open a pouch on his belt and muttered, "Which of us was the fucking combat medic?"

"Damn, Shay. I thought you did a number on the first two bastards, but you *really* fucked up this volturian," Thargen said.

Shay turned her head to look at Thargen. He was drenched

in blood, his face tattoos hidden amidst the crimson, and was in the process of flipping Nostrus's body onto its back with his boot. Her body jerked slightly as Urgand tore the jacket around her cuts. She curled her lips into her mouth and bit them against the flashes of pain.

"One for the discomfort," Urgand said as he pressed a tiny gun to her thigh and pulled the trigger. There was a click and a prick on her skin. He opened the device, removed the small cartridge from its chamber, and deftly loaded another before lowering the gun and repeating the process. "And one to keep you moving."

A strange combination of warmth and coolness spread outward from the spot he'd injected her, slowly creeping in both directions along her leg.

"This the guy you told me about? The bodyguard or whatever?" Thargen asked, glancing at her.

Shay nodded. "That's him."

Thargen closed his mouth and sniffed in hard, producing a growling sound in his throat. Then he leaned down and spat a big, phlegmy wad of saliva into Nostrus's face—or what was left of the volturian's face. "Take that to the afterlife, you fuck."

Urgand pinched the sides of the cut on her hip together with the fingers of one hand as he ran some sort of sealant gel along the wound. The gel's sting was worse than the pain of the cut by a wide margin, making her suck in a sharp breath.

Drakkal pressed his face to Shay's neck and shoulder, nuzzling her over the bite scar he'd given her. It provided her a moment's distraction and comfort as the vorgal worked.

"Combination disinfectant and temporary sealant," Urgand said without looking up. "It'll hurt until the pain dampener kicks in."

"A little warning beforehand would have been nice, but thanks." Shay wrinkled her nose and hissed when he applied the sealant to the cut on her side. She looked up at Drakkal again. "How did you escape? How are you here? What about Vanya?"

"She's dead." Drakkal moved his left hand up to her head and combed his fingers through her tangled hair, stopping as they neared the back of her head. "A head wound, too, *kiraia*?"

"That one's not too bad," she said, even though that spot hurt like hell; when everything hurt, it made all of it less immediate. Fortunately, whatever Urgand had injected her with was gradually dulling all that pain.

"I wish he were still alive so I could kill him myself," Drakkal snarled.

Shay's lips twitched into a smile. "You're so hot when you talk like that."

One corner of Drakkal's mouth tilted up, and he shook his head. Love and relief shone in his eyes, though they weren't enough to overpower the worried gleam that had been in his gaze since he'd arrived. This wasn't done yet.

Her smile fell, and Shay closed her eyes and laid her head on his chest. "I'll be fine. I just want to get Leah and go home. I want this to be over."

"Soon. Very soon."

A pair of calloused but gentle fingertips settled around the cut on her cheek just before the gel flowed over it. With the sting dulled, all she felt was a cool, slightly refreshing sensation, welcome after the heated fight with Nostrus. Once that cut was done, Drakkal carefully guided her head forward. Urgand repeated the process with the cut on the back of her head. She felt Urgand move away when he was done.

Her pain had already receded into something distant, something she could safely ignore, and now her exhaustion was doing the same. A tentative sort of energy flowed through her limbs; she still felt like shit, she knew that at heart, but she could keep going. A few minutes ago...well, she'd been nearly out, hadn't she?

Drakkal moved his hand down to cup her jaw and tilt her head back toward him. She opened her eyes to meet his fiery gaze.

He bared his fangs. "Let's get our daughter, *kiraia*."

TWENTY-SEVEN

"*Murgen just left the examination room through a back door,*" Arcanthus said over the comms. "*I suppose he finally realized the severity of the situation.*"

Drakkal growled a curse but didn't allow himself to slow. He was walking at a brisk pace with Shay beside him, his right arm around her back and hooked beneath her armpit. She'd leaned on him less and less as they'd continued deeper into the zoo—undoubtedly the result of the booster Urgand had injected her with. She'd crash and feel like shit again once it wore off, but all that mattered now was that she could keep moving.

"What about Leah?" he asked.

"*She's still in there,*" Arc replied. "*The techs are arguing... annnnnd never mind, they just ran into a supply room to hide. Left her on the exam table.*"

"What's happening?" Shay asked, tightening her arm around Drakkal's middle.

"Is she all right, Arc?" Drakkal demanded.

"*As far as I can tell. She looks like she's still out.*"

"Murgen ran off," Drakkal said, squeezing the grip of his auto-blaster with his left hand and glancing down at Shay. "They left Leah behind, but we think she's okay."

Shay nodded.

Sekk'thi and Thargen, who had taken the lead in their new formation, turned the next corner. Drakkal followed with Shay just behind him, and Urgand took the rear. The wide door to the examination room stood twenty meters ahead. The door that led to Leah.

"Have any guards remained behind?" Sekk'thi asked.

"*No. The two that were in there are escorting Murgen away,*" Arcanthus replied.

When they arrived at the door, all five of them fell into position. Shay didn't resist when Drakkal angled himself to shield her body with his, though she did lean slightly to the side, aiming her blaster around him. The door opened on a sterile, silent room filled with sleek medical equipment and several examination tables and adjustable chairs.

Thargen and Sekk'thi moved into the room with auto-blasters raised, checking corners as they went. Drakkal and Shay advanced in their wake, and his eyes were drawn immediately to one of those tables, atop which Leah lay beneath stark white light.

"Clear," both Sekk'thi and Thargen declared. The door closed after Urgand entered the room.

Drakkal and Shay hurried to their cub, finally splitting apart to move to opposite sides of the table. Leah lay naked and unmoving but for the rise and fall of her little chest, head turned to one side and eyes closed. Her skin was too pale.

"*Is Leah okay?*" Samantha asked over the commlink, her voice filled with fear.

Shay picked Leah up and cradled her in her arms, holding her close. Her strained, worried expression eased, and she closed her eyes. When she opened them to meet Drakkal's gaze, they were filled with tears. "We got her back."

"We think so, Sam," Drakkal said softly. His chest tightened with raw, powerful emotion—elation, relief, sorrow. They should never have had to deal with everything they'd been forced to endure. No one should ever have had to deal with it. If he could've somehow spared his family from all this suffering, if he could have somehow found Shay and claimed her without triggering this chain of events...

He leaned across the table, bracing himself on an elbow, and placed a hand on the back of Shay's neck. Dipping his head, he placed a soft kiss on Leah's forehead. He lifted his face a moment later to kiss Shay on the lips.

She returned the kiss, but a soft sob escaped her as she drew away, pressing her lips against Leah's head. Her tears fell freely, cutting trails through the blood smeared on her cheek.

In the months he'd known her, Drakkal had only seen Shay show such emotion, such vulnerability, a handful of times—few enough to count on one hand, and he had a finger fewer on each hand than her. It broke his heart a little, but it also bolstered his love for her. He understood now what he'd been too naïve to comprehend in his youth—showing these emotions was not a sign of weakness. In many ways, in many cases, it was amongst the most admirable signs of strength.

"Don't want to interrupt," said Arcanthus over the commlink, *"but I think Murgen is heading for a safe room deeper in the facility."*

"You saying he's trying to hide instead of run away?" Thargen asked.

"A lot of people with his kind of wealth do the same," Urgand said. "Used to see it all the time when I ran in private security. They have these rooms in their manors that are like little self-sufficient fortresses. They can just wait in luxury for help to come."

Drakkal clenched his jaw, dropped his arm from Shay, and stepped back. There was still another emotion roiling inside him with the others, stronger and deeper than all save his love for Shay and Leah. *Rage.* It was driven in part by instinct, which had not yet been satisfied—which wouldn't be satisfied until the threats to his family were eliminated for good.

"Cren, how are you three doing up there?" Drakkal asked.

"*Moving up to the last group now,*" Kiloq replied over the comms.

"*These guys fight like amateurs,*" Koroq added.

"All right." Drakkal turned to look at his companions. "Urgand, can you check Leah and make sure everything looks good as best you can tell?"

Urgand nodded and walked to stand beside Shay.

Drakkal turned to face his other companions. "Sekk'thi, you're on watch. Cover the door. Thargen...go take care of the staff hiding in the supply closet."

Thargen sighed and let his shoulders slump. "Are they even armed?"

"*No,*" Arcanthus said.

Releasing an even heavier sigh, Thargen stomped toward the supply room door on the left side of the room. "Fine. But only because we had some real fighting earlier."

"They might not fight back," Shay said, "but they're the ones that were poking and prodding me and Leah. The ones that Murgen wanted to *experiment* on us."

Thargen's expression fell subtly, conveying an oddly cold fury that was a rare sight from him. "Oh, I *hope* they fight back." He swung his auto-blaster on its shoulder strap, stowing it behind his back.

"Arcanthus, I want you to guide me to Murgen," Drakkal said as Thargen entered the supply room.

Arc chuckled. *"And here I thought you were about to give me a challenging task."*

"You want a challenge? Try to go five minutes without sounding like an arrogant prick."

"A fair *challenge, azhera. That's asking the impossible."*

Smirking, Drakkal turned back to Shay and reached across the exam table. His smirk faded as he placed his palm over her cheek and gently brushed the pad of his thumb under her sealed cut. "I'm going to finish this. Be right back."

Her blue eyes blazed as she pressed her face into his palm. "Make him *hurt.*"

The weight behind Shay's words was not lost on Drakkal. This was not a demand for cruelty—it was a demand for vengeance, for closure, for *justice*. A demand to right the scales, which had been wildly misbalanced for too long.

But the heart of this matter was simple—Murgen Foltham had caused Drakkal's mate and cub suffering, distress, and pain. The degree of that suffering mattered only in relation to how much pain Drakkal would now inflict upon Murgen. There were no more deals to be made, no more second chances to be claimed. There was no more forgiveness to be offered.

Drakkal closed his eyes just long enough to take a deep breath, filling his lungs with air perfumed by his family's scent, which surpassed all the other smells in this room based on its familiarity alone. He didn't want to leave it behind—didn't want to leave *them* behind—but he had to finish this.

Opening his eyes, he offered Shay a solemn nod, lowered his hand, and swung his auto-blaster back into his hands. He turned and walked toward the back door. "Arcanthus, show me the way to this fucking *zhe'gaash.*"

"You want me to close off the corridors and trap him somewhere closer?" Arc asked.

"No," Drakkal replied without hesitation. "Let him get far away from Shay and Leah. Let him get to his safe room. I want him to believe he's safe, want him to believe he's secure, so I can show him that all his fucking money doesn't mean anything. I want to see it on his face the moment he realizes it's over."

"Remind me not to piss you off in the future."

At Arcanthus's direction, Drakkal plunged into a network of long, dimly lit corridors that were wholly at odds with the rest of Murgen Foltham's zoo. These corridors were drab, gray, and narrow—barely wide enough to fit the hovercarts used elsewhere in the facility. Exposed pipes, ducts, and conduits ran along the ceiling in a haphazard bundle that altered as components branched off and turned inward to join the flow.

It briefly brought his mind back to his days on Caldorius. How many such passageways had he walked in the bowels of those arenas? How many times had he been made to sleep in chambers that had the same sort of grungy, mechanical innerworkings on full display, knowing all the while that the owners and the ravening audiences enjoyed comfort and relative luxury during every moment of their lives? Murgen Foltham and his colleagues, his *guests*, were too good to endure the sight of these places under normal circumstances. These were the territory of slaves and servants, of the subordinates. The territory of the less fortunate.

Drakkal didn't care if it was petty, but the thought of Murgen scurrying through these corridors like a terrified sewer skrudge was immensely satisfying. Foltham deserved to spend his last moments brought low, deserved the fear Drakkal hoped he was feeling right now.

Turning where Arcanthus indicated, Drakkal entered another corridor and increased his pace. His breath came quick and heavy, his muscles burned, and ever-intensifying heat radiated outward from his chest to suffuse his limbs. Despite his weariness and soreness, he felt *alive*, his senses amplified and on high-alert. He could detect Murgen's scent on the air, strengthening with each step forward. This was the realization of his instincts, the fulfillment of his current purpose—as a hunter, a mate, a protector.

"*Next right,*" Arcanthus said. "*They're thirty meters ahead, just about to reach the safe room entrance.*"

Voices drifted to Drakkal from around the corner, barely above whispers and difficult to decipher—but he recognized one of them. The deepest, most frantic of the voices belonged to Murgen. A loud rumbling echoed down the hall, as though a heavy door were opening.

Drakkal slowed, raised his auto-blaster, and turned the corner, squeezing the trigger even before he'd had time to visually register his targets. A torrent of plasma sped along the corridor. The sound of the firing auto-blaster was the only warning Foltham's guards received.

Both bodyguards spun to face Drakkal. The closer of the two fell almost immediately, hit by at least five bolts within half a second. Drakkal advanced toward them at a brisk stride, keeping the trigger depressed.

Wide-eyed, Murgen pressed himself against the opening door. The remaining guard was raising his blaster. Before he could return fire, a trio of plasma bolts hit him in the arm, chest, and eye.

Murgen ducked and fell through the doorway, vanishing from Drakkal's view. The door slammed down with a thunderous finality.

Glowing rings and lines stood out all over the floor, walls, and overhead ductwork, slowly fading as they cooled. Drakkal strode forward and fired a few more shots into each guard as he neared them. He stopped in front of the large blast door through which Murgen had fled. Extending his left arm, he banged his metal fist on the door.

The sound carried along the corridor in a deep, booming echo; no sound dampeners here, not for the staff.

The keypad on the doorframe flashed.

"You're not getting through this door, azhera," Murgen said through the intercom. "It's made of the strongest tristeel in Arthos, and can withstand a direct hit from an orbital strike!"

"Seems excessive," Drakkal growled.

"What's excessive is what I'll have my security personnel do to you once their special task force arrives. You don't have the intelligence to fully comprehend the consequences of what you've done, you slavering beast. I suggest you flee while you can."

Drakkal's rage continued to burn hot around an icy, unshakeable core—that calm and patience he normally had such mastery over. Murgen's words didn't fan those flames; they couldn't anymore. Ultimately, they were the same as their speaker—loud, arrogant, and empty.

"You've no idea who you've crossed, azhera," Murgen continued. "Do you have the slightest notion of how many credits I'm willing to pay toward your prolonged suffering? Do you understand who I am?"

As Murgen continued talking, Drakkal asked in a low voice, "How long you going to make me wait, Arc?"

"What? Who are you talking to?" Murgen demanded.

"Part of me wanted to see how long he'd go on like that," Arcanthus said over the commlink. *"And I wanted to give you an opportunity to respond."*

"*Kraasz ka'val*, he'll have my response the moment the door's open."

Murgen barked laughter. "This door won't open until your body's cold and dead, azhera."

Though the sound was so faint that Drakkal couldn't be sure if it had occurred, he thought he heard Arcanthus laugh—and Samantha scold him for taking so long.

The keypad on the doorframe flashed a series of glitchy, scrambled characters, and the heavy blast door rumbled. A moment later, the door began rising.

Murgen made a shocked, unintelligible exclamation; Drakkal heard the garbled words both through the intercom and the widening space beneath the door.

As soon as the door was high enough, Drakkal met Murgen's gaze. The large durgan was standing in a lavish antechamber that was decorated in a fashion befitting of the manor high above. The walls were maroon with gold accents over dark paneling, the floor a gleaming polished stone, black with deep scarlet veins.

Murgen's eyes were so wide they looked on the verge of popping out of his skull. "H-how did you...h-how—"

Drakkal unslung his auto-blaster's shoulder strap, detached the energy cell, and tossed both the weapon and the cell aside. He took a step forward.

Murgen's throat flesh swelled with an alarmed, grating screech. He shambled backward and tripped over his own feet, waving his big arms in desperation to reclaim his balance; both the screech and his attempted recovery were at odds with his immense size. "I'll give you anything. Anything! N-name your p-price, azhera!"

Balling his right hand into a fist, Drakkal surged forward and swung his arm. His knuckles struck Murgen's cheek. The durgan's fleshy jowls shook with the impact, and his head snapped to the side, rerouting his stumbling retreat into the same direction.

"Please, p-please," Murgen stammered, raising an arm to shield his face. "You can have anything you w-want."

Drakkal's next strike caught Murgen in the gut, knocking him back several steps before he finally fell hard on his ass. Drakkal pursued him at a steady, relentless pace, responding to Murgen's pleas only with fists—and, soon enough, claws. Murgen's begging grew more frantic and babbling with each passing moment. Drakkal only increased the strength behind his attacks as Murgen's desperation grew.

If Murgen were saying words, the azhera no longer heard. That old, red haze had settled over his vision, welcome and familiar, and the only sound he paid attention to was that of his own steadily beating heart.

Each time Murgen struggled to his feet, Drakkal knocked him down again. The scents of blood and sour sweat dominated the air. Soon, Murgen was screaming between his labored breaths, and the sounds pushed Drakkal harder, faster. He no longer saw only Murgen Foltham—this was also Vanya and the slavers who'd captured Drakkal long ago, this was all the cruel slave owners and arena masters he'd met on Caldorius, this was Vaund and the whole Syndicate. This was everyone who'd ever wronged Drakkal, Shay, Leah, and his family, everyone who *would* ever wrong them.

When Murgen fell again, Drakkal didn't give him a chance to get back up. Releasing a powerful, reverberating roar, Drakkal pinned Murgen on the floor and unleashed the fullness of his rage.

He wasn't sure how much time had passed when he finally stilled his arms. He wasn't sure how long it had been since Murgen's screams had forever fallen silent. Drakkal's chest and shoulders heaved with ragged breaths, and the exposed fur on his arms and face was drenched in warm, fresh blood. He wasn't sure what he was supposed to feel now.

There was that deep-running heat, of course, but it was already dispersing—if only slowly. He pushed himself to his feet. His many aches and pains chose that moment to make themselves known anew, but Drakkal felt...lighter. This situation was not yet concluded—there was cleaning up to do to ensure none of this came back on his people or on the prisoners locked in the zoo—but the final threat to his mate had been eliminated.

He turned toward the door and exited the room without offering Murgen a backward glance. Drakkal planned to only look forward—toward Shay and Leah.

It was time to bring his family back home.

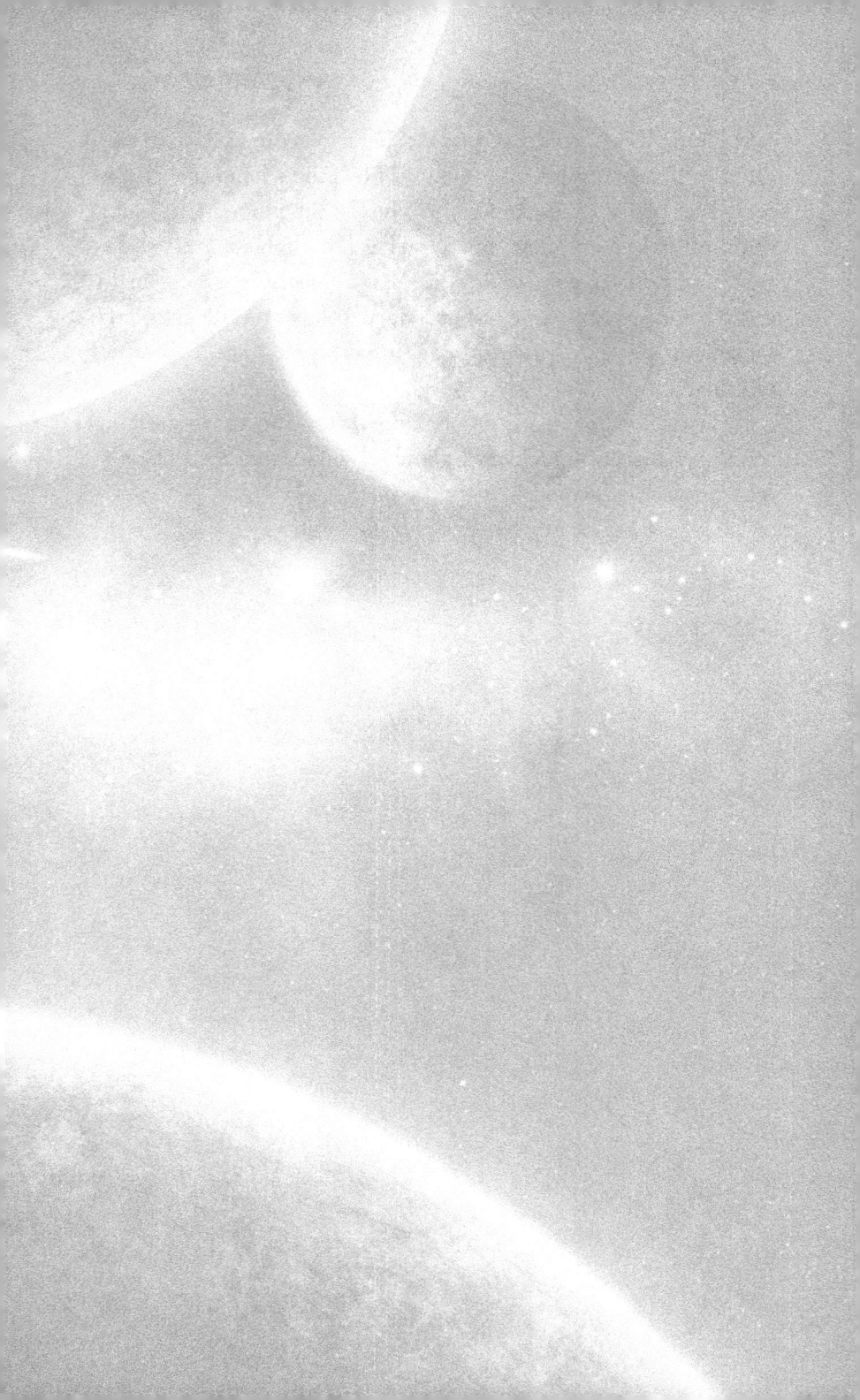

EPILOGUE

Eight Months Later

EVERYONE WAS GATHERED in the break room, forming a circle around the little girl sitting on the floor. Leah was surrounded by gifts and wads of torn wrapping paper. It was her big day, her first birthday, and Shay couldn't stop the tears from randomly stinging her eyes.

My little girl is growing up.

It seemed like only yesterday that Leah was still in Shay's womb, the baby Shay had never planned for but had devoted her life to. Of course, that feeling was probably strengthened by the fact that she usually felt like she had no idea what she was doing—babies really *didn't* come with instruction manuals, and finding sources of information while there were still so few humans in Arthos had proven challenging.

But she had this crazy, wonderful family around her, and they'd all been amazing. This birthday party was just another example on a long list—half the people here didn't understand why humans celebrated birthdays, didn't understand why anyone went through the trouble of wrapping presents only to tear off the paper and throw it away, but they were going along with it anyway. For Leah.

Leah had grown so much over the last few months. Though she was taller and more mobile now that she'd started walking, she still had her adorable baby chub. Today, she was wearing a puffy blue dress Drakkal had purchased for her, and her dark hair—which was now down to her chin—was pulled up into pig tails and tied with tiny matching bows. Her eyes were a bright blue to match Shay's, and every time Leah smiled, dimples appears in her cheeks. The little girl already knew how to use those dimples to her advantage. There wasn't a male in this room who wouldn't drop whatever he was doing to cater to Leah's whims—including Thargen.

Leah clawed at one of the wrapped gifts, her delicate brows angled down in frustration. Razi stepped forward and lowered himself to the floor in front of her, reaching out with his large hands to make a little tear in the wrapping paper so she could open it. She smiled up at him, flashing those troublemaking dimples, and ripped through the paper, tossing it aside. Once she'd been shown the joy of tearing off wrapping paper, she'd taken to it like a natural. Opening gifts was clearly more interesting than the gifts themselves.

But Leah paused with this gift, her eyes serious and focused as she reached into the open wrapping. She withdrew a small stuffed animal—a cartoonish cat with suspiciously familiar gray-brown fur and markings.

Leah grinned, struggled to her feet, and waddled to Drakkal, holding the cat high.

Drakkal glared at Razi, who grinned just as big as Leah.

Laughter erupted from everyone—the sort of good-natured

laughter that Shay enjoyed so much—with Thargen's booming the loudest.

Drakkal's frown was comically exaggerated, but when he bent down and scooped up little Leah, he was all smiles.

"Got your own little kitty, huh?" he asked.

Leah giggled and declared, "Ki-ki!" She held up the cat in one hand and patted Drakkal's cheek with the other. "Ki-ki."

Everyone went silent. Shay's mouth gaped as she stared at her daughter in shock, excitement, and envy.

"Her first word is *kitty*?" Arcanthus asked, his softly-spoke question shattering the silence.

"Ki-ki," Leah agreed, leaning forward to press her face against Drakkal's furry cheek and giving him a loud kiss.

Drakkal's smile widened, and he tilted his head down to gently nuzzle Leah's hair. "Yes, little one. Ki-ki." He lifted his gaze to the others in the room. "Now you all need to pay up. I won the bet."

"What?" Shay asked, brows lowered. "No, you didn't!"

Sekk'thi scowled and dug out a credit chip, tossing it toward Drakkal, who caught it while still maintaining his hold on Leah. "I call foul."

"I thought it was supposed to be whether she said mama or dada first," Samantha said.

"No, it was if her first word would be me or Shay," Drakkal said. "She said kitty. That's me."

Shay poked his ribs but couldn't keep the grin off her face. "You're such a cheat."

"I'm *not* a cheat, *kiraia*. It's not my fault everyone insists on calling me that. She's probably heard that word more than any other."

Leah wiggled in his arms, and Drakkal bent to set her carefully on her feet. She hugged her stuffed cat and walked back to her presents, plopping down onto Razi's lap. The big gray cren smiled tenderly down at Leah and picked up another gift for her to unwrap.

Shay smiled. Leah wasn't lacking in big, strong, scary-ass uncles who were such softies on the inside. She had them all wrapped around her little finger—Drakkal most of all.

Samantha cleared her throat. "You guys will have another chance at that bet before too long."

Shay's eyes widened as she looked at her friend. "Really?"

"Why would that be?" Arcanthus asked, arching a brow. "She doesn't get a second first word."

Drakkal shook his head and snorted. "Really, Arc?"

Arcanthus's brows fell, and he turned his face to Samantha. After a second, realization rounded his eyes. "Samantha?"

She smiled up at him, glancing briefly at Urgand, who was seated next to Sekk'thi on the sofa. "Urgand said I'm around eight weeks. He's not sure what the gestation period is for a human and sedhi hybrid, but he said the heartbeat is strong."

The corners of Arc's mouth curled upward to reveal the tips of his fangs, and his eyes softened as he gazed down at his mate. His cybernetic hands settled on her hips and slowly moved up to cradle her middle, his thumbs lovingly stroking her belly. "Ah, my flower, I cannot wait to see you blossom further."

Samantha reached up and cupped his jaw, and the sedhi lowered his head, bringing his lips to hers as he pulled her close.

"Well that's not going to be a fair bet at all," said Koroq.

"Why's that?" Kiloq asked, nudging his gift toward Leah, who eagerly dragged it closer.

"Sam's been cleaning us out playing Conquerors for two years," Koroq said, "and you know for a chunk of that she didn't really know what she was doing. That terran has luck on her side."

Leah gleefully tore apart the wrapping paper to reveal a brightly colored tablet. Her attention remained on the wrapping instead of the toy; she crumpled the paper and tore it more, giggling to herself.

"You're just a sore loser," Kiloq said.

Koroq glared at his brother. "And you're just ugly."

"I look just like you."

"Exactly."

Thargen shoved a forkful of cake into his mouth. "That's the last gift. Now can we admit that my present was the best and finally break out the booze?"

Shay laughed and shook her head. "Okay, firstly, you gave her a knife."

"Yeah. Pretty clear I win."

"No, no you don't. That thing's half as long as her!"

"She'll grow into it, right?" Thargen tapped his temple, just in front of his scar. "Thinking long term, terran."

"She's not touching that thing for *years*, vorgal," Drakkal growled.

"Secondly," Shay continued, "this is a baby's birthday party. We're *not* breaking out the booze."

Thargen's jaw fell, and he threw up his hands. "What is this, a damned nursery now? First the azhera—who has knives for fingers—says no knife for the kid, now you say nothing to drink?"

"We *all* know how you get with booze," Sekk'thi said.

Thargen jabbed a finger at her. "I get *fun*."

"The sort of *fun* you mean isn't appropriate with a youngling underfoot," Arcanthus drawled, curling his tail around Samantha's leg. "If you'd like, I'm sure Samantha would be up for some Conquerors and *gurosh* later."

"Um...no," Samantha said, patting Arc's chest affectionately. "I'm pregnant. No drinking for me."

Thargen turned back to his cake, picked up the remnants with his hand—it was at least half of a big slice—and shoved it into his mouth, smearing frosting on his lips. He chewed noisily as he stood up, licking pink frosting from his fingers, and said, "Been a while since—*mmm*—I went out. Damn, this is good... I'm gonna—*mmm*—go get a drink."

"Take it easy out there," Urgand said, frowning.

Thargen waved a hand dismissively before crouching in front of Leah. He patted her head—thankfully *not* with the hand he'd just been licking—and smiled. "Keep everyone out of trouble, kid. They're bigger babies than you are."

Leah beamed up at him with a giggle.

Thargen's eyes softened, and his grin widened. "Yeah, you know it. I'll, uh...find you a *more suitable* present, I guess. See ya later."

"That does not mean a blaster, Thargen," Sekk'thi called after him as he exited the room.

His deep, booming laughter sounded from the hallway just before the door closed.

Drakkal's arms slid around Shay from behind, and he pulled her against him, lowering his chin to rest atop her head. She settled her arms over his and smiled. She never tired of this, any of it—the closeness, the companionship, the *love*. It was all here, in this room...

But it was the closeness, companionship, and love from Drakkal she enjoyed most of all.

Kiloq gathered all the ripped wrapping paper into a pile. Leah stood up from Razi's lap—with a bit of help from him—and dove into the paper with a high-pitched laugh.

Shay glanced at Samantha and Arc, who were now cuddled on one of the sofas, speaking softly to one another with their love plain on their faces. There was awe in Arc's eyes as he again covered Sam's belly with his hand.

Over the last several months, Arcanthus and Drakkal had been working to steer their business away from illegal activities. Shay wondered if that process would speed up now that Sam was expecting. They'd already become even more selective in accepting clients than before, and they'd even helped a few of the former prisoners from Murgen's zoo with ID chips free of charge.

Most of the animals and intelligent beings there had been left to the Eternal Guard's care; the Consortium had programs to help victims of kidnapping and enslavement that extended even to species not yet integrated on Arthos, but a few of those prisoners had wanted to leave with Drakkal, Shay, and the others. Arcanthus and Drakkal had worked to get those individuals established, to help them acclimate to life on an alien world—a world of technology far surpassing anything some of them had ever seen on their homeworlds.

Fortunately, no one had started a crusade to find Murgen's killers and bring them to justice after it had all gone public—none of the other wealthy elite wanted to risk calling attention to themselves by speaking out, lest their own dirty secrets come to light. Not that they would've found much anyway. Arcanthus had brought in cleaners within an hour of Murgen's death; they'd removed all the physical evidence while Arcanthus wiped the computer records and surveillance recordings, effectively making it like none of them had ever been there, including Shay and Drakkal.

Just like it was difficult to believe Leah had been born a year ago, it didn't seem like months had passed since the incident at Murgen's. Those experiences had helped Shay finally understand what her father had meant when he'd said those life and death situations never really faded from your mind. They stuck with you forever; you just had to learn how to live with them.

But here, now, surrounded by her friends—her family—she could look back and be grateful for all of it. Those hardships had led to *this*.

As if sensing her thoughts, Drakkal slid his hand down to Shay's belly, covering it possessively, and pulled her against his body just a little more firmly. Heat stirred in her core.

He moved his face to the side of her head and brushed his lips over the shell of her ear. "I've got you, *kiraia*. Always."

Shay smiled and raised a hand, sliding her fingers into his mane as she turned her face toward him. Her lips grazed his. "I know you do." She turned fully in his embrace and looped her arms around his neck. Their eyes locked. Those familiar fires burned in his gaze; their effect on her had only seemed to strengthen as time passed. Her heart fluttered and her breath quickened.

"*Kraasz ka'val*, Shay, I *love* you," he said in a low rumble that vibrated into her before he cupped her backside and slanted his mouth over hers in a hungry, scalding, breathtaking kiss.

AUTHOR'S NOTE

Thank you so much for reading *Untamed Hunger*! We hope you enjoyed it.

And if you've stuck with us this long, be sure to check out Thargen's book, Savage Desire! That vorgal could use a little love.

Again, thank you all for following us and reading our stories! We love you. If you're on Facebook, come join our private reader group!

ALSO BY TIFFANY ROBERTS

THE INFINITE CITY

Entwined Fates

Silent Lucidity

Shielded Heart

Vengeful Heart

Untamed Hunger

Savage Desire

Tethered Souls

THE KRAKEN

Treasure of the Abyss

Jewel of the Sea

Hunter of the Tide

Heart of the Deep

Rising from the Depths

Fallen from the Stars

Lover from the Waves

THE SPIDER'S MATE TRILOGY

Ensnared

Enthralled

Bound

THE VRIX
The Weaver
The Delver
The Hunter

THE CURSED ONES
His Darkest Craving
His Darkest Desire

ALIENS AMONG US
Taken by the Alien Next Door
Stalked by the Alien Assassin
Claimed by the Alien Bodyguard

STANDALONE TITLES
Claimed by an Alien Warrior
Dustwalker
Escaping Wonderland
Yearning For Her
The Warlock's Kiss
Ice Bound: Short Story

ISLE OF THE FORGOTTEN
Make Me Burn

Make Me Hunger

Make Me Whole

Make Me Yours

VALOS OF SONHADRA COLLABORATION

Tiffany Roberts - Undying

Tiffany Roberts - Unleashed

VENYS NEEDS MEN COLLABORATION

Tiffany Roberts - To Tame a Dragon

Tiffany Roberts – To Love a Dragon

ABOUT THE AUTHOR

Tiffany Roberts is the pseudonym for Tiffany and Robert Freund, a husband and wife writing duo. The two have always shared a passion for reading and writing, and it was their dream to combine their mighty powers to create the sorts of books they want to read. They write character driven sci-fi and fantasy romance, creating happily-ever-afters for the alien and unknown.

Sign up for our Newsletter!
Check out our social media sites and more!
http://www.authortiffanyroberts.com

Printed in the USA
CPSIA information can be obtained
at www.ICGtesting.com
LVHW041804050724
784731LV00037B/254